Following a first-class degree from Cambridge, Sandi Toksvig went into the theatre as a writer and performer, before becoming a founder member of the Comedy Store Players. She is well known for her television and radio work as a presenter, writer and actor. She has written six books for children and her first adult novel, *Whistling for the Elephants*, was published in 1999. *Flying Under Bridges* is her second novel.

*Also by Sandi Toksvig*

Whistling for the Elephants

# Flying Under Bridges

## SANDI TOKSVIG

WARNER BOOKS

A *Warner* Book

First published in Great Britain in 2001
by Little, Brown and Company

This edition published by Warner Books in 2001

The author gratefully acknowledges
permission to quote from the following:
P. 58 Copyright © *Guardian* by Martin Wainwright

A CIP catalogue record for this book
is available from the British Library

ISBN 0 7515 3133 2

Typeset in Sabon by M Rules
Printed and bound in Great Britain by
Clays Ltd, St Ives plc

Warner Books
A Division of
Little, Brown and Company (UK)
Brettenham House
Lancaster Place
London WC2E 7EN

www.littlebrown.co.uk

To Alice

Books are not solitary enterprises. My thanks to the following for their invaluable advice and assistance – Ursula Mackenzie, my editor, friend and mentor, without whom I wouldn't write a word; Pat Kavanagh, my splendid agent; Viv Redman, for immense patience with fine-tuning the text; Juliet van Oss for fantastic error-spotting; Patsy Silburn and Glen Wolford for work on the early material; everyone at Little, Brown; Germaine Greer for her splendid writing over the years; and, as ever, my wonderful children.

One need not be a Chamber – to be Haunted –
One need not be a House –
The Brain has Corridors – surpassing
Material Place –

Far safer, of a Midnight Meeting
External; Ghost
Than its interior Confronting –
That Cooler Host.

Far safer, through an Abbey gallop,
The Stones a'chase –
Than Unarmed, one's a'self encounter –
In lonesome Place –

Ourself behind ourself, concealed –
Should startle most –
Assassin hid in our Apartment
Be Horror's least.

The body – borrows a Revolver –
He bolts the Door –
O'erlooking a superior spectre –
Or More –

'Ghosts', Emily Dickinson

# Preface

Two women, one story. An everyday tale of morals, marriage and murder. Both women from the same town, the same school, the same generation. For a long while their lives went in completely different directions. Fame, acclaim and the fast lane for one; husband, kids and the suburbs for the other. Nothing in common but their past until the summer they met again. Soon one became a killer and the other was not surprised. It could have happened to anybody but it didn't. It happened to them and by the time the snow fell they were both trying to understand.

# Chapter One

1 January
Holloway Prison for Women
London

My dear Inge,

### In the Beginning

In the beginning was the word . . .

(JOHN 1.1)

Do you think there is a Bible quote for everything? That's my one
for today – about the beginning. It seems appropriate. Happy
New Year and all that. It's a funny bit of the Bible really because
it doesn't come at the beginning of the Book at all. It was written
after lots and lots of things had happened and that's what I feel
like. As though I've got to go back to the beginning even though
I am so far into the story. I do want to find the 'once upon a time'
bit of what happened but it's not easy. I just think if I could
explain it to you then you could explain it to Shirley. Is she all
right? Give her my love, won't you? So long as it doesn't upset
her. I mean, don't if it will. You decide. I miss her, but I don't
know what's right any more. I'm so glad you're looking after her.
Everyone wants to know 'the facts' but even I find it hard to get
it all straight in my head.

I know Shirley still wants to think it was an accident but maybe she should know the truth. I have nothing else to give her. I still can't believe I'm here. I'm in prison. It's unbelievable. I'm in prison for killing somebody. Everyone keeps talking at me and I am trying. I am trying to find the words. In the beginning was the word.

In some ways I think it's quite simple. I mean, guests ruin weddings all the time, although I will admit it is probably less usual for them to do it by killing the groom. I do want to be honest about what happened. I didn't entirely mean to kill him. Well, I may have meant to but I didn't plan it. I was, after all, the mother of the bride, which I think anyone would say carries a certain responsibility. I've had a letter from the women's group I used to meet with. I think they were trying to be supportive but their basic message seemed to be that the whole thing has done nothing for me socially. As if I care.

I'm tired. I just want to sit. I just want to be left alone, but there are questions, endless questions. The barrister seems a sweet girl. Too young to have to wear black every day. Nice hair and given to a good suit but she hasn't got a clue. She's a bit older than Shirley but I think of her when we meet. I think of Shirley. I think of Shirley all the time. How did I end up here? She would have been married now . . . if I hadn't killed her fiancé. My daughter, married.

'Do you mind . . . Mrs Marshall?' The barrister blushes at me. She obviously minds terribly. 'Would you say you were a woman of a certain age?' She nods at me and I half think she is going to wink as well. I'm not at all sure what we are blushing and winking about. I'm forty-five. I tell her I'm forty-five. I don't know if that's a certain age or not. I don't seem to have been a useful age since I was eight and finally old enough to have my own bicycle. After that it seems to have been pretty much downhill. Quite a lot of years of being too young and then decades of being far too old. I don't ever seem to have been just right. Now I am getting hairs on my chin. I am growing into an old woman with a beard. A woman small children won't want to kiss. There's another sign of age. I think about being kissed by small children, not Richard Gere or Errol Flynn. The barrister stumbles forward into my inner life.

'I was wondering about the . . . menopause.' She almost whispers the word. It is too ghastly and yet we must consider it. Something that is too far away for her to contemplate looms over my every move. I look at her young body choking with ovarian health. Little eggs bursting all over her inner bits while my crop withers and shrivels on the vine.

'It might be . . . helpful,' she manages as we plod on. You can see her point, especially at these prices. The menopause would be helpful. What a relief if we could blame the whole thing on some hormonal imbalance. That I was imbalanced at the time. It's so much tidier. I might even get off. My sister Martha would say it is what men want to believe if we women step out of line. We poor females at the 'mercy of our defective carcasses'. I suppose the good thing about being a woman (from a legal point of view) is that there is always something to blame. Menstruation, pregnancy, childbirth, the menopause – it all adds up to 'hormonal imbalance'. We do droop and drip endlessly. Germaine Greer says (I know, you're shaking your head and saying, 'Oh Eve, not Germaine again,'), but Germaine says that men believe that every one of a woman's working parts comes with a 'built-in predisposition to malfunction'. We are God's faulty design. Nothing so proud and substantial as a male organ but a vacuum that is useless unless filled. Listen to me. Who would have thought?

'There have been numerous cases where women . . .' The young black-suited woman flicks through fat books and dust settles in the air. I could clean that. I am good at dust. She finds comfort in her legal tomes because she does not understand me. I have done something women don't do. I have been violent and now we must sit quietly, women together, and find that it was all due to 'the adverse effect of my biology'. Maybe it was. I don't know. Maybe it is the menopause. Maybe it is postnatal depression. Latent, of course. I had my last baby twenty years ago but I'm sure there is some precedent in her fat books. The solicitors have got a woman to represent me on purpose. I think it is supposed to soften my image but she looks at her books rather than me. I suspect I frighten her, although I don't mean to. Am I the witch waiting in every woman? Is there a shadow of me in this bright university mind and dull suit?

The barrister is just one of many who have probed and prodded since I was arrested. No one can 'understand' and it is very important to everyone that they do. I am in the middle of 'having reports done', which hasn't happened since school. Do you remember?

*Eve is a keen member of the form. She has good application but with little obvious result.*

Keen. I've always been keen but this is the first time I've ever actually *done* anything.

The psychiatrist is another prober. I see him after the barrister has departed in legal despair. A flurry of pink ribbon waves around the departing legal shoulders. The lawyer wants to tie me up while the shrink wants to unravel me. He is a very earnest old man with a rather pleasing middle-European accent. I listen to his constipated vowel sounds and I find them rather comforting. I mean, if you were in a film with a psychiatrist then he ought to be a bit German, don't you think? It is the only textbook thing about the untextbook thing that I have done. His heavy accent suggests power. Questions which will be answered and properly. The Dutch or the Belgians never conquered the world because the accent was all wrong. In the beginning may have been the word but I don't think it was a Flemish one. The fact is if someone told you in Flemish that they planned to rule the world, you'd tell them not to be so silly. I wonder what it is about Austria and Germany that makes its people want to go into mental health? Of course the Von Trapps didn't. They were Austrian but they escaped over the mountains and ran summer music camps in Vermont. I should have liked that but I had no mountains . . .

I've just come back to my letter from exercise period. What the hell was I writing about? The Von Trapps? Maybe I *am* going mad. Maybe I was mad. I have been so busy using my brain to run other lives and now I find I have this huge empty space under my skull and a *To Let* sign on my forehead.

The shrink, the mental inquisitor, holds my hand rather too long when he shakes it and insists on staring me in the eye when we talk.

'Tell me,' he asks, 'what do you see when you look at me?'

Mainly I see that he has a big nose but I keep it to myself. The nose has a huge wart on it. A vast growth, like an alternative nose with a large hair growing out of it, but I don't mention that either. Opinions have been getting me into enough trouble. It's funny him having a long hair growing on his face like a fairy whip. He can't mind or he'd pluck it out. I suppose he's a man so it's all right to have hair like that. I'm not allowed any on my chin. We women must pluck and tidy ourselves away while men are quite happy to let bits of themselves swing around for all the world to see.

We talk about everything very slowly. Perhaps I could do some embroidery during our sessions so I've got something else to look at besides the two noses.

'What do you see when you look at me?'

'A man,' I say, because it is polite and straightforward and I can't think any more.

He nods. 'You cannot ignore that I am a man.'

I don't know whether it is a piece of analysis or a statement of fact.

'Let me just be sure that I have the facts straight, Mrs . . .' He looks at his notes. I am so forgettable but I am polite. He can't see without his glasses so I help him.

'Marshall. Mrs Adam Marshall.'

'Mrs Adam Marshall.' He writes everything down in pencil as if I might be tempted endlessly to change my mind about what I've said. We could always go back and rub things out. I'd like that. I'd like to rub my whole name out.

'The body of the deceased was found . . . and I believe the word you used was "crucified", against a holly bush in your front garden.'

I shake my head. 'No, that's not right.'

He raises his eyebrows. 'You did not use the word "crucified"?'

'It was wisteria not a holly bush.' The pencil pauses for a moment and I am tempted to help him with the spelling of wisteria which may, for all I know, be unknown in middle-European garden centres.

'*Wisteria sinensis*,' I say, as he pauses. 'It's originally from Central China.' He stares at me. 'Member of the pea family. A deciduous climber with divided leaves and trusses of lilac-blue flowers. Beautiful for house walls.'

'How do you know that?' he enquires.

'I read things and I remember. I don't do anything with them. I just remember.'

He writes something down. I suspect it is not a gardening note. Then he looks up and stares me in the eye again.

'I see. So, tell me about yourself.'

I think, this won't take long. And then I stop for a minute.

'It's difficult to know where to begin,' I say.

'Aaah,' he intones and nods. His large nose beats time above his lip. The hair from the wart dangles like a fine fishing line. He should have a moustache or a beard. There is a big space between his nose and his lip. Not a handsome man. About sixty. He's probably heard it all. All the loonies. I don't really want to tell him anything. I take some sewing out of my bag. I like cross-stitch. You have a pattern and you just follow it. You just follow it exactly and at the end you have something beautiful. It isn't complicated. Old Freud is staring at me. I realise I haven't been paying any attention.

'Sorry, what was the question?'

He writes something down and then stares again.

'Tell me who you are.'

Who are you? Such a simple question and yet it gives me a bit of a jolt. I can't remember ever being asked. Well, not since I joined the Brownies. We had to write an essay about ourselves while Brown Owl went outside for a cigarette, but that's going back a bit. *Who are you?* Such a tricky question to answer. Mrs Adam Marshall – Mrs Adam Marshall – that's how the AA addressed me on my new card, which arrived the week you did. I am Mrs Adam Marshall. The really strange thing is that it's taken me twenty-odd years to notice that I'm not really me any more. I mentioned it to Adam.

'Do you realise my whole name has disappeared?' I said to my husband, my lover, my partner in life. 'That I don't have a single name I started with?'

Adam sucked on his teeth, which is a new habit. It's not attractive. 'You shouldn't be worrying about these things,' he said. 'People are past all that women's lib nonsense. Good job too.'

Which is all very well for him. I mean, he's not Mr *Eve* Marshall, is he? I thought Shirley would think it odd too, but she didn't.

'It's a new millennium, Mum.' She shook her head at me and crunched a Hobnob. 'It's time to move on. There are other issues. You know you really ought to be a "postfeminist" by now.'

That was what my grown-up daughter thought. Postfeminist. It's a funny expression. I think it suggests that I've already passed through a feminist phase, and yet I don't remember it. You had yours, didn't you, Inge? I envy you that. Perhaps my feminism is in the post and hasn't arrived yet.

The psychiatrist is waiting patiently. I suppose I had better say something.

'When the post comes, it's addressed to Mrs Adam Marshall. That's me, I suppose and . . . well, there's not much to say. Bit of a nothing, really. I can't even seem to manage to stay on the church flower-arranging rota.'

I laugh, but apparently it is not funny. He does not laugh. Perhaps he is very religious. It's everywhere these days. Still, for all I know he may never laugh. I am embarrassed. I was quite a laugh at school, wasn't I, or have I forgotten that too?

'Of course the flower rota wasn't entirely my fault. Mrs Milton got so funny about the whole shop business and . . .' I drift off. None of it seems important now. Do you remember Mrs Hart at school? Geography and PE. Odd combination really. It's not like you need ordnance survey to find the sports field. Anyway, whenever someone had some little problem or other, she would look down her nose and say, 'I see. And where do you suppose this fits in the great scheme of things?'

The answer was always nowhere. The trouble is I can't seem to see the great scheme of things at all.

The psychiatrist prompts me back into my inner recesses.

'Mrs Adam Marshall?' he says quietly.

'Mmhmm,' I reply. 'Yes. It was only when Inge moved back to Edenford that I noticed my whole name had disappeared.'

Big nose scribbles away. His pencil bounces across the pad. I have no idea what I've said to cause such a literary surge. Perhaps I shouldn't have mentioned you. Perhaps he is a fan.

'Adam does a lot of correspondence,' I say while I wait for him to catch up. 'Mainly to the *Edenford Gazette*. He had the first cuckoo last year.'

I use the word 'cuckoo' deliberately. I think it would be rather a good one for a shrink. He could give me that searching glare and say, 'Zo you zay "cuckoo", and are you ze cuckoo person?'

But he doesn't. He is resolute in pursuit of my reason for being. I like cuckoos. They just sort themselves out and don't give a damn. And why? Because their parents didn't give a damn. Just lay the egg in some other bird's nest and let someone else raise their kid. Then the cuckoo hatches and shoves all the other eggs out of the nest. No guilt, no retribution, no Hail Marys, just . . .

The psychiatrist gives me a long Germanic look and says quietly, 'And do you mind? About your name?'

I suddenly feel nervous. 'I shouldn't, should I? I mean, it's silly. It's just a name. I didn't think about it. Not for years. I know there are women who don't bother any more. You know, keep all of their name always, but I'm sure it mattered to Adam.' I stop and think.

I should have known straight away. We had only had one date when Adam mentioned it.

'I hope you're not one of those . . . women's libbers,' he said. I remember because I was holding the screws while he worked on the security bars for Mother's pantry window. Adam always dabbled in security even before it became a living. I think he spent his childhood making sure other people's rabbits didn't escape. Mother always worried about the pantry – what with her prize-winning jams and pickled eggs. When she found Mrs Bartlett's boy from next door, who'd never really been right, looking through the pantry window, she had burglar bars fitted.

Adam's first job was in plaster-relief mouldings. That's how I met him. Mother wanted a new ceiling rose after that trouble in the lounge when the bath upstairs ran over while Aunt Luce had her seizure on the toilet. Odd to think I got my husband from the *Yellow Pages*. Mother never liked him. She always said she rued the day she patched her parlour and took up Adam's offer to protect her preserves. Then, of course, he went into insurance and never looked back.

I tell the psychiatrist all this and there is a long pause and I don't know what to do. No one has ever taken this much interest in me before. I realise that I have stopped sewing and the blue thread has drifted out of the needle. The situation looks hopeless. I look at the wayward yarn, feeling as though I've never threaded anything before. The psychiatrist is waiting. I'm not sure that we're getting anywhere and I don't want anyone to blame Adam. It really wasn't his fault, so I add, 'Don't think that Adam and I don't get on. We have a lovely life. I mean there's . . . the house . . . it's all double-glazed.'

The psychiatrist carries on staring at me. He obviously doesn't think I've finished. I fumble with the thread, but his eyes are boring into me.

'Of course, there were lots of people who said, "How could you?" when I married him. "How could you marry a man named Adam?" I have to say I still wonder myself. You see, I'm Eve. Adam and Eve. Well, it was hardly something to put across the front windscreen of your Cortina. And, of course, we live in Edenford. Adam and Eve of Edenford. It was awful. Shame, because everything else about him seemed so . . . acceptable. He's older than me (fifty-five next birthday, but he doesn't want a fuss). I liked him. He was kind and I couldn't very well say, "I quite like you but we can't possibly get serious unless you change your name." So that's me. Mrs Adam Marshall.'

I want to talk to the psychiatrist about my dreams. Perhaps he could help me. We have to sit here anyway. I dream it is pitch black and I am scared, but then I find a torch. The batteries are weak. I should have changed them. That is my fault. I am stumbling around a dark room and I suddenly realise that I am inside my own head. The room is quite empty except for a long row of old-fashioned metal filing cabinets. They are all neatly labelled but the drawers are open. The drawers are open and all the files have spilt out on the ground. The floor is covered in scraps of information but I can't get any of it back into the filing cabinet—

'What else?' demands Big Nose.

'What else?' I can't think what else. 'Well, I'm forty-five. Forty-five.' God, we're going to get back on to the menopause in a minute I think, so I change the subject. 'I suppose I have achieved some things. Let's think. I have a son called Tom and a daughter, Shirley. Well, obviously you know about Shirley. She was . . . anyway, I'm somebody's mother.'

'What do you think about your children?'

What do I think about them? What a ridiculous question. I don't *think* anything. They are in my blood, in my limbs, under my skin. I don't think about them, I am them. Think? What does any mother think about her children? They are what I've done with my life. They are my contribution to the world. I haven't written anything, invented anything, built anything. I did once think of an idea for a cot bumper which played a tune when the baby hit it with its head but, of course, it never came to anything. No, I have made two children. I am very good with coughs and scraped knees and a complete whiz at chicken pox. Of course now I am also a killer. Is that what Shirley will come to think? Does she need to think it was an accident? I can tell them that. I can, Inge.

My inquisitive friend is staring at me. I think it must be rather dull for him listening to people whinge all day. No wonder he looks so miserable.

'Tell me about your daughter,' he says.

But I can't. I can't think about Shirley. I can't talk about her. Not yet. I try to change the subject.

'Did you know,' I say brightly, 'there's a woman in the cell next to mine who is on remand for throwing a brick through her own window? Don't you think that's bizarre? I mean, how can she be a menace to society? I tell you what I think it is. It's because we're not supposed to. Women. Be violent, I mean.'

'Why do you say that?'

'Well, we're not. Men kick and punch things and that's all right. They're meant to. We're supposed to worry about the colour of our kitchen tiles. And I'm not saying that's wrong. I thought it mattered too. My kitchen took an age. To me it was the most important room in the house.'

'Why?'

I look at the learned enquirer. Only a man could ask such a question.

'Because I spend the most time there.' I carry on with my

sewing. He sits staring at me. I don't know what I'm supposed to say.

'I took ages with the tiles. The man at the All Squared Tile Centre drove me mad. Hadn't a clue. "I know what I want," I said to him. "I want mushroom tiles." You know, that lovely, soft, just-picked colour. He had no idea. Backwards and forwards with ceramic samples until at last we found what I wanted. Adam put them in. He says they look brown.'

'Are these the things you think about?'

They aren't, of course. I haven't thought about my kitchen at all until now. The time when all that mattered seems such an age away. Everything has changed. I don't know what to tell him. I think about strange things now. I've been reading the Bible. Shirley gave it to me. I used to read the *Encyclopaedia Britannica* but they won't let me have that many volumes at once in here. I don't understand it. The Bible. It's nice, lots of it, but I want to know why there doesn't seem to be a single woman's opinion from Jesus's time. If the Virgin Mary was the mother of God, might she not have made some notes? I don't say this because I realise it's silly. I mean, she had other kids. She must have been just as proud of them. Anyway, she was probably too busy round the house. The Old Testament has Ruth and Esther. I thought Esther was a woman writer because there's a whole bit in it at the beginning about what some curtains looked like, but then it talks about 'Queen Esther' as if she were someone else entirely. Ruth has her own book, but it's very short and I can't work out if she wrote it or if it's just about her. The thing is . . .

'So you are a mother,' he says.

'Yes.' And I want to scream. Of course I am a mother or I wouldn't have done this and—

'And your own mother?'

'She's dead now, but it took some doing.' My attentive listener's head snaps to attention. I realise what he's thinking. Perhaps this case is more exciting than he thought. Perhaps I am the Rosemary West of the Home Counties. He sees a book in it, maybe a film from the book, chat shows, Oprah Winfrey . . .

It seems a shame to shatter his world. 'I mean, she was sick for a long time,' I say. 'Nothing to do with me.'

He crashes back to the prison service. 'What was she like? Your mother.' I try to think. Mother was just Mother, but I know that won't do.

'She worried. She was always worrying. What people would think, what they might say. She wanted to be a star, but she wasn't. She was just a sort of dim light that never went out. One of those light bulbs that you can't really see by but you feel you shouldn't change yet either.'

I don't want to talk about my mother. I just want to tell him that it is all my fault and I do feel bad and yet I didn't have any choice and . . . if that's what everyone wants to hear, that's what I'll tell them. It's what I told the police. It really doesn't matter what happens to me now. I did what I had to do. I'm not important in all this. That's the point. It's the end of my session and we never get to the point after all. I go back to my little room. None of it seems to get to the point. I killed my daughter's fiancé and I don't think she'll ever understand. Please, tell her that I love her.

Love,

Eve

# Chapter Two

The beginnings of things are sometimes hard to find. In the beginning was the word and the word was God. And before that? Nothing apparently, but human lives aren't really like that. They twist about taking unexpected turns and link up in the strangest ways. Like trying to find the end of that tangle of string in the kitchen drawer, it is not always clear-cut where a particular story in someone's life starts. Certainly the changes that were to come about in both Eve and Inge's lives occurred long before Eve finally ended up in prison. You could probably look back and pick any number of days in the early summer of that same year and say that was when events began to unfold. The story has to start somewhere, so take that day in May, May 3rd actually, when Inge Holbrook drew up at Television Centre.

It was a mark of her achievement that she was always allowed to park at the Horseshoe, a turn in the drive right outside the BBC's main building with only five or six highly prized car spaces. Inge Holbrook, gold medallist for Great Britain, four hundred metres sprint, 1976 Olympics, still fantastically fit at forty-plus, but too famous to be made to walk from the multi-storey. She slipped her silver Mercedes SLK Kompressor in next to an idling limousine and stepped out. She looked fabulous: blonde (since 1987), tanned (since Christmas in the Caribbean), long legs (since for ever) and an aura of success, which can never fail to be attractive. Inge was one of the 'faces' of the corporation and she enjoyed every minute of it. She headed for the entrance known as the Stage Door. It was the old main entrance at the heart of the building. The BBC had spent millions making a new glass entrance and foyer, but had brilliantly placed it miles from anywhere anyone wanted to be. Everyone tried to avoid using it. A curious symbol for the entire place. If you wanted in at the BBC, it was best to try to sneak an entrance at the side.

As Inge headed for her meeting, a harassed-looking man in spectacles and a grey suit ploughed out of the automatic doors, followed by a long-established black comedian. They were in a heated debate, which they stopped only for a moment in order to acknowledge Inge as she passed.

'A decision, I just want a decision,' the comedian kept repeating.

The two men headed for the waiting limo and the suit got in while the funny man shuffled off to be hilarious with a cab driver from the rank.

Inge waved to the women at reception and took the lift up to the fifth floor. She walked along the silent corridors of Light Entertainment. The doors of the tiny offices were all tightly shut. Even the small glass panels bearing the occupant's name had been papered over from the inside so that no one could see in. Behind them everyone was presumably being lightly entertaining, but not so entertaining as to let any of it seep out to the nation. It still felt strange for Inge to come here. This had never been her floor in the past. She had come up through sports presenting but sport was now officially an entertainment. Inge was no longer a journalist but an entertainer. The corridor wound round in a giant circle as Inge passed huge colour photos of herself at Wimbledon, at the FA Cup, the Olympics, winning at the Olympics. Her life, career and hairstyles played out for ever in front of the world.

Paul Roe, Controller of BBC1, had a large office at the far side of the building with, as a mark of his importance, an even larger waiting-room. He also had two secretaries. One to jump when he called and the other to look impressive with the coffee machine. Inge strode in and managed to make them both jump.

'God, Inge, sorry, you're here,' said the senior one called Trish. It was an English sign of instant subservience to have the word 'sorry' in an opening sentence. Inge didn't know if Trish was 'sorry' Inge was here at all, 'sorry' in general or just 'sorry' in case something might turn up to be sorry about. It was hard to tell. Trish had a voice unique to a particular breed of women who work in outer offices. It was ingratiating and yet pitched high enough to encourage the gathering of dogs from distant parts.

'Coffee?' squeaked the junior one called Sue in an even higher and more impossible range. Inge always wondered about these voices. They were emitted by very thin women who seemed intent on taking up as little space in life as possible. Both physically and vocally they occupied the minimum square footage necessary for existence.

'Black, thanks.' Inge smiled at them, she smiled at the coffee machine and she smiled at a small, wild-haired man hunched on one of the leather chairs in a corner. Inge smiled a lot. She was famous for smiling. She was accessible. She was the people's friend. It was what made old ladies she had never met before hug her in Tescos.

'I'm afraid Paul is running a little late,' squealed Trish. 'I'm so sorry.' And she was sorry. Inge smiled and everyone was sorry. It was the correct balance of power. They were sorry and Inge was gracious. Inge smiled some more and took her coffee. Paul was always running late. Everyone at the BBC ran late. Inge had never run late. She wondered about it as an excuse at the Olympics.

'Sorry I didn't win a medal. I was running a bit late.'

Inge moved to the hairy lump in the corner. He twitched and seemed unsure whether to get up. She put out her hand.

'Hi, I'm Inge Holbrook. I don't think we've met.'

He stood and managed to fall over his own feet, knocking his coffee from the glass table.

'God, sorry, yes, of course, I mean, I know.'

'And you are?'

'In development.' The twenty-something young man blinked at her and swallowed hard as he took a grey hanky from his pocket and attempted to clear up some of the spilt drink. He wore ancient, creased, black trousers upon which it was impossible to tell where the coffee might have landed. Inge smiled.

'I meant your name.'

This was clearly a new concept to the man in development.

'*My* name?'

'Um,' said Inge encouragingly.

'Nick. I'm . . . Nick . . . in development.'

'So you said.' Inge sat down and sipped her coffee. 'And what do you develop, Nick?'

'Ideas mostly, you know, for . . . Paul.' He said the name with sufficient reverence to need to sit down again.

'Programme ideas?'

Nick nodded and wiped his hands, wet with sweat and coffee.

'How long have you been doing that?'

'Oh, three years.'

'And what sort of programmes? What might I have seen?'

The question seemed to cause a minor seizure.

'Do you mean on air? Oh.'

Nick-in-development paled at the thought of actual programmes and was probably only saved a major blood vessel rupture by the appearance of Paul Roe.

The man responsible for the entertainment and information of a nation stood framed in the doorway. He was slim-hipped, slim-haired and hung on to the last remnants of his thirties by wearing a smart white shirt and Gaultier tie with faded but pressed denims. The jeans were tight and Paul often found it necessary to adjust his genitalia against the inside seam. He did this openly and with no thought of concealment. Inge thought it must be strange to have a penis. To have a part of your body which is never quite where you want it to be. No woman ever walked into a room and suddenly discovered that her left breast had inexplicably moved on to her shoulder blade.

There was no one in Paul's office with him. There was no way of knowing what had caused him to 'run late'.

'Inge! Sorry! Trish, you never said!' he admonished senior squeal, while giving another cupped flick to his pants.

Trish took the blame instantly.

'Sorry,' she said. Paul shrugged his shoulders and smiled. Then he took Inge's hand, kissed her warmly on both cheeks and led her into his inner sanctum.

'Have you met Nick from development?' asked Paul, as he waved Inge on to the leather sofa.

'Yes, yes, we've been . . . chatting.'

'He's got some very exciting ideas.'

Inge was keen to get on, but it wasn't going to be easy. She had long ago decided that British men and women have completely different approaches to meetings. Because the women usually have the meeting to get through, three children to collect, a dog to worm and the nagging worry that something was left boiling on the stove, they tend to be rather cut and thrust about the whole thing. Meanwhile the men tend to favour an approach based on the UK road network. They know where they are supposed to be going, but can't see the point of a straight road. They are quite happy to go round many roundabouts en route while discussing the merits of the straight-arm driving technique. Much foreplay, little substance. Inge didn't like preliminaries. It was this sense of urgency that had made her a world-class runner. She took off from the starting blocks.

'I wanted to talk about Wimbledon for next year,' she began. 'I've been thinking about some junior presenters round the outside courts and—'

'Ah.' Paul carefully pulled the padded leather chair on wheels from behind his desk. He placed it to one side of the large mahogany work surface. It was a mark of friendliness.

Inge knew where this was heading. 'Not Wimbledon? Surely not Wimbledon?'

Paul shook his head in despair. 'I know. I'm sorry. Sky just outbid us. Went this morning, I'm afraid. They'll announce tonight.'

Inge was almost speechless. 'Paul, how could this happen? The BBC *is* Wimbledon. God, there'll be no sport left. We've already lost the Premier League, ITV are going to dance rings around us at the next Olympics, Channel Five got the bloody boat race. If the BBC don't cover Wimbledon, what are we going to have left? Carpet bowls?'

Nick shook his head and muttered, 'Eurosport, I'm afraid.'

Paul looked down at the very carpet where, but for financial constraints, bowls might have been played. He shook his head for a moment and then bounced up and made for the door.

'Wine, shall we have some wine? Trish! Get some wine.' Paul circled back into the room. 'I found this terrific new wine warehouse under the arches in King's Cross. They've done the place up. It was falling down and—'

Inge found it hard to care less about Paul's fallen arches. 'So if not Wimbledon, then what?' she asked.

Paul smiled a slight smile of irritation. He liked talking about his wine warehouse discovery. He nodded, adjusted his bollocks for comfort and headed back for the straight road.

'Indeed. Well. This is going to be a very exciting time for you, Inge. We have great plans. I think I speak for the entire corporation when I say that you are one of the most loved and trusted faces here at the Beeb and we are going to move you up and up. Now, Nick has got some very exciting ideas. Nick?' Paul clicked his fingers to wake Nick up from his reverie. 'The show . . . Nick! Tell her about the show.'

'Yes.' Nick cleared his throat and gave a small cough. 'We, Paul, obviously, and I, have come up with an idea for you to host a brand-new Saturday-night show called . . .' he paused for effect, '*Don't Even Go There!*'

Paul beamed, Nick beamed, Trish came in and served the wine. Everyone was thrilled.

'Isn't that a great title? I just love the title,' boomed Paul.

'Great title,' echoed Trish the mouse.

'Chardonnay?' enquired Paul. 'It's a lovely little oak-smoked—'

'No, thanks.' Inge waited for Trish to go back outside. 'Great. It's a great title. What's it about?'

Paul picked up a sheaf of papers and started leafing through them.

'According to our Audience Approval Ratings, we thought about . . . seven o'clock for half an hour.'

Inge shook her head. 'Sorry, the idea, for the show.'

Nick blinked and Paul swallowed some wine.

'Obviously it's not finalised but . . . Nick?' Paul looked to his trusted deputy.

'Yes, well, it's a panel game with you hosting and other famous sporting personalities competing in two teams—'

'Like *A Question of Sport*? I mean, that's been done. Sue was brilliant.'

'Same sort of set but totally different concept. Obviously that was sports people answering, you know, questions about . . . sport. This will be different.'

'How?' persisted Inge, still reeling from the Wimbledon announcement. None of this was what she had expected from the meeting. Nothing was what she expected any more.

'Well, obviously the actual content of the show is in development.' Nick faltered for a moment but then rallied with an idea. 'But I did think of one section called *Sports Balls*, where we find footage of famous sportsmen who fall or whatever and show their, you know, balls, except because it's seven o'clock and family and that, we block that bit out and the audience will all say—'

'Don't even go there!' Inge finished the sentence for him.

Paul and Nick nodded and drank some more wine. Paul smiled at her. 'I knew you'd like it. I think we're looking at a catch-phrase for the nation. The public will love it. They love you.'

That was the day Inge learnt that the corporation had no more sport for their most famous sports presenter to present. Everything was going to have to change. It should have been all right. Inge was famous. Everyone knew Inge Holbrook. She probably should have known better than to move back to Edenford.

# Chapter Three

It's when you go to the supermarket that you see the true triumph of women's liberation. Each out-of-town superstore is packed with women leading full and satisfying lives. These are the women who have achieved the serenity of motherhood, the satisfaction of a creative career and the ability to achieve orgasm during the spin cycle of one of their many efficient household appliances. Women who know how to fondle a melon into ripeness, a child into slumber and a man into ecstasy. Is it true? Wander down any aisle and find out.

While Inge's career was being loved and going 'up, up, up', her old schoolfriend Eve Marshall was doing the weekly shop at the giant out-of-town supermarket. She looked like any of the other countless women who had pulled up in their Ford Fiestas and their Vauxhall Cavaliers to replenish their food stores and sustain their loved ones. Slightly overweight, slightly unfit, slightly distracted. Minimal make-up, maximum perma-press. These are the women who aren't supposed to exist any more. They were supposed to have woken to the clarion call of liberation given in the 1960s and 1970s and reached out to fulfil themselves. Instead, these women had stolidly followed in their mothers' silent footsteps. The women knocking on the glass ceilings of corporate affairs might find it hard to imagine these suburban lives, but they are still being lived. Some with more equanimity than others.

The wire shopping trolleys stood waiting in serried ranks next to the homeless man selling the *Big Issue*. He had been rather popular when he'd first started. Many of the women had found paying 50p a convenient way to feel they had dealt with the homeless but, annoyingly, the man kept coming back. No one had said anything, but there was a quiet consensus amongst the shoppers that he was pushing his luck. Surely he had been there long enough to have found a home by now? How many 50ps could it take, for goodness' sake? In quiet disapproval at the vendor's persistent life on the street, most of the women shoppers had stopped buying the paper. Now the thing had gone up to £1 and that had really overstepped the mark. One could feel sympathetic but there was a limit. Even Cancer Research only came out with their collecting tins one day a year, and cancer was something anybody could get. Even, annoyingly, well-off people with private health care.

Eve wasn't shunning anyone. She just didn't see the homeless man. She didn't see anybody. She was trying not to think about shopping. Actually, she was trying not to think. She had recently decided that thinking did her no good at all so she was trying to shut down her brain, but something always sent it whirring off again. A woman in front of her was pulling at a trolley that clung to its metal colleagues, desperate not to be put to work.

'Dreadful, aren't they?' Eve said brightly to the struggling woman. 'Did you know that the shopping trolley was invented in Oklahoma City in 1937 by the owner of the Humpty Dumpty Store? Oh yes. The first ones were made out of folding chairs. The feet were put on wheels, then there was a basket on the seat and you pushed the whole thing with the back.' Eve's audience was unimpressed. Eve smiled. 'Had to be invented by a man, don't you think? I've got a book called *Facts You Didn't Know*,' she called, as the woman salvaged her trolley and disappeared into the shop.

Eve sighed. What a useless piece of information. Facts You Didn't Know and Didn't Care About. She eyed the wheeled basket selection. She had a theory about shopping trolleys. There had been a time when she thought they all had one wonky wheel, but then she had decided that would be an odd thing to invent. Lately she had concluded it was personal. There was just one defective trolley and she always chose it. Eve moved slowly towards one of the carts and then darted to another by surprise to see if that made a difference. She moved off towards the automatic doors and her trolley lurched and tripped over its inevitably faulty wheel.

The place was full of two types of women: those with lists and those without. Those with had their heads down and were busy efficiency shopping around the acres of sustenance. Those without had arrived in the hope of inspiration. That the Muse de Manger, St Creuset, might suddenly appear over the wet-fish counter. Eve was listless in every sense. She couldn't be bothered to write a list any more and she could hardly bring herself to drag round the aisles. She hated shopping. She passed the flowers and moved into the fruit and veg. The supermarket had provided a paradise of fresh produce to lure her into the bowels of the shop. Here was freshness, here was goodness, here was that just-picked wonder of Mother Nature, which her family cried out for. Eve supposed she ought to buy some but she resented it.

'The lure of the lemon and the call of the kiwi fruit drag us ignorant women in to buy fresh things, which rot in a bowl on the dining-room table, and tinned things, which don't. They think we are stupid and it will make us buy more. We are and it does.' Eve spoke to herself in her head. It was a new habit. She had so much to say and no one much to say it to.

She looked at the fresh herbs and the exotica. A large sign asked her 'Why not do something successful with a star fruit?'

It was an impossible question to answer, so Eve moved on. There was a special on plums. A woman with screaming twins in her trolley jammed the aisle ahead. The poor woman was trying everything to quieten her shrieking pair of babies. She waved rubber toys, made curious noises with her teeth, shook the trolley in a gentle sway, but the babies just screamed. The woman was at a complete loss. Eve looked at the babies. Perhaps they weren't the woman's children at all. Perhaps, as there were two of them, they were some special offer she had picked up at the front. Buy one, get one free. Eve couldn't get past, so she picked up some of the plums beside her and put them in her trolley.

From where she stood, Eve could survey the lie of the land. She knew it would not be a good day. In an attempt to add to the joy of the supermarket experience, the powers in charge had moved everything.

'Look everyone, here's something fun – Bakewell tarts are now in the crisps section!'

Once she was released from Fresh Produce, Eve moved methodically up and down the aisles until she reached Household Goods. Whoever was in charge of this section had made something of an effort. A display of tin foil had been rather artistically laid out to encourage people to cook turkey out of season. Fans of foil were splayed out to look like metallic Christmas birds on a bright, orange board. Eve had stood for some time in front of Paper Goods trying to decide whether 100 per cent recycled toilet tissue was more or less environmentally friendly than Sustainable Forest paper, when she suddenly looked up and caught sight of herself in the fold of a foil bird. She was frowning and all she could think was that what really needed recycling was herself.

It was sort of shocking. Life-changing moments ought to be big, cataclysmic affairs, things that shake and change the shape of your world, but if your life is already made up of minutiae then perhaps the big change arrives with a tiny herald. All that happened was a glance at the arse of a bird made of kitchen wrap, but Eve could hardly get her breath. She saw herself, really saw herself, for the first time in years. It was not some glance in the morning mirror to see if she absolutely had to wash her hair. It was a long look in a distorting display and she knew suddenly that she looked old and fat. She looked like somebody's mother. In that instant, that insignificant instant, Eve suddenly wanted out of her own life. She walked on in a haze of discontent and depression.

The vicar, Reverend Davies, was in Frozen Food, rummaging through the veg section. The man had rather an unfortunate harelip, so no one could have been the least bit surprised to see him selecting washed and peeled carrots for his tea.

'Ah, the lovely Mrs Marshall,' he beamed, clutching a dripping bag of orange rabbit food. Reverend Davies's top lip was hardly there at all. His mouth seemed to be entirely made up of bottom lip and huge front teeth. The effect was to create something of a spray when he spoke. The Lord loved him but not enough to provide orthodontic work.

'The flowerth are looking lovely in the north aisle. I alwayth thay there'th nothing tho thummer-like ath thunflowerth in theathon.' Water dripped from the carrots and from the end of Eve's nose. She always forgot not to stand too close when the Reverend came up with a sentence containing a lot of Ss. Later she would think that perhaps she should have paid more attention to Reverend Davies. This was God's envoy. This was her passport to Paradise. Perhaps he could have helped her. The pastor of St Mary the Virgin of Edenford. Unfortunate name for a church, she always thought. Made it sound as if Edenford had just the one virgin.

'Thee you for the Thummer Thocial?' he enquired, with a fresh gush of saliva. Maybe it was a test from God and Eve failed. She nodded her answer and moved on to drip dry amongst the custard tarts and bottled waters. Eve didn't know why she did the flowers at the church. Reverend Davies came round one day for jumble and she didn't have any so she ended up doing the flowers instead. She wasn't a churchgoer at all, but Eve liked arranging the large bunches. She liked cutting the fat stems of new flowers so that the sap ran down on the wrapping paper. She liked watching the green stems dive into the clean water in the tall vases.

The shopping trolley dragged Eve from one zigzag to another, finally leaving her jammed against a display of foreign goods. She had selected nothing for any meal whatsoever. Just the special-offer-near-at-hand plums. In a dump-bin by the till the Lords of

Food were trying to shift starter kits for Mexican food, so Eve bought one of those and left.

The cat was waiting when Eve got home. It hid behind the hat stand in the hall watching her unload the bags. There was no love lost between Eve and that cat. Adam had bought it for her one Christmas. He never asked Eve if she wanted a cat or, indeed, what she thought about cats in general, because it was meant to be a surprise. It certainly was. Eve didn't like cats at all. They seemed to her snooty creatures and somehow the cat, Claudette, seemed to know this. It bided its time. Eve was just bringing in the last lot of perishables when it pounced. For a moggy it had exceptional athletic ability. From behind the hat stand Claudette flew into the air and landed in the middle of Eve's shoulders. Eve dropped the shopping and the box of plums spilled out over the floor. Claudette clung on for a good minute and Eve could have sworn she heard her laughing. Then for no reason whatsoever the cat just dropped to the floor and buggered off. She did it all the time. Never when anyone was watching. Just when Eve was alone.

Plums. Plums everywhere. The one product Eve had bought to show how fresh and healthy her life was. She bent down and gathered up the bright red fruit, but there was one stuck under the radiator and Eve couldn't get to it. Eve couldn't get to it partly because it had rolled too far under and partly because of Tom's stuffed otter.

Eve's son, Tom, dabbled in taxidermy and the stuffed-animal presence of his hobby was felt throughout much of the house. He had left the otter there to dry one winter and never collected the thing. It was an odd creature, captured in a moment of whatever makes an otter insane with delight. It had been stuffed to sit up on its hind legs with a smile to make a dentist moist with pleasure. It sat grinning at Eve while she lay on the floor with a knitting needle and tried to poke the plum out. At last she managed to jab the Houdini of the fruit basket with the end of the needle and the point came out all red. Like it was bleeding. Eve had been bleeding a lot recently. Most days she was preoccupied with either going to or coming from 'sorting myself out'. She had seen the doctor. He had told her 'something must be done', but she didn't want to go again. She couldn't bear the indignity of it. The flat on your back trying to 'relax' of it.

'If you had a hysterectomy, Mrs Marshall, then it would all be over,' the doctor said, as if he could possibly know anything about it.

Why do so many men go into gynaecology? What leads a young man to a life up to his elbows in vaginas? It would all be over if she had the operation. They would vacuum out Eve's functions and it would all be over, but she just couldn't. She just couldn't and she didn't know why.

'It's a very common operation,' continued the doctor. 'Why, in America a third of all women have had their wombs removed by the time they are sixty.'

Eve looked at the man who was dealing with her mysterious body. He stood there, confident that he alone could untangle Eve's defective structure. His white coat merely hid his blue tights and red underpants. He was able to cure the uncurable. Stop a woman seeping in a single bound. A professional ready to lance her body as if it were an abscess.

Eve never discussed it with Adam. She knew he wouldn't like the actual word. Womb. He couldn't bear anything to do with women's problems. It was bad enough that he lived in monthly terror that she might discharge something on the sheets at night. Constant bleeding would be intolerable. Eve was unclean.

She lay on the floor looking at the plum blood. She thought of her face reflected in the foil and it occurred to her not to get up at all, but she would have been too easy a target for Claudette so she rose and went to the loo. These were big daily decisions. This was Eve's life.

# Chapter Four

My dear Inge,

## *And Lillian and Derek begat Eve*

It is not the old that are wise, nor the
aged that understand what is right.

(JOB 3.9)

Thank you so much for your letter and the photograph of the flat. It looks lovely. All that Caribbean sun. It's funny. I always wanted Shirley to travel. I just didn't think it would be like this. I don't know why she went with you. I don't suppose any of us knows why anything happened, but thank you. I know you'll look after her.

The psychiatrist wants to know about my childhood. He keeps saying that there has to be an explanation. It's what we all want, isn't it? We don't like things we don't understand. I think that's why people have religion. To get rid of the uncertainty of everything. Something bizarre happens and people nod and say, 'Well, God moves in mysterious ways,' and that's that sorted out. I have an explanation for what happened but I'm sure it won't do, so the shrink and I relentlessly seek out an answer. I don't know what it is he wants – a bad nappy change when I was four or a difficult relationship with tricycles or something. There just has to be some blame. What happened has to be somebody or something's fault.

'Were you happy as a child?'

And I think about that and the answer is – yes. Very. Mum and Dad were the happiest couple in our street. He was so gentle, my dad. Do you remember him? Never said a word against anyone. He was a builder. A good builder. An unusual builder because everyone loved him.

'Please, Mr Cameron, we're desperate. You're the only one we can rely on.'

Cameron Builders and Decorators, which sounded like an army but it was just him. He built and decorated all day and then came home and did the same for Mother. The garden was stunning. He used to work in it all weekend and Mother would come out and say, 'What have you put the azaleas there for? They can't go there.'

And he would smile at me and say, 'How's my lovely Eve? How's Daddy's girl?'

I still miss him. The smell of his jumper. The feel of his arms around me. He played the piano and sometimes Mother would stand in the door with a dishcloth and stop for a second to listen. It was the only time she was quiet. I thought things were perfect till he died. I thought I understood how he and Mum worked. I don't know if you knew but Dad passed away at the end of February last year. It was near the end of March when we went to Mum's for the will reading. I'm sure everyone thought it would just be straightforward, but it wasn't. It was a terrible day. Partly because of the will and partly because Adam caught his willie in his trouser zip. I don't think he and I were ever the same again after that.

## *Adam's Defective Trouser Department*

... you wives, be submissive to your husbands ...

(1 PETER 3.1)

I remember we were late leaving for the lunch but I could hear Adam was in a terrible state.

'Eve! Eve!' he screamed from the bedroom in anguish that could only be life-threatening. I was busy in the bathroom. I'd been having a few problems, bleeding and that, but Adam was calling, so I patched myself up quickly and sprayed sprays of different kinds to hide any possible smell. It's a worry for women, isn't it? Smell. Anyway, I hid my secret pads and bits in the under-sink cupboard. Adam never looks in that cupboard. It holds the risk of *cleaning things*. Then I ran to our room. Adam was standing in the middle of the bedroom with tears streaming down his cheeks. His face was all twisted with pain. I thought he'd had a heart attack.

I ran to the phone. 'I'll get the doctor.'

'No!' he squeaked. 'You can't!'

'Why ever not?'

Adam could hardly speak. 'It's caught.' He moaned through a sort of coughing sound, and indeed it was caught. The very edge of Adam's 'little friend' had caught in the zip of his trousers. I always think it's a very odd part of the male body. Funny little dangly thing with a will of its own. I haven't said that to anyone else. Maybe these are the crazy things. It was not a time for me to think such thoughts. This was very serious. If we did not remove our little friend from his trap, it was quite possible the house might fall down.

'It needs cream,' I said.

'You can't touch it!' he screamed through clenched teeth.

'Lie down,' I said, and went to get the Oil of Ulay. Adam lay face-up on the bed and I gently wiped on cream with some cotton wool. The middle of the morning – what would people think? It was a very slow operation but we managed to secure freedom. The lesion left behind was tiny but devastating. Little lamb. He could hardly walk.

We sat looking at his penis with great reverence. I couldn't remember the last time I'd seen it in daylight. Poor thing looked rather tired. I've never written the word penis before. Penis. Sounds much tidier than the real thing. Do you remember Miss Cadman, English Lang and Lit, fifth year? It took her a whole term to tell us that a 'pity' in art was a nude. We all thought she was going to faint dead away when you made her explain what it meant. Penis. Pity. Don't tell Shirley all this. It isn't necessary. I don't think children want to know that their parents have genitalia at all, let alone bits which they've injured. I wondered if we couldn't have insured against damage to the thing? We had insurance for everything else.

'Do you think it's serious?' Adam asked, as he examined the wound thoroughly.

'No' I said, aware that I was bleeding again. Gushing and seeping.

'You mustn't tell anyone,' he kept saying through clenched teeth. Who was I going to tell? We were going to lunch with Mother.

News, Mother? Well, Adam caught his privates in his zip this morning. I know, fifty-five! You'd think he would have got the hang of it by now.

We went to have coffee in the kitchen. He thought it would calm him down. Despite his pain, Adam tutted as I picked up the newspapers from the hall table. He thinks it is a new extravagance on my part that I have the *Guardian* delivered as well as the *Daily Mail*. I tell him I don't want the *Daily Mail*. I want to see what's happening in the world.

'There's no point in reading all that foreign news because there's nothing we can do about it,' he says. Adam mostly likes the local paper and cuts out long bits about planting your onions out early. 'You should stop worrying about something that is none of your business and concentrate on things you can do. Like the garden,' he said, while I poured the coffee. He was right. I shouldn't be sitting there. Not while there was fruit to be removed from under the hall radiator.

We settled down. He flicked through the *Mail* while I read my paper. I remember because that's what always happened.

'There's a Japanese cult in the paper who say there's going to be Armageddon in September,' I'd say, and he'd reply, because he wasn't listening, 'I don't think we're doing anything in September.'

Then Adam chuckled to himself and stabbed a finger at his tabloid. 'This is good,' he said. 'This is very good. They've got this photo of a Filipino man who's been caught eating his dead partner's hand. What do you think the headline is?'

'I don't know,' I said.

Adam could hardly tell me for laughing. 'What Are You Doing for the Rest of Your Wife? Isn't that great?' He looked disappointed at my reaction. 'I thought you'd like it. It's foreign news.'

I looked at him, my husband.

'Adam, do you love me?'

'What? Don't be silly. What's brought this on? Don't I look after you? Give you a nice home?'

And he does. He has stood by me. He came to visit me here and we both pretended nothing had really happened. We pretended that someone will realise the car was terribly faulty and it couldn't possibly have been anything to do with me.

I went back to my paper. They only have the rubbish ones in here so I have nothing else to read. I don't know if I mind. I am beginning to wonder what the point of all the news is. I mean, it floods into our houses day after day and none of us do anything about it. What is the point in knowing if we're just going to carry on the same as usual anyway? Did you know that the Turkish government is doing horrid things to the Kurds? I saw a programme on it and I kept thinking, What should I do about this? What can I do? These people might join the Common Market.

I used to watch the television news in the kitchen. Adam bought me a portable for my birthday. I know he wanted it for gardening programmes, but Dixons happened to be running a special offer the week of my birthday so it rather fitted in.

*Fact – the first real television station was built in Berlin in 1935 in anticipation of the Olympic Games where Hitler behaved so beautifully. The BBC did the first live journalistic reporting in 1937 for the coronation of King George VI. Imagine living in an age when seeing royalty on the telly was a rarity. The smallest video screen available is less than one inch across – about the size of a postage stamp. It's called Private Eye and was dreamed up by some American called Allen Becker. Apparently you have to hold it really close to your eye to watch. Tricky if you want friends round to watch Wimbledon.*

I think Adam thought a telly in the kitchen would keep me quiet at night. I don't sleep, you see. Not properly. Haven't for ages. It's the dreams. They won't leave me alone. I think it mainly started when Shirley was born. I used to lie awake with her cot right next to my head, listening to her every move and willing her to breathe till morning.

Sorry, I got distracted. They like to keep us busy in here. I've been for another 'session'. Big Nose, the psychiatrist, and I have been discussing the 'reasons for my crime'. Apparently, he says, it is good that I've never done it before. I can't think why. I mean, I never had the chance before. The barrister says that it is good that I am 'intelligent, articulate and personable'. Middle class seems good too, although she doesn't say so. I think that comes as a given under 'articulate'. The psychiatrist is rather more cheerful today. Rather more confident that we can find an excusing mental condition for my aberrant behaviour. I imagine it would be nice to render me harmless with some pathological excuse.

## The Temptation of the Sunday Supplements

Thou has set our inequities before thee, our
secret sins in the light of thy countenance.

(PSALMS 90.8)

I have made the barrister, Miss March, less confident.

'Before that . . . day . . .' We both know which day she means.
I nod conspiratorially as she lowers her voice to a whisper. 'Had
you ever done anything which you, yourself, might consider to
be . . . wicked?'

I lean forward to match her and lower my voice. 'Well . . .' She
can hardly bear the suspense. Sits tapping her mobile phone on
the desk.

'Yes,' I finally say. The pause has been worthwhile. She almost
drops the phone. I'm being mean and it's not right. It's only that
everyone is watching me all the time. I wish they would get it all
over with. I am quite happy to say I did it but it seems that won't
do.

'I see,' she says, with a rough clearing of her throat. She is
faced with a serially bad person. 'And what was the nature of
these offences?'

'Oh, I didn't say they were offences. Just a bit wicked. That's
what you said – something wicked.' She clears her throat again.
It makes me almost maternal.

'Would you like a fruit gum?' She shakes her head so I pick up
my tapestry and begin sewing. I think I seem calm but I'm not
really. I have terrible flashes of feeling quite sick. I don't know
how things got to here. It's not where I belong. It's not how
things should have turned out and I have been wicked before.
Not big things. Just stupid things because everything was always
the same. Because nothing ever changed.

I was born in 1955. I was a teenager in the sixties, I was heading for grown up in the seventies. Everything was supposed to
have changed since my mother had me. Since she regretted

everything about her life and me. I went to school with a lot of girls with plans. We all had plans and then when I had my children I met my friends again. I met them in the same playground where my mother had waited. I met them waiting for their children. Regretting. You see, nothing had changed. It was all talk. But I didn't regret. Not till the very end.

The lawyer starts tapping again. Maybe she thought we were getting somewhere. 'What sort of wicked things?'

'Oh nothing, just daft really. I started sending off for ads. You know, from the newspapers, Sunday magazines, that sort of thing. There's quite a lot in the *Sunday Telegraph*. Well, I had started reading all the papers and then I noticed all these ads – shoes for the wider fitting, stairlifts for the terraced home, trousers with elasticised waists in non-crease man-made fibres, holidays for the elderly-but-active sun-seeker, nylon sofa covers and snuggle bags for wet dogs in the back of saloon cars. The first one happened because I was cross about the charity shop. I filled in Betty Hoddle's name and address on a coupon for incontinence pants in a range of autumn colours and sent it off. After that I started sending all sorts of things to people in the town. Plastic drain cover brochures, sonic pest repellents, anything really, although I did try to match the item to the person I was sending it to.'

'And what was their reaction?'

'Well, I've no idea. I mean, no one knew it was me. It seemed rather harmless in the great scheme of things. I suppose it was irresponsible but it's not like I took to drink or anything.'

'Had you been drinking at the time of the . . . incident?'

'No. Not at all.'

'That's good.'

'Yes.'

Everyone is very pleased that I hadn't been drinking. That would have made the killing very unladylike, which would have been even worse. A man killing someone while he was drunk might have used it as a defence, but for a woman it painted her as even more satanic. That's what the girls on my wing tell me. They're really very nice for criminals. I had not been drinking, but the fact is I have been wicked. It is a bad thing. It fuzzes the lines between whether the jury will vote for me or not. I have been naughty. Miss March has been clear with me.

'But you had been violent before.'

'I don't think so.'

Miss March looks at her notes. 'I have here that one evening in your parents' house you knocked your sister out with a blow to the head.'

'I can explain. She wanted me to. You see—'

'The fact remains, Mrs Marshall, that the world is divided into two types of female defendant – those who merit compassion and those who don't. It is very important that we get the jury on your side. These incidents will not help. Now would you say that you were good at your job?'

'I didn't have a job. I was a housewife.'

'Yes, but were you good at it? You understand the probation officers will go and see what sort of house you maintained.'

'*I* maintained?'

'Yes. How your family will or will not cope without you has an important bearing on the final judgment or the sentence you might expect.'

Quick, Ladies and Gentlemen of the Jury, you must return me to the bosom of my family or they may burst with germs. I try to think about my house. It seems very far away. Was I good at running it? Did I maintain a nice home? We never ran out of toilet paper and I put blue air-fresheners down all the drains. Would that save me staying in jail? Did anyone value it? Certainly not Adam or Shirley. Neither one of them would have seen running the house as 'a complex task requiring high levels of management skills'. If Adam had done it things would have been different. The house would have been filled with little plaques for Employee of the Month with his name all over them.

*Fact – the Stoics believed that disciples, who were often from very wealthy families, needed to do menial work before they learnt anything. They taught that until a person had learnt to bear physical hardships and the social embarrassment of doing a slave's labours, they couldn't acquire wisdom. I must be very ready for learning.*

I look at Miss March. She is young. She has made it. I am merely a rung on her case ladder to success. Why didn't I become a barrister? I wasn't stupid at school. Why did I sit at home for so long feeling the hairs on my chin? Why did it take so long for me to wonder what I was for? To want to know why I had come?

In my house I could see out of the kitchen window from my chair at the breakfast bar. If I had the chair just right I could see out and watch the television at the same time. Our house is on a new estate. The Much Sought-After Palmer Estate with its Convenient Shopping Facilities. So convenient, in fact, that I could see them at the end of the road. From one chair I could take in my entire horizon – the house, the shops and the TV. There are eight houses on the way and inside each one sat a housewife, sipping coffee. We didn't get together much, any of us. Too much to do. Hypnotised by the fear of lingering odours in the fridge or unwanted pet hairs on the hall carpet. The estate has moulded miniature gardens. We were like those little pockets of air in bubble-wrap – separated into claustrophobic isolation.

I kept a small mirror on the breakfast bar for my chin work. Almost every day there seemed to be a new hair that had sprouted. I pulled them out with a very fine pair of tweezers I kept just for the purpose. I went through a lot of tweezers before I found the right ones. I got them out of Adam's Swiss Army knife. I didn't tell him, but it is a loss that we discussed for some time. The hairs are tough and when you pull them out there is a great, fat, white root on them that was buried in my chin. I hold them up to the light from the window and examine them. They are sturdy things. Dandelions of the face that will not be eradicated no matter how often you weed them away. I sometimes wonder if it wouldn't be best just to let them have their head, so to speak. Just let them grow and see what kind of facial growth I could achieve. I quite fancy a twirling moustache.

'Aha!' I would cry with a flourish of handlebar hair. 'It is time to conquer the germs, to annihilate the enemies of hygiene.' I stand with my gun hand ready on the trigger of a disinfectant spray. 'You cannot hide from me. I am not alone. I have a robot army of machines, oceans of water and detergent and an array of technicians who, with a single phone call, will leap to my aid.'

I rush to the bathroom ready to destroy. My moustaches flail in the air. I raise the lid of the toilet and cry, 'You cannot escape. Incoming at nine o'clock. Brrrrrr!' The droning of an attack in full flight departs my lips as I dare to approach that most sinister of places – under the rim of the toilet bowl. I spray and death comes.

It's just like that. Then, when at last it is time for coffee, I know that I can rest. My cupboards are neat and orderly. My jellies are ranked in colour order. I can find a small tin of baked beans with my eyes shut and then . . . I start again because I do not want to think.

'The housewife who must wait for the success of world revolution for her liberty might be excused for losing hope.' Germaine Greer. Bloody Germaine Greer. Hadn't she got something better to do than fill people's heads with rubbish? If I'd never joined those classes none of this might have happened.

The barrister leafs through her notes. 'Your husband says things had started to slip before . . . the incident.'

'He does?'

'Yes. He says he found . . . rotting fruit under the radiators . . .'

*Fact – the plum is part of the rose family. The plum tree flower has an enlarged basal portion called the pistil. The pistil is the ovary of the fruit. The outer part of the ovary ripens into a fleshy, juicy exterior, making up the edible*

*part, and a hard interior, called the stone or pit. The seed is*
*enclosed within the stone. According to the earliest writings*
*in which the plum is mentioned, the species is at least 2,000*
*years old. Ancient writings connect early cultivation of*
*these plums with the region around Damascus.*

I've been trying to take up smoking while I'm in here but I
can't seem to get the hang of it. I've tried lots of times before. I
wondered if I could use those nicotine patches smokers use to
stop, and build up to smoking gradually? It would be something
to do while I sit – smoking. I'm forty-five and never puffed a fag
behind a bicycle shed.

God, stick to one thing at a time. The news. I know the news
is not my business, but it used to keep me awake at night. All
those Kosovan refugees with nowhere to go. Muslims who hate
Christians who hate Muslims . . . Shirley used to tell me I should
pray. The last time we were in the kitchen alone together she
wanted to hold my hand with her eyes shut.

'I'm making it my mission for you to see the way, Mum,' she
said, while I was trying to get some garibaldis out of the bottom
cupboard.

I'm sorry, I'm drifting. I want to tell you about the day of the
lunch because it matters. We had to wait for Adam's 'little friend',
his injured member, to settle down before we could get in the car
to go. He wasn't at all well.

'I don't think I can drive,' he muttered through clenched teeth,
so we went in my car. I knew he was badly wounded because he
hates me driving. It's not just me. He hates anyone else being
behind the wheel. Sits sucking in his breath every time I turn a
corner. It makes me nervous so I rather lurched out of the drive.

'It's not my fault,' I said, feeling defensive at the first suck of
his breath. 'There's something funny about the automatic gearbox. I know it's supposed to change gears on its own, but not
when you're not expecting it.'

'Eve, you must get this car seen to,' Adam said for the millionth time. And he was right. I should have. It was another thing I had put off having fixed. I looked in the mirror to pull out and I could see that I was frowning my supermarket frown.

'The mechanic always treats me as though I am stupid,' I said, narrowly avoiding hitting a bus. Adam sucked on his teeth. I didn't tell him that I had written off for a book about cars from *Reader's Digest*. The ad said it explained everything and you got a free forty-piece socket set. Perhaps I could be less stupid. We sat silently for a moment.

'Adam . . .' I began. 'I've been thinking about . . . my time.' We both sat quietly while we thought about this idea. This notion of *my time*. I moved on slowly. 'Now that the children have grown up—'

'Grown up? Tom's never going to grow up!'

'He's no trouble and he's not at home any more. I was thinking about doing one of those Open University courses. You know, art or something.'

'Art or something? Eve, what is the point of that? Where's the point in art? Why don't you stick with what you're good at?'

'All right, what am I good at?' This made us both think. He's not unkind, Adam, so he really did try.

'Lots of things.' He thought for a minute. 'Like . . . cupboards. Kitchen cupboards. You're very good at organising cupboards.' The car lurched through another unexpected gear change. Kitchen cupboards. That's what he thought I was good at.

I have to go now. Tom's come to visit. He's been wonderful. We talk and that helps. Love to Shirley and some for yourself.

As ever,

Eve

# Chapter Five

Inge moved to Edenford at the end of May. The morning of the Friday before her departure from London found her staring at the breasts of the BBC's senior, female newsreader. The removal firm had left her a pile of old newspapers to wrap around the china. They had offered to do it as part of the service, but Inge wanted strangers in the house for as little time as possible. The yellowing collection of newsprint included the seamier Fleet Street papers that Inge never bought. Now she was sitting on the floor staring at what passed for news in these publications. The breasts she was looking at were slightly out of focus, but clearly breasts and it was quite clear who they belonged to.

Carol Hart, senior newsreader for the BBC, was reclining on a yacht wearing only the bottom half of a rather finely conceived bikini. Her breasts lay exposed to the sun and indeed now to the world. It might not have been news were she not recovering from reconstructive surgery following a major breast-cancer scare which had hit the headlines. She had nice breasts. The plastic surgeon had done a good job. She looked great. Carol was loved by the nation and now the nation could love her breasts. She had gone away to recover and now the nation could rejoice. Even people who didn't buy the paper could rejoice. The breasts were on the front page.

Inge knew Carol and knew that she had brought a complaint against the paper but everyone also knew it was a waste of time.

The breasts were in the public domain and Inge was using them for packing. The other tabloids, who had failed to get the paparazzi pictures in the first place, had generally responded with moral outrage. They were outraged at the paparazzi, they were outraged on behalf of Carol Hart, they were outraged on behalf of all recovering women (photographs of breasts in various stages of repair), they were outraged on behalf of anyone with breasts (fine photographic evidence), they were outraged at the cost of surgery to get such fine breasts (examples of splendid breasts through the ages) and they were generally a decent and fine publication which Middle England could embrace. It went well. Middle English women were pleased with the outrage, Middle English men were pleased with the breasts.

Inge shuddered. The papers had never gone to town on her but she knew it was only a matter of time. A couple of the gossip columns did have some inches on her but it was a replay of an old rumour about her and Mark Hinks, the footballer. She and Mark were friends, they were both single, they often went out together and each time it caused talk. Would they, wouldn't they? Did they, didn't they?

Inge looked around the place she had called home for the last ten years. The smart flat with its high loft ceilings was full of boxes now and some of her best mugs were carefully wrapped in the exposure of other people's lives. Inge packed the china into a cardboard box and sealed it shut. She had nearly finished but she still didn't know if they were doing the right thing. She had never wanted to leave the flat or London. It was so perfect. So central. So safe. She had never thought she would go back to Edenford, the sleepy Home Counties town where she had been brought up. Edenford. God, it seemed such a long time ago, but they needed the garden, needed the air. Inge had never sold her parents' house after her mother died, and when the tenants moved out it seemed like fate. It seemed as though things had been decided for her, but Inge was dreading it. Dreading going home.

When the phone rang she called, 'I'll get it,' although she

doubted Kate would have the energy to take a call. Inge wasn't expecting anyone to ring and immediately she felt afraid. She couldn't have said what she was afraid of, but something in her stomach turned over. It wasn't a new feeling. It happened when the phone rang, when the post thudded through the letterbox, when the morning paper landed on the mat. It used to happen when the doorbell went, but in this apartment building the porter didn't let anyone up without getting clearance. Despite that safeguard, Inge lived in a permanent and inexplicable state of slight fear. It was as if she knew that someday something would happen to bring everything crashing down around her head. It never had, but that didn't mean it wouldn't. She had lived like this all her professional life. It was the norm.

The porter was at his most businesslike.

'Someone from the BBC, Miss Holbrook. I expect you'll want me to show them straight up. A Miss Jenny Wilson.'

'Wilson?' Inge couldn't think of anyone called Wilson. Maybe one of those waiting-room women. Maybe something was being sent round. Maybe . . .

'No, wait. Let me have a word.' There was some muttering as Miss Wilson came to the phone.

'I don't normally allow anyone in my booth . . . Mind my paperwork . . . No, don't sit on the chair, it's specially adjusted for my back . . .' The porter was professionally unhappy. He handed the receiver over reluctantly and a bright, booming voice thundered down the line. The porter needn't have bothered with the phone. The caller had a vocal quality that did not require the use of amplification in order to be heard from the foyer.

'Hello, there. Jenny Wilson, BBC Talent Department.'

Inge moved the phone a few inches from her ear and frowned. 'I'm sorry, you are . . .?'

'Jenny Wilson, Talent Department.' In the background Inge could hear the porter muttering, 'BBC pass, BBC person or I wouldn't even have called up.' He did not like having his judgement questioned or his phone taken from him.

Inge was still confused. 'Yes, sorry, Miss Wilson, did we have an appointment?'

'It won't take a moment. Shall I come up?'

Panic filled the back of Inge's throat. There was no need for it but it came unbidden. 'No, No!' she replied hastily. She wanted the woman to go away. She didn't know her. She wasn't booked. But Inge was terrified of seeming standoffish. Of word getting out at the BBC that maybe she wasn't the warm, accessible human being she so wanted to be. 'I'll be right down.' Inge hung up and took a deep breath. Why the hell was she seeing her? The woman didn't have an appointment. Inge brushed her fingers through her hair and looked in on Kate. She was sleeping. Perhaps she wouldn't even notice Inge had gone.

Inge took the lift down ten floors and headed for the porter's small office. A very large woman filled the doorway. She had more chins than seemed a fair share for one person and appeared to be wearing a marquee as a summer dress. It was bright orange with massive cerise flowers. Had it not been of such a violent hue it could easily have been rented out to hold functions.

'God, it is!' boomed the woman. 'It is! It is! Inge Holbrook as I live and breathe.'

'Inge Holbrook,' repeated the porter, smiling. 'In our very building. I tell no one but it is a fact.' He leant confidentially towards Miss Wilson. 'I am silent as a grave but I know a great deal. It'll be a sad day when Miss Holbrook moves out of here . . .' Inge frowned at the man who blanched at his indiscretion and tried to recover. 'Not that she is . . . moving . . . and if she were, then you wouldn't hear it from me . . .'

Inge smiled at the woman. 'Hello?'

The woman thrust forward a massive, plump hand. 'Jenny, Jenny Wilson. You were expecting me?'

'No.'

The woman shook her head. 'No, you were. Jenny Wilson, talent team?'

Inge shook her head. 'Sorry, I'm not with you.'

'Oh, but you are. You are not only with me, but top of my list.'

'Well, she would be,' agreed the porter, who seemed to feel he was now part of the conversation.

The woman smiled broadly. 'You didn't know I was coming and that makes it all the more clear to me why I am needed.' She flashed a BBC staff pass at Inge. 'Shall we go up? A little more private?'

'Good idea,' agreed the porter and pressed the lift button. 'Much more private.'

'I was just going to get a coffee . . . at the coffee shop . . . next door,' Inge managed hurriedly. 'Why don't you join me?'

Jenny Talent beamed. 'That would be lovely.'

The porter shook his head with disapproval. 'Not nearly so private.'

Inge led the way as her large companion followed, causing an upsurge of wind as she walked and her marquee flapped. The coffee shop occupied one small corner of the apartment building's ground floor and was often the only place Inge managed to get any sustenance. The owner knew her well and swiftly seated the pair at a quiet back table. On one side was a large bank of cushioned seating.

'Lovely place,' boomed Jenny as she plumped down, covering every inch of the seating space. She beamed at Inge who took a chair on the other side of the table. 'I hear there are great plans afoot for a new programme,' Jenny continued.

'Well, I think some people in development are . . .'

Jenny leant forward and whispered confidentially, '*Don't Even Go There!*'

'Yes. Of course, I don't think anyone quite knows . . .'

Jenny nodded. 'Going to be a wonderful documentary.'

The waitress came for the coffee order giving Inge a moment to pause. Once they were alone again she turned to Jenny.

'Documentary? I thought it was a panel game.'

'Was, indeed, *was*, but they've moved on. Development.' She looked at Inge's bewildered face. 'Oh dear, not keeping you in the loop, are they?' She raised a hand in the air as if to part the very waters of the Red Sea of confusion. 'Not going to happen now I'm on board, I can assure you. Anyway, fabulous idea. How many of us just love to watch sport?'

'Well, it is popular.'

'Oh yes, but how many of us have longed over the years to actually participate in a major sporting event but haven't actually had the . . . what can I call it?'

Inge tried for the obvious. 'Fitness?'

Jenny shook her head in a movement that caused ripples down her body. 'No. Opportunity. But now all that will change. Members of the public will apply and, if selected, you will train them to take part in an actual event like Wimbledon, the Olympics, the FA Cup, that sort of thing. Obviously they won't play in the whole thing. I mean, we can only afford to train them for a week but, you know, they will get their moment. It will be tough but before they begin you will warn them . . .'

'*Don't Even Go There!*' mumbled Inge with her eyes closed. When she opened them again Jenny was still brilliant with pleasure at the concept.

'I think it could become a catch-phrase.'

Inge didn't know where to begin. 'What do you think the athletes will think about this? Because if you actually get to the FA cup final, would you really want Joe Bloggs from Derby to be on your side?'

Jenny, thrilled to be asked for an opinion, considered the matter carefully. 'I think sports people are very realistic these days. It's big business. They'll know it's good publicity. Anyway, they all love you.'

She waited for Inge to bask in the love but the BBC legend was tired.

'And how is it that you know about this and I don't, Jenny?'

'Indeed. Indeed, how?' Inge's companion removed a sheaf of papers from a large shoulderbag and began to riffle through them. She really was an enormous woman. It was like having coffee with the Alps.

'You see, Inge,' she began, 'this is what I am here to stop happening.'

'I'm sorry, Jenny, I don't—'

'No, clearly. You didn't know I was coming, you didn't know about the show and that is my brief. To see that this never happens again. Let me explain.' She assumed a look of deep seriousness and a low tone of confidence. 'Inge, as you will know, the BBC is very concerned about the talent drain. You know that clever people like you are spending their formative years with the BBC and then drifting off to just any old television channel the minute some more money pops up. Now we don't want that, but we do want you to be happy. That's why Paul has set up the Talent Team. We at the Talent Team are here to make sure you are happy. Each established face at the Beeb is going to be given a "talent guardian". In your case that will be me. It will be my job to make sure you are happy, to see that you have what you need, that no meetings come as a surprise . . .' Jenny laughed at this hilarious joke and shook like a blancmange. 'You and I will really get to know each other, and at any time, should you be on BBC premises or attending a function on behalf of the BBC, I will be there to make sure you are properly looked after.'

Coffee arrived, which caused a short pause in the proceedings. Jenny looked around the shop. 'What a handy place. Is it true what the porter said, that you're moving? Seems a shame. Do the press office know?'

'No. The thing is—'

Jenny waved her hand in the air. 'Don't worry. We'll get to that. Perhaps a small statement. Now, I am here to help you, so we need to go through one or two essential questions.' Inge reached for the milk and sugar but Jenny put out her hand to stop her.

'No, Inge. This is where it begins. I am here to look after you. Every time you enter a BBC building, I, or someone from our team, will be there to make sure you are happy. So, and I think this shows how much we plan to be there for you, how do you have your coffee?'

'Sorry?'

Jenny patted Inge's hand. 'You tell me and I do the milk and sugar. It's no trouble. I've got a space on my form for it.'

# Chapter Six

Eve liked to learn things. She loved facts and she was good at remembering them. There was nothing she liked better than absorbing some obscure piece of information and then passing it on to someone else. But lately this party trick had started to worry her. She had been explaining to someone in the charity shop that 'More French people die of diseases of the digestive system than any other European nationalities' when Mrs Hoddle, who was sorting clothes in the back, had said very loudly, 'Isn't it a shame that some people confuse gathering information with being clever!'

Perhaps it had just been a passing remark, but the more that year went on, the more Eve learnt and the less she felt she understood. It wasn't until later that Eve realised her mother had made a huge culinary mistake in God's eyes on the day of the will reading. The Bible was absolutely clear about shellfish. Those 'bottom dwellers' of the sea were a definite no-no. Prawns should never have been served.

As Eve drove herself and Adam to lunch at her mother's, Adam sighed. She thought it was about the faulty car again.

'I'll get it fixed,' she said.

'Oh, it's not that.' He sighed again. 'Just thinking about this new job. I may have to go into the office later.'

'Right.'

Adam sighed yet again and reached for the cassette player.

Shirley Bassey filled the journey, singing loudly about the fact that she was no one.

The great Shirley Bassey no doubt wallowed daily in the impact she had had on many lives, but she was perhaps unaware of the integral part she played in Adam and Eve's marriage. When Eve married Adam she might have guessed the full extent of his obsession with the Welsh singer as they had a serious discussion about his bride-to-be processing up the aisle to a recording of 'Big Spender'. Over the years it had become clear that if Dame Shirley ever arrived in Edenford with a gleam in her eye, Adam, Eve's devoted husband, would be off in a second. Eve looked at Adam out of the corner of her eye while she drove. He sat with his hands cupped over his injury.

She loved him and he loved her, but perhaps not with the passion he reserved for the two focuses of his life – Shirley Bassey and avocado plants. It was a curious combination, but Adam had made it a life's work. He had all of Shirley's recordings and he was hoping to be 'avocado self-sufficient' by the following year. It was, at least, an ambition.

Every time Eve and Adam had an avocado, he would take out the pip, put a matchstick in either side and hang it over a glass of water. Once it had sprouted he'd plant it in one of the big tubs on the bedroom windowsill (south facing – best light). Eve hated them. She watched them grow thin and tall and could feel them suck the sunlight out of the room. They had never had an avocado from them in the many years he had been doing it, but Adam was not a man easily swayed from his path of purpose.

He had the same single-minded attitude to many things. Like not eating certain Eastern foods. 'They're bound to have used cats and dogs for the meat,' he would say, and Eve would think about that. To her it seemed ridiculous. Why would anyone bother? It had to be twice as difficult chasing around in the dark for a stray moggy than popping down Dewhurst's of a Saturday morning. Why would any restaurant not just go to a butcher? Save all that 'Here pussy, pussy', followed by fur stripping and eyes down every time you saw a hand-made 'beloved pet missing' poster on a telegraph pole. 'A pound of mince and a nice chump chop please,' simply had to be easier. But Adam was sure he was right and that was that.

Eve's mother had made a special effort with the lunch. Her husband's will reading was an important family occasion, although no one was expecting fireworks. There was no anticipation of anything exciting. He had been a local builder. There was unlikely to be a secret slush fund in the Cayman Islands. Still, Mrs Cameron had really laboured over the meal and it was important that everyone realised the full extent of the effort.

As Adam and Eve arrived at the family home, Ravel's 'Bolero' was booming out of every casement. Adam, his eyes closed with pain, his hand cupped as a flesh codpiece for his injury, waited for Eve to ring the bell. It still seemed odd to Eve to ring the bell at her own home, the place where she had grown up, but it was polite. There was a small cry from the kitchen and in a moment Mrs Cameron could be seen through the glass front door, wearing her frilly apron, flour in her hair and with a face as red as a baboon's bottom. Mrs Cameron had a bad limp, but despite this she appeared to be attempting to glide across the parquet floor.

'Dum, da, da, da, dum, da, da, da . . . dee, da da dee da da deeee!' She opened the door with a flourish, her arms busy conducting the music as she glided towards daughter and son-in-law. Adam moved to kiss her hello but Mrs Cameron held up a hand.

'Wait . . . best bit coming up.' The music swelled and Eve's mother twirled across the floor as best she could, dragging her left leg behind her. Fortunately Ravel's piece is a short one, but Adam and Eve must have stood for at least three minutes while she danced before them. Finally the record finished and Adam applauded. Mrs Cameron blushed and took several modest bows.

'The Jane Torvill of your day,' said Adam, smiling.

'I could have been, I could have been, but then my lovely Eve . . .' The sentence trailed off. Eve's mother could have been a star if it were not for Eve. That was the rest of the unfinished sentence. But for Eve and a terrible jump in the county ice-dance championships, which had finished her leg and her career.

'If only Eve had had the gift.' Adam knew the conversation and helped keep it going each time. Eve silently blessed him.

'My lovely Eve,' said her mother. 'She was worth it, but yes, it would have been nice. I think we knew by the time you were four, didn't we, darling? You could no more skate than . . .'

'Reinvent the mousetrap.' Eve finished the sentence and everyone laughed at how she had ruined everything.

Mother gave a little sigh and wiped her nose with a hanky from her apron pocket. 'Anyway . . . Hello, my dears!' Not one for physical contact, she handed out pretend hugs all round which only soothed the air. 'Bless you, bless you both.' She made a little sign of the cross in the air. The papal greeting of Edenford.

'How lovely. All my family. Did you have trouble with the . . . who ha?'

'The car? No,' Eve said, trying to ignore Adam's slight limp as he went up the steps. He was limping on the opposite side to Mother. She realised that if they walked too close together, they could bang heads.

'No?' Mother looked quizzical. 'It's just that you're the teensiest bit late. Nothing important, but I was hoping you would help set the table . . .'

There was always something. Eve smiled. 'I'll do it now.'

'Oh darling, of course, I've done it myself. Don't worry, it was a pleasure.' Mrs Cameron sighed with the burden of her pleasures. 'Adam! Congratulations on your promotion. You clever boy!'

Adam smiled and you could just see how he must have looked when he was picked for the second eleven at school. 'Thanks. I may have to go into the office later.'

Mother nodded. 'Of course.' The pressure of the insurance business. Adam was now a divisional manager and the division could hardly manage without him. 'Thomas?' Mother enquired.

'He's busy,' Eve said quickly. Tom didn't 'do' family functions and Eve was tired of hearing about it. It was his life and he was entitled to it. He was doing what he thought was right and Eve was proud of that.

'Of course.' Mother leant forward and whispered although there was no one else around, 'Still living in a tent?' Eve nodded. 'Still gripped by that foreign religion, is he?'

'It's not him, just some of his friends. They're Buddhists, Mum. They're really very nice.'

'It's still foreign.'

'So's the pope' replied Eve, ever defensive of her son. She was immediately admonished.

'May God forgive you!' Confident that he would, Mother changed tack. 'Come and look at this.' The small party limped off to the dining room. Leaning against the wall was a huge brown paper parcel. A great rectangle about four foot high and two foot across. Mother patted it.

'It's your father,' she whispered to Eve, and wiped a tear from her eye.

'What is?' Mr Cameron's ashes had yet to arrive from the crematorium and Eve half thought that perhaps they had been sent flat packed. Mother carefully peeled off the paper and folded it for reuse at Christmas. Inside a heavily ornate gilt frame was an enormous picture of Eve's father, Derek Cameron. He was standing in the garden, moving an azalea and smiling slightly. The photograph had been blown up to poster size and was slightly blurred. It made him look cross despite the smile.

'This way he can always be with us,' sighed Mother. 'Adam, I neeeed you,' she implored with a hint of little-girl squeak in her voice. 'I want him in here. On that . . . who ha.' She pointed to the wall above the sideboard. 'Would you?' It was a signal to open the floodgates of manhood.

'No problem, Lillian. Be done in a jiffy.'

She removed a hammer from her apron pocket and handed it to him. 'I'll get you a who ha . . . picture hook.'

Adam headed off to be clever with tools and Eve went and stood uselessly in the hall. Mother scuttled past her daughter.

'Don't scowl, darling, it's not attractive.' She disappeared into the kitchen. Eve could hear her uneven tread on the parquet floor as she almost certainly prepared to do wonders with a melon baller. Mother had limped ever since her daughter could remember. When she was little, Eve used to imagine her leaping in the air perfectly whole and coming down on the ice a broken woman. It had made Eve feel guilty all her life. Mother had told her many times that had she not been pregnant with Eve then she would never have fallen. If she hadn't been pregnant, Mother could have been someone. A sequinned toast of the town. Instead she had borne Eve and Eve had borne disappointment. Eve looked in the hall mirror. She was scowling again. Perhaps she had been born scowling.

Through the arch into the dining room Eve could see the table laid for lunch. The large mahogany surface was entirely covered with a plastic lace tablecloth. The cloth was to protect the table. In forty-five years Eve could never remember seeing the actual table. What was the point in having it if all you did was protect the wretched thing? What was the point?

Mother had made an arrangement of bright flowers out of multi-coloured tissue paper. She had learnt to make them in the sixties and had been making them ever since. They were everywhere. Fake flora and fauna in every nook and cranny. Flora and fauna and God. Having given up the sequinned world of ice-skating, Mother had turned to Catholicism for the show business part of her life. It hadn't been much at first. A few little icons when Eve, Martha and William were growing up. Rather more candles than might be deemed necessary for a power cut, that kind of thing. But since her husband had died it was becoming obsessive. There were velvet pictures of Jesus, which in the right light showed his bleeding heart. Rosaries hung from every framed prayer. Eve's favourite item was a large clam shell, which, when plugged in, opened to reveal the head of Pope John Paul I. The head would rise a few inches, light up and play 'Ave Maria'. The pope rose and shone, rose and shone. Eve, useless Eve, stood and played with it for a few minutes looking at the Holy Father. Mother always seemed to know what Eve was doing or thinking. 'Leave His Holiness's head alone, Eve. We don't want him to get broken.'

Indeed they didn't, so Eve left the leader of the Catholic world and wandered into the kitchen to be useless in there. Mother was very carefully cutting up tomatoes for the salad. She had developed a new respect for salad vegetables since she had read a report in the paper about a holy tomato being found in Huddersfield. The article was on the fridge under a St Sebastian magnet from a holy shrine in the Basque country.

### Pilgrims View Holy Tomato
#### Huddersfield salad ingredient joins list of symbolic fruit and veg
##### By Martin Wainwright

*The holy tomato of Huddersfield yesterday joined religion's rich tradition of curious edible symbols, taking its place beside the Jesus tortilla and the aubergine of Allah.*

*More than 200 people have so far travelled from London, Birmingham and Manchester to enjoy brief glimpses of the fruit wrapped in cling film in a terraced house fridge.*

*The excitement centres on fibres and marks in the flesh which appear to spell out the Koranic messages: 'There is no God but Allah' and 'Mohammed is the Messenger'. Although Arabic's sinuous lines are well suited to the natural patterns of fruit and veg, the tomato is a particularly accurate template.*

*'God must have made me buy it,' said 14-year-old Shasta Aslam, who bought a 60p bag of tomatoes on her way home from school. She had been astonished to read*

*the familiar texts as she sliced the fruit in half – the third*
*of three tomatoes in a salad for her grandparents at their*
*home in Lockwood, two miles from Huddersfield centre.*

*The round red Moneymaker, which is admired in brief*
*door-opening sessions to keep the fridge cool, follows an*
*aubergine found with a similar message in Bolton,*
*Lancashire. Linked mysteries include the celebrated milk*
*drinking by Hindu statues in London last year and a*
*series of tortillas showing Christ's head in California.*

Mother cut up another potential symbol and examined the
inside thoroughly.

'Where did you get these?' Eve asked.

'Who ha, what not, Asda.'

'I don't think it's likely, Mum.'

Mother sighed and put the last cut but unhelpful, unholy
tomato in the salad bowl.

'No, you're right. Maybe not from Asda.'

'I mean at all.'

It was the wrong thing to say. Mother turned and pointed at
her child with the vegetable knife. 'Don't you be so sure. I know
it mostly happens in foreign countries but if it can happen in
Huddersfield then . . .' Mother and daughter left unsaid the many
possibilities of revelation that existed for fresh produce in the
Home Counties.

'You don't take me seriously,' muttered Mother, as she wrung
water from a spring onion.

Eve smiled. 'Oh, I do, Mum. If anyone should find inspiration
in a tomato it ought to be you. You deserve it.'

Mrs Cameron eyed her daughter carefully. She was not, on the
whole, in favour of the idea that anybody *deserved* anything. It
was God's will and it simply had to be borne.

'You're frowning again,' said Mrs Cameron, and limped back
to the sink. Eve and her frown sat down at the kitchen table. The
surface was spread with travel brochures advertising the wonders

of Lourdes and its many dramatic possibilities. Lourdes was Mrs Cameron's new ambition. She had originally wanted to go to Heritage USA – the 21st Century Christian Campground of Jim and Tammy Faye Bakker in America. It had been rather a splendid offering, which included a Heavenly Fudge Shoppe, a Noah's Ark Toy Shoppe and a Walk of Faith leading to an air-conditioned replica of the 'top room' where the Last Supper was held. Sadly the whole place had gone bankrupt after federal officials had had the effrontery to disagree with the amount of money God wanted the Bakkers to have in their private account. Eve leafed through the holy town's offerings while her mother shook water off some radishes. Eve knew better than to offer to help. As a child she had been welcome, but now Eve was an adult and this kitchen was another woman's territory.

'Doesn't it look exciting?' Mrs Cameron said, bringing a cloth to wipe the table where Eve had leant on it. 'My salsa class from St Francis's is thinking of going. We hope we might be able to help Mrs who ha . . . Hartnell.'

'I thought she only had one leg.'

Mother nodded. 'Exactly.' Eve tried to imagine the monopod Mrs Hartnell taking one trip to Lourdes, having a miracle and salsaing home. Lobsters can regrow a claw if it falls off. What was God thinking when he gave that to them and not to us? Did that make lobsters more important in the scheme of things? Eve shut her eyes and tried to imagine Mrs Hartnell growing another leg and . . . A key in the front door accompanied by some Australian whine stopped the full picture emerging.

'Oh, Willie, darling, for God's sake, you could have parked much closer. I told you there would be a space.'

Eve's older brother William and his wife Pe Pe had arrived.

'I don't want anyone scratching the car, sweetheart. Do you know what the average cost of a simple scratch repair is, my pumpkin?'

William was the family success. He had done very well. After Mr Cameron had retired, William had taken over the family firm and turned Cameron Builders into a huge enterprise. The company was involved in all manner of things now, some of which seemed to Eve to be nothing to do with building at all.

'Taken over the whole of the underground sewage routing for the council,' he had announced on the phone to her recently. 'It's very technical. All the latest computers.' He was obviously pleased or he wouldn't have phoned, but Eve couldn't think of anything to say. The subject of sending toilet business away under the roads day after day seemed to her to have limited conversational appeal.

To look at, William was something of an odd fellow. Even as a boy he had been given to wearing a tie on days off. He appeared now in blazer and flannels with his tie crushing his white shirt firmly shut around the neck. Eve thought perhaps the ever-present tie was to distract attention from his tragic hair. Why don't men who are going bald just let it happen? The back wasn't too bad, but he had wisps of fine hair at the front that seemed to cross his forehead as a bit of a dare.

William was married to an Australian called Philippa, except the family were all supposed to call her Pe Pe. Apparently everyone called her Pe Pe as a child and she still thought this was a good idea. She insisted on calling him Willie. Pe Pe and Willie. Eve thought it sounded like a child's introduction to potty training.

Pe Pe was William's third wife. He changed them at about the same rate as Eve and Adam did the car. This particular wife helped represent William's move up in the world. Like him, she was very successful, but in a different field. Pe Pe wrote self-help books about being happy. The books sold all over the world and presumably that helped make them both happy. Before she had taken on the good humour of the globe, Pe Pe had been a champion swimmer. Miss Butterfly Stroke from the 1989 Melbourne Games or something. Certainly she had the arms for it. She had been in England for about ten years and Eve wouldn't have been the least bit surprised to find she had swum over.

William had his own key to Mother's house 'in case of

emergencies'. He had a key to Eve's house too and Shirley's flat. Quite possibly he had keys to the entire neighbourhood to check their sewage routing.

'Little Evie!' he barked as he saw his sister emerge from the kitchen into the hall. He gave her a bear hug which enveloped Eve in the musky smell of too much aftershave. Pe Pe appeared in a sheath of a dress sprayed on as an homage to the wonders of vacuum sealing. Her perfectly sculpted body and perfectly sculpted hair shimmered into the house. A three-dimensional ad for vitamin supplements and the ability to put your toe behind your ear in yoga class. She beamed and smiled as if they all actually got on. Pe Pe smiled non-stop. She smiled at her father-in-law's funeral, she smiled now for the will reading, she would no doubt die smiling.

'Eve, how delightful. You look delightful.' Eve thought for a minute she was going to punch her on the arm. She scowled and caught sight of herself in the hall mirror standing next to her Australian relative. Delightful. A goddess standing beside what looked like a Teletubbie with a hangover.

'Where the hell is Adam? Got a little promotion present for him!' William winked and dug his sister in the ribs. What a jolly time everyone was having for a will reading. Mother appeared with a small plate of canapés, so carefully arranged that they defied anyone to take the first one.

'He's putting up a picture in the who ha,' she explained.

William rushed from the hall. 'Better lend a hand. Better lend a hand.'

'Philippa, my dear.' Mother and Pe Pe kissed the air. 'Take these in, would you?' Mother handed her the canapés and went back into the kitchen to look for St Paul in the celery.

Pe Pe and Eve went to sit in the sitting room where Pe Pe took off on some long story while disarranging the canapés into her mouth.

'We've had the result of the sperm tests,' she announced, smiling broadly as if they had won an award. Eve tried to imagine what tests you could possibly set sperm. How could they hold a pencil? Did some of them get nervous beforehand? Did the tests count against success in later life? Pe Pe didn't need Eve's contribution. She swept forward, her majestic bosom giving the impression of figurehead and galleon under full sail in one sculpted piece.

'There's a problem with William's production apparently. There just aren't enough of them.'

Eve's brain clicked away. It was like a defective but relentless computer. She knew that men made sperm twenty-four hours a day. That the average man could release four hundred million sperm at every ejaculation, but it only took one to—

'The doctor showed us under a microscope. There should be hundreds, but William's are a bit like waiting for a bus to come along. It's happening to lots of men. They say it's stress. Too much pressure to be a modern man. Really, we women ask too much of them . . .' Pe Pe dived headlong into the wonderful world of William's sperm and Eve's part in their downfall.

She could just see Adam and William in the dining room. Maybe Adam's injury had brought out the worst of the man in him. He valiantly defended his wounded manhood with a lot of laddish acting, which William also excelled at. More like two workmen faced with some tricky building maintenance than family members.

'. . . so I said to Engleby – you remember Engleby, branch manager at Littleton – "Haven't seen old Hopkins around much." Spilt all the beans.'

William examined the picture, while Adam made the hammer comfortable in his hand. 'Really? Hello, Lillian.' Mother appeared with the starters and a wet cloth. She carefully wiped the edge of each plate as she put it down on the table.

Adam carried on. 'Yes. Dead.'

'Engleby?' asked William.

'No, Hopkins. Bit of rumpy-pumpy with the secretary. Popped off in the act.'

'Bad heart?'

'Well, nice in his own way. Oh, I see what you mean. Yes. Dicky ticker.'

William clutched the picture to his chest. 'Couldn't she have phoned someone?'

Adam shook his head. 'No. Heavy fellow. Lillian, dear, the picture hook?'

'Oh yes.' Mother hurried off.

'Who was heavy? Hopkins?'

'Yes. Took her two hours to get out from underneath him.'

'What was she like?'

'Oh nice, you know.' Adam undulated his hands in the air in the shape of an absurd hourglass. That was a pretty woman. A woman who existed from the neck down and was made up entirely of breasts and bottom. Eve remembered when Adam had felt that way about her. When he had admired her breasts. Stroked them and talked to them. Then they did what they were supposed to do. They fed the children and began to embarrass him. They darkened, stretched and withered. Fell victim to gravity and the daily trap of foam and wire. Adam never felt right about her breasts again after Eve fed Shirley at the office picnic. She was three months old.

'How could you let me down like that?' he yelled all the way home in the car.

'Let you down? What was I supposed to give her? A chicken leg?'

Now Eve's breasts were not sexy. They were a pillow for Adam's head. He was nice about them, about her waistline. He said he liked the fact she was 'motherly', but Eve was not at all sure that was what she wanted to be. Motherly. It suggested sensible shoes, pants with a double gusset and body hair in unexpected places. She didn't want to be his mother.

'. . . We have to try to capture what little sperm there is to do the job.' The Australian fertility lecture continued without any need for Eve's assistance. 'The thing is that sperm can survive outside the body at room temperature for at least two hours, so the doctor says . . .'

Mother reappeared with a small hook. Adam took it and held it up to William. 'Looks like we arrived in the nick of time. Going to use this hook were you, Lillian?'

'Well, I don't think I've got another.' She looked at the hook closely. 'I can't understand it. That's the one the 'Last Supper' used to hang on. If it was good enough for our Lord . . .'

Adam whispered out of the side of his mouth to William, 'Looking lovely as usual but no idea.' He turned to Mother and spoke rather too loudly, as if she were slightly infirm. 'You can't be too careful, Lillian, you have no idea the claims we get in from damage done by people hanging pictures incorrectly. I see it all the time. Don't worry, we'll manage. Any chance of a drink?'

'Of course, Adam, of course.' She went off to subdue drinks into appropriate glasses. Adam took the painting from William. 'Now, what have we got here?'

William sucked in air through his teeth at the complexity of the job ahead. 'Well, I think you're right about that hook for a start.' He took the picture back from Adam and weighed it in his hands. 'That's a number-one hook she's got there. Can't carry this kind of weightage. You want at least a two or three hook if we're talking this kind of poundage per painting.'

Mother returned with a tray of glasses and a warm bottle of Blue Nun. 'Haven't you done it yet? It's only the one picture. I do want it up before the lawyer gets here.'

Adam and William grinned to each other. 'Only the one picture!' exclaimed Adam. 'Don't you worry your pretty little head. Be done in a jiffy.'

'Well, I want it just here.' Mother pointed to a spot on the wall.

Adam smiled. 'Wish it were that simple, eh, William?' William began tapping the wall with both hands as if he suspected it might have TB. 'Wish I had my pipe detector. You seen those,

Adam? Electronic device. Just sweep it across the wall and beeper goes off if there's any kind of pipe in the way.'

'Marvellous.' Adam held the painting up where it was to go and then put it down again. 'Good point, you know, about the pipes. I wonder if Lillian has any plans for the house.'

'Electrics as well. It also does electrics. I think people don't realise that forty-three per cent of household fires start with people doing DIY through electrics.'

'Perhaps we'd better wait. Get that detector thing.'

'Yes. I usually carry it in the car. Can't believe I didn't bring it with me.'

Adam put down the hammer and moved to pour them a drink. Pe Pe's eggs were on full alert.

'No alcohol, Willie!' she called from the sitting room. 'Remember your production!'

William sighed and splashed soda in a glass noisily. He and Adam went out into the garden. Adam seemed to have lost his limp. Eve knew she shouldn't have done it, but while they were gone she went and hung the picture where Mother wanted it. In the middle of the wall above the sideboard. Pe Pe kept talking while Eve banged in the picture hook and put up her father. He looked down at her from his new vantage point. It was strange. Now he seemed to be smiling. Maybe it depended on the angle. Eve wasn't ready to have him look at her yet. It was too soon. Still, it was better than what used to hang there. Mother had taken up oil painting by numbers some years ago and had done a huge canvas of the Last Supper. It was when she was going through her phase of first needing glasses but refusing to wear them. Some of the numbers had gone a little awry. Consequently, Jesus's face was a slightly strange orange colour as if he'd come direct from an all-night tanning parlour. All the apostles appeared to be suffering from slight indigestion, which was not surprising as the food on the mildly red table was primarily blue.

Eve put the hammer away. Mother saw her do it but never said a word because Shirley arrived. Shirley, Eve's beauty, her triumph. Nineteen years of perfection. She looked immaculate in a way that Eve had never quite managed. Neat skirt and jacket with a delicate silk blouse. Her hair was cut into a shoulder-length bob and hung exactly where she had commanded it. Shirley had taken a job at one of the High Street building societies during her 'gap' year before university. She was good and had taken to dressing with a kind of shop-front authority. Eve and Shirley hugged the way Eve had always hugged her children. As if her life depended on it. Shirley patted her on the back and moved away.

'Hello, Mummy. Hello, Nana.' Mother and Shirley hugged the air around each other and Shirley smiled again at Eve.

'I've bought Father a present . . . for his promotion.' She went out into the garden to find Adam. Eve could see him opening his gift and smiling. She stood watching through the plate-glass window in the dining room. Adam's promotion. It was a funny idea. He'd got a promotion for selling insurance policies. He had scared enough people into paying money so they could be less scared. What if you die? What if you can't work? What if your house burns down? What if you get a terminal illness? What if your wife does, or your kids or your dog? Insurance for everything and anything that could happen.

Eve had never had a promotion. Not for doing anything. She had spent twenty-five years administering not just food but nutrients, not just comfort but bonding, encouraging social skills, teaching everything from speech and table manners to road sense and human relationships. That's what Martha told her. Eve hadn't realised. She had probably even got better at it as she got older but no one ever gave Eve a promotion. No one ever said, 'Have a raise in salary, Eve. You've earned it. Here, have a new plaque with your name and title on it for your kitchen door.' She did it because it was her job. She did it because somebody had to. Because she was . . . what was it? The angel in the house. Eve could see herself reflected in the window. Her floating image seemed to be wherever she looked – in foil, in a mirror, in the window. She had not seen herself for a long time and now suddenly she was everywhere.

Pe Pe had taken little breath in her conversational monologue, so Eve felt obliged to go back and listen. Mother still had the toy box and the old doll's house that Father had made in the sitting room. Perhaps she thought some of the family still needed occupying. Eve picked up a 'Swimming Barbie'. It was a curious doll. Eve had forgotten about her and her athletic ability. Barbie hadn't lost her touch. Her arms were still able to swivel round her head in a frightening manner. Eve tried to imagine her as a real woman. She had read somewhere that Barbie's breasts were supposed to be the ideal female shape but she didn't seem right. Eve held out the doll and looked at her. If Barbie were a real woman, Eve reckoned she would be six foot tall with size one feet. All her perfect breasts would do was make her unable to stand up in even a mild breeze. Wheelchair Barbie.

There was a lot of Barbie in Pe Pe – stupid name, same hair origin, bouncy flesh tone. Eve wondered what Pe Pe's breasts were like. Perfect, no doubt, like the rest of her. Germaine Greer says there are different types of breast, but really the ideal is that they are exactly the same size. Eve couldn't remember ideal for who. Pe Pe's looked the same – they were both huge. Desmond Morris said that women developed breasts so men would have sex with them from the front. Nothing to do with feeding then. Pe Pe's certainly suggested sex from the front. In fact they suggested sex with everyone on the front. Pe Pe talked about sperm and babies but Eve wanted to say to her, 'How do you get so fit and still have such big breasts?'

They were remarkable endowments. Give her a black eye if she ever took up golf. Eve wondered which shape they were: the fried-egg shape (broad spreading base with nipple held close to underlying muscle), the sweet-potato shape (narrow based and comparatively long) or the standard shape – which is apparently rare – perfectly hemispherical with nipple exactly at the centre point. Adam wouldn't mind any of them. He always used to say he was a 'breast man', like it was a cut of roast. He loved that wet T-shirt competition at the club, but not breastfeeding. Not in public.

'I read somewhere that there is a tribe in New Guinea who use tight girdles on men as well as women so that the men have hourglass curves too.'

'What?' Eve realised that Pe Pe was staring at her. 'What are you talking about, Eve?'

'New Guinea,' managed Eve, surprised to find that she had spoken out loud. 'I should like to go there. Actually, I should like to go anywhere.'

Pe Pe went out to the garden. Perhaps she wanted to make sure William was still making sperm on his day off. Perhaps she too thought Eve was mad. It was funny William and Pe Pe not being able to make a baby. They were so good at everything else. Such a Martini couple. Mrs Harris at Number 28 had five children and she and Mr Harris didn't even speak most of the time. Apparently the last was an accident, which always struck Eve as an odd expression. She wondered what it meant. Perhaps Mrs Harris had fallen off a kitchen stool and on to her husband's penis when he happened past? She wondered why people had sex when they were not even getting on. Adam and she hardly had it when they were thrilled to bits with each other.

Martha was late as usual and arrived at the same time as the solicitor. He was a young man, maybe twenty-five, very smart and sleek. A dark, three-piece suit, but very modern and a careful haircut. Eve knew Mother would like him because he looked like a missionary. In fact, when Eve opened the front door, she half suspected he'd come round to sell copies of the *Watchtower* and tell them why Jesus ought to come into their lives.

He put down his briefcase, smiled at Eve and seemed to set his eyes to twinkle as he put out his hand. 'John Antrobus. Hogart, Hoddle and Hooper.'

Eve smiled. Wasn't that nice? Hogart, Hoddle and Hooper. All the Hs at law school must have got on. She managed to keep the thought to herself.

'You must be the granddaughter,' he said, twinkling away.

Eve giggled. She hated herself but she giggled. 'No, the daughter.'

'Good heavens,' he breathed.

Eve and John shook hands and he gently placed his other hand on top of the handshake as if to confirm the whole thing. It was May when their hands bonded. Before Christmas he'd be dead and Eve would have killed him.

But that day Eve was polite. Middle-aged, middle class, polite. 'My daughter's going to be a solicitor. She's going to university in September. We're just waiting to hear which one.'

Eve's younger sister, Martha, stood impatiently behind John Antrobus as she waited to come in. Martha was uninterested in him. She was wearing a selection of clothes that were fighting a heavy rearguard action against becoming an ensemble outfit. Large swathes of natural fibres suggested Eve's sister had dressed while fleeing a burning building. She also wore a turban for reasons Eve never fathomed. They were not a turban sort of family. Not in Edenford, but then Martha had not been around for some time. She taught women's studies at a university in Bangkok and had only come home for the dealing out of her father's spoils. She was staying at the University Women's Club in London and was impatient to get back there. She did not understand her family and, to be fair, they did not understand her. Martha's only concession to them all was that she had brought a gift of a pineapple, two melons and a lemon.

'I thought fruit would be good,' Martha said, when John finally stopped twinkling and stepped into the house. The kitchen door flew open and Mother appeared wiping her hands on a tea towel.

'Oh, Martha, sweet of you but I've got fruit. The one thing we didn't need.'

Eve smiled. Everyone except Martha smiled, as if the whole fruit thing was just fine.

'Christ!' said Martha, and stomped off with her pineapple to get a drink.

Mother was mortified. 'So unnecessary. I'm so sorry.'

Eve made the remaining introductions. 'Mother, this is Mr Antrobus from the solicitors.'

He shook Mother gravely by the hand. 'I know it's a difficult time, but may I say you are an inspiration to us all.' Mother nearly fell on the floor with delight. She preened as he moved on. 'Perhaps we had better get started,' he said, getting more sonorous by the minute.

'Oh no. Lunch. We must have lunch,' insisted Mother.

'I couldn't, really.' Mr Antrobus held up his briefcase. 'You see, it's a little awkward. Perhaps not as straightforward—'

There was no arguing with Mother. 'Nonsense. Lunch!'

The Great Provider called everyone in and the men did lots of handshaking with the man from the law. Martha sat smoking at the table until Mother began unnecessary coughing. Mother brought in an unnecessary damp cloth and put it beside her plate. She lived in mortal fear of spillage, hence the large plastic table-cloth, just in case.

Adam and William sat in the carvers at either end of the table while the rest of the family gathered at the sides. Mother went back for something. She always went back for something. She sat and stood so many times during a meal that as a child Eve had felt confident someone had placed a small electric charge in her seat. She was an age in the kitchen so Eve went to see if she could help. Mother was wrapping the remains of the hors d'oeuvres in cling film, struggling to get three leftover olives neatly contained. Eve knew better than to interrupt. She watched her mother wrap the three olives as if the family's future sustenance depended on them.

'Everyone is waiting,' she said at last.

'Waste not want not,' Mrs Cameron replied, taking her time to preserve one cheese cracker and a single centimetre sliver of liver pâté left from the canapés.

At last Mother settled herself for her meal. She carefully wiped her mouth with her napkin. She was the only woman Eve knew who did that before she started eating. Adam already had a spoonful of starter halfway to his mouth when Mother intoned, 'For what we are about to receive may the Lord make us truly thankful.' There was an embarrassed and English wave of muttered 'Amens' from most of the table, but a rather firm response from John. Eve made a mental note to check his car. Probably had one of those silver I'm-a-Christian-so-don't-road-rage-me fish on the back of it. The family picked up their spoons to begin.

Mother carried the conversation baton. 'So, Mr Antrobus, how lovely of you to come here on this sad business.'

'Please call me John.' John smiled at Shirley who smiled back. 'You all seem to be coping very well.'

Mother nodded, thrilled with her own fortitude. 'The strength of a good family.'

'Indeed. Nothing like it.'

'Nothing at all,' muttered Martha.

Mother ignored her youngest daughter and wiped a small tear that threatened in her right eye. 'Also I think we feel that Derek is still watching over us.' She smiled bravely at Father's portrait and his beloveds munched on.

'You're new to Edenford?' asked William.

'Yes, yes. Lovely town.'

'And what does Mrs Antrobus do?' probed Pe Pe, smiling.

John looked confused. 'My mother?'

Pe Pe gave a little pleased chuckle. 'No, I meant your wife, but I take it you're not married?'

'No, but I'm in the market.' John glanced at Shirley who looked down at her plate. He didn't glance at Eve. She knew why. Eligible young man. Attractive young man, but her pheromones screamed double gusset, closed access. It would be nice to be in love again. Just once more. To be that excited. That special.

Mother picked at her food with extreme care. It wasn't that she had inspirational hopes for the starter. Even she seemed to know that God wouldn't stoop to a message in a melon ball.

No, in the last year Mrs Cameron had developed a new relationship with her digestive system. It had become very precious.
Food had become something to follow as it made its way
through the system and then wait for anxiously until its reap-
pearance at the other end. She was obsessed with the idea of
being regular. Consequently she had become thinner and thinner. She was a shadow of her former self but even then only in
very bright sunlight. There was very little of her left for the
Lord to love.

Adam, however, wolfed his starter. 'Hogart, Hoddle and
Hooper? Didn't you just have some trouble in the office?'

Eve wanted to kick him. 'Don't start, Adam.'

'Something about a woman getting pregnant.'

Mr Antrobus nodded. 'Tricky. Good solicitor, but she wasn't
married. She had no one to take care of the baby.'

Martha decided to take an interest like a cat might open an eye
to a three-legged mouse. 'Are you not in favour of women working, Mr Antrobus?'

John blushed. 'It was playing havoc with the office.'

Adam sucked in some air disapprovingly. 'Chinese father,
wasn't it?'

'Yes. Yes, I believe so.'

'Adam!' Eve warned, but he was all innocence.

'What? I like Chinese people. I'm always very polite to Mr
Wong/Fong, whatever, when I collect the takeaway. I just don't
want to eat the bloody meal with him. What's wrong with that?
Maybe the woman should have thought about other options . . .'
Adam trailed off.

'Well, she couldn't have an abortion,' boomed Pe Pe, whose
present pursuits made such an idea unthinkable.

Mother nodded sympathetically. She didn't really like the subject at the dinner table so she simply whispered, 'It's against
God's will. Now would anyone like to . . .?' Change the subject,
she was probably going to say but William had the facts at his
fingertips.

'Did you know there are over one and a half million abortions in the United States every year? I was reading a very disturbing report. It's not all done by qualified surgeons, you know. No, quite often abortionists are literally the dregs of the medical profession who couldn't make a go of it successfully in private practice. There was one state where a dermatologist opened an abortion chamber.'

It was the sort of conversation that left nowhere for anyone else to go. Why was William reading such a thing? Why a dermatologist?

'So, Mrs Hogart, Hoddle and Hooper, let me see – your skin is dry, you are a solicitor and you're having a baby. I can cure all three with a simple abortion. I simply place this nozzle attachment on an ordinary vacuum cleaner and—'

Mr Antrobus cleared his throat. 'Anyway, we paid her off. Well, she couldn't expect to carry on efficiently.'

'Why not?' Martha enquired. No one knew, so Adam moved on.

'Well, Mr Antrobus—'

'I want to know why not,' persisted Martha.

'Leave it, dear,' instructed Mother. Martha clenched her jaw and fought back by lighting another cigarette.

'John, please, call me John.' Mr Antrobus smiled at Adam who smiled back.

'John, of course. I do hope you'll take an interest in local affairs.' He looked around the table. 'I trust you will all be helping me in the elections at the end of the year? We've got some very exciting platforms for the town.' Adam was a local councillor. Eve couldn't imagine what exciting platforms he could be thinking of. The last election had hinged on a heated campaign to stop people leaving dogs' mess on the verges near the church. Eve's husband crunched through a melon ball as he spoke. 'I've got some very exciting ideas.'

'Adam did the notice board, you know,' confided Mother. 'The one on the Green. It was Adam's idea.'

Adam smiled modestly. 'Simple idea, really. I thought let's have a notice board on the Green for everyone in Edenford to keep in touch with council activities. I only wish it had been that simple. You see, I wanted something nice in oak to match the beams in the War Memorial Hall . . .'

'Adam's on the Heritage Committee.' While Adam held court, Mother provided the subtitles.

' . . . but the planning people decided we couldn't have oak. It had to be something "fire retardant" and that obviously wouldn't be oak, which is made of, well . . . oak.'

'Nightmare,' prompted John.

'Absolutely. I mean, I'd already ordered it and it cost two hundred pounds. Thankfully it was sorted with some fire retardant creosote or something. It did look nice.'

'Apparently the smell will wear off.' Not all Mother's subtitles were helpful. Adam ignored her.

'We had a bit of a ribbon cutting with the Green Committee when it was put up. Councillor Hodson made a speech, which was nice.'

'Shame about the dog.'

'Lillian!' Adam was getting irritated, but he kept smiling for John's benefit. 'It was nothing. Really, the creosote was still just a trifle sticky and Mrs Hodson's terrier got its back leg stuck to one of the posts while the junior school were playing something from the . . . what was it?'

'Michael Jackson's *Thriller* album.' It was a sound Eve would never forget.

'That's it. Lovely arrangement for descant recorder.' Adam adored that board. He kept walking past and patting it. It had had more contact from him than Eve had in years.

'The vet says the dog will be fine . . .' Adam swallowed and sucked on his teeth at the same time before finishing his sentence '. . . any day now.'

There was a pause as the table reached a dead end in this conversational bypass.

'It's so nice to have lunch with an ordinary family.' Mr Antrobus smiled at the gathering. Mother smiled back.

'Ordinary?' laughed Adam. 'I don't know. Mother here nearly served the meal on skates!'

Everyone laughed and in the mirth of the moment, Adam accidentally shot a melon ball across his plate and on to the floor. Mother blanched. Her precious carpet. She hadn't thought to put a plastic sheet on the carpet. Adam stooped down to pick it up.

'Sorry, Lillian. Effect of gravity, eh? Same thing happening to Eve's body, isn't it?' He laughed at his own joke and Eve wanted to fly away there and then.

Martha had had enough jollity. 'You shouldn't let him speak to you like that, Eve.'

'Martha,' managed Eve.

'It's a joke, for Christ's sake,' exploded Adam. 'Sorry, Lillian, but I mean really.'

William was getting impatient. 'Look, I wonder if we shouldn't get the will reading over with. I expect there will be matters to discuss . . .'

'I doubt it, dear,' said Mother.

'Mother, this is important. I need to know where the business stands. If Pe Pe and I are going to have a baby—'

Mother clapped her hands. 'You're going to have a baby!'

'Well, not yet.' Pe Pe explained. 'You see, William is having a problem with his sperm and—'

William went ballistic and threw down his napkin. Melon juice spun in the air, hovered and descended on the carpet. 'There is no need to tell everyone.'

'I'm sorry, darling, I only . . .'

William headed for the garden to commune with his testosterone. Pe Pe smiled at us all and gave a slight sigh.

'He'll be fine. He has some issues but he's dealing with them.'

Mother hated issues so she went to fetch several damp cloths and see to the main course, while Adam set about topping up glasses. He limped to the sideboard to fetch the near-empty bottle of Blue Nun. The mere mention of another man's troubles in the trouser department had reminded him of his own brush with zipper death and he held his hand protectively across his nether parts. Shirley closed her eyes in quiet contemplation and Pe Pe played with a flower on her dress sheath. Perhaps she would write one of her books to help William. *Seven Simple Solutions for Non-Swimming Sperm* or *How to be Happy with Fewer Sperm.*

There was a short silence until John said, 'It's to do with stress, you know.'

Adam poured himself the last of the wine and smiled uncertainly. 'What is?'

'Men having trouble with their sperm. It's a modern thing. Apparently it's the stress men have to deal with today.' John munched on his bread roll as if these were conversations the family had round the dinner table every day.

'That's what I was saying to Eve,' declared Pe Pe, thrilled to have found an ally. She simpered at the guest, while the rest of the table tried to decide where to head next. 'But what is the answer?'

'Keep healthy,' said John. Adam sucked in his stomach and nodded agreement, while John continued, 'I think men have a duty to the next generation to look after themselves. I have regular checks on my sperm count as well as the usual cholesterol and blood pressure. That way when I do get married, the woman will know what she's getting.'

Adam thought about this. 'Like selling a house with the survey done? Kind of insurance against things going wrong?'

'Exactly.'

No doubt everyone knew Pe Pe would go too far with this unsolicited information. 'And how is *your* sperm?' she enquired.

'Oh perfect, thanks, just perfect.' John smiled reassuringly round the table and everyone was terribly relaxed.

Mother brought in the main course.

'A little treat!' she announced with a flourish. 'Tiger prawns!' She put down a large tray of creatures who had in their time swum rather better than William's sperm. While he served, Adam picked up the conversational ball again.

'Do you play golf, John?'

'Well—'

'You should, you know. Great game to help you get on. Great club here. Tricky to get in but I could have a word. Great bunch of lads. As a matter of fact, it's on the cards that I might just be captain this year. I'm not saying it will happen but there has been talk, hasn't there, Eve?'

Eve couldn't deny it. 'Yes. There has.'

'So I might be in a position to help you out.' Adam ripped the shell off a large prawn before launching on. 'What sort of music do you like, John? Personally, I think you have to go a long way to beat the Tigress of Tiger Bay.'

To his credit John looked puzzled. 'Sorry?'

'Bassey! Shirley Bassey. You a fan? Well, who wouldn't be? She's sixty-one you know. You're shocked, aren't you? It's hard to believe she's even seen forty. That's what comes from not letting yourself go.' Eve was sure Adam looked straight at her. She knew that look. That look that said she hadn't so much let herself go as driven her body to the quayside and waved it goodbye. Adam pulled the head off his prawn with some vigour and swanned off for five minutes on the relative merits of *Goldfinger* against some more modern material.

This was followed by a short treatise from Pe Pe who was about to embark on a series of seminars on how to achieve a more meaningful orgasm. 'Isn't that what we all want?' she said. 'To feel good about ourselves, to have good physical health, emotional fulfilment, gratifying sex and positive ageing.'

Martha was not convinced. 'Pe Pe, you sound like a bloody women's magazine. What about our brains, our intellectual lives?'

John was right there with Pe Pe. 'I couldn't bear not to be fit.'

'I can see that,' she replied, eyeing his thighs beside her. 'Stay fit and you won't be stressed. It's the theme of my new book – it's not stress but too little joy that's killing people.'

'Bollocks,' said Martha, which was either her opinion or an attempt to get back to the subject of William's sperm. Pe Pe smiled at her in her tolerant and loving way.

'Martha, I know you are a very feeling person, but you should use your emotions as a biofeedback mechanism to stay in touch with the causes of your unhappiness.'

That gave everyone something to think about.

William came back to the table in time for pudding. It was trifle. No one really wanted any and there was at least half a bowl left when John started to read out the will.

'It's not very long,' he said.

'I'll get coffee,' said Mother.

'No.' John shook his head. 'I think you'll want to hear this,' and he began to read. 'I, Derek Cameron, being of sound mind and body, do hereby make this my last will and testament. To my son, William, I leave Cameron Builders and Decorators, all its assets and any goodwill remaining in the business.'

William helped himself noisily to another prawn. It had been what he expected. John took a sip of water and read on.

'To all three of my children, William, Eve and Martha, I leave everything else, including my house. To my wife, Lillian May Cameron, I leave nothing. I have given her everything I could. For forty-eight years she has had everything she wanted. I did everything she asked and now I am free. I was a good husband, a good father and I hated my life. With the money I leave them I ask my children to get on with their lives. Please don't make the same mistake I did. Don't sit and wait till it is too late. I did and I am sorry. I love you. Dad.'

There could not have been greater shock at the table if a chapter of Genesis had appeared in the grapes and cheese.

'The house?' Mother managed, gripping her beloved and unblemished table.

'Yes,' nodded John. 'I'm afraid everything was in your husband's name.'

'Well, of course, but . . .'

John couldn't have been nicer. He reached out and patted Mother gently on the hand. 'As the children are fully grown I'm afraid there's nothing . . .'

Eve knew Mother would do something, she just didn't know what. Everyone was looking at her when she sort of went rigid and her eyes glazed over. Then she fell forward into the pudding basin. It went everywhere. It is a terrible fact of life that when something really serious happens it often has its comic side. Mother had had a stroke. It was dreadful but as she fell she got a maraschino cherry up her nose. Eve thought she was dead and found herself wondering what she should do with the three olives she'd wrapped up so carefully. And Eve thought about her life. And her father smiled down at them all. In that moment both the father and the mother that Eve had always known disappeared from her life. Nothing seemed certain any more, and all the time John was watching.

# Chapter Seven

My dear Inge,

### The Darkness

And God said 'Let there be light'; and there was light.
And God saw that the light was good . . .

(GENESIS 1.3)

I am writing this at two o'clock in the morning. It's not easy. It is dark at night in my cell. I've never slept in the dark before. I lie here and worry about stupid things. About whether they will let me have clean pants every day. I think a lack of clean pants is the one thing that would drive me to distraction if I were ever kept in difficult circumstances. Some of the women cry through the night. Maybe they're crying for what they've done. Maybe they're crying for what they've never done. I wish I had a candle. I love candlelight. It is amazing how the small glow of light from a candle can transform a place.

*How far that little candle throws his beams!*
*So shines a good deed in a naughty world.*

Do you remember that? It's funny. All that O-level English and that's the only bit that stayed in my head. I like the idea of the world being simply naughty. Not wicked or evil, just a bit of a tinker. Much more comforting than what's actually going on. That's what my Sunday supplement ads were – just a bit naughty. I didn't start out to be wicked.

Thank you so much for the picture of Shirley. She looks so thin, but I thought I saw a little smile. Was that a smile? I couldn't tell because she had her hand up against the sun. The place looks lovely. I can see why you and Kate loved it so. Is that helping you too? I hope so.

I battle on with trying to find the right words. Shirley gave me a revised standard version of the Bible some months ago. It has printed in the front that it was 'translated from the original tongues'. It's hard to know just what that means. How do you tell words that are inspired by God from those that aren't? I mean, it can be the same words, grammar and everything as if it were written by humans. And if humans can make mistakes, which we can, then could somebody have been wrong about which are the holy words and what they mean? Of course, there are people who think they don't make mistakes. The pope doesn't. He's not allowed to. He's a man but his job makes him infallible. That must be nice. Like having one of those Home Highway Internet connections to God.

*Fact – during the Kosovo War, the pope, His Holiness the Pope, refused permission for Catholic women in danger of rape by Muslim soldiers to use the pill. If they became pregnant it was the will of God. Some 20,000 women were abandoned by their families for carrying alien children. Abortions are a sin but some carried the children to term and then killed them. The Catholic Serbs did not want Muslim babies in their midst for they were making a Greater Serbia. Why would God send such a message to the pope? Couldn't he get through to anyone else?*

I keep thinking about the lunch where Mother had her stroke. I think I seemed very ordinary at that lunch. Just middle class and ordinary, but I'm not. I'm not just a polite middle-class lady who's been secreting trinkets from the High Street into her raincoat pocket on the quiet. I don't mind prison. Perhaps it might even be rather nice to stay. There's no cooking and I can read. I like reading. I might learn French. I was going to have evening classes in French once, but Adam said he couldn't see the point. He told me *cheval* means horse and it's like that all the way through. They have a different word for each one of ours. The psychiatrist asks me what I think about John now that he's dead and I say, 'Well, I'm sorry, of course, but he was very religious. I mean, if he was right he'll be just fine by now.' He would be fine in death but he would have ruined Shirley's life, only I don't say that.

'What happened after your mother had the stroke?' The psychiatrist never seems to tire of his job.

### Get off your Bed and Walk

... if you will not hearken unto me and will not do all these commandments ... I will appoint over you sudden terror, consumption and fever that waste the eyes and cause life to pine away ...

(LEVITICUS 26.14)

I don't want to talk about Mother. I want to talk about my dreams. The little I do sleep is so full of strange dreams. Last night I was in a plane. Actually, first I was standing next to the plane. It was one of those old-fashioned ones with two wings. What do you call it? A biplane. I was laughing and people were taking pictures with really ancient cameras that flashed and banged. I was thin, which was nice, and I jumped up on to the plane, which was scary. Then I got in the cockpit. The plane started and I was in charge. I was ready to fly but I looked at the controls and I didn't know how any of it worked. I woke up sweating and I couldn't remember where I was. I lay there wondering why I can't seem to sleep and then what good would it do anyway.

Nobody really knows why we sleep. The body doesn't actually need to shut down 'the system' for as long as most people find they need to sleep. I think it must be some kind of safety valve to let the brain sort out all the input from the day. Time to put one's internal system in order. Unfortunately the office of my mind seems to be perpetually strewn with scraps of paper and untidy bundles of discarded information. I know all these things and they are of no use to me. Why did God give me a brain? To sort tea towels by colour so they don't run in the wash?

Margaret Thatcher needed only a few hours' sleep each night to feel refreshed, which I think is all the proof you need that she wasn't a real person. I always thought the most telling aspect of the Brighton bomb at the Grand Hotel was that at 3 a.m., when it went off, Thatcher was at her desk working, while Denis was fast asleep. The other curiosity was that Norman Tebbit was carried out with the top button done up on his pyjamas. What a fun chap he must be.

What did happen after Mother had the stroke? Well, they were nice in the hospital. Edenford General. Perfectly pleasant to me and Mother. I wasn't worried at first. She'd had a stroke but the doctors said there was every reason to suppose she might recover, although when I was with her it seemed hard to believe. She had descended into a hell where I could not find her. I tried. I did try. I went to visit every day and she would be sitting up in her bed jacket loudly calling, 'Who ha! Who ha!'

The stroke had left her unable to see at all without her glasses. She was confused and frightened and flailed about, still refusing to put them on. She was also speechless apart from the phrase 'Who ha', which she had once used when she forgot the occasional word. Now it seemed to be the only thing she could remember. She sat up in bed calling 'Who Ha! Who Ha!', an old woman who looked like my mother, dressed like my mother, but who in the middle of the night had had her soul stolen by an incontinent and blinded owl.

She had the most staggering ability to urinate. It's not something you want to know about your mother or any grown-up really. The nurses were very busy and I had to keep getting Wet Wipes to sort her out. We were supposed to meet with social services but William had a conference and Martha can't/won't deal with hospitals. When the man arrived, Mother was asleep. I sat looking at her. Her whole face had sagged down on to the bed. She looked a hundred years old. This was my mother. I tried to imagine that I had started life inside her, grown inside her, first heard the world through her, but I couldn't see it. We seemed to be nothing like each other. What had she done to my father to make him remove her from the will? How could he have been so cruel? Why didn't he just leave? Why did he wait till after the end? I had so many questions and nowhere to take them.

The social worker was very nice, very young, very tired. I got him a cup of tea from the machine.

'How old is your mother?' he asked.

'Sixty-five, I think, yes, sixty-five.' Four years older than Shirley Bassey. Who ha, who ha . . .

He flipped though endless paperwork. 'Right, and the prognosis?'

I smiled. 'Good. They seem to think she could recover. She's just . . . confused at the moment, that's all.'

'Oh dear.' The young man sipped his tea.

'Oh dear, she's confused or oh dear, she'll recover?'

'No, that's good, it's just we have to decide what to do with her in the meantime.'

I didn't understand. 'Do with her?'

'Well, care . . . Who will care for her?'

'Won't you? Social services?'

He shook his head. 'Not entirely. We're not a cure-all,

you know.' He looked at me, frowning, and became a bit less businesslike. 'Have you dealt with the elderly before?'

The elderly. My indomitable mother was suddenly 'the elderly'. I shook my head.

'Let me explain. Your mother could live for some time.'

'I hope so.'

'Yes, but you see . . .'

*Fact – during the 1970s and 1980s, industrialised countries experienced unexpectedly large declines in mortality among the elderly, resulting in larger-than-projected numbers of the very old. In the United States, the so-called frail elderly group, aged 85 years and older, increased nearly fourfold between 1950 and 1980, from 590,000 to 2,461,000. Given the high incidence of health problems among the very old, such increases have important implications for the organisation and financing of health care.*

'Our budget is very limited . . .'

*Fact – the elderly now constitute the largest single client group using personal social services worldwide. In all advanced industrial societies, the proportion of infirm elderly is on the increase and, although they constitute only a small minority of the retired population, their claim on social services is disproportionately heavy.*

'Obviously we want to help but we have very limited resources. Does your mother have any money?'

'No.'

'None at all?'

'None. It's all been rather sudden. My father . . . no, none.'

'It's just that there isn't a vacancy in the local council homes at the moment. Maybe in three or four months—'

'Three or four months? Look, my mother worked all her life, I mean, not in a job as such but—'

'Mrs Marshall. Let me explain to you that half of all personal social service expenditure in this county is spent on the elderly. We are doing the best we can but the numbers just keep going up. There are too many frail old people and not enough places.'

*Fact – improvements in health care are reflected by the increase in longevity for people in England. Life expectancy increased from 68 years in 1961 to 71.8 years in 1985 for males, and from 73.9 years to 77.7 years for females.*

The young man warmed to his theme. He had obviously done his homework. A social degree in getting old and getting stuffed. 'I suppose it's a sign of society doing well, isn't it? People living so long. Did you know that in ancient Rome and medieval Europe the average life span is estimated to have been between twenty and thirty years? Life expectancy today has expanded in historically unprecedented proportions. The chances of surviving to be over sixty-five are quite staggering.'

'What's the point if you've got nowhere to go?'

'Of course, if you could go privately . . .'

It was money. It was all about money. 'How much are we talking about?' I asked.

'Minimum – three hundred and fifty pounds a week, all-in. It's very nice. They have regular meals, get their laundry done, bit of entertainment . . .'

'That's a lot.'

The young man was running out of steam. 'Chiropody . . .' he faltered as we said goodbye. I went back to Mother's bedside.

The nurse was nice. She sat stroking Mother's face.

'Shame,' she said. 'All that experience in there. All that life. Will she be going home with you?'

'I don't know. I mean, I wanted to . . .'

'I know. People don't any more. Everything's changed.' She leant down to the bed and spoke to my sleeping mother. 'What happened to the family, eh, Lillian?'

The nurse went home. She went home without Mother and felt fine. I sat beside my old mum and looked at her. Martha had sent fruit, so I cut open an apple. Before I ate it, I examined the thing all over. A miracle. I realised I was looking for a miracle. And that's what you can do, Inge. That's the choice. You can sit and wait for a miracle or you can get up and do something by yourself. It was all I was reduced to.

Tell Shirley I love her. Tell her I'm sorry. Tell her I am trying.

Love,

Eve

# Chapter Eight

Two very funny removal men arrived early on the Saturday morning of Inge's move and managed to be funny all day long. Every time Inge came into the room, one of them would start a mock racing commentary.

'And Inge Holbrook is coming up on the outside. She's looking good, carrying a small packing case . . .'

Or if one of them lifted something particularly heavy, the other would present him with a medal that was accepted with a thick Russian accent.

'Comrades, I am proud to be a member of de Russian vomen's team. I tank god for vodka, vomen and steroids. Tank you, tank you.'

Hilarious. Inge smiled and smiled. They played shot-put with the tea bags, relay races with the sugar spoon. Not for one minute did they just let her be a woman who was simply moving house. They couldn't seem to forget who she was or get used to her presence in the room. She let ride the jokes, she even let ride hearing one of them on the mobile telling someone to 'guess where he was' and she let ride how long it all took. By the time the men left, Inge, friend of the people, was exhausted and the flat was empty. Her home had been packed and taken away and Inge was afraid. She looked at the large, empty loft, all set for the next *professional couple*. For people on the up, people with careers, places to go, people to see.

Inge checked her watch. There wasn't much time before the truck would be heading off for Edenford. She shook herself into action. There was no point in getting sentimental. She was doing the right thing. Kate was sitting on a folding chair, waiting in the hall. She had a compact camera in her hand.

'Come on, grumpy, smile!' she commanded, as Inge appeared in the doorway. Inge grinned as Kate flashed a quick snap.

'Do you have to immortalise everything?' Inge enquired.

'Absolutely.'

'Do you know what this move has cost in shifting photo albums alone? Thank God we never had children.' Inge gently put her hand under Kate's shoulder and helped her to her feet. Kate rose slowly and reached out to stroke Inge's face.

'Your children would have been beautiful.' The two women smiled at each other. 'You'll be glad of them. The albums.'

Inge felt the tears rise behind her eyes but she wouldn't let them flow. 'Yes, yes I will. Now come on, you old camera bag.'

Edenford lay about an hour south of London if you put your foot down, but Inge took her time. Kate slept as they drove and she didn't want to disturb her. Kate the lovely, Kate the cursed, secret Kate. Truth be told Kate was perhaps not the prettiest woman in the world. She carried the light tan colour of her Caribbean roots, with dark, curly hair and deep, brown eyes. Nearly fifty, her face was a little too lined and perhaps a little too round for real beauty. Inge tried to remember what it was she liked about her. Why she was turning her life upside-down for her. It was something indefinable. Kate was a person so filled to the core with life that it made everyone who met her feel good about themselves. That was her skill. Making others feel worth something. When anyone spoke to her, she would concentrate so fiercely on what they were saying that for a short while the speaker would believe their own significance. She gave Inge significance. It was a great gift.

A tone deaf version of the 'William Tell Overture' began bleating from Inge's mobile. Her stomach tensed for no reason. It was ridiculous. Inge grabbed the phone off the dashboard.

'Hello?'

'Darling, it's Barry. Well, tell him I'm not accepting that. Unless we get the extra thousand he can forget it.'

Inge waited. She had had this call almost every day of her professional life. Barry Trancher, her agent, would call her and then carry on the rest of his business as if he hadn't. He always spoke partly to her and partly to anyone who happened to be in the room with him. It had taken some time to get used to.

'Hello, Barry.'

'Where are you, darling? I can never find you. You must tell me where you are,' his slightly high-pitched voice whined at her.

'I'm moving, remember?'

'Of course you are. Helen, send Inge flowers . . . don't know . . . moving sort of flowers . . . no, not emotional ones . . . what the fuck is an emotional flower? Moving . . . you know . . . house . . . flowers. Honestly, you can't get the staff. Moving, that's lovely. Now, I've had a call from contracts at the BBC about the new project—'

'Don't even go there.'

'Darling, I have to. I know it's the business side of things and you hate that but—'

Inge laughed. 'No, Barry, that's the name of the show.'

Barry coughed and moved on. 'Well, obviously I know that. Now, we can go one of two ways with this. We can go for the kind of all-in contract you've had before, you know, you work for the Beeb, they pay you, you do whatever they ask or . . . well, tell him I'll call him back. I don't care if he is in sodding Marrakesh . . . or we can go contract by contract. Now because this is a game show—'

'Sorry, Barry,' Inge interrupted. 'Game show? I thought it was a documentary?'

'Doco? No, no, it's a game show . . . with the . . .' Inge could hear Barry desperately rummaging through paperwork in order to remember. '. . . kids . . . that's it . . . kids.'

'What kids?'

Barry tried to be calm. He had clearly thought this was going to be a quick call. 'The ones, Inge, who are going to take part.'

'I'm sorry. I was told it was a documentary with members of the public getting fit.'

'No, no, that'd never work. No, it's a game show where teams of the public and/or celebs watch kids trying adult sports and guess which one will win. You do interviews with the kids and they say cute things, but if they get a bit cheeky, you say—'

'Don't even go there.' Inge had had enough. 'Barry, this is ridiculous.'

'Please, I haven't even done the money yet. Coffee, where the hell is my coffee?'

Inge waited for Barry's coffee. 'Not the money. The show. All they have is a title. They don't actually have anything to broad-cast. I'm not a bloody comedian. I can't afford to—'

'You can't afford not to do anything. Inge, I deal with this night and day. You have to understand that things have changed. I have clients, established clients, who can't even get their calls returned. Just let me get you signed up and we'll worry about what you're making later when you're actually making it. Well, what's he doing in Marrakesh? Sweetie, I'll call you back.' Inge's phone went dead.

'What shall I do, Kate?' she said out loud.

'Quit and have a life,' replied Kate from behind her closed eyes.

'I thought you were asleep.'

'No, I merely lie dormant waiting to plague you.'

'Good.'

Inge and Kate drove on to their new life and a silver Volkswagen Golf followed close behind.

Edenford was almost certainly unprepared for its new inhab-itants. Of course it was generally known that TV's Inge Holbrook had grown up there, but no one had ever imagined she would come back. It wasn't that sort of place. Throughout recorded time in the town, anyone who had gone off and 'done something in history' had done so without ever finding the need to return. The town had done its bit over the years. In the old people's day centre, down by the river, the fading ladies and men would often gather over a Peek Frean and mutter, 'The town never really recovered from the war. We gave then. Those fine young men who marched up the High Street. Not one of them ever returned.'

Strictly speaking this was true. One hundred and thirty-four men were listed on the War Memorial as having the excuse of death for staying in France after the great conflict of 1939–45, but the fact was that a hundred and thirty-nine Edenfordians had originally joined up. No one ever mentioned what happened to detain the other five.

The town was perched on a large, cobbled hill above the banks of the River Eden. It boasted a decent theatre, a leisure centre, a celebrated golf course, the largest Conservative Association membership in the south-east and more estate agents than a brief glance at the population might suggest was sustainable.

Inge's parents had bought their house when they got married. It had cost £3,000 and was considered expensive. Built in the 1850s, it had a doll's house look about it. Square front, door in the middle and high sash windows on either side on two floors. A white picket fence enclosed the front garden, which was a mass of country flowers. Lavender, hollyhocks and wild poppies vied for space and made any reckonings on the central sundial an impossibility. It was not a place to keep time but to let it flow gently past. Inge had been happy here as a child and she hoped to feel safe coming home.

Inge parked in the gravel drive and led the way to the front door. Inside, the rather smart hall had a sweeping oak staircase with the large sitting room off to the right and dining room to the left. At the back was her father's old study, the kitchen and a large conservatory. It was here that Inge seated Kate so that she could look out over the back garden with its neat lawn, the row of shaded apple trees and the small summer house at the far end. It was peaceful. The air was good. It was a good decision.

The removal men had lost none of their fabulous humour on the road down. They arrived with jokes, demands for tea and a surprising amount of the furniture chipped or scratched. Inge went into organisation mode for the next few hours. She was just bringing down a box marked 'kitchen' from the bathroom when a woman appeared at her front door. Everything about her was fantastically fit apart from her vowels. She was Australian and she whined. She could have whined for her country.

'Inge, good day, what a delight, what a complete delight. Pe Pe Cameron from the tennis club.' Pe Pe stuck out her hand so that Inge had no choice but to put down the box and take it from her. They shook firmly as two fit people feel obliged to do.

'I know you're just settling but the nice boys you have helping you said you were in here and I wanted to be the first—'

Inge let Pe Pe's hand go and smiled. 'You're very kind.'

Pe Pe frowned. 'Kind?'

'To welcome me.'

'Oh yeah, that. No, really, I know everyone is going to swamp you with invitations, but I wanted to be the first. Now, this week-end my husband William and I . . . William Cameron? Cameron Builders? If you ever need anything doing . . .' Pe Pe glanced around the hall with a look that suggested everything needed doing, and quickly, '. . . he'd be delighted. We are holding a little soirée at our home for the benefit of the tennis club kids' pro-gramme and we would be just thrilled if you would come and draw the raffle. Now, it's at seven on Saturday and—'

'That is so kind,' Inge interrupted and smiled. Pe Pe smiled. It was kind. They were two very smiley women. 'But I've only just moved in and—'

'It's for the kids. For charity.'

'Right.'

'At seven on Saturday. You can't miss the house. Biggest one at the end of Church Hill Road.'

'Right.'

They both smiled again. Pe Pe gave her a look that showed a definite desire to be shown around. She smiled once more at her famous new neighbour and made one last enquiry. 'Will you be bringing anyone?'

'No. No. No.'

Finally Pe Pe left with more smiling and firm handshaking. Inge shut the door and leant her head against it. Why didn't she just say no? Oh God, this was just the beginning. People coming to her door, talking to her, not leaving her alone.

'Giving the door a header, eh, Inge?' The removal men wandered, seeming to go nowhere, carrying nothing. 'On the head, to me, to me.' They played mock football down the hall and disappeared into the kitchen to put the kettle on. Inge sighed and went out to the conservatory to see if Kate was all right.

Kate was more than all right. She was laughing. A young lad was sitting with her and they were both laughing. He was a handsome fellow. Maybe fifteen, with the nice, lean muscles of a young man to be. Kate looked up and held out her hand to beckon Inge in.

'Inge, this is Patrick. Patrick is now in our employ so you must both be nice to each other. He is going to mow our lawn for us. Patrick, this is Inge.'

Patrick had been leaning against a small bookcase but he got up and stood stiffly to a kind of attention as Inge approached. Inge put out her hand. He carefully wiped his on his shorts and then they shook hands gravely as new business colleagues ought to.

'I heard you were moving in and I thought maybe you could do with someone. We've got the house at the back. There's a hole in the fence and . . . We've just moved here ourselves and Dad says good help is hard to find when you're new, so I thought . . .'

So it was decided. Patrick would come once a week to do the

lawn and once a week to help Kate with any other odd jobs she might think of. Patrick went back through the fence and Inge and Kate sat and looked at their new garden. While they sat watching the back, someone else was watching the front. Beyond their white gate a silver Volkswagen Golf sat idling.

# Chapter Nine

The biggest thing happening in Edenford that summer (apart from the much anticipated Edenford Players Production of *Fiddler on the Roof*) was the building of the town bypass. It had caused quite a controversy in the town. There were other things happening that could have roused the blood of the town – 44 million people in Africa with Aids, Romanian refugees no one wanted, children's hospices closing due to lack of funding, the oldest golf club's absolutely desperate need for new mats on the driving range – but the bypass was the big news. Adam had led the campaign and took personal pride in every inch of road as it was laid. Eve was less thrilled. They did need somewhere for all the traffic, but the route chosen was through the Bluebell Wood at the back of the town.

If she had been asked, Eve, of course, would have said that she didn't want the four-lane highway to go through the woods. What she might not have said was that she quite wanted it to go right through the town. Through the town and right down the middle of her house. Then she and Adam would have had to move, do something new, but Adam had never asked her what she thought so she had never said. The construction workers began clearing the fields in early spring, cutting great swathes of space through the grass and woodlands. Eve used to go every day to watch. Watch the destruction.

The bypass was what had brought Tom home. Adam and

Eve's son Tom was now twenty-one. He was Eve's pride and Adam's disappointment. Tom's favourite childhood haunt had always been Bluebell Wood up in the hills behind the town. The hours he and Eve had walked there, built bivouacs and sat munching picnics. Then he had grown up and gone off to save the world. Never the academic, Tom preferred the outdoor life in one endangered site after another. He was a warrior for the world. When Edenford town council passed plans for the road, Tom had returned. He had come home and set up his tent. Now he lived in the middle of what should have been a dual carriageway. Work had come to a halt and the town was divided about what was happening. All Adam knew was that his son and his friends were stopping progress and Adam, local councillor and horrified father, was appalled.

Eve visited her son every day. She brought him and his friends food and clean clothes. She told Adam she did it because she was Tom's mother. She told him it was nothing to do with the bypass. Eve stayed out of the politics.

Apart from visiting Tom in the woods and her mother at the hospital, life proceeded as normal for Eve. It was her silver wedding anniversary the week Inge and her mother arrived back in her life. Adam and Eve, the couple Mrs Cameron had never wanted to see united, had lasted twenty-five years. Eve made a special meal with candles and matching napkins. She thought it looked lovely. She thought it would be what she would have every day if she were rich. She also bought a special perfume called Zen – a scent which expresses the quiet, purity and tradition of Japanese beauty.

It made Adam cough and they didn't last long – the candles. Eve had made Mexican fajitas and Adam said if he had to have food that needed rolling up then they would have to put the main light back on. Adam was very excited, which was unusual.

'Imagine, Eve, several thousand acres of shopping space.' Cameron Builders was building a new shopping mall just outside town. It was going to be a huge development. 'Imagine the possibilities for insurance in a building like that. There is no end to the things that might go wrong.' Adam sucked on his teeth and removed a small piece of grilled red pepper with his fingers. He wiped it on one of Eve's nice blue napkins. 'Mark my words. This will put Edenford on the map and look at this.' He whipped out a pure white invitation with a gold border. It read:

> *To Mr and Mrs Adam Marshall.*
> *Cameron Developments invites you to the*
> *Annual Edenford Tennis Club Night For Kids*
> *June 2. Cocktails: 6–8pm*

It was lovely stationery. Adam got up and leant the invitation carefully against the soup tureen on the Welsh dresser.

'We're a shoe in. Your brother is in charge of the whole project. I will casually bring it up at the tennis club do and he will, casually, say to me – "Adam, this project will founder if we don't have the right kind of underwriting." We are talking thousands, hundreds of thousands.'

Adam sat mentally counting the money he was going to make. Shirley had gone up to the hospital to see her grandmother so that the anniversary couple could go out after supper. They didn't go far. Just up to the driving range where Eve had a tonic water and watched Adam hit a bucket of balls. It was not what she had imagined when they were young. Adam was having trouble with his swing. It was his little 'injury' that was the problem. They didn't really discuss it. He had taken to walking around with his hand permanently cupped in front of his genitals. Eve said if it was that bad he probably needed to see a specialist but he didn't want to talk about it.

What with her mother's night things, which the hospital seemed disinclined to wash, Tom's clothes from his outdoor life, Adam's white shirts and her own 'problem', Eve now found she had a lot more laundry than before. It was boring sitting watching it go round at home so she took to going to the Laundromat to have a little break. Of course she had her own machine but more and more, for no reason, she felt she couldn't breathe in the house. Her nice house with the mushroom tiles.

Sometimes she would take a book with her. Mr Wilton, from the second-hand bookshop, gave her boxes of books for the charity shop. They could never sell any of them. It was all odds and sods with pages torn out. Things he couldn't sell and couldn't be bothered to get rid of – *The Female Eunuch*, the Bible with the first bit missing. Eve would take the cardboard box with her and sit reading while the wash went round. It didn't matter what the book was. She was constantly amazed by how much she didn't know about everything. She would sit there reading and whenever she looked up she could see herself in the window – a rather plain woman with two loads of whites and one of coloureds.

Eve knew she had never been good-looking. That the nearest she had ever got to being a *femme fatale* was being involved in a really serious car crash. She felt a female failure. She had never stopped a heart beating with her beauty. She doubted she could stop an egg beating and it wasn't just the new hairs on her chin. It was a sad fact for a woman to face that she would never inspire a single love poem.

Her one adventure with romance had been Adam and then they got married and that was the end of the story. Now the rules were clear. He didn't need to romance her but she had to work to keep him. All the magazines said so. Every wife was a devil for having cellulite, she must not 'let herself go', she must think of witty and appropriate conversation to have over well-prepared meals, and he might smell of sweat and labour but she might not. Not ever. She must succumb to perfumes, balms and bath oils, colours for her hair, her lips, her cheeks and her eyes. Above all, she must not look down in the bath and find that her stomach refused to sink below the water.

Eve never told Adam she was going to the launderette. It would have disturbed him. She knew he liked to think he knew where she was at any given moment. He liked to think of her at home, waiting, preparing, so Eve went to the launderette at weekends when he played golf. Adam needed his golf. He worked so hard all week and it gave Eve time to catch up on the jobs she hadn't had time for. And then there was the money. The launderette was a waste of money. She had a perfectly good washing-machine. Eve had to secrete the launderette money from the Omnipotent Administrator who kept all household accounts. Adam was a stickler for accounts. He knew what he had spent on bath sealant in 1976.

Eve nearly ran into Pe Pe on her way to do the wash and had to duck into the Post Office while she went past. She felt like a spy clutching her bag of evidence, and then Mrs Hoddle from the charity shop was in there so Eve had to buy some airmail paper. She didn't need it. She didn't know anyone abroad to write to. Pe Pe might not have said anything but she'd definitely have told William and William would have told Adam and then Eve knew she would never hear the end of it. It was Adam who had chosen the washing-machine for Eve. Adam knew about these things. He had a lifetime's subscription to that consumer magazine *Which*, so Eve was always kept in the know about what was a 'good buy'. It was a 'sensible piece of insurance' never to buy anything large without checking with Adam's back issues first. Eve sometimes longed to buy something and make a hideous mistake, but she didn't have the nerve.

On the radio Pasty Cline was singing a song about feeling blue. They played country-and-western music very loudly in the Laundromat. Mrs Ede, who had been working there for ever and could sort the entire town by sheets and pillowcases, was rather deaf now but she still liked her music. Eve quite liked it too. It was partly why she went. She never had it that loud at home and Adam didn't like country-and-western. Eve liked all those songs about unrequited love for women, cars or dogs. All that passion. So unlike Edenford. Eve didn't know if she would die for love. She wouldn't die for Adam because he wouldn't notice.

Eve sat and listened and thought, I'd like to sing but I haven't the talent. Why did I not get given that? I'll be forty-six next birthday. It's odd to think that when Patsy Cline was my age she'd been dead for twenty years.

Eve picked up a copy of *Cosmopolitan* magazine. There was a girl on the front wearing a leotard that suggested she had no genitalia of any kind. She certainly had never had an unwanted hair in her life. Eve's feet hurt. She looked down at them. They were wearing sensible heels. Heels. Why the hell was she wearing heels to the launderette? They didn't look like her feet at all. Her body seemed to start as herself and then finish as somebody else. She was wearing stockings.

'But I don't like stockings. I've never liked stockings,' Eve mumbled to her own feet. Eve looked at the woman in the magazine and she looked at her own feet and she realised she had become a sort of female impersonator.

The June issue of *Cosmopolitan* had much the same articles as the one Eve had read at Pe Pe's house before Christmas. There was a general presumption that single women in their twenties were whiling away a lot of solitary hours in the gym, which was good because the office was no longer exciting for women but rather a place of sexual harassment and the cause of exhaustion and distress for working mothers. Anyone who wasn't already a working mother was obviously aiming to be one, so there were articles about how to catch a man (including a pull-out map showing cities where men outnumber women. Top Tip of the Month – move to a city on the map and then spill a drink on the man of your choice); several articles on how to keep your man once caught, with follow-up advice on the signs of impending date rape and the spread of sexually transmitted diseases.

A woman sitting opposite was reading *She* magazine.

'Did you know that American women spend more than ten billion dollars a year on make-up and beauty aids?' She flicked on through her article and sighed. 'It says in here that women buy eighty per cent of everything that is sold anywhere in the world.'

Eve nodded. 'Doesn't surprise me. Men don't even buy their own underpants.'

The woman held up a photograph for her to see. 'There's that Claudia Schiffer. Lovely looking girl. My Bert really fancies her.' She tutted and put the magazine back in her ample lap. 'Imagine him making love to that. Claudia would be horrified.'

Old Mrs Ede boomed into the conversation like Concorde riding roughshod over the air waves. 'I like watching the clothes go round in the wash. You don't know whose clothes have just whipped around in there before yours. Maybe a murderer getting rid of evidence or a wife spinning away lipstick from her lover. Don't you think?'

Eve didn't know what she thought. 'Adam's got a bad egg stain on his beige golf jumper,' she said.

Mrs Ede nodded sympathetically. Stains were a lifetime's devotion to her. She had a cigarette stuck to her bottom lip and ash dribbled down her front as she spoke. At least she was making more work for herself.

The woman with the *She* magazine was unmoved. 'It says here that 1 in every 2.3 marriages in the UK ends in divorce,' she said.

The women all tutted together. It had been a difficult day for Eve. She had had one of those smart-arse cashiers at the supermarket who race you with the scanner while you're trying to sort fresh from frozen into separate bags. She looked so smug when she slapped down the bill and Eve was still panting her way through bagging the household essentials.

'Did you know that supermarkets put longer floor tiles in front of expensive items so that shoppers will feel more relaxed and so are more likely to buy things?'

No one heard Eve speak. It was all nonsense. Not about the floor tiles. That was true. About the launderette. No one spoke. It is the 'age of proximity without communication'. Eve had read that. No one spoke. No one was going to. There was just deaf old Mrs Ede, the woman reading. She, Eve and someone else's feet on the end of Eve's legs. And it was the feet that made Eve get up and leave. She couldn't walk very fast in her heels but she tottered away from the launderette, she wobbled away from her spin cycle, she teetered away from Patsy Cline and straight into the nearest shoe shop on the High Street. Using her rarely touched credit card, Eve bought a very expensive pair of trainers and instructed the sales assistant, who had a ring through her nose, that she could, 'Chuck those heels in the bin.'

Newly shod, Eve stepped out into the cobbled street. Her feet felt totally different, her legs felt different. She felt bizarrely liberated and began to run. She ran and ran and ran, straight into Inge Holbrook.

Inge and Eve had been inseparable at school and it should have been a great reunion but Eve didn't see Inge at first because she was hidden behind a huge bundle of sheets. It was only when the two of them banged into each other and the sheets went flying that Eve realised who it was. Inge Holbrook. She looked just the same as she had at school. Blonde and athletic, attractive even in an old sweatshirt and jeans. Eve had a sudden flash of her getting out of bed at school and looking stunning even in the terrible pyjamas they had made everyone wear. It made her smile.

'Inge?' There was a slight stir in the street as Eve spoke. Many of the shoppers had seen Inge walking but so far the consensus had been to stare slightly without making actual contact. The woman straightening the rack outside What She Wants tensed and the man on the hot-potato stand cocked his ear to see if he had heard something. Inge turned and looked at her assailant. Recognition took a moment so Eve helped her.

'Eve . . . Eve . . . Marsh . . . Cameron. Five X. Remember? Five X? I sat at the back with Susan Belcher. How we all laughed when we found out her family lived in a house called Windy

Corner. The Belchers of Windy Corner.' Inge was still frowning and Eve felt a bit embarrassed. Quite a few people were looking now. 'Yes, well, we were easily pleased in those days.' Inge looked at Eve again and then put her head back and laughed.

'Good God, Camie, how unbelievable.' Camie! Eve was thrilled. She hadn't been *Camie* for thirty years. Cameron . . . camie knickers . . . camie. Everyone called her Camie at school. Of course, after she left school she had thought *Eve* was more sophisticated. Now she realised it just sounded old. Eve and Inge smiled at each other. Huge, great, wide, genuine smiles. Eve tried to think where to go next. There were so many years to cross.

'Lot of sheets you've got,' she said. Inge nodded.

'My friend's not well.'

Eve nodded sympathetically. 'And my mother. My mother, she's not well.'

'I'm sorry.' There was a pause.

'I'm sorry about your . . . friend.'

'Yes.'

The two women, one famous and one not, were by now causing a slight stir. Inge whispered to her old chum, 'You have to help me, Eve. I can't remember where the launderette is and I don't think the public can quite believe I have sheets.'

After setting the laundry off they headed to the Right Bite Café and had a coffee. It was unbelievable. Not only was Inge back in Edenford but in her old house, right next to Adam and Eve. They were neighbours and it was wonderful for both of them. Eve, who had longed to talk, at last found someone who was willing, and Inge, who was afraid to talk, at last found someone she felt safe with.

'I remember you that first day,' Eve said, 'wearing your boater like Maurice Chevalier instead of some suet pudding like the rest of us. Straight away, Miss Campden sat you at the front to keep an eye on you. Then I got moved to the front too. What with my eyes and everything. That's how we sat next to each other. Poor Miss Campden. How she loved to read out Rupert Brooke. Do

you remember? "The cool kindliness of sheets . . ."' Inge joined
in and they laughed as they repeated together,

'. . . that soon
Smooth away trouble; and the rough male kiss
Of blankets.'

Inge winked at Eve. 'I think Miss Campden had a bit of a run-
in with a Yank during the war.'

'Oh, Inge!'

'I do. Finished up with a pair of stockings and that faraway
look in her eye.' Eve laughed out loud. It felt so good. Inge smiled
at her.

'So, are you married?' Eve asked, and then wondered why she
had. Who cared if there was someone else. She didn't care about
there being someone else.

'No. No, I'm not. I'm busy. Too busy.'

Eve nodded and moved on. 'By the way, I heard Miss
Robertson died. You remember – biology, wore a tweed skirt all
through that heat wave. It was Miss Robertson who told us
babies came from sex. I thought at the time that it all seemed
most unlikely and probably quite uncomfortable and I can't say
I've changed my mind much. I was ages getting the facts straight.'

Inge grinned. 'Miss Robertson had so many hairs on her chin
I used to find it difficult to concentrate.'

Eve put her hand over her own chin and nodded. 'It was that
same summer we discovered about riding our bicycles over the
cobblestones down Larchfield Lane. Do you remember? Sent tin-
gles right through you.'

'Do I remember? Susan Belcher couldn't get enough of it. I can
still see her – all plump legs and navy knickers, bumping down
across the cobbles, especially the uneven ones, gripping her
saddle with her thighs till she hit the kerb at the end and gave a
great squeal as she collapsed on the handle bars. I think about
that sometimes.'

Eve had forgotten. She had forgotten so much of what Inge talked about that afternoon. They had more coffee, went to dry their wash and then came back for cake. It was wonderful. Inge's face was so beautiful. Not a mark on it.

'And do you remember Miss Robertson making us cover up all the windows with masking tape and back copies of *Science for Schools* magazine before the sex education lessons? She didn't want the fourth form to see, but it made it rather dark so to be honest I couldn't see too well either, and it certainly wasn't something you did with the lights on. I remember a lot of hazy film with amoebas and tadpoles and Miss Robertson sweating profusely. The rest is a blur. Later we untaped the windows and dissected a chicken, which Miss Robertson was taking home for supper.'

'Where did you go for the sixth form?'

Inge shook her head at the memory. 'St Ansten's – my parents were so worried about my hormones that they confined me to an all-girls boarding school. The whole subject of sex was taboo. I spent two years at St Ansten's working out why we weren't allowed long-handled hairbrushes in the dorm and why no girl was allowed unaccompanied into the hockey equipment room.'

A woman at the next table had been pretending not to listen. She got up to go and as she passed by Eve and Inge's table she stopped.

'Oh God, it is, isn't it? Don't tell me but it is.'

Inge stopped speaking. For a brief while she had forgotten to be careful. She leant across the table to Eve. 'Eve, I think you've been recognised.'

The woman laughed as if Inge had said the funniest thing in the world. 'Inge Holbrook! I know I shouldn't but I'm going to. May I?' The woman pushed her bottom on to the bench seat next to Eve so that Eve had to move along. The woman's whole attention was on Inge. It was as if Eve wasn't even there. 'My name is Paula, Paula Ross, and I run the campaign for bereaved people with special needs – I'm sure you've heard of it. Anyway, we are holding our first annual ball in the autumn and I just know you would be the perfect speaker. We had asked that newsreader but you know she's had such trouble with . . .' The woman mimed the words 'breast cancer' and moved on. 'You don't have to decide now, naturally, but I can't tell you how marvellous it would be. Here's my name and address . . .' The woman scribbled on a napkin. 'Do call any time. Now, where can I get hold of you?'

Inge dutifully wrote out her agent's address and handed it over. The woman looked positively tearful. 'Marvellous, it's going to be marvellous.' And then she was gone.

Inge waited till the door of the café had closed behind the intruder and then both she and Eve started to giggle.

'Oh God,' sniggered Inge. 'Do you think she heard us talking about sex?'

Eve looked at her old friend. Inge said it all so naturally. Eve couldn't believe she was sitting in the Right Bite Café in Edenford High Street talking about sex. She wasn't sure she had ever talked about sex with anyone. Mother had never really explained it, except to say that sex was something two people did only when they were very much in love. This seemed strange to Eve as a child. Everyone knew that Harry Minter and his wife, Marie, who lived across the road, did it all the time and he was horrible to her. At parties he would sit with his hand round the back of her neck and squeeze it every time she said something he didn't like or if she wanted another drink. Then they would go home and you could hear them going at it hammer and tongs in the sandpit in their back garden that they'd bought for their kids.

Eve couldn't stop smiling at Inge and then Inge asked Eve what she did and she had to say, 'Housewife,' and it sounded so awful. She said so. 'It's awful, isn't it?'

'And then what?' Inge replied.

'What do you mean?'

'What will you do next?' Inge leant across the table towards Eve. 'I'm going to learn to fly. One of those little planes you can take up on your own. Kate and I want to go to California. I shall learn to fly and . . . you know the Golden Gate Bridge?'

Eve nodded. She knew what it looked like. She'd never been but she'd seen pictures. 'You want to fly over that? How wonderful.'

'Over it!' exclaimed Inge, so that the other table stopped their conversation about the problems inherent with flat roofs and listened. 'Anybody can fly over it. I want to go underneath.' Inge left Eve with that thought and swooped back to the past. 'Do you know, at school Matron used to come in and wake us in the morning and we had to get out of bed instantly the door opened? I heard she died a few years ago and I couldn't have been more delighted. Isn't that dreadful? Kate's a Quaker and . . .'

Eve wasn't really listening. Eve was thinking about her life, about her house. I could be a cabbage in that house, she said to herself. Eve, you could do something with your life. You don't have to just sit here like a pudding. Eve's Pudding. It was like a light had gone on in her derelict building. It changed everything. In fact the whole avocado business would never have happened if Inge hadn't turned up.

# Chapter Ten

14 January
Holloway Prison for Women
London

My dear Inge,

## Being No One

. . . seeing in the distance a fig tree in leaf, Jesus went to see if he
could find anything on it. When he came to it, he found nothing
but leaves, for it was not the season for figs. And he said to it,
'May no one ever eat fruit from you again.'

(MARK 11.13)

I don't understand that story. It wasn't the season for figs. The
tree could hardly be blamed, yet it got cursed to never make anything good again. What's it about? It just seems like temper but
that can't be it. If anyone came along to my tree there'd be no
fruit. That's what I am. I'm the cursed fig tree.

You know that I don't blame you for anything that happened, don't you? Something in your last letter didn't feel right.
I mean, it's important that you know none of this was your
fault. You're my friend. You're the person I trust to look after
my daughter now that things are so bad. I don't blame you but
everything changed after you came. That day, after we met, you

went home with your laundry and I should have done the same, but I felt so shaky I didn't know what to do with myself. I saw myself sitting, spending my life sitting. I have spent my adulthood waiting for others to do what they had to do. Sitting at the table waiting for Adam to come home for his dinner, sitting in the school playground waiting for the bell to ring and sitting waiting for my children. Waiting. Sitting. I didn't mind so much for Shirley. She was going to be a dancer. Did you know that? Jazz, ballet, tap, we did it all, well, she did. I watched. I loved it. All the girls running around, needing help to put their hair in buns, sewing costumes. The big shows at the end of the year. Waiting in the wings. Watching my angel floating out in front of everyone.

'Your daughter's got real talent,' people would say. 'You must be so proud.'

And I was. I waited and I was. I used to dream about seeing her in the West End or some film, you know, like Leslie Caron without the accent. I hadn't done anything but she was going to. She was going to.

After we chatted, you and I, I couldn't sit for another minute. I knew I'd had too much coffee so I went along to the library. I don't know what I was looking for. A book to change things somehow.

I was dithering in the careers section when I met Theresa Baker. We'd never really had a conversation even though she lives only a few doors up. Anyway, she was looking up something in tile grouting and we rather bumped into each other. Theresa's really quite the riskiest thing in our close. She's not married to her partner. That's not the risky bit. No. She had a 'placenta party' after her last home-birth. Apparently in the old days women used to fry up the whole thing and eat it. Packed with protein. The whole street was invited. It was twins so I expect there was plenty to go round but we didn't go. I didn't go because, well, I was busy and Adam didn't go because I didn't tell him about it.

Anyway, she said, 'Hello, Eve, getting the latest Joanna Trollope?'

'No. No,' I said, even though it was always a possibility. 'No. I need a book on starting your own business.' The librarian heard me and immediately went looking. Theresa frowned at me but my mouth kept moving on its own. 'I'm starting my own business. Doing organising for people. You know, people who are too busy to work and run their homes efficiently. A wardrobe and cupboard organiser. I'm very good at kitchen cupboards.'

'Gosh.' Theresa chuckled. 'What an extraordinary idea. Actually I could do with that. Let me know what you charge.'

Charge? Charge? Money? 'Yes, yes I will.'

'By the way,' she said, 'you going to your sister's classes?'

'Classes?' I said, trying not to sound as if I didn't know what Theresa was talking about.

'Women's Studies, at your mum's house.'

*Fact – 25 per cent of all housewives are clinically depressed.*

I'll get to the women's classes in a minute because they're important, but first I have to say that I don't believe that statistic about housewives for a moment. That means seventy-five per cent feel fine. I read in the paper today that a new study has shown that women who are depressed ought to spring clean the house. Everyone in prison is madly looking for my depression. In here we are all either mad or bad and at the moment I haven't been categorised, which makes things uncomfortable for the authorities. It would be good to blame my behaviour on the menopause except for two things: apparently no scientific association has ever been clinically demonstrated between depression and women's hormone levels. And (I think this one is the clincher) I hadn't had the menopause yet.

I can't say I had depression as such but they give disturbed animals in the zoo Prozac. Germaine says – this suggests misery in response to unbearable circumstances rather than something constitutional. The trouble is my circumstances were not unbearable, just predictable. I hadn't done anything with my life and by the time I realised, it felt like it was too late. I've been crying and the shrink says that's okay. It's what we women do – seek relief in tears. Men do it with masturbation he told me, which was more information than I needed.

I cried when Diana died, Princess Diana, and I didn't know her but I knew that feeling. That sitting on your own feeling she must have had and she was beautiful. The whole town got together and erected a plaque at Anderson's Garage. She once stopped for fruit gums on her way to a polo match. I don't think she actually bought them herself but that wasn't the point. The mayor unveiled the plaque and Mr Anderson played memorial music over the tannoy system, which is usually used to warn people that they are inadvertently about to fill up with diesel.

I am allowed to be sad. Sad is fine. It's the crazy bit that they're all on the look-out for. It was crazy what I did, killing someone, but I wouldn't do it again. Then I keep thinking about what will happen if they do let me go. Will I just go back and sit in my kitchen? Look out of the window and pluck hairs from my chin? The psychiatrist has shown me that I need to change my world. Martha showed me that, come to think of it, but I don't know how. All I knew was that I could change Shirley's world. That I could change things for my daughter so that she didn't end up just sitting. I don't know what will happen to her now but I know she isn't married to that man. To that man who would have made her sit and wait all her life. That's what I need her to understand.

'Do you think you were a good mother?' they keep asking, and I don't know. I thought so. I mean, it was what I did, but Adam blamed me for Tom. He so wanted a son to follow him into business. To build on his insurance empire. To see that nothing ever happened to anybody for which they did not receive some financial reward. When Tom went his own way, Adam said it was my fault for encouraging him. They blame the mother for everything. Not the father. I read that some people in Finland had done a study and they found that being unwanted by your mother was the crucial factor in the subsequent development of schizophrenia. It's such a responsibility. Right from the beginning they tell you that a glass of wine can cause neurological problems in the foetus. That you need to provide the 'optimum uterine environment' or your kid will be clueless, but not to worry too much about it because stress is bad for the baby.

I want to explain about Tom because I think it will help everyone understand how I felt about Patrick. You see, human beings can feel things so deeply. I know that but it wasn't part of my life. I felt I had been skating on thin ice all my emotional life. Never getting under the surface and I didn't want that for my kids. I wanted passion for them. I wanted something extraordinary because what I had was only ordinary. I'm not blaming Adam. It's just how things were. You had passion, Inge. You must know what I mean.

## Womb with a View

> To the woman he said, 'I will greatly multiply your pain in childbearing; in pain you shall bring forth children, yet your desire shall be for your husband, and he shall rule over you.'
>
> (GENESIS 4.16)

Miss March, the lawyer, is much more confident than the psychiatrist. He favours a pencil but she writes everything down in pen.

*Fact – the Bic pen was invented by a French baron called Bich. He dreamt up the smooth-flowing ball-point in 1953 and probably never had to write a cheque again. There are now three thousand million of them sold each year. The Japanese invented the felt tip and the self-propelling pencil. The fountain pen may have been around in 1748 when*

*Catherine the Great wrote in her diary about using an 'end-less quill', but then she also died making love to a horse so she may not be a reliable historical witness.*

Miss March thinks I am nearly ready to testify but she is very worried about what I should wear. It is very important that I look demure. She has the facts at her manicured fingertips. Imagine that – a lawyer and time to do her nails. Basically it's the non-killer look that she's going for. Certainly I mustn't wear anything that might suggest any strength about me and she doesn't want me to mention the classes Martha held.

That's what I was talking about, wasn't it? Sorry. Anyway, I didn't mean to go to the classes. It happened by accident. Mother was still in the hospital and needed some fresh night things, so I popped over one evening to her house, our old house, to get them. It's just an ordinary semi. I'd grown up there but that night I didn't know the place. Jesus on his bits of velvet had disappeared and in his place were a lot of candles and posters for flower remedies and tea tree oil, that sort of thing. From the minute Mother moved out Martha hadn't wasted any time. She had swept down from her London club and changed everything. Even the basics. Out was draylon and in were natural fibres and untreated wood. I think you could have boiled most of the furniture and got quite a hearty meal.

There were about six women in the sitting room when I arrived. They were drinking red wine and wearing a lot of flowing things. I didn't seem to know any of them except Theresa Baker from the library, who was clutching a box of Sainsbury's red. Theresa handed me a glass of wine while a woman in swirls of multi-coloured batik held forth.

'Oh, it's the most awful business. They need the pregnant mares so they routinely slaughter foals, re-impregnate the mares as soon as possible and start all over again.' A tiny ferret of a woman in one corner looked quite faint.

'Hello,' I said brightly. 'Sorry to interrupt, just come to get—'

'You're just in time,' declared Martha. 'You all know my sister Eve. She's perfect. Ordinary as the day is long. We need your opinion, as an ordinary woman.'

'What on?'

'Urine farms,' said Theresa Baker, pouring more wine. 'For hormone replacement therapy. You know, HRT.'

I looked blank, so Mrs Batik, who'd started the whole thing, ploughed on. 'They harvest natural oestrogen from the urine of pregnant mares. The mares are fitted with a collection cup, which is attached to the horse who is then confined to a narrow stall for the whole eleven-month pregnancy. It's huge business. There are over eighty thousand mares in US urine farms. And why do women do it? Hmmm?'

She seemed to look straight at me. I rummaged through back issues of *Cosmo* in my mind and made a stab in the dark.

'Does it make your skin look younger?'

'Oh that, yes, and keeps your eyes moist, improves your husband's sex life, stops glaucoma, Alzheimer's, but at what cost?'

I didn't know but I thought it sounded pretty good on the surface.

'Are we nearly ready, Theresa, only I've got to—' whispered the ferret woman.

'Yes, yes, just waiting for Brian to go out. He's off to the pub.'

Martha leant over and whispered to me. 'Brian's Theresa's partner. There's something wrong with the boiler and he's just looking at it.'

We sat and waited for Brian to be brilliant with boilers followed by being ready to leave. I should have gone then but I hadn't finished my wine and there was a slightly uncomfortable silence that I couldn't think how to break. We'd done urine farms and didn't know each other well enough to move on till Brian had gone. Martha is younger than me and so were the other women in the group. Not by much, but I felt out of place. I don't normally drink but I couldn't think of anything else to do. We all had a good sup till finally Brian appeared in the door.

'All sorted,' he said, looking awkward. 'Well, you girls have a good time. We chaps'll be in the pub!' He laughed rather heartily. 'Right. Bye then.' Brian waved goodbye and after a moment we all waved back. Then we sat and waited for the front door to close before my sister began.

'Right, well, welcome to the Edenford Women's Study Group and to what I hope will be a regular Tuesday gathering. A meeting where we will come together not to change the world but to reassess our place in it.' So far so good, I thought. I quite wanted to reassess my place in the world. Indeed, I wasn't at all sure that I even had one. I had never seen Martha at work and it was fascinating to watch as she flowed on.

'Right, how many of you managed to read *The Female Eunuch* and *The Whole Woman* before you came?' She held up a copy of *The Whole Woman* by Germaine Greer. I'd read about it in the paper but I hadn't seen a copy till then. It wasn't something Mr Wilton carried in the bookshop. That was where I first heard about it. 'Now you won't need me to tell you that the key to this book is the castration of women.'

There was a lot of general nodding so I had some more wine.

'And we need to examine that, quite literally. Why are we castrated?' Before anyone had a chance to answer, Martha was off. 'I think it has a great deal to do with the fact that as women, our genitalia are hidden. How many of us in this room have ever really examined our sexual organs?' Despite the large amount of batik and the small number of brassieres in the room, it wasn't a question that evoked a big response.

'I think,' said the little ferret woman, 'that the problem is with communication. I mean with men and their language.'

I nodded because Adam and I often seem to speak a different language, but so too, it seemed, did the ferret woman. 'I mean,' she said, 'that everything about sexual relations with men is put in the language as a sort of poking, isn't it? Something that happens *to* us not with us.'

'Fucking,' said Mrs Batik.

'Screwing and shagging,' said someone else.

'What about rooting?' said Theresa. What about it? I thought. I'd never even heard of it.

The ferret woman was on a roll. 'I think we need to change our whole attitude to sex. We need to embrace the penis, not just take it.' There was a pause after this. I don't know whether we were supposed to think about what she said or just contemplate the very idea of her having sex at all. She seemed such a little, shy thing.

'Exactly!' exclaimed Martha, as if the whole evening were going to plan. 'Thus self-examination. For too long the womb has been seen as a source of weakness and, indeed, wickedness. A source of hysteria, menstrual depression and unfitness for any sustained enterprise. What we need is womb-pride.'

What I needed was not to cook the dinner every day but it seemed like a bad time to mention it.

'That's what I'm saying,' said the ferret. 'I'm not just some hole waiting to be filled. I'm not just a vacuum. I'm a woman.'

'What is the worst word anyone can think of?' asked Mrs Batik.

I quite liked the question. It reminded me of midnight feasts at school when no one had been able to stay awake past ten o'clock and it all got a bit silly.

'Bugger,' I said.

'No. Worse than that,' admonished Mrs Batik. No one wanted to say, not even the ferret, so Theresa did.

'Cunt,' she proclaimed, and then looked through the door to make sure Brian hadn't come back. The word was like a trigger for Martha.

'Exactly. You see,' she said. 'You're all shocked. So where does that leave us? We can't say the name of a part of the female body but everyone's quite happy to sit and watch death and destruction every day on their televisions without doing a thing about it. Day after day, endless reports of atrocities, nobody gets their arses off the sofa. One mention of a cunt on the television and everyone would be writing to Anne Robinson.'

Theresa chose that moment to draw me into the discussion. 'Eve, what do you think?'

'I think we might change the subject,' I managed rather weakly.

Martha nodded. 'All right. Let's talk penis size.'

I was too far from the door to leave and she seemed to be talking straight at me. I had some more wine while my sister, my little sister in my parent's sitting room, went on.

'Why is it that men are allowed to be obsessed with the size of their sexual organs while women are supposed to keep theirs nice and tidy? Men want to swing through the world like an elephant's trunk sucking up peanuts, but no woman wants a twat the size of a horse collar – and I quote here from Germaine.'

'We were born the companion of man and became his slave,' said a woman in white, who so far had said nothing but had eaten all the twiglets.

'I think inside each of us there is a voracious, questing creature waiting to get out,' added Theresa, who sounded like she was quoting too.

Martha kept nodding like one of those toy dogs on the parcel shelf of Ford Fiestas. 'Now, I know it's a tricky area for beginners, but we're going to plunge right in with a self-examination class. Probably not something many of you have given much thought to. A little scary, but trust me. I have been teaching Women's Studies in the Far East for many years and they think nothing of it.'

Well, I thought self-examination was something to do with the Open University and I had thought about that, so for a moment I was glad I'd come. Anyway it turned out to be something else entirely. Martha was very matter of fact.

'You will all learn the value of this!' she announced triumphantly. 'This,' she said 'is a speculum.' And she produced a thing made of clear plastic with two handles. A bit like a nutcracker really.

'Now it's very simple,' she explained. 'You simply take the

speculum and pop one end up yourself and then open the handles wide and look in with a mirror.'

I felt quite ill. I think if she'd done a practical demonstration I'd have passed out. But they were only a pound and I thought I'd better buy one just to show willing. I'd never felt so foolish or ignorant. The rest of the meeting passed in a bit of a haze. All I remember is Martha's final benediction as I rode out of the door on a wave of cheap wine and horse urine.

'Remember, Eve!' she called after me, 'liberty is terrifying but it is also exhilarating.'

When I got home I left the speculum thing in my handbag but I couldn't stop thinking. What if I had one of those diseases they'd been talking about? Maybe that was why I kept bleeding. I didn't want someone else poking about inside me but maybe I could have a look. See if there was something wrong. A woman should know her own body. Look for my 'voracious, questing creature'. It's what I was thinking about when we went to the tennis party.

There were two things in the paper the morning of the tennis party. One that caught my eye and one that actually got Adam's attention. The first was on the front page and it was about the Romanians. Romanian refugees. The Home Secretary was looking for towns to volunteer to take some of them.

'They could come here,' I said. 'Edenford's got plenty of room.'

'Play havoc with the traffic,' said Adam.

'I don't think they've got cars,' I said. 'I don't think they've got anything.'

'No, no.' Adam was impatient. 'They do that window-cleaning thing. You know, stand in the street and try to clean your car window for money. Plays havoc with the traffic.'

Adam sat down at the table with his notebook and pen. He was forever cataloguing his Shirley Bassey memorabilia. He had been collecting the stuff for thirty years. We probably had more of it in our house than Dame Shirley did in hers.

The other story in the paper was actually about Edenford. In the national newspaper. Adam was thrilled. A young woman had been beaten up at the National bus depot in the late afternoon.

'Not even dark,' he kept repeating. 'Not even dark.' The local radio phoned and Adam, as a local councillor, had to be interviewed. It was quite exciting.

'Edenford has always been a safe place. A family place. This will not be tolerated,' he declared. Then Radio 4 was having a slow news day so they called and he declared it again. By the time we got to the evening I think he actually believed it.

I don't know whether it had all been too exciting but by the time we were getting ready to go out, Adam was in a great state.

'Eve, we need to talk,' he said. He sat down on the bed. 'I've seen the specialist and it needs cream.'

'What does?' I asked, trying to decide between a black dress and a blue one. I should have been paying more attention. I thought Adam was going to cry. Adam was wearing his nice grey suit that doubles for funerals with the right tie. It's easy for men, isn't it? Women are not expected to be seen in the same dress twice but it was so long since we'd gone out that I couldn't remember which dress was due for an outing.

'My injury, my injury! How can you forget about my injury?'

'I'm sorry.' We looked at each other, unsure how to move forward. I had forgotten. Adam had had an appointment with the penis specialist that afternoon. I had offered to go with him but we had both pretended not to hear when I said it.

'Do you want me to put the cream on for you?' I asked. He nodded and got up to lock the bedroom door and draw the curtains. Even with the light on it made it rather dark and I couldn't see the injury at all. I put a lot of cream on, all over, while he lay on his back moaning. I kept thinking how unsexy it all was. Then we got dressed. The trainers didn't go with either of the dresses so I had to dig out another pair of heels. Adam didn't notice what I wore. He was ready long before me. I went outside to find Adam hanging campaign balloons and ribbons on my car aerial. The election wasn't for months but they flowed in the wind over the boot of my car.

'Might as well arrive with the flag flying,' he said, and pulled the last piece of string a bit tighter. Men like fiddling with straps and fixings on cars. I think it has echoes of pioneers setting off across the plains. There's a ring of Scott of the Antarctic about it. Adam was a bit too vigorous. One minute the decor was flying high and the next the car aerial snapped backwards and trailed behind us like a much decorated sting on a giant metal bee. The car lurched across town. The gearbox was dying.

I have to go to one of my sessions.

The psychiatrist is beginning to narrow the field in his questions to me.

'Did you hate John when you killed him?' he asks.

'I suppose I must have,' I said.

'And is that a common feeling for you? Have you hated many people?' I thought about it. Did I really hate anyone?

'Maybe Jane Asher.' It was a joke but I am not to be funny. I am never to be funny again.

Love,

Eve

# Chapter Eleven

William and Pe Pe's house stood on the top of Church Hill Road. It had terrific views of the town and fields in the distance. It was an amazing place. Keeping up with them was a job no one in the town would undertake lightly. Pe Pe looked stunning. She had had her body Moulinexed into yet another black sheath, which clung to her in a reminder to all of what bodies were supposed to look like. Her make-up was perfect. A smooth sheen of colour that opened her eyes and pouted her mouth. Eve looked at her and knew she looked a disaster. A terrible old blue dress and eye make-up that could have been slapped across her lids by a myopic traffic warden on duty at the time.

'Lucky bugger,' Adam whispered to his wife.

'Who?' asked Eve, although she knew full well.

'William, of course.'

Lucky bugger, indeed. It was a boy's idea of luck. How lucky to have a wife other men covet. Pe Pe wandered about fulfilling her part brilliantly. She was there for the other men to appreciate. For them to envy William having her at his disposal. Eve thought about her women's study class and had a very unfeminist thought. She longed sharply to be a sex object for just one evening. She envied Pe Pe that night. They could not have been two more different women. Pe Pe was a female sex object and Eve believed she was a female most men would object to having sex with. She wondered what Adam thought of having her on his arm. Eve was much younger than him and that used to help. He probably had never expected her to get old too.

The party was a gathering of everyone who was anyone from the town. Neat little name tags had been filled out in advance. Pe Pe's read *Mrs William Cameron* and Eve's read *Mrs Adam Marshall*. Once more she had a sense of disappearing. It was new. She had never minded before but now Eve cared terribly. She desperately wanted to be someone she remembered from twenty years ago.

The house was fabulous. Everything was straight from a centre spread of *House & Garden*. If one of those ghastly television make-over teams laid a finger on the place you would kill them. The hall was enormous, with a great mountainous staircase up to a galleried landing. A frozen acrylic banister had been twisted and turned up the oak stairs like a liquid waterfall running over a deep, blue carpet. Adam and Eve received their name tags from some 'staff' and moved to shimmer into the shag-pile room. William had got a photographer to 'snap' everyone as they arrived. Of course, Eve tripped. She did not glide in on Adam's arm but landed head first in six inches of double Worcester. Adam did try to grab her as she fell but he was also protecting his privates and it was left to Pe Pe to deal beautifully with the *faux pas*.

'High heels!' She laughed one of those crystals laughs that women have to practise to perfect. 'Such a monstrous invention. They bring you up to a man's height and then make sure you can't keep up with him.' She and Adam roared at her quip and they moved into the room while Eve returned to the vertical. She looked around the crowded room. It was a husbands- and wives-fest. Everyone had come in a couple. There were no spinsters, no unbought merchandise. The men were there to network and the wives were there to look charming, be supportive. They were awash in the cult of coupledom, where to be single was to be one of the unchosen ones. The chosen few had to band together. Admit nothing. Smile. The wife who would dare to confess that she was unhappy was throwing in the towel. It was not done. The women all worked at being a wife, year after year. It was an investment no woman would dare to lose by admitting defeat. If the chosen ones were defeated, the unchosen would smell retreat and circle around.

Eve knew what Adam wanted. He wanted her to be a politician's wife, an insurance salesman's wife – look good but not too good, dress well but not expensively, speak when spoken to, come when called and laugh at his jokes. Never be caught sneering/frowning/yawning/slouching/looking anything but perfectly groomed. He would never have said so but Eve knew it all the same.

Why didn't she leave there and then? Head off for pastures new? Eve could no more admit to that room that she was unhappy than sculpt herself like Pe Pe. The only thing she had ever laboured at was being a wife and mother. If Eve didn't have that then there was nothing left. There was a commotion in the hall. Lots of high-pitched squeaking blended with low-pitched men taking coats and offering drinks. Inge had arrived.

Pe Pe was almost overcome with excitement. The crowd parted like the Red Sea as she led Inge, her prize guest, into the large sitting room.

'I expect you'll want to check your hair,' she said very loudly, although Inge's hair looked perfect. 'May I show you the way?' Pe Pe smiled graciously at her guests as Inge obediently followed in her hostess's wake. 'We've just had the house feng shuid. That's why there's no mirror in the hall.'

'Sorry?'

'You know, feng shuid – it's Chinese. A lovely little man comes and rebalances the energy in your house. You can't have a mirror in the hall. It literally bounces good fortune out of the home. He said—'

Inge never heard what the wise Oriental had to say. She spied Eve and rushed over with open arms. 'Hello, Camie.'

They hugged while Pe Pe stood watching, her mouth the only part of her face still smiling.

'Do you want a drink?' asked Eve.

Inge nodded her head at Pe Pe and whispered, 'I'd love one but apparently I have to check my hair.'

'I'll come with you.'

Eve and Inge lined up beside Pe Pe, who once again led the way.

'You look stunning, Pe Pe,' Eve said, because it was true.

'Well, needs must. I know he's your brother but I don't want to give Willie an excuse to run off with anyone else. Third wife syndrome!' She eyed the other women in the room as they departed. Each one a potential thief. Each spinster of this parish a dangerous piece of unbought merchandise.

'Poor Martha,' Pe Pe commented under her breath. 'Never married, you know. It's so sad because . . .' There was a horrible pause as Pe Pe realised that Inge had never married. Up close and off the television she suddenly saw her in a slightly different light. Perhaps inviting her had not been such a wonderful idea. She was really very attractive. Inge excused herself into the loo.

In the bathroom mirror the energy bounced out of Eve. Pe Pe and she looked in together while Pe Pe fixed something unnecessarily. Eve looked at this endlessly smiling woman. This woman who slept with her brother.

'Pe Pe, are you happy?'

'Eve, I am happy because I intend to be. Happiness is not accidental. It is purposeful. It is something you have to create all day long.'

'How?'

Pe Pe applied a new layer of lip gloss as she spoke. 'Every morning I tell myself a story for three or four minutes about the kind of day I intend to have. I promise myself a good day. I focus on beauty and joy. The story keeps me on track as the day unfolds. You have to let the negative stuff go. Each day I have a new opportunity to be happy. Just about everyone can be happy, Eve.' She looked at Eve as if she half thought her sister-in-law disproved the theory. 'Intending to be happy is the first step. Take the party tonight. Go out there and keep asking what joy can I find in this situation? Maximise all experience.' She snapped the lid on to her lipstick as Inge emerged from her retreat. 'And smile.'

A marquee had been set up in the garden and there was a band for dancing. Women performing that neat sleight of hand where they glide backwards, controlling every muscle and yet making it look as though the man is shoving them effortlessly round the floor. Eve knew she couldn't do it. It was too much like ice-skating.

Inge was swept away on a tide of enthusiasm. Everyone wanted to meet her. Everyone wanted to talk to her.

Eve tried conversation with several people during the evening. 'It's my mother, you see. I have to look after her. She's in hospital but she'll be out soon,' she said to one half-interested woman. 'When she's better I'm thinking of going into business with—'

'Oh, you should put her in a home. That's what we did with mine. It's a pity because she used to be such fun. Loved a flutter on the horses. Used to bet on anything. Actually it was one Christmas we realised it had got out of hand and she was on her way out. She put gambling chips in the pudding instead of sixpences and they didn't take well to all that boiling.'

The surprise of the evening was that Theresa Baker was there with her partner Brian. They seemed the wrong sort of people for Willie and Pe Pe but it appeared Brian was due to make some murals for the shopping precinct. He and Theresa were allowed to be a bit odd as he was an artist.

Pe Pe had caterers. She also had a tailor-made Poggenpohl kitchen, but as far as Eve knew she had never used it. She beamed at everyone. She looked fabulous. Like Venus de Milo before that unfortunate arm thing. The whole town appeared to have turned up. John Antrobus was there. And Eve's family, of course. Her daughter Shirley and her sister Martha, who was holding court in a corner. Eve couldn't think what to say to her. She was terrified that she'd ask whether she'd used the speculum.

Everywhere waiters whispered and glided about with things on silver plates. All the dishes were decorated in a tennis theme, while small children dressed in Wimbledon whites rushed around selling raffle tickets. Eve could see Adam trying to get William to one side but he kept getting cornered by John. They were having some very intense discussion.

'It's sushi,' beamed Pe Pe, over a plate of wet fish. 'It's so good for you. I'm thinking of writing a book about it.'

'What are you going to call it?' snarled Martha. 'If you knew sushi like I know sushi?' Pe Pe's beam never faltered. She was a dental dream.

'I sense anger in you, Martha, and I can help you with that.'

Eve sensed anger in Martha too and she couldn't help her with that, so she went to find somewhere to sit down. Inge was deep in conversation with the president of the tennis club.

'We are so grateful to you, Miss Holbrook,' he gushed. 'This is going to make all the difference to the children.'

Inge smiled. 'Well, the more under-privileged kids we can get into sport, the better.'

The man's *bonhomie* faltered. 'Under-privileged?'

Inge nodded. 'The money from tonight. To get kids into tennis.'

The president laughed politely. 'Oh, that. No, it's for our first team to go to Paris and play against a lovely French team at a private lycée. To be honest there's not a parent in the club who couldn't afford the trip but we thought it would be good for club morale to have a fund-raiser.'

After about an hour and a half, William called for everyone's attention.

'Ladies and gentlemen, ladies and gentlemen, we shall now be drawing the raffle. Into the conservatory, please, everyone.'

The conservatory was new and until that moment had been kept firmly shut. Pe Pe hustled the tennis children into a short guard of honour, while William opened the large double doors to the room. He marched in, clapped his hands and lights came on in a vast glass palace just off the sitting room. It was stunning. He clapped his hands again and classical music began playing softly.

'The latest technology.' He clapped his hands again and the lights went off until he clapped them on once more. In the centre of the room was a large table covered with a white silk cloth. Pe Pe ushered everyone into the room while holding back Inge as guest of honour. Inge was grateful. The woman speaking to her was the one from the café. She had not left Inge alone for an hour.

'The people at the garage knew where the house was, so I did call round to give you details about the ball but there was only your housekeeper in,' said the woman.

Inge looked confused. 'I don't have a housekeeper.'

The woman smiled, thinking perhaps Inge was too busy to remember. 'Yes you do. I met her. Coloured woman. Very pleasant.'

That's not my housekeeper.'

'Are you sure?'

'Thank you all for coming,' began William.

'You won't forget about the ball?' the woman called to Inge, as she was forcibly separated from fame by Pe Pe. 'It will be so fabulous.'

The room hushed to listen to William. 'Welcome to what can only be described as a fabulous charity evening. We are here so that the kids of Edenford can play tennis . . . in France, and who better as our guest of honour than that tennis champion—'

'Athletics,' said Eve, quite loudly.

'—and great sports commentator, now resident here in Edenford . . .'

This caused a general murmur with at least three people saying, 'Oh yes, her parent's house, you know, on Maple Lane.'

'. . . Inge Holbrook.'

As a pièce de résistance, the two lines of children whipped out tennis rackets from behind their backs and held them up to form an arch for Inge to walk under. It caused a wave of applause and

Inge to have a brief moment where she thought she'd lost an eye. As soon as the clapping started the room technology kicked in. All the lights went on and off and Mozart had a stuttering fit. It was perhaps not as smooth as Pe Pe had intended. Inge bent low and emerged in the room with the walk of a hunchback. William stepped forward with a large crystal bowl of raffle tickets.

'Now then, before anyone asks me what's under the white silk, it's the model for the new Edenford Shopping Mall – as brought to you by Cameron Builders – but I've covered it up because we are not here to talk business. We are here for charity.' More applause, more stuttering music, more lights flashing on and off. 'Thanks to the many generous people who have had their arms twisted by my magnificent wife . . .' William pretended to rub his own arm. 'Ow!' he said, and everyone laughed. '. . . we have some very exciting prizes. First prize – two tickets to the mixed-doubles semi-finals at this year's Wimbledon championships, kindly donated by Cameron Builders . . . Inge, the winner, please.'

Inge reached in and pulled out a number. The prize went to a small boy in a suit, who said very loudly, 'But Mum, I hate tennis.'

He was persuaded that this was not the case and Inge moved on to second prize.

'A day-trip to Paris on the Eurostar, first class, including a meal for two at the famous Maison Catherine in Montmartre. Coincidentally on the same day that our lovely first team will be there. Kindly donated by Cameron Builders. Inge, the winner please.'

Inge reached in again and pulled out a white counterfoil. She had no trouble reading the name. It was written in the neatest, smallest print she had ever seen. 'The winner is John Antrobus.'

John stepped forward and kissed Inge on both cheeks. He shook William's hand in a double-handed grip and waved his prize ticket for the crowd to see. The prizes were a little less exciting after that. Someone got their drive re-tarmacked for free and quite a lot of people went home with bottles of oak-smoked chardonnay.

Eve won nothing so she wandered off to the bookshelves. It was not a time to chat with Inge. The shelves were crammed with Pe Pe's bestsellers and other works of importance. Most of them were quick-fix guides to sorting your life out. Inner improvement for people in a hurry. Eve had laid before her an entire industry dedicated to selling the concepts of self-improvement and self-acceptance for impatient people.

There were books on all sorts of things. Some of it was fairly standard like acupuncture, organic beef cookery, aura reading and even holistic dentistry, but then it rather skewed off the tracks of believability. There were tomes on healing gems, healing crystals, fourth-dimensional chromatic healing, magic healing lamps, magic wands, numerology, techniques for recalling past lives, tantric-sex therapy, vocational-awakening group exploration, Native-American shamanism, three volumes on ayurvedic medicine of Ancient India, two on astral travel, several on I Ching loving light massage, and a very disturbing book giving advice on 'walking on a bed of hot coals to a destination of new spiritual realities and deeper capacities to love'.

'Junk food for the mind,' said a voice behind her. John Antrobus was standing there smiling.

'Oh well,' replied Eve. 'I'm a busy woman. I was just trying to see how quickly I could improve myself. I thought perhaps there was time before any more excitement. Well done on your prize.'

'You two finding inner happiness?' enquired Inge, finally left alone for two minutes.

'Hmmm, we are but we feel we need to do it quickly.' John scanned the shelves and picked up a volume. 'How about *14,000 Things to be Happy About*?'

Inge shook her head. 'Far too many. This is better. *Simplify Your Life: 100 Ways to Slow Down and Enjoy the Things that Really Matter*.'

John examined the book and then said, 'I still think one hundred is a bit steep. I mean, I have a life as well.'

'True, true.' The trio kept looking.

'*Ten Principles for Total Emotional and Spiritual Fulfilment*,' called Eve. '*The Nine Choices of Extremely Happy People*,' replied John.

Inge came back straight away with, '*The Seven Habits of Highly Effective People*. And . . . it's a gift edition which should make you even happier.'

'No,' Eve said. 'I've got it – *Five Easy Steps for Discovering What You Really Want and Getting It* or *Dianetics: In a Couple of Hours I was Over the Pain of the Sudden Death of My Best Friend*.'

John acknowledged that getting it down to five was good but he had the clincher in his hand. '*The 15-Second Approach to Setting and Achieving Lifetime Goals: Transform Your Life, Be More Relaxed, Live More Fully and Have Time to Follow Your Dreams. Extraordinary Results in a Minimum Amount of Time*.'

'I like this one,' declared Eve. *Shelter for the Spirit: How to Make Your Home More than a Drop-Off Zone*.'

'That's good but here's a cracker – *Yesterday I Cried: Celebrating the Lesson of Living and Loving*.' Inge began to read out loud. 'Eve – find the courage to celebrate yourself. Yesterday I cried for the woman I wanted to be. Today I cry in celebration of her birth. Yesterday I cried for the little girl in me who was not loved or wanted. Today I cry as she dances around my heart in celebration of herself.'

The three of them were crying with laughter when Shirley came over smiling.

'Mum,' she said. 'That's the first time I've seen you laughing since Granddad died.'

'I suppose it is.' Inge and John watched as mother and daughter hugged each other and Eve stroked her daughter's hair. Since Shirley had taken her building society job she had moved into a flat with a friend. It was lovely that she was independent but Eve missed her so badly.

'Well, this will make you smile.' Shirley beamed. 'I've got in at Durham and Exeter.'

Eve didn't know what to say. It was as though everything she had ever done had fallen into place. Her daughter, her baby, was going to be a lawyer. She was going to university; she was getting out.

'Oh, well done.' Inge reached out and pulled Shirley into a hug. Eve's head was bursting with a hundred ways they should celebrate when she heard John cry, 'We must celebrate!'

'Absolutely,' Eve managed through her tears of complete joy.

'It's essential,' declared Inge.

'I know,' he said, 'let me take you to France for that slap-up lunch I just won. Go on, it'll be fun.'

Shirley looked at Eve and, of course, she couldn't say anything. It would be fun. Eve liked John then. She really did. He had taken time to talk to her and she was grateful.

The rest of the evening rather deteriorated after that. When Eve went to look for Adam, she found him beside the unveiled model of the shopping centre. It would be a massive development. Huge acres of glass held aloft by arcs of wood and steel. Adam looked terrible. Eve thought he was going to faint. She went over and held his hand.

'Scandinavian design. We can't look back. It's the future. William says so.'

'It looks nice.'

'He's arranged the insurance cover direct in the City. Too big a job for me, he says.'

'Oh Adam, I'm so sorry,' Eve said. Adam squeezed Eve's hand. She was touched. He needed her. That was when John strode over to Adam. When he was just about to need her.

'Mr Marshall, Mrs Marshall. John Antrobus, Hogart, Hoddle and . . .'

'Hooper,' Adam concluded. 'Of course, John, how are you?'

'I'll tell you, Adam. May I call you Adam? I am excited. I was listening to you this morning on the radio about that terrible incident at the bus depot here in town and I really think you are on to something. I was wondering—'

William called Eve before she had a chance to hear what John wondered. Her brother with the Scandinavian stream-line and big things in the City wanted to talk to his two sisters in his study. He sat smoking a huge cigar while Eve slipped on and then off his leather sofa. She knew it was expensive but she couldn't see the attraction of leather furniture. You slide off it in the winter and stick to it in the summer.

'We need to talk about Mother,' William announced, as if it were another development project. 'When is she released, Eve?'

'It's not a prison . . . Soon, but there's nowhere for—'

Martha paced up and down. 'I want to move into the house permanently.'

'What house?' Eve asked.

'Mum and Dad's.'

'Permanently? What happened to living in Bangkok or Hong Kong or whatever? What happened to living a long way away?'

William stood up. 'Great. Then you can have her, Martha.'

Martha shook her head. 'Absolutely not. I have work to do. I need to get on with my writing. I can't be distracted. Besides, I shall be teaching women's study classes. I can't be disturbed.'

'Martha, it's not your house,' Eve managed.

'Listen, Eve, you have a house. William has a house. I have nothing. I have never had anything.'

'You never wanted anything. You didn't want . . . what was it . . . any "capitalist shackles".'

'Oh, bring that up.'

'But where is Mum going to live? It's her house.'

William shuffled his feet uncomfortably. 'Actually, it isn't. Dad quite distinctly—'

Eve interrupted. 'Well, I don't understand that. Why would he leave her out of the will? It doesn't make sense. Anyway, we don't have to follow it. Mum can stay there if she wants.'

William was getting irritated. He had guests to gloat over. Martha looked at the hem of her top while her brother dealt with the matter.

'No, Eve, we can't. As my father's eldest son I am not about to see his wishes ridden roughshod over. I don't know why he decided what he did, but I for one intend to honour his last request. That leaves us with the problem of what to do with Mother. Now, obviously, Pe Pe and I can't have her. We're far too busy. So, Eve, she'll have to come to you.'

Martha and William both looked at Eve as if it were settled. 'No. No. I can't. I won't.'

'Why ever not? What is the matter with you? She's your mother. What else do you have to do?'

Eve looked at her brother and sister and knew even then that she would lose. 'I'm starting my own business,' she muttered.

William smirked at Martha. 'Your own business. Doing what?'

'I'm going to organise people's cupboards. Adam says I'm very good at . . .'

Martha and William exchanged a look and Eve knew it was the end. Mother was as good as moved into her house. She didn't want her. No one wanted her. Why her?

When Eve came out of the study Pe Pe was half sitting, half lounging on the sitting-room sofa with Inge, Adam was repeating his radio interview to a small group and John Antrobus was deep in conversation with Shirley.

Pe Pe, heady with her success, had perhaps gone a drink too far in her celebration. For one night at least, her concern with sperm and egg production had abated. Her words were even less distinct than usual but she had the intensity of conversation that only alcohol can fuel.

'I feel I can talk to you, Inge. You're very sympathetic.'

'You're very kind. I'm afraid I really must head off—'

'You see, you and I, Inge, are in the same boat. Both attractive, both in the public eye and what do people expect? Cheerfulness! Bloody cheerfulness.'

Inge smiled. 'Well, you do it very well. It's been lovely but I really must—'

Pe Pe leant forward and held firmly on to Inge's arm. 'Do you know how I do it?'

Inge shook her head. 'Something about telling yourself a happy story?'

'Bollocks. No.' Pe Pe took a large, sustaining gulp of Soave and whispered one word. 'Operation.'

Inge didn't think she'd heard properly. 'Sorry?'

'Dr Habib, Harley Street. He's a marvel. Botox. That's what they call it. It's the same toxin as botchi . . . batchili . . . food poisoning. They inject it in your forehead and you stop frowning and then some kind of glue in your cheeks to keep you smiling. Lasts for six weeks. Marvellous. He could help you.'

Pe Pe produced a pamphlet from a small drawer in the coffee table. Inge began to protest but Pe Pe stuffed the leaflet into Inge's handbag. Inge looked at Pe Pe's expensive smile and felt sick. She couldn't think what she was doing here. Raising money for rich kids who didn't bloody need it. She couldn't think why she wasn't with Kate. She couldn't think. The guests were gradually making a move to leave. Eve passed by the sofa and gave Inge a chance to extract herself. Everyone began to engage in the mini goodbyes that precede an actual departure from such a distinguished event.

Mr Hoddle cornered Eve in the hall. Horace Hoddle was not Eve's favourite person in town. He was so proper, she could never think of anything to say to him. His consonants spat at you and his vowels came out as if they had spent a short time on an oral rack. But you had to be nice to Horace Hoddle. Everyone had to be nice to Horace – captain of the golf club, chairman of the local Rotarians, chief fundraiser for the Edenford Conservative party and general demigod at Hogart, Hoddle and

Hooper on the High Street. Not a handsome man, but he always made the best of himself. Neat little moustache, neat little hair and neat little sentences.

'Ah, Mrs Marshall.' He looked her up and down like a potential purchase. 'Interesting ensemble.'

'Thank you.'

'I see your Adam has made a bit of a name for himself today on the radio.' His face pinched as he spoke. 'Good, very good. Tell you the truth, never thought he had the right stuff. I'm afraid your son Tom has done nothing at all for Adam's profile, but after today . . . maybe, maybe . . .'

They left the rightness of Adam's stuff in the air and made their final farewells. Pe Pe had risen unsteadily from the sofa and was handing out free copies of some book as everyone left so Eve took one. Eve couldn't tell what Adam's mood was. He was silent as she drove them home, balloons and ribbons streaming behind.

As soon as they got in, Adam went straight into the garage and turned Shirley Bassey up loud even though he was still wearing his suit. Something was up but Eve couldn't chase him to find out what. Mother was coming. Eve just knew Mother was coming.

Kate was in bed when Inge got back. The old chessboard Inge and her father had often played on was set up in the conservatory, with a note scrawled from Kate. 'Don't touch! Patrick and I are in a marathon game!'

Inge wandered out into the garden. The boy, Patrick, had done a nice job on the lawn. Everything smelt fresh and good but Inge knew it wasn't. She knew she couldn't live here.

# Chapter Twelve

Eve's mother was due to arrive the next day, a Sunday, two weeks after the party. Shirley was back from her trip to France and asked if she could come to dinner with John. They had a present for Eve, and Shirley had some good news. Eve didn't want it all on the same day but she didn't want to turn Shirley down. At first, when Shirley had moved into her little flat, she had dropped in every night for a quick chat, but lately she'd been too busy. Which was good. Eve was pleased. Of course she knew what the news was. At least she thought she did. Some kind of scholarship at the university.

Eve was making a cake to look like a graduation diploma when John Antrobus appeared at the back door.

'Morning, Eve, fabulous day.' He bounced in like a newly washed Tigger. 'You're looking lovely.' Eve thought for one nerve-racking moment that he was going to kiss her hand but he slapped his fist down on the counter instead. 'What have you done to that Swiss roll?' It was a good question. It didn't look like a diploma. More like a dinosaur turd with white icing. Bloody Jane Asher. John picked a piece of icing off the cake and smiled, as he licked it off his finger.

'Supper's not for ages,' Eve managed.

'No, I know. Come to see Adam first. Where are you hiding the old man then?'

He should have been at the office. There were no days of rest for divisional managers, but just then Adam pulled into the drive. 'Hello John, good of you to come. Eve, darling, any coffee?'

'In the pot.'

'Right. Both white with, please. I think we'll need the kitchen table. Will you forgive us for a moment?'

They wanted the kitchen. They wanted Eve's kitchen. She poured the coffee, poured the milk, measured the sugar, stirred. Indeed she thought of drinking it for them, but she wasn't wanted. Eve wandered out to the garden like a refugee. Then she went over to Inge's for coffee.

Since Inge had moved in next door they had seen each other most days. Sometimes just over the hedge in the garden, but quite often for coffee. It was nice. Like having a real friend. Inge came to the door frowning, but then she saw Eve and smiled. She suddenly looked all blonde health and happy. Eve liked the Holbrook house. She always had. It was so neat and cosy. Since Inge had moved in, there always seemed to be a fire going in the sitting room, even when it wasn't needed, and books everywhere. Eve could feel her shoulders sink six inches as soon as she crossed the threshold. She had spent so many happy hours here as a schoolgirl. It didn't feel any different now. Inge wasn't famous. She was just Inge. Eve half expected Inge's mum to appear with a plate of cakes and some fresh lemonade. Inge put the kettle on while Eve sat looking at her cookbooks.

'Special night?' she asked.

'I want to make the kids something nice. Shirley's got some news. To do with her university, I think,' she said. 'It's silly but cooking for Shirley always makes me nervous. My own daughter. And then Tom, my son. Well, he's a vegetarian now and I can never think what to make. I'm sure it's very healthy but it does seem troublesome to me. He seems to like things that need soaking overnight and by the time I think about it, it's always already morning and dinner is just round the corner.'

Inge nodded. 'I think you need to be very organised to be a vegetarian. I'm not surprised that Linda McCartney was one.

She had the money, didn't she? I'm sure she never had to think, Oh well, at least a chop will be quick.'

The two old friends sat next to each other and leafed through the cookbooks. Eve tried to imagine the late Linda McCartney having an ordinary conversation about what to have for dinner. She was sure she must have. She just couldn't imagine it. Inge pointed to a picture of a nut casserole.

'I never think the cookbook pictures of veggie food look very nice. Everything seems so brown. It doesn't seem to matter what you make, it all ends up looking like it's been eaten once before.'

They were laughing when the strains of Shirley Bassey wafted over from Eve's house.

'Adam,' she explained. 'He's making posters for the election. He's standing again. It's only the town council but once Adam's decided on something . . . Marshall your forces – vote Adam. Adam Marshall!' In blue letters on yellow paper. I haven't said anything. Adam thinks it's time something was done about Edenford.'

'Why, what's wrong with it?'

'Well, it's changed a lot since we first moved here. There is a rougher element now and I see his point. What with the mugging at the bus depot, and then last year's pantomime was an uproar.'

'What happened at the panto?'

It was a slightly rude story and Eve wasn't sure about it. She hesitated.

'Go on,' said a soft voice from the doorway.

Inge looked up, surprised to find Kate up and about. 'Eve, you've met my friend Kate?'

'No, hello.'

'I think I've always been asleep when Eve's been over but I've heard a lot about you.' Kate grinned at her. 'So what happened? At the panto?'

Eve blushed. 'Oh well, I shouldn't tell it, but it was Robin Hood, and Robin had just captured Maid Marian for the first time. And he did what Robin Hood always does; he turned to the audience and said, 'What shall I do with her, boys and girls?' And three boys at the front, from the modern houses up by the garage, shouted back . . .' Eve hesitated for a moment, '. . . fuck her!'

Inge and Kate both laughed and laughed and Eve suddenly realised it was funny. It was terrible but it was funny too.

'Tell her about that school show you went to, Inge,' prompted Kate, still laughing.

'Oh God. I was asked to open or close some senior-school open day, and as part of the event they had done a rather refined production of *The Importance of Being Ernest*, to which they invited the local primary school. The play has a tea scene in which two rather posh ladies are exchanging remarks, one of which is, "I don't believe I've ever even seen a spade." It was quite a rough area and I don't think some of the younger children had ever been to see any theatre before. I was sitting at the front and the audience had been fairly attentive until this scene. As the rather grand actress said the line about the spade, a small boy sitting right behind me said in a disgusted voice, 'You cunt!'

The three women wept with laughter and all the time Eve was thinking that she had heard the word before. This was not the first time. Of course, no one had ever said it to her in their kitchen but she had heard it.

'Wasn't everyone furious? What about the teachers?' Eve asked.

'No. I think I persuaded everyone that Oscar Wilde would have loved it. He was quite a naughty boy himself, you know.'

Eve didn't know that but she did know that she glowed. They were sitting discussing Oscar Wilde. Drinking coffee and trying to decide what Oscar Wilde might or might not have liked. The three women were silent for a moment. That nice, comfortable silence that friends can have. The only sound was Inge's ancient family lawnmower being pushed rhythmically up and down in the garden outside. Through the kitchen window they could see the young lad, Patrick, clipping the grass. The lawnmower was probably forty years old. Eve hadn't seen one like it in years. It had a stout wooden handle, two wheels and, suspended between them, a curling blade. There was nothing technological about it. It was warm out and Patrick was wearing nothing but a pair of cut-off denim shorts. The muscles in his back stood out as he forced the old machine into its labours. The women watched him as he moved across the garden, up and down the lawn and round the handful of apple trees. The light filtered through the leaves and glinted off his shaggy blond hair. It was a pleasant sight. He was not yet enough of a man to be alien to them and not so much a boy that he needed their care. His hairless chest and flat stomach seemed newly sculpted. His bare feet had yet to be trodden into imperfections. Eve thought it was like having an angel mow your lawn.

'He thinks he might be gay,' said Kate.

The women came back into the room. Inge poured some more coffee while Eve concentrated on getting an exact measure of sugar on her teaspoon.

'New trainers?' asked Inge.

'Yes. I am going for comfort,' replied Eve.

Inge nodded. 'Quite right.'

'Goldfinger . . .' came blaring out of Eve's house. Adam was practising his campaign speech.

'People of Edenford, we are cast upon a sea of change . . .'

'Why don't you just do salad?' suggested Inge. 'Eve's son is vegetarian. She can't decide what to make. I thought salad.'

'Salad is good,' responded Kate, still looking out of the window.

'What?' Eve wasn't paying attention.

Inge had got salad in her head and wasn't about to let it go. 'Tonight. For Tom. Just do salad. You can't go wrong with salad.'

'Yes,' said Eve. She didn't want to do salad. Now that her mother had gone off for a short hop with the fairies, she found she was checking vegetables for her. Checking them for signs, inscriptions of the Old Testament, black and white photos of St

Paul, that sort of thing. She couldn't tell Inge. She couldn't tell anyone. It was crazy.

'Maybe you and Kate would like to come . . .'

Inge got down off her bar stool and put her cup in the sink. 'No thanks, Kate's not feeling too clever, are you?'

'I'm fine. Maybe another time.'

'Salad,' said Eve. 'I'd better be off. See you tomorrow.'

As Eve headed out, Kate called after her, 'Oh, Eve, do you know Pastor Hansen? Up at the Ten Commandments Church?'

'That's that new one, isn't it? I don't think so. Why?'

'He's Patrick's father. I just wondered . . .'

'No, no I don't.'

And Eve left.

There were papers all over the kitchen table. Adam was sucking on his teeth while John stood beside him.

'I think that's it, I do think that's it,' he kept saying. 'Ah, Eve, look at this.'

The poster was only a mock-up but it was still quite frightening. There was a black and white photograph of a woman out on her own at night. She was being menaced by something and was terrified. The slogan was straightforward.

*Don't let Edenford become a nightmare.*
*Vote Marshall. Sleep safe at night.*

Then there was considerable detail about the mugging at the bus station and what Adam intended to do about it. It was a far cry from notice boards and dog-fouling.

'John's idea,' beamed Adam. 'Get people to realise they need to protect this town and all it stands for.'

John shrugged his shoulders. 'Not at all. Nothing to do with me. It was Adam who said it on the radio. I'm just trying to help a good man get re-elected. Do my bit for the community.'

The good men went back to work and Eve was marooned in her own house. She looked in the freezer to prepare for the evening meal. Beside a tupperware container of spaghetti bolognese and wrapped in cling film there was what appeared to be a bright blue budgie. Eve looked at the bird for a moment, then she put on her coat and went to see her son.

Tom was grown up now, and it was so nice that he lived round the corner. Of course he lived in a tent under a tree, but Eve knew it wouldn't be for long; just till the bypass was sorted and then he would move on. Eve thought about her son as she walked. Tom. She had always known Tom would do something with animals and nature. There was nothing more calculated to upset him than watching his dad carve the joint on a Sunday. From his earliest days he had been obsessed with trying to save every living creature. When he was five she had caught him trying to revive the Christmas turkey after it had come out of the oven. Even then, at that young age, he had been the fully developed person he was now. It was strange. Parents think they can form their children but the children arrive with other ideas.

As Eve left the paved town behind and wandered up into the woods she could feel her back relax and spirits lift. A row of diggers and trucks stood idle and groups of men in hard hats were discussing plans and tactics. The police had been called several times and now one lone bobby kept an eye on the protesters. Tom the protester. Tom her son. She saw him sitting cross-legged in front of his tent, with work spread out around him. His long, knotty hair hung around his shoulders. He had explained it to her. It was a Rastafarian thing. Apparently if you stop washing your hair, after a few months it stops getting any dirtier. Eve still longed to plunge him in the bath and get the scissors out. It wasn't the look of it that bothered her, but she was his mother. She was supposed to keep him clean. It was her job.

Tom was busy stuffing a duck but not in the Delia Smith sense. He had taken up taxidermy at the age of twelve after his much-loved hamster had unexpectedly choked on a carrot top. Unable to bear the pain of his loss, Tom had set about teaching himself the ancient art of dead animal preservation. First in his bedroom and later in the loft, which Adam had converted for him. His father had tried to be supportive at first but it was a tricky subject. The smell of formaldehyde was appalling and then people heard about Tom's hobby and took to dropping cardboard boxes of road-kill or near road-kill on the front doorstep. In the end, Adam had given him an ultimatum. 'Tom,' he had announced to his son and heir, 'you are sixteen and this is still my house. You either stop this disgusting business or you move out.'

Tom moved out and on, until now. Until Bluebell Wood. He seemed happy. He lived the life he wanted. He would find a battle that needed fighting, quietly turn up and stay until the matter was settled. It made him content. It gave him purpose. Eve wished Adam could be pleased for their eldest but she knew Adam couldn't get over the disappointment of his son not following him into double indemnities.

Tom's taxidermy was strange but very good. Very good if you like that sort of thing. A lot of the displays he made were very realistic. Not mice having tea parties. None of that sort of thing. There was nothing Beatrix Potterish or cute about any of it. It was all rats digging away at sacks of grain, otters damming things and lately he had taken to doing more exotic displays. Everything had to be real, with as many elements of correct vegetation as possible. It wasn't just dead animals in poses but entire habitats. Little naturalistic scenes of wildlife going about their business, surrounded by bits of twig and, in the case of one small rodent, actual running water. The badger and his burrow had occupied a major corner of the bathroom until Adam put in the power shower.

Tom was pleased to see his mother. He stood and hugged her. He was taller than her now and she felt the rough cotton of his loose top against her face as she held him close. A small fire was burning near the tent and a battered old kettle was just beginning to whistle.

'Can I make you some tea?' he asked, as he might have had he lived in a house on the estate. He made nettle tea and poured it into a tin mug. Because she was his mother, Eve had brought

Tom some clean pants and socks, which she laid carefully on top of his sleeping bag in the tent. Then Tom laid out a blanket for Eve and she sat down. It was summer now and the place was in full bloom. No one could have decorated their house better.

'Consider the lilies of the field, even Solomon in all his glory was not arrayed like one of these . . .'

Tom's friends and fellow protesters were gathering wood or chatting under the trees. Eve could hear the birds and the crackle of the fire and she wished Adam could be there. She wished he could be there and enjoying it. A small pack of the hard-hat men wandered past and stared at Tom with open disgust. Eve's son was the enemy of progress. A dangerous, unwashed, possibly unhinged eco-warrior. Eve waited till they had gone.

'How's the protest?' she asked.

Tom sat quietly and stared at the halted construction vehicles in the distance. 'It's okay, but I think they're getting ready for some kind of move. Two of the guys have moved into the trees, but I don't know . . . Know what this is, Mum?' Tom asked, holding out the dead bird he had been working on.

'It's a duck,' Eve said. No flies on me, she thought, although there were a couple on the duck.

'It's a female duck,' he corrected. 'Very female.'

'Well, it had to be one or the other,' Eve said. She did try to take an interest but her knowledge was limited. Tom shook his head.

'Oh no, the animal and vegetable world is not universally divided into two sexes. No, some creatures are male and female by turns; some fungi and protozoa have more than two sexes and more than one way of coupling with them. There are lots of all-female species – gall-making wasps, sawflies, at least nineteen species of lizards and there is an all-female variety of fish in the Gulf of Mexico. Did you know that Amazon mollies pirate sperm from other species to fertilise their eggs but produce only females?' Eve didn't even know what an Amazon mollie was. 'Beehives and ant communities are full of sisters working side by side but there are no all-male species at all.'

Eve tried to be light-hearted. 'I'm not surprised. They can't manage on their own.' It was meant to be a joke but Tom just agreed.

'Sorry, Tom, I guess I don't know much about it.'

'But that's the secret, Mum. We must all admit our ignorance and set out to learn, rather than pretend we already understand the mysteries of the universe. Actually, what we really know about the world is very limited. There is nothing that closes our minds to new information and new insights more than the feeling that we already understand. You get sucked into seeing things the way you've always seen them. Then you start making assumptions about things because of what you knew before. You generalise and soon you have some prejudice about how things ought to be.'

'I don't know if I'm with you.'

'Well, have you ever seen a crow without black feathers?'

'No. No, I haven't.'

'Does that mean there isn't one?'

'I don't know.' And Eve didn't. She didn't even know what all-female Amazon mollies were. 'Is there such a thing?'

Tom shrugged. 'I've never seen one but I don't think that means that there couldn't be, somewhere. I don't think that we should assume that a crow has to have black feathers. We shouldn't presume that we know how things are going to be.'

Eve watched him working on his duck. Trying to learn about life from the inside of things. Digging away under the skin. He held the dead bird with great reverence and they both stared at the deceased creature. Eve tried to think of another question.

'How did it die?'

'She's from the lake here in the wood. It happens every year. The females get pregnant and they lay four or five eggs. By the time the ducklings are born the mothers are very weak. And when they're weak the males come and rape them. They rape them and they hold them under the water till lots of the females drown. They drown and there's no one to look after the ducklings.'

'Where are the babies?' Eve asked.

Tom smiled. He lifted up the flap of his tent and pulled out an old cardboard shoe box. There, nestled on a jumper Eve had knitted many years ago, were four mottled brown baby ducks. They were asleep, cuddled and curled into each other.

'Oh, Tom!'

'I know.' Tom took his mother's hand and guided it to gently caress one of the motherless birds. Then he grinned. 'I did try to find them another mum. I spent six hours in the rain wandering about. I thought maybe some relative or other. Do you have any idea how many ducks look exactly alike?'

Eve roared with laughter. It was just the sort of thing her Tom would do. It was kind and a bit silly. Tom carefully put the box back in the tent.

'I don't think they'll make it but I'll try,' he said.

'I know.' Eve was proud of him. She sipped her tea as Tom went back to his work. After a few comfortable minutes' silence, Tom looked up at his mother.

'I don't understand about the ducks. About the rape. It doesn't feel right. It makes you doubt what you know about the world. Don't you think?'

Tom went back to his work and Eve thought about his questions. He had always had a thousand questions to which she and Adam had had no answers. They were questions that had never occurred to them. Tom had taught himself taxidermy from second-hand books gathered anywhere he could find them. They were the only possessions that travelled with him. Works from the Maison Verreaux in Paris and Ward's Natural Science Establishment in Rochester, New York. Gripping summer reads like *The Manner of Collecting and Preparing Fishes and Reptiles* by W. Shilling, *Practical Taxidermy* by J. H. Batty and his personal favourite, *Death Becomes Them – A Complete Guide for the Amateur Taxidermist*.

Tom's work tools lay spread out on a large waterproof sheet beside him. There were shears lying open next to an old penknife, tweezers, a vice fitted to a sawn log, a small brush, a spool of nylon cord, some modelling clay, linseed oil, plaster of Paris, forceps, needles, what Eve knew to be a skin holder with a locked handle, a bone saw and what seemed like hundreds of artificial eyes staring up from small plastic boxes. Everywhere a sprinkling of powdered borax covered the surface, as if the police had been in for fingerprinting.

'I wanted to ask you, darling . . .' Eve began cautiously. She didn't want to seem prejudiced in any way. 'About the budgie in the freezer at home.'

'Oh yes,' said Tom, laying his project duck out before him. 'Sorry about that. I'll collect it. It wasn't quite dead but if you just press the thorax with your fingers for a few seconds it stops the circulation. It was Mrs Pard's. I tried to save it but I think it was in a lot of pain.'

For a brief moment Eve wondered where her cat Claudette's thorax was, but she didn't want to ask. She felt she should be going home. There were a million things to do and no matter how many times she saw him working with moribund animals Eve never got used to it. Tom pulled a piece of wadding from a pile and began stuffing it up the duck's arse.

'Got to stop any blood or excrement running out,' he said.

'Yes,' Eve managed. Tom opened the bird's beak and began filling it with padding as well. Then he closed it firmly and wrapped a small piece of thread around it to keep it shut. The bird lay on its back with its head lolling to the right. Tom began separating the feathers from the hollow of the breast down to its packed anus and then made the first incision.

'Mustn't pierce the flesh,' he explained.

'No, I know,' Eve said, although she didn't. Tom gently sewed a piece of tissue to each side of the incision to stop the feathers getting soiled. Then he took a small saw and cut the end of the spine leaving the tail feathers attached. He hung the bird on three fish-hooks suspended from a chain attached to a pulley on a small wooden stand and proceeded to cut the wings with some sharp scissors. From the bird's feet he began to lift the skin up off the body towards the beak without detaching it completely. Eve knew what was next. He would cut the neck at the base of the skull. Remove the brain and draw out the tongue and palate. He would pull out the eyes and replace them with modelling clay before removing the flesh from the top of the skull with a scalpel. Eve couldn't watch. She couldn't wait for him to wipe it all over with a dry cloth sprinkled with borax.

Tom stopped and examined the duck's innards. 'See, Mum? The ovaries are all developed on the left side of the body.' Tom pointed to a series of minute egg yolks gathered in a granulated cream-coloured mass. All those baby ducks come to nothing.

Eve looked away from the stuffing to Tom's neck. His head was bent over his work and she could see the fine hairs on his neck. She remembered a holiday when he was about five. They were at a small lake near Windermere. Tom was naked and running through the shallows in the late afternoon sun. He had his arms raised to the sky and he was singing, 'I love my lake and I love my mum, I love my lake and I love my mum . . .'

He'd stopped splashing and looked at Eve. 'Mum, can we keep today just as it is? For always?'

Eve wanted to kiss him then. She still wanted to. Hold him close for ever and have nothing change. She was overwhelmed with love for her son. He caught her looking at him and she covered up.

'Tom, I was just checking you haven't forgotten about dinner tonight. Shirley's got some news for us.'

'Vegetarian?'

'Well, yes, but I'm going to make rabbit for your father.'

Tom nodded, and as usual Eve didn't know if that meant yes or no. Adam minded terribly about Tom, but as she sat there Eve thought that at least her son was getting on with his own life. At least he was devoted to something. At least he was leading the life he wanted. She just wished he had someone to share it. She wished he had some passion for another human being. She kissed him as she left.

'Be careful, darling. I love you.'

'I love you too,' he said.

When Eve got home, John and Adam were still enmeshed in their work. She couldn't get on with the meal so she went upstairs to sort out her handbag. That was when Eve found the speculum again. She sat on the bed and held the plastic examination device. She thought about the duck with its eggs and its inner life laid bare on her son's lap. She thought about her own insides and how little she knew about them. She thought about how faulty they clearly were and that maybe it wouldn't hurt to have a look. Adam looked at his penis but then that was on the outside.

Adam was still busy so she lay on the bed and thought, I might as well try.

It wasn't as easy as she had imagined. Eve was a bit nervous and perhaps a bit light-headed from all the coffee at Inge's. She removed her skirt, her tights and her pants and lay down with her blouse on. She had just got the thing . . . *in* when the doorbell went and possibly that made her panic a bit because then she couldn't get the wretched thing out. The doorbell kept ringing and she kept thinking Adam would get it but then she realised he must have gone out. Eve thought it must be important so she managed to get to her feet and look out of the bedroom window. It was Simon the postman and Eve could see he'd got her socket set – the free one she had been waiting for with the book on car maintenance. She didn't want him to take it back to the post office so she left the stuck speculum where it was, pulled on her skirt and had to sort of hobble to the stairs.

It was hell getting down. The thing seemed to squeeze in more firmly with every tread and then Eve had to sign the delivery paper and the postman said there was money to pay. Eve said there wasn't as it was a free gift and she wasn't going to pay anything. Eve knew Simon to be very particular but never more so than that day with a speculum shoved up her nether parts. She would have paid him the wretched twelve pence if for a moment she had thought she could walk to her purse. It was quite possible that Eve's whole body was in rejection when she finally got back upstairs. Her back had hardly touched the bed when the wretched thing shot out between her legs, across the room and decapitated one of Adam's avocado plants on the windowsill.

The whole thing had made her feel most peculiar. She had completely forgotten to look with a mirror when the thing was in place and now it had done serious vegetable damage. She washed the speculum in TCP and put it in the Oxfam box in the garage. Then Eve stuck the avocado stem back together with sellotape but it still looked very droopy. She sat on the edge of the bed looking at Adam's depressed plant and thought that there had to be an easier way to be a feminist.

# Chapter Thirteen

16 January
Holloway Prison for Women
London

My dear Inge,

## *Stuffed*

And of every living thing of all flesh,
you shall bring two of every sort into the ark . . .

(GENESIS 6.19)

Miss March, the ever-attentive barrister, is worried. 'You won't be wearing the trainers?'

'Sorry?'

'The trainers you have on now,' she says, pointing to my feet. 'I'm afraid you can't wear them to court. Of course we will discuss the outfit but do start to think about it. It makes a huge difference you know. If the jury see anything masculine in your dress or posture or speech . . . well, it's taken as defiance and that won't help. That won't help at all. I must emphasise that it is a very unfeminine offence that we're dealing with,' she says, as if there were a range of offences in a catalogue that I might have been better off choosing. 'It's unfeminine because it involves aggressive behaviour.'

'Members of the jury, how do you find?' says the learned judge.

'Guilty, my Lord.'

'On what grounds?'

'Footwear alone, my Lord.'

*Fact – Dr Walker, a woman surgeon serving in the American Civil War, was arrested and imprisoned for wearing men's clothing. She had won a bronze star for her wartime services but this did not stop the horror of her adoption of what she called 'rational dress'. This involved her wearing a top hat, frock coat and cravat, which I don't think is entirely rational for war but then it probably beats hell out of a corset and large hooped skirt. The fact of her being a woman was only discovered after she was wounded and captured by the Confederates. They discovered her true sex and let her go. She was in and out of prison after that for popping on trousers until she founded a women's commune on a farm near Oswego. It was women only and they all had to swear to wear men's clothing and be celibate. They had their own judges and police system, and bicycles and horses were available for recreation, although no one was permitted to ride sidesaddle. Before her death, Dr Walker finally received a special dispensation from Congress granting her the right to wear men's clothes. She wasn't entirely noble. As well as her fight for sartorial freedom, she also insisted on having her photograph taken in a makeshift coffin with a stuffed hummingbird. Just when you think you've found a hero they turn out to be as flawed as the rest of us.*

Mother came to stay in July. Adam had been to the printers with John. When they came back I was drinking a small sherry in my kitchen. I'd been over to see you and I couldn't get started after that. Tom and Shirley were coming for dinner, Shirley had her big news and William was dropping off Mother from the hospital. I started to feel cross. I was sick of cooking. Why couldn't Adam cook for his children? I tried to remember when was the last time Adam had made me coffee or changed the sheets or . . .

John helped Adam set up Mother's bed in the dining room. I couldn't watch. I had to do something. There was so much going on in my head. I was worried about Tom, dreading Mother moving in and one of you had told me Patrick thought he was gay and I couldn't stop thinking about it.

I had that feeling again of being trapped in my house. I thought I would burst with restlessness. As I went through the hall, Claudette . . . that's the cat. I'm sorry if some of this seems so mundane. I'm sure that's what the shrink thinks. The thing is it may be the detail of my life but the deed is in the detail, that's what he doesn't understand. Anyway, Claudette chose the moment of my getting up to launch herself at me from behind. She scratched and spat for a while and then slunk off. I wondered if Tom could do something with her.

He stuffs animals. Not all the time but too often for most. Well, you've seen them. They're all over the house. The otter at the front door, a rather sinister fox in the guest loo, an eagle with a gleam in his eye resting on the television in the sitting room, three field mice cavorting on the landing and unnamed birds swooping on every windowsill.

*Definition – Taxidermy: the lifelike representation of animals, especially birds and mammals, by the use of their prepared skins and various supporting structures.*

I did wonder if he could do something with Claudette but I suspected the creatures were supposed to be dead first. Claudette made me think of Tom. I was thinking about Patrick and now I thought about my own son. Not that I thought Tom was gay. I mean, I wouldn't have minded. I wouldn't have minded any kind of passion for my boy. Oh, he's wonderful with animals and nature and the world but nothing just for himself. I don't remember him ever having a girlfriend. I don't remember him ever having anybody. I told the psychiatrist that I quite wanted Tom to have Stendhal Syndrome. I asked him if he knew that one but Big Nose shook his head. I knew he'd look it up as soon as I left. Fancy having time to be a psychiatrist and not knowing all the syndromes. I told him about it.

'I read about it in the paper. There was this very nice young man from Oxford, second year I think, who went on holiday to Florence. Anyway he was forcibly admitted to the psychiatric wing of some hospital because of Stendhal Syndrome. Apparently he doesn't speak much any more but does marvellously detailed drawings of the genitalia of other patients.'

*Fact – Stendhal Syndrome is very rare but is a recognised psychiatric condition. Named after a French novelist who had a very extreme reaction to the church of Santa Croce. In recent years a number of visitors to great centres of art like Florence have had unexpectedly intense emotional reactions to certain masterpieces when seeing them for the first time. The sufferer becomes 'emotionally disorientated' after viewing a moving piece of art. The effect can be so profound that the visitor loses the power of speech and several people have been found wandering about Florence and Rome completely incoherent and unable to look after themselves.*

Apparently he was struck down in the Uffizi Gallery in front of Giotto's *Madonna in Glory*, which I looked up. It's Mary and the baby. Nice picture. She looks like a mum. The young man was taken to hospital after he was spotted crawling in the undergrowth of the Bóboli Gardens with a pizza on his head. Since then he hasn't spoken at all.'

'At all?' says the shrink.

'Well, except to ask for more pepperoni,' I say.

'Pepperoni?'

'No, sorry. I made that bit up. The pizza, you see? It's quite taken him over. All he does all day is draw what the paper called 'pornographic' sketches. Mainly giant penises, I think. Do you know what's funny?' Big Nose shook his head. Nothing it seems is funny. 'There have been no Italians among the Stendhal Syndrome patients, but then the Italians aren't too big on repressed emotion, are they?' I stopped and knew I was being stared at.

'Eve, why do you keep all this stuff in your head?' he asks.

'Because it's true. It's a fact. It's extraordinary. It's out there in the world and . . .'

'And?'

'And I'm not.'

## Charity Begins at Home

And a leper came to Jesus beseeching him, and kneeling said to
him, 'If you will you can make me clean.' Moved with pity, he
stretched out his hand and touched him, and said to him,
'I will; be clean.'

(MARK 1:40–42)

I was bleeding again and I had to sort myself out all the time. William, Adam and John were installing Mother in the dining room when I came downstairs. They got her into bed and then disappeared for a beer in the kitchen. Mother sat up and began the routine that from then on never wavered.

'Who ha, who ha!' came the call, whether she wanted tea, a biscuit or the loo. She had become a small child again. Now she paid me back for every sacrifice she had ever made for me. Claudette lay ready for attack in the hall. I dodged past her and into Mother's den. My mother. She was so helpless, this woman whose life had been one long opera of her own devising. I didn't understand what had happened. My father, my gentle, kind father.

I wiped and fed her, cleaned and changed her. I don't think anyone should wipe their mother's bottom. 'Who ha!' she called, and banged things to get my attention. She was my grown-up child. Once she was sorted I sat with her till she fell asleep. I was going to have sparkling dinner parties in the dining room once the kids had grown up. Now it smelt of death. My own death. The wallpaper was yellow and I couldn't remember if it had always been yellow or if it had gone yellow. It didn't look like my sort of colour at all. I could feel my chest tightening. I couldn't look down because my feet weren't my own and now I seemed to be in someone else's house. I don't know how it had happened but I was in the wrong body in the wrong house. I started sweating and tried to think about something else.

Rabbit stew. Salad and rabbit stew. Tom could have salad and the rest of us would have stew. Adam loves rabbit. Adam loves rabbit . . . I sat reading the paper till I was sure Mother had gone off.

The *Guardian* front page had a story about some of the Romanian refugees. They had been to Glasgow and back through some administration error. Families travelling through the night to places where no one wanted them. They were angry and there had been some trouble. Now the opposition was calling for detention camps for all incomers whatever their status. I suddenly decided I couldn't just sit any longer. So I got up, put away my cleaning things and . . . sat down again. I could feel blood trickling from me. Another pair of pants ruined.

Adam came upstairs while I was changing. He came into the bedroom looking very serious. The avocado plant, I guessed. I'd accidentally killed one of his avocado plants and I thought he'd seen it. But he hadn't. It was worse than that.

'Eve, we need to talk.' He looked so grim that all sorts of stupid things ran through my head. Maybe he was having an affair or dying. I imagined my whole life being turned upside-down and I didn't mind. I didn't mind at all.

'It's about my injury,' he whispered.

'What injury?'

He almost banged the dressing table in temper. 'Don't make this more difficult than it is. My . . . personal injury . . . from my trousers. I am worried about it. I think maybe we should test it out. You know . . . *test it out* . . . this evening.'

It was not entirely romantic but I was too busy standing in front of the decapitated avocado plant to really notice. 'Right. Good idea,' I said.

He and John went into the garage to do men things while I got on with the supper. I really didn't want to cook. Especially not two meals. I got the rabbit for Adam out of the freezer and defrosted it in the microwave. It was smaller than I'd thought so I made frozen chicken escallops with mash and gravy for me, Shirley and John, and something readymade and brown from Marks & Spencer for Tom.

Shirley came home. I'd been up in the woods with Tom that day and it made me look at Shirley again. They're so different, my kids. I mean, I know that they both came from Adam, but you wouldn't guess it to look at them. I shouldn't be the least bit surprised to discover that the milkman had actually fathered one while I was asleep. They're both wonderful, but where Tom is so . . . relaxed, Shirley is so organised. She always looks neat, well turned out. While Tom was bunking-off school in the woods, she was always studying, doing well. My daughter was going to be our little lawyer and my son was probably going to need one. I hugged her and wanted to ruffle her hair. Untidy her a bit. She handed over her gift for me.

'Camembert, Mum! All the way from Boulogne. I got Nana a present too,' she announced. 'Actually we got hers in Dover – some paints. She used to love to paint.'

'That's a lovely idea, darling.'

'It was John's idea. He suggested it.'

Great. The man was brimful of ideas. Perhaps he had thoughts on what to do with a used speculum. It's a long story. I didn't get a chance to ask. John came out of the garage and he and Shirley went into the dining room and spent a happy hour with Mother, a tray of poster paints and an old roll of woodchip wallpaper from under the stairs. Free of paint-by-number lines and able to see with her new glasses, Mother produced some rather fine things. Actually, they were wonderful. Great splashes of blue and orange paint with streaks of red and yellow. The sort of thing Shirley had done at playgroup. I put a very bright one up on the fridge with a magnet shaped like a Cornish pasty.

Tom arrived full of good cheer. 'That's wonderful,' he breathed when he saw Mother's painting. He stood looking at it. He kept grinning at it and no one could get his attention. Adam wheeled Mother in to join us. We had to eat in the kitchen now that she slept in the dining room. The WRVS had given us a wheelchair, which was nice but it had a wonky wheel so it made great gouges in the kitchen wall whenever Adam tried to move her.

'Oh, Adam, she doesn't have to come in,' I said.

'Nonsense,' he said, because he didn't deal with her all day. 'She needs the company.'

'Who ha, who ha,' said Mother urgently. I'd got the hang of the different tones of 'who ha'.

'She wants her handbag. Shirley, darling, go and get Nana's handbag.'

'Mum, couldn't Tom have washed his hair? Can't you get him to wash his hair?'

'A hair wash would be the least he could do,' echoed Adam.

'Nana's bag!' I repeated, wishing they'd leave Tom alone.

Mother sat up to table, clutching her bag and looking bewildered. I had tried with her hair but it was no use. Now that she didn't eat properly and her hair stuck up, she looked like a surprised stick insect. Tom stood transfixed in front of the fridge. It was the perfect Oxo family meal.

'Tom sit down. Have some salad. Do you good.'

Tom looked briefly at the food. 'You shouldn't take it for granted that you're entitled to eat fresh salad all year round.

People don't think about the cumulative environmental damage that is done by planes and trucks as they rush fruit and veg to us out of season.'

'The old swimming baths are up for sale,' Adam announced, while I dished up.

I smiled at Shirley. 'I can't wait, darling, you're going to have to tell me the news. What have you decided? Durham . . . Exeter . . . it's not Oxford, is it? No. A scholarship?'

'It's not about university, Mum.'

'It isn't?' My stomach tightened. Something didn't feel right. Adam seemed to be having a conversation on his own.

'I don't know what you could use it for but it's a big space.'

John reached over and patted my hand. 'It's all right, Mrs Marshall. It's good news.' He smiled at me, he smiled at Shirley, actually he smiled at everyone. 'Shirley has been saved.'

'Saved?'

'I've found God, Mum,' said Shirley.

Adam chortled and finally joined the conversation, saying rather too heartily, 'Found God! Didn't know he was missing.' This observation was followed by total silence.

'Your idea, John?' I managed.

Shirley smiled at him. 'Well, we talked about it on the way to France and then John introduced me to the church this morning. It was like a miracle.' John and Shirley gooed at each other.

'This rabbit tastes funny' said Adam, poking it with his knife.

Tom had taken the painting off the fridge and was staring at it. He looked at the table for a moment and said, 'I think it could be one of my squirrels.'

'But it didn't have any skin on,' I said.

Tom nodded. 'No, I used that for something else.'

I felt bewildered. Not about the squirrel, although Adam said it had ruined his digestion. It could have been worse. The freezer is full of odd things. I might easily have thought the budgie was just a very small chicken. I was bewildered about Shirley. Of course it was fine to find God but she looked different. Distant somehow. I kept staring at her and she and John kept smiling. That was why I wasn't paying attention to Mother.

Mother was not eating. I had put a plate of food in front of her out of habit but I was expecting to feed her when everyone was finished. She could just about move her right side. With her left hand she was clutching her handbag and slowly reaching out with her right to grab bits of rabbit stew and chicken escalope, dripping with gravy, and place them in her bag. The mash was next and then some of the vegetables.

'Mother!' I yelled loud enough for Tom to come away from the fridge. 'What are you doing?'

'Who ha, who ha,' came the reply.

'Oh, God.' I got up but I was in a rush to stop the last of the gravy being scooped up as well. Never the graceful mover, I tripped as I stood and fell headlong into Adam. I put my hand out to save myself and landed right in his lap. He leapt up with the pain to his injured member and pushed me away. Still intent on Mother, I hurtled forward and tried to grab her bag to stop her filling it. For a woman of sixty-five who had had a stroke, she was remarkably strong. As I grabbed the handle she pulled it away from me but I couldn't let go. My hand had caught in the strap and I fell forward, pulling Mother from her wheelchair and on to the floor.

'Who ha, who ha!' yelled Mother, and let go of the bag. The wretched container, pregnant with supper, flew towards the fridge where Mother's art work was covered in a mix of gravy, potato and bits of squirrel.

After the terrible supper we had coffee in the garden. The low sun didn't help the slight headache I had and I felt quite sick. Tom went back to base camp and John took Shirley off for a pray or something. When Adam and I got into bed, I was feeling really low. He limped in from the bathroom holding both hands across his manhood.

'Please, don't ask me to perform,' he moaned. 'I can't. I just can't.'

I didn't. Instead I lay looking at his broken and sellotaped avocado plant.

'Adam,' I said, 'I've been thinking.' Which, of course, didn't quite cover the day I'd had. 'I was thinking that I could do with some more help around the house.' If we could talk about his penis then I could make a big, bold feminist statement. The only thing I had really got out of my consciousness-raising was that Adam did nothing to help and we both lived here. I wanted some time to myself. I wanted to come in some days and find my dinner ready. I wanted to share—

'You're right' said Adam. Well, I could have fallen on the floor. 'You do too much and we need to make a change. I'm sorry, I should have done something about it before.' He leant over and patted me on the arm. 'I'll get you a cleaner.'

A cleaner? I was reading in the paper that a group of scientists have discovered that some schools of whales have different accents from others. They taped some whales in the Pacific and then some in the Atlantic and somewhere else and they all use the same sort of noises but slightly differently. The scientist said it was the same language with a different accent. I think Adam and I had the same accent but different languages.

Love,

Eve

PS. I just got your card. I'm glad Shirley doesn't understand the fig tree story either. I don't know why but it makes me feel better. At least she's starting to talk. I miss you both.

# Chapter Fourteen

Under the new Talent Team scheme, Inge's talent was protected the minute she entered the BBC building. She had barely passed through the stage door at Television Centre when Jenny Wilson – talent guardian to the stars – was standing in front of her with a Styrofoam cup of coffee.

'Black, one sugar,' she boomed, and beamed as she handed over the beverage to Inge. This required Inge to put down the briefcase, handbag and newspaper she was carrying.

'Thanks, I . . .'

Jenny frowned at her charge. 'You don't look pleased? Oh God, don't tell me, was it two sugars?'

'No. One is great.'

'You do have coffee in the mornings, don't you?'

'Yes, I just usually wait till I get out of the foyer.'

Jenny put back her head and roared with laughter at this fine remark. She liked Inge a lot. Inge was a very nice woman. She was a pleasure to guard. A large clock above the bank of foyer televisions came into Jenny's field of vision with shocking focus.

'Oh my word, we're late! Quick, quick. We cannot keep Paul waiting.' Jenny raced off towards the lifts. 'I'll get the lift. Leave that to me. Excuse me, you there, hold the lift! We need the lift for Inge Holbrook.'

A deeply impressed young man allowed himself to be crushed to near-death in an attempt to halt the progress of one of the lifts.

He smiled weakly from between the metal doors as Inge attempted to pick up her case and paper while balancing the hot coffee.

'Inge, the time!' admonished Jenny.

Inge rushed forward rather faster than her coffee cup. For a brief cartoon moment the drink hovered in the air and then descended down Inge's cream trouser suit. It was black coffee. There was nothing cream about it. She let out a loud yell that was followed by an even greater cry from Jenny.

'Oh my God, oh my God, Inge Holbrook is injured.' Jenny rushed to the reception desk. She was a big woman and the movement had a ripple effect across the room. Everyone who had been waiting now started watching. 'Tannoy, immediately. We need a first-aider or a doctor. Whatever you can get. Inge Holbrook has been injured!'

No one rushed to help but Inge was now the centre of everyone's attention. Fortunately Jenny had purchased the coffee some time in advance of Inge's arrival and it had not exactly been boiling. Inge removed a hanky and dabbed at the damage.

'I'm fine, Jenny. I'm fine.'

Jenny rushed from the desk to her charge. 'A wheelchair? What about a wheelchair?'

'No. Nothing. I'm fine.'

Jenny wrung her hands in a fine imitation of old time melodrama. 'It's my fault. I was worried about the time.' She pointed to the clock. Inge looked up.

'That's the time in New York,' she said quietly.

No first-aider turned up and the only doctor in the building was there as a television presenter so no one thought to call him. When things settled down, Inge and Jenny once more headed for the lift. Jenny was aware that her first greeting in the building had not been a big success. She stood silently for a while, watching the numbers in the lift light up.

'Inge?'

'Yes?'

'Could I ask you a favour?'

'Yes.'

'Please don't say the coffee was my fault. I know it's a lot to ask but I'm new and—'

'It's fine.'

Jenny looked as if she were about to cry. 'Thank you. Everyone said what a nice person you are but I had no idea. I thought it was just, you know . . . publicity. Thank you.'

Inge had an English woman's stomach for emotion and could have jumped for joy when the lift doors opened and released them from the confines of their almost intimate moment. The two women headed down the corridor towards Paul's office. When they reached the door, Jenny reached out one of her chubby hands and grabbed hold of Inge's arm.

'Inge, this morning has made me realise something,' she said. Inge couldn't possibly think what it could be. Perhaps the need for a change of career? Perhaps a thunderbolt that what she was doing for a living was ridiculous? Perhaps the notion that one fewer visit to the cake shop would pay off? Jenny nodded her head confidently. 'I can see I'm going to have to be prepared for emergencies. What is your blood group?'

The meeting with Paul went well. Inge apologised for her appearance and her own stupidity in spilling coffee down her suit. Paul was most sympathetic and most effusive. He and Nick from development were sure that *Don't Even Go There!* was going to be huge. A woman from the press office joined them and said she knew it was going to be huge. She knew this because all the focus groups said it was going to be huge. Paul had statistics from a questionnaire completed in the streets of Swindon that said it was going to be huge. Ever aware that size does matter to boys, Inge was never the less more interested in being clear what the show was about.

'It's a documentary, right?'

Nick from development shook his head. 'I don't really like to call it that,' he muttered. 'I think we need to be cutting edge.'

Paul soothed his way into the conversation. 'It's very exciting, Inge. It's going to be a doco-game show. All the hidden camera technique of Big Brother – you know, people being watched constantly and yet they're taking part in a game show. It's very exciting. It's going to be huge.'

Inge nodded and smiled. 'So members of the public train for a sporting event of their dreams and we watch . . .'

Nick stood up and started pacing. 'We're nowhere with this. Why are we nowhere with this?'

Paul raised an eyebrow. 'Jenny? Has Inge not had the proposal? Where is the proposal?'

Jenny paled and began to murmur, 'Oh God, I knew there was something. I got the coffee but . . .' Jenny rummaged in her large shoulderbag and removed a document with a laminated cover. She handed it to Inge. Meanwhile, Paul moved to sit on the edge of his desk. He leant over, adjusted his balls to the move and made a small note on a desk pad. Then he looked up and smiled.

'No matter. I think it was Bill Cotton who once said to me that the best television ideas are the simple ones and this is so simple. We take three famous sporting celebrities who have children. They all swap children and train the other person's child to compete in a sporting event. We make a documentary about the training, which we show while you ask the kids questions about what happened. You know, get that cute kid stuff and then the final is the actual competition. Doco-game show.'

Inge took in the idea slowly. At least it was to do with sport. At least it was something she vaguely knew about. 'And what sports people have you got?'

Paul looked to Nick who looked to the press officer who looked up from her notepad. 'We're just checking appropriate profiles now. The market research people . . .'

The meeting broke up with Inge feeling none the wiser about what was happening or when. She had been making television for twenty years. She had made some good television. Now she felt they were all just making television for the sake of it. Because that was what they all did for a living and not because it held any actual value. That perhaps her greatest contribution would be to encourage people out into the sports field because there was nothing to watch on the TV.

The press officer stopped Inge on her way out. Inge felt her stomach tighten.

'We'll be lining up some publicity for you, Inge.' The woman flicked through her notepad. Through the door Inge could hear Paul on the phone.

'No, it's fine, Barry. She's fine. I'm just a little worried. I think something's happened. She's letting herself go. You should have seen the state of what she was wearing today.'

The press woman found what she was looking for. 'Obviously we've been inundated with requests. You are very popular.' The officer sighed as if she couldn't imagine anything more annoying. 'I want to try to get an angle. Do something a bit different. The *Mail* are running a nice thing about single career women. It's called *Why I Never Married* and all you have to do is a quick photo and an interview about . . .'

Inge didn't hear any more. She left the building in a daze. She drove home in a daze. When she got in, Kate was playing chess in the conservatory with Patrick. The day's post was piled high on the kitchen table. Much of it had been sent on from the BBC.

*Dear Miss Holbrook,*

*I am writing to you about my four-year-old daughter Imelda who recently died of a brain tumour. My wife and I are determined to make her short life a valuable one so we are going to start a hospice for children called Imelda's Place. We know that you will appreciate how much this is needed. Your warm nature shows us that you would be just the person to act as patron of Imelda's Place and . . .*

*Dear Inge,*

*I am your biggest fan. Is there any chance of a photo?*

*Of course what I'd actually like is any underwear you
wore during one of your races. Just kidding! Are you ever
in Wolverhampton? Only I'd be happy to let you buy me
lunch . . .*

*Dear Inge Holbrook,
   In an otherwise enjoyable programme about the history of Wimbledon, I was appalled to hear you remark
that mixed doubles has never had the same fan base as
other aspects of the game. For thirty years I have run a
magazine entirely devoted to . . .*

*Dear Miss Halbrook,
   My wife and I are big fans. This year I am taking on
the captaincy of the West Wittering Golf and Social Club
and we would love you to come and speak at the annual
captain's dinner. Obviously we can't afford to pay you but
we can promise you a delightful evening . . .*

*Dear Inge,
   Do you have skin cancer? No? Then you're lucky but
here are some photos of kids who are not. You could
help. Give your time or money and one of these kids
might just live a little bit . . .*

There were the letters and there were the bills. Inge had got
used to earning a lot over the years and she had never been careful with money. Lately she had been buying Kate all sorts of
treats and for once she was noticing how high her credit card bills
were. She had to work and for the first time she realised she no
longer wanted to. She didn't want to do anything. Inge had spent
a career trying to please. Being nice, being 'fun', being friendly
and it was enough. She couldn't do it any more. From her earliest days she had carried her country's hope on her shoulders
when she ran. Now people still turned to her but she couldn't

save the world. She couldn't save anybody. The pile of post sat looking at her. Inge reached into her handbag for her cheque book. Caught up in her leather wallet was the leaflet Pe Pe had given her at the party. Inge sat and looked at it. This was what the world was reduced to. Pamphlets, leaflets that could secure your home, damp-proof your walls, make you fit/thin, check your guttering, bring God straight to your door and . . . make you smile.

> *Do you frown all the time? Are you frowning while you read this? Wouldn't it be fabulous to be one of those people who smiles their way through life? Now you can be and you can do it without discovering the secrets of eternal happiness. No, it's not a visit to a Tibetan guru but simple cosmetic surgery.*

So much for Pe Pe's self-help to heaven and happiness. Her mush was held up by glue and the skill of a man with a scalpel. Inge wandered out to the conservatory where she could hear Kate and Patrick chatting. Kate had her earnest voice on. She rarely talked intently with anyone except Inge and Inge was surprised.

'I don't know, but there's plenty of time for you,' she said.

Inge stood in the doorway. 'Tea for anybody?'

Patrick looked up from the chessboard and grinned at her. He was a handsome fellow. 'I'd love a coke,' he said.

'Of course you would.' Kate reached out and tousled his hair. 'You must be sweating from all that gardening.'

Patrick pulled back laughing. 'Hey! You're the one who keeps wanting a rematch.'

'That's because I'm the one who keeps losing.' Kate sighed as she carefully laid her black queen on its side.

Inge fetched them all a drink and they sat in the garden, watching the sun go down. Inge had rarely seen Kate so relaxed. The boy was good for her and she was glad.

'Who taught you to play chess, Patrick?' Inge asked.

'My dad. He says it's a game for kings.'

Kate snorted. 'Did he not mention gardening boys then?'

'You're just a bad loser,' grinned Patrick. 'I've told you, you don't attack enough. You just respond. You have to plan ahead or you won't win.'

# Chapter Fifteen

The morning after Eve's mother moved in, Adam fitted a burglar-proof gate to the front door. It came from a shop that stocked specialist gates and safes for the paranoid suburbanite. Stalwart Security – Safe As Houses. As far as Eve was concerned all it meant was that now she had to unlock two things to get in. The focus of Adam's election campaign on safety in Edenford was translating itself into a very personal matter. When not out knocking on doors to secure votes, Adam was busy making sure his entire house was attackproof. Sometimes Eve found it almost impossible to get into her own home. She suspected that Adam would have quite liked it if someone had tried to burgle them as a test. He had scrapped the Neighbourhood Watch stickers that had been on the hall window in case it deterred potential villains. Eve watched him work. Screwing and fitting.

'I'm securing our house as an example,' he declared, while Shirley Bassey warbled from a cassette player on the patio. 'Been talking to the boss down at Stalwart Security. He's very impressed by my campaign – helping to make Edenford safe.'

'Mmm,' Eve said, heading up the path. 'I thought it was safe.'

'The bus station,' Adam admonished his wife. 'Just remember what happened at the bus station. Anyway, Stalwart think I might be useful to them.'

'How's that?' Eve felt fairly sure people from a security firm could secure their own places.

'Advisory capacity. Talk to people about the need for security. What products are available. There are a lot of women living on their own, you know.'

'A salesman then?'

'No, Eve, a security adviser.'

'Oh. Right.'

Adam shut the new gate. It gave a loud click like a sound effect from *Prisoner Cell Block H*. Adam pushed his weight against it. 'Edenford could become a model for the whole country. A safe place for parents and children. A real place for the family.'

There was a Safeway box on the front step with a dead hedgehog in it. One of the neighbours had left it in the night. Eve sent a message up to the woods via one of her dog-walking neighbours. Tom arrived on foot to get the box. He kissed his mother as she got in the car and he headed up the path.

'What do you think of the new gate, Tom?' Adam asked his son rather desperately.

Tom looked at the collection of steel bars. 'You've crushed the hydrangea,' he said, pointing to where the new gate post had been driven into the ground. The plant was split in two.

Adam laughed. 'Don't you worry about that. We can always get a new hydrangea but we can't replace your mother!'

Tom shook his head. 'We're in trouble. We're all in trouble.'

Adam seemed thrilled with this. 'Exactly! That's why we need to protect ourselves.'

Tom pointed his finger at his father. 'The people of the past two hundred years have pursued technological growth and personal satisfaction to such an extent that thousands of other life forms have been destroyed. We have done irreversible damage to the soil, the rivers, the lakes, the oceans and the atmosphere. We are thieves who have stolen the means of livelihood from future generations just to increase our own comfort and pleasure.'

It was probably a quote but, original or not, it was hardly an easy statement for Adam to find a comeback for. Tom picked up his hedgehog and went back to the woods.

'It's only a hydrangea!' Adam called after him. 'That boy's much too serious,' he said to no one in particular. Eve pulled out of the garage while Adam slapped his hand against the new security measure with pleasure. As she jerked the car out of the garage she could see that the wisteria on the wall behind her was going to be nice this year. Eve rolled down her window. She needed the air. She needed the escape route.

'Take a tank to get through this,' Adam shouted as Eve pulled off. She had just turned into the street when he started and yelled, 'Eve, where are the keys for the new gate?'

'You left them on the hall table,' she called and drove off. Eve gave a little laugh. Adam was locked out of his own home. She had a sudden image of him driving a tank to get in. It was naughty but it was just a little thing.

Eve went into town to go to the butcher's and then on to the charity shop. Since the incident with the squirrel, she no longer trusted anything that was in the freezer. The car lurched along, seeming to change gears at whim. Now that Simon the postman had delivered her free socket set and she had her book on fixing the car, she thought she might have a go at it that afternoon. This was what Eve was thinking about when she went to the big meeting at the charity shop.

Edenford was a rather average town. Some big-name shops plus everything that the average Home Counties shopper needed – butcher, chemist, newsagent, the Fireplace Shop, the Good-As-New Dress Agency, the Knick Knack Nookery with 'candles for any occasion', Ozbal's Grocery Shop, the fish-and-chip shop – Bernie's Plaice – and the charity shop.

Britain is full of charity shops and it is hard to say what actual good they do. Certainly they raise some money for a few noble causes but that may not be the actual point. More than 80 per cent of RSPCA volunteers are women and that's probably low across the charity board. It may be that the shops are there to give rudderless women a sense of purpose. That their actual function is not to shift old ball-gowns but to be a place where women can endlessly knit and sort in order to make themselves feel useful.

There were several charity shops in Edenford, of course, but Susan Lithgood was the most prestigious. Well, obviously she wasn't the charity shop. It was named after her. She was not anything now. She was dead. It had been the Susan Lithgood Shop for Lepers when it first opened but there was a big storm in '86 and the leprosy part of the sign fell off. Which seemed appropriate somehow. Susan Lithgood was a local woman who had made leprosy her life. She had never actually met anyone with the disease, as she never left Edenford, but she raised thousands for the afflicted in Africa. Eve had only met her when she was very old and not the woman she once was. By then leprosy had lost its focus for Susan and her main preoccupation became incontinence, which can be a terrible trial.

Mrs Hoddle, wife of Horace Hoddle of Hogart, Hoddle and Hooper, gave the address at her funeral: 'I know that we are all indebted to the vision of Susan Lithgood and I know she would have said "Rejoice Rejoice", and we can rejoice for how glad she would have been to have died in one piece and not in dribs and drabs with bits falling off like those poor black people in the hot countries.' Then everyone shook collecting tins from the shop in time to 'Abide With Me'.

For any self-respecting member of the community, the Lithgood shop was the only one to work in. Started by a local woman and run by local women ever since. No men. Not ever. Just women. It's what women do. Eve was very aware that not all the women did it just to be nice. It was more like every hour spent there deposited a bit more in their 'good member of the community' account. Emma Milton was typical of the shop staff volunteers. She was at least fifty-five, the mainstay of the shop and devoted to knitting blanket squares. She had never married. She had too much selfless giving to do with her needles. Maybe all the women were gathering up points for the afterlife but it was also in the back of everyone's minds that Mrs Lithgood had received an OBE just before she died. That was an ambition. Such a reward would make life worthwhile. Eve didn't know why she needed the shop but she did. She didn't particularly want an OBE but the shop was what she did on a Wednesday. She always knew that she would never die on a Wednesday because she had too much to do.

That morning, while Adam limped and moaned around the kitchen, Eve had been watching the news. They kept showing some terrible war that was raging in Africa. Children with guns. Then there was a man, a foreign man, one of those Romanians, who'd been arrested in Glasgow for begging or something and he was looking so cross and upset and his wife was crying.

Eve kept thinking, Why does all that news come into our houses unless we're supposed to do something about it?

She arrived at the shop carrying a stuffed stoat that Tom had made for the window display. He had donated quite a lot of animals over the years. Eve didn't like to tell him that they never sold but they did make a nice display for the scarves and necklaces.

The meeting had been called to determine the future. Now that Mrs Lithgood was gone, no one was quite sure what to do with the shop.

It was an odd collection of women. They were mostly older than Eve and it suddenly occurred to her that she didn't belong. Didn't really belong anywhere. She was too old for the speculum-shoving women of Martha's classes and too young for the do-gooders of the High Street. Most of the charity-shop women were well into their fifties and beyond. Old women, used souls with bodies worn at the edges. It was as if several families had dropped them off in black bin liners, no longer wanted. There was Emma Milton, knitting as usual, Doris Turton, representing the Women's Institute (an organisation it was hard to fathom still existed), Helen Richler, wearing something from a long-out-of-print catalogue, Betty Hoddle, who always wore a hat, and Eve.

Doris had WI business. She came straight up to Eve and said, 'Eve! We're having a competition and you must enter.' She said it as if Eve had some remote chance of winning, which, of course, she knew she hadn't. 'It's for the best flower arrangement involving a candlestick.' Immediately lots of possible designs flashed through Eve's mind but none of them were really suitable. Perhaps another use for the abandoned speculum? Betty Hoddle called the charity shop meeting to order.

'Ladies, we are gathered to determine the future.' This seemed unlikely but ever since the funeral Betty had enjoyed speeches. 'The Susan Lithgood Shop for Lepers has been a vital part of this community for over twenty years but it is time to move on. The fact is that there isn't the call for leper work that there once was.'

Emma Milton looked up from a row of plain knitting. 'Really?' The idea that they might have actually raised enough money to have solved the problem had never occurred to her.

'Really,' replied Mrs Hoddle. 'We may be doing fine work collecting for the lepers but there are no longer the lepers in the world who need our assistance.'

'I don't know if that's true,' Eve began. 'I was reading about—'

The intervention went unheeded. Mrs Hoddle was on a roll. 'The charity shop must move forward. Find a new cause that we can sustain.'

There was a long silence while everyone thought about this. The truth was that no one had ever really been comfortable about lepers and now that Susan was gone they fancied a change. Maybe something a bit more . . . well, endearing.

'What about the Kurds?' said Doris. 'Aren't they having a horrid time? I've seen it on the television.'

Television or not, Mrs Hoddle was adamant. 'I'm afraid not. We couldn't possibly do the Kurds. We don't want to upset Mr Ozbal.'

'Mr Ozbal?' Eve said, confused.

'Yes. We don't want to upset him.'

Emma Milton was also confused. 'Why would collecting for the Kurds upset Mr Ozbal?'

'He's Turkish,' explained Helen.

Doris looked shocked. 'Oh, I thought he was Greek.' There was a moment's pause.

'It could be Greek,' conceded Mrs Hoddle.

'I don't think we should take the risk,' declared Emma. Everyone agreed. Mr Ozbal ran the little grocery shop on Church Street. Greek or Turkish, he didn't mind what time he stayed open and no one wanted to annoy him.

'He's so useful,' said Doris.

'What about Aids?' suggested Helen but no one took it seriously. She was only saying it to get at Emma whose brother had become HIV positive on holiday in Goa but absolutely refused to discuss it. Helen was something of a stirrer. She tried once more with, 'Leprosy was the Aids of Jesus's time, you know,' but she was on a hiding to nothing. Then Betty Hoddle asked if Eve had an opinion and she was rather surprised to find that she did. Have an opinion.

'We ought to collect for all those poor people from Romania we keep hearing about,' Eve said straight out and possibly rather too loud. 'The refugees with nowhere to go. We could get clothes and books and toys for the children and then . . .' she paused for effect . . . 'we could bring them here to Edenford.'

The Milton needles went mad. The potential for blankets had never seemed so enormous.

'Where would we put them?' asked Doris, who did have a spare room but liked to use it for her ironing.

Eve was ready. 'The old swimming baths. They're for sale. We shall put them in the old swimming baths.'

Everyone seemed really excited by the end of the meeting. Eve was thrilled. The old swimming baths were perfect. They were unoccupied, they had plenty of shower and toilet facilities and the empty pool itself would make a wonderful big dormitory. All the women loved children, or at least the idea of children. The thought of saving grateful little wretches with big eyes was very appealing. Mrs Hoddle and Eve were nominated to do the logistics and find out how much money they needed to raise.

Martha's next class for women was on the following Tuesday evening. It was the same crowd – Theresa Baker, Mrs Batik (who turned out to be called Fran), ferret woman, two women in matching tracksuits and the woman from the fish shop. Eve went partly because she wanted to find out if everyone had done the speculum thing and partly because Martha had asked if she could do some light snacks. Everyone had decided to make the whole thing more social, so each woman was to provide some snack or drink for the class. Martha didn't cook so it was left to Eve. Martha was in a temper when her older sister got there.

'Have you seen this?' She slapped one of Adam's leaflets down on the table. The terrified woman in the black and white photograph looked up at the assembled study group.

*Don't let Edenford become a nightmare.*
*Vote Marshall. Sleep safe at night.*

'It's not right. It's just not right,' muttered ferret woman.

'Pandering,' snorted Fran Batik. 'It's just pandering to women's fears.'

'Women shouldn't have to live in fear all the time,' declared a tracksuit.

Martha was very clear. 'This, ladies, is a clever plot to keep women off the streets of Edenford.'

Eve thought it unlikely. It was only Adam trying to get back on Radio 4. It wasn't that clever.

'But we won't submit to it,' declaimed Theresa.

'No,' said Martha quietly, 'we won't, but that doesn't mean we won't be ready. Right, let's get started. Now, this appalling leaflet is just part of a calculated campaign in the media to tell all women that you can't walk safely anywhere any more.'

This seemed a bit rich. It had only been the one mugging on a Saturday night. 'I don't know, Martha. This is Edenford not Bangkok.'

Martha looked at her sister, suddenly sorry she had asked for the snacks.

'All right, Eve, let's start with you. Could you defend yourself?'

'Well, it would depend what someone said about me.'

Martha sighed. 'In the street, Eve. Come on, I can help protect you.'

Eve giggled. 'You used to say that when we were kids but at least you had a Captain Marvel ring then.' Martha turned away in disgust.

'Fran, let's imagine – if someone came at you what would you do?'

Fran looked apprehensive. Everyone in the room was a little unsure where this was heading.

'How good-looking is this person?' giggled Fran.

Martha ignored this. 'Come on, Fran, have a go at being attacked by me. Don't worry about me. I'm trained so I know what to do. I'll come at you and you defend yourself.'

'Now, Martha, be careful,' warned ferret woman, who had brought the punch bowl and didn't want an accident.

Martha stood up and planted her feet firmly on the hearthrug. 'Right, Fran, you pretend you're just walking down the street.'

Everyone looked at her and, really, she had no choice but to get up. Fran stood opposite Martha and tried to be helpful.

'I'm just walking down the street?' Martha nodded. 'Okay.' Fran started walking and then stopped.

'Sorry, Martha, where am I going?'

'I don't think it matters.'

'No, it's just that I walk at different paces depending on where I'm going. You know, fast to the coffee shop but slow to the dentist, that sort of thing.'

Everyone started to agree and contribute their own paces in relation to location until Martha couldn't stand any more.

'All right, all right.' The room settled down. 'You're going shopping.'

Fran set off again across the carpet and Martha began to move towards her. Fran stopped again.

'Sorry, Martha, what am I going to buy?'

'It doesn't matter.'

This made her cross. 'Look, you may know all about attacking people in the street and all that but I do know about shopping and—'

'Shoes, you're going to buy shoes.' Fran was a sport and held her hands up to accept this.

'Fine. I don't need shoes but it's fine.' Fran began to walk again while Martha snuck up behind her. Just as Martha was about to strike, her potential victim turned to face her and began speaking very loudly.

'Six ounces of cheese, three celery sticks, one onion finely chopped and two pints of chicken stock.'

'What the hell is that?'

Fran looked hurt that no one had recognised it. 'It's part of a soup recipe.'

Martha was incredulous. 'Someone is going to attack you in the street and you defend yourself by quoting a soup recipe?'

Fran was indignant. 'It's Jamie Oliver and it worked, didn't it?'

Martha was losing it. 'Oh, for goodness' sake. Eve, what would you do if a man came at you?'

Eve thought about it for a minute. She really did want to be helpful.

'I don't know,' she said. 'I think I'd probably comment on his hair.'

'Why?' exploded Martha, exasperated.

'Well, men are funny about their hair. He comes at me and I say, "Your hair's looking a bit funny at the front." He goes like that,' Eve reached up with both hands to brush her hair back, 'and I knee him in the groin while he's got his hands up.' There was general murmuring of approval at this idea but Martha was having none of it.

'This is disastrous. Now let's just try some basic self-defence techniques, okay? Fran, I'm going to attack you from behind.' Martha was impatient now and didn't wait for anyone to agree. She simply leapt behind Fran and grabbed her. 'Got you,' she yelled menacingly.

Fran leant back in Martha's arms and sniffed. 'What is that perfume? It's lovely.'

Everyone sniggered, which was a mistake because Martha was now beside herself. 'Will you take this seriously? This is important. It could save your life.'

There was a silence. Everything had gone too far for a decent women's study group.

'Look, Martha,' Eve said, feeling some responsibility as a family member. 'I know it's important. I just don't want to think about it. It makes me so furious. Why should we walk around thinking we have to defend ourselves at every minute?'

Martha nodded. 'That's good, Eve, get mad. Come on.'

'I'm not angry,' continued Eve, 'I just want to know why I can't simply walk in the park and enjoy it without looking over my shoulder.'

Martha began bobbing up and down close to her sister. 'And it makes you furious.' Martha reached out and jabbed Eve on the arm. Eve spun round. She was beginning to get drawn. 'Why does it happen, Eve, huh? Huh?' Martha poked her again.

Eve clenched her jaw in irritation. 'I'll tell you what I think,' she said. 'I think a lot of it is a conspiracy. I think it's a load of men who write newspapers, blowing these stories up out of all proportion to make us frightened and keep us in the house. Well I'm not having it. I will not be afraid.'

'So come at me! Come at me!' shouted her sister, punching at Eve and then spinning round behind her. Eve was mad now. Eve was mad about a lot of things. She didn't stop to think. She spun round, took one single punch and knocked Martha clean out.

# Chapter Sixteen

My dear Inge,

### The Joys of Sex

But I say, walk by the Spirit, and do not gratify
the desires of the flesh.

(GALATIANS 5.16)

I think the psychiatrist believes that we are getting down to the nitty gritty.

'Do you and Adam have a good sex life?' asks Big Nose, who thinks nothing of poking his big nose in anywhere, willy-nilly, as it were.

'I don't know,' was my answer. 'I think so. I mean, till his . . . accident.'

We seem endlessly to stray on to the subject. I don't know if I had a good sex life. I never had sex with anyone except Adam. He wasn't very demanding after the children came along. I think he was happy. I mean, he made all the moves.

'I suppose it must be hard for him to take all the responsibility for sex in your relationship.'

'Yes, well, I just never really thought of it. I mean, it was always up to him. It's like that with men, isn't it? You sort of think they can't help themselves, don't you? That's what everyone tells you. That it's not their fault. They're driven. That's why they have all those magazines, even in petrol stations where the most I'm ever looking for is a mini Scotch egg from the cold cabinet.'

'And what did you want?'

What did I want? It was a question that never came up. I wanted to sleep alone in clean, white sheets. Egyptian cotton ones from the linen specialist. Anyway, I knew he wanted to . . . have an early night . . . ever since the big party. You know, because of Pe Pe looking so splendid and him not getting the job from the mall and his injury and then him getting ready to save Edenford and everything. He had a lot to prove to himself.

It's a funny business, sex, isn't it? Maybe not for you. I mean, I wouldn't know. Perhaps it was all more . . . sympathetic for you. You were with someone who must have felt what you felt. I mean, I imagine. I sometimes think the worst thing that ever happened to us is that Adam read an article about foreplay in *Cosmopolitan* while he was waiting at the dentist's. He brought it home and put it on the kitchen table.

'This business here, Eve,' he said, poking a finger at the magazine article. 'I do work at making you . . .' Well, he could hardly say it, '. . . satisfied?' Of course, I nodded. I mean he does work at it. Endlessly.

He's absolutely scrupulous about the entire operation. Starts at the top, kneading and twiddling my breasts like he's tuning the radio and keeps it up until I give a moan that suggests he's found the right frequency. Then he works his way down as if he were visiting the stations of the cross until finally he can't stand it any more.

'Here comes the train into the tunnel!' he shouts, as if I might not have expected it and then there's two short blasts of the whistle and he passes on into the night, leaving me still standing on the platform.

I kept thinking about the wrong things. About what I read in the launderette, about what was said at the charity meeting, about what I heard on the news, about Martha's classes. I lie on my back when Adam makes love to me. Not because we haven't tried more exciting things, but I've put on weight and I am getting older. I think if I lie flat out then gravity spreads things back on the bed rather better. I mean, I think I must look better being bored down on rather than coming at him from above. I don't know if you would understand. It matters. It's a buyer's market. If Adam goes off me he could still find somebody else but what the hell would I do?

*Cosmopolitan* says it's important to stay sexually active when you get to a certain age. Apparently regular sex stimulates the blood flow into the vaginal area thus reducing dryness. Who finds these things out? Anyway, the fact is the muscle contractions during orgasm promote the health of the vagina. You must have sex or get a sick vagina.

I didn't want to be thinking about those things. I didn't want to be thinking about anything. I wanted it to be different. Different like in a romance novel. I wanted harmony, to melt together, no one making any sacrifices or making them and not minding. Neither one of us having to disappear for the other. I wanted to be swept up in masterful arms, to be protected from the horrors of the world, to have Adam's lips bring rapture. Martha says women have to hold out, not for orgasm but for ecstasy. Mostly I just hold out for us to finish. That's not to say that there wasn't a surprising amount of smut in my mind, yet whenever Adam suggested we have an 'early night', I couldn't seem to be bothered. Oh, I know relationships go through stages and it can't ever be as exciting as that first time up against the pickled eggs in the larder. It was like that then. Like riding your bicycle over cobblestones. Now I just lie there wishing we had a remote control for the telly so I could at least change channels while Adam builds up his 'head of steam' as he calls it. And then sometimes I do feel like it but I've only just changed the sheets and by the time I've decided that I can be bothered to wash them again, Adam's got engrossed with his avocados or something and the moment's gone. I shouldn't be telling you these things. It's just that I've got no one to talk to. I'm drowning in still waters. Susan Belcher's a chiropodist now. I don't really like feet. I always think of them as the frayed edges of the body. Actually I'm not overly keen on the body in general. Especially mine. I eat too much chocolate.

'What do you do afterwards? After your . . . intimacy?' asks the shrink.

What did we do? 'Nothing really. He's a good man, Adam, but he doesn't really . . . he puts his head on my shoulder and says, "Was it all right for you?" and I always think, How can you ask me that? I mean, weren't you there?'

I don't think any of this matters. Adam and I didn't have sex after his injury and then he got arrested for molesting that woman, which was all a misunderstanding but it really did him in and . . .

I look at the shrink and wonder what he is getting from all this. We spend so much time together that my sewing is coming on a treat. He looks at me as if he knows I have something to add. So I do.

'Why do you suppose it is that the initial on the lid of a tube of Smarties is never your own?' I say, but he doesn't answer.

*Fact – you are statistically more likely to be bitten by a shark than you are to be arrested for impersonating a police officer at an airport.*

I was cleaning the downstairs loo when Horace Hoddle came round unexpectedly. Adam was furious because there was an empty loo roll in the hall. He wrestled a bit with the security gate to let Horace in while I went to put coffee on. The two men were deep in conversation when I came back.

Adam was doing confident acting. 'No problem, Horace.'

Horace smiled a thin-lipped affair at me. 'Coffee. How delightful, but I don't, thank you.' He patted his trim stomach. 'Got to watch the caffeine levels.'

I put the useless tray down on the table.

Adam was beaming. 'Good news, darling, the golf club committee are doing a musical revue at the end of the year.'

Horace smiled. 'Yes, indeed. It's a charity event. We're raising money partly for the hospice and also for new driving mats, which are desperately needed on the practice range. Adam has very kindly agreed to take part.' Horace lowered his voice although there was no one else around. 'I have high hopes for your husband, Mrs Marshall. I think he could well make captain . . . at some point . . . and I think it would do him a lot of good if the members saw what fun he can be. We all know he is hard working but we need to see the club leader in him. Fun, eh, Adam, that's what we want.'

Horace stood up. With his black suit and pinched face he looked like the grim reaper at a coffee morning. Fun? It seemed unlikely. We all gave cheerful goodbyes and he departed, leaving Adam on a cloud.

'Eve! Captain! I know we hoped but . . .' His forehead creased, 'Fun? What can I do that's fun?' I had several interesting suggestions but there wasn't time for those.

'You could sing or . . .' I was going to add walk on water, both of which seemed equally remote as possibilities, but it was too late. Adam had seen the future and seized it.

'Of course! Bassey! I don't think it's a secret in this town that there's absolutely nothing I don't know about Shirley Bassey. I can sing. I can be fun! This *is* fun – I, a councillor and a security adviser by day, will sing one of her songs at the musical revue!'

## Going to the Top

Let every person be subject to the governing authorities . . .

(ROMANS 13.1)

As I waited to cross the road to J. C. Bergman's Estate Agents, a huge green truck thundered past. Adam had helped to make the High Street into a one-way system to stop the big lorries clogging up the road. Now they didn't clog the place at all. They just killed people on the way through. The truck had a massive advert painted on the side. *What are you doing with your visit to planet Earth?* it blared at me as I stood in my Etam raincoat. The correct answer apparently was sleeping well on a Drift 'n' Dream mattress. It didn't seem enough somehow.

Mr Bergman was on the phone. Actually, he was on two phones at once, so I sat and waited. He had a brass plaque on his desk with his name engraved on it – J. C. Bergman. Funny initials for a Jewish person, I thought. Mr Bergman was very Jewish. He wore a little black circle on the back of his head, held on with hair grips. He was going bald and it was obviously becoming a daily problem to find a good location for the grips. I wondered what completely bald Jewish men did. Could you use Blu-Tack or maybe have a circle painted on? I knew what the skull cap was for.

'It shows my constant devotion to God,' he'd once told me. At least I think that was Mr Bergman. I might have remembered it from *Fiddler on the Roof*.

I didn't know anyone in town who was Mr Bergman's friend. I don't think it was because he was Jewish, although I couldn't think of anyone else in Edenford who went to synagogue. There isn't one for a start. I wondered if he thought of himself as one of the 'chosen people'. Funny of God to pick just one group like that. I mean, it was just an accident that he belonged. Maybe when Mr Bergman looked at me he didn't think I was as good as him. This made me feel defensive. I could have been Jewish if my mother had been Jewish. How bizarre to judge somebody just because of whose legs they came out between. And it caused wars. All these artificial divisions in humanity. Countries spending money on getting ready for war instead of welfare and health. Tom had told me that, 'Any religious system built upon the justification of social inequality on the basis of birth is an obstacle to civilisation and . . .'

I realised Mr Bergman was looking at me.

'So, Mrs Marshall, you thinking of moving? Must be twenty years since I sold you your house. Still, a change is good. I think about it myself. I too dream of new horizons. I plan to move one day. Be with my family.'

I had been sitting thinking too much. 'Israel?'

Mr Bergman looked confused. 'Sorry?'

'You're thinking of moving to Israel?'

'Why?'

'To . . . be with your people.'

'I come from Colchester.'

'Right.'

We sat for a moment, silenced by my stupidity.

'I came about the swimming baths. The old baths. Adam says they're for sale.'

The estate agent leaped to life. 'Indeed, indeed. Indeed, I have details. Great development potential, but not cheap, not cheap at all.' Mr Bergman rummaged in a filing cabinet and brought out a small sheaf of papers. 'Yes, yes. Not cheap.'

'How not cheap?'

'Half a million and the council has to approve the intended use. You'd need the council on your side.'

Half a million! How could we raise half a million? But at least I did have the council on my side. I'd had a councillor by my side for twenty-five years. It was the least Adam could do for me.

I stopped at the Crown for a quick sandwich and a tonic water. There was much laughter going on in the back room.

'Having a party?' I asked Jill, who runs the place.

She raised her eyebrows disapprovingly. 'Sounds like it. It's supposed to be a men's meeting, but they're certainly ordering more beer than most meetings.'

'Men's meeting?'

Jill nodded and pointed to a poster on the bar as she went off to serve coffee to some old women.

> *The Centurion Club*
> *Men! Are you tired of being pushed*
> *around by the modern world?*
> *Come and meet your fellow sufferers*
> *Tuesday lunchtimes at the Crown.*
> *For details contact John Antrobus 889675*

The door to the meeting room opened to allow a couple of men to get to the bar. The room was full of smoke and laughter. I could just hear one man calling out, 'Hey, why did the pervert cross the road?' and another answered, 'Because he couldn't get his dick out of the chicken.' There was wild laughter and in the doorway I could just see Adam and William standing together.

I went to the charity shop with renewed determination and the particulars on the pool.

'It's a huge amount of money,' they all exclaimed but we knew we could do it. Now the fund-raising had to start in earnest.

'Don't worry about the council,' I said. 'I'll speak to Adam. They won't give permission for anyone else to buy it if they know we're trying to raise the money.'

'Six toilets!' Emma was impressed, but then she does have a tendency to bladder infections and worries about sanitary provisions.

'The WI did very well a few years ago with a nude calendar,' said Helen.

'I thought it was in poor taste,' sniffed Doris, who still smarted from being overlooked as Miss March.

'We shall need masses of jumble,' declared Mrs Hoddle. 'And

someone will have to take charge of the official paperwork. I suppose that will be me.' She sighed bravely.

'And blankets! They'll need blankets.' Emma darted off into a corner to click with brand new needles bought for the occasion.

There was some discussion about us having a sale to get people's attention but in the end it was decided that might be a little odd for a charity shop. Things are quite cheap anyway. We knew we could do it. The refugees were as good as saved. They were as good as moved into the Edenford Swimming Baths.

I wanted to talk to Adam straight away to get his support but he was away. Adam had started doing occasional business trips for Stalwart Security. He always brought me something back. If he had been on a plane it was usually something from the in-flight magazine but sometimes it was things like a very nice basket of coconut bathroom stuff from the Body Shop and the receipt so I could take it back. And always some new device to safeguard the house. The prison people would have done better to have left me at home. There were days when I could hardly work out how to get to the garden.

His security campaign had really caught everyone's attention. There were demands for better streetlighting, curfews for teenagers, registered cabs for lone female passengers. The posters were everywhere.

*Don't let Edenford become a nightmare.*
*Vote Marshall. Sleep safe at night.*

### Safety First

But understand this, that in the last days there will come times of stress. For men will be lovers of self, lovers of money, proud, arrogant, abusive, disobedient to their parents, ungrateful, unholy, inhuman, implacable, slanderers, profligates, fierce, haters of good, treacherous, reckless, swollen with conceit, lovers of pleasure rather than lovers of God, holding the form of

religion but denying the power of it. Avoid such people. For
among them are those who make their way into households and
capture weak women . . .

(2 TIMOTHY 3.1–6)

A young policeman came to the door when Adam was away.

'Mrs Marshall?'

'Yes?' I said through the security gate, which seemed to be on some kind of timer.

'Constable Carter. Your husband asked me to come round when we had the details on the bus station mugging.'

'Yes.' I tried the gate again to no avail. 'I'm afraid you can't come in.'

He nodded sagely. 'I quite understand.' The constable flicked through a notebook. 'It has been deduced that the perpetrator was one Dennis Harrison of Reading in Berkshire. It seems he was travelling through with his girlfriend when they had something of a domestic dispute.'

'So it wasn't a mugging?'

'Not as such, no.'

'And it wasn't someone from Edenford?'

Carter looked at his notes again. 'No. It was the Edenford bus depot but not an Edenford citizen, as such that would be correct.'

There was no mugging. Just some trouble with people passing through. It was nothing to do with Edenford. John came round to get some more leaflets for Adam's campaign and I told him.

'It was nothing to do with Edenford.'

John smiled at me and squeezed my hand. 'Isn't that marvellous, Eve?'

'I suppose. I mean, at least Adam can stop frightening everyone.'

John shook his head. 'I don't think you understand the public service Adam is doing. He is protecting the people.'

'But they don't need protecting.'

'No, Eve, they won't need it if they are already on their guard. It doesn't matter who mugged who. It happened in Edenford and we shall stop it happening again.'

I watched him tapping bundles of leaflets on the table as he arranged everything in neat piles. He had the most perfectly manicured nails I had ever seen on a man.

'You're running the men's meetings, aren't you?'

'The Centurion Club. It's nothing. I did it for William actually.'

'William? My brother?'

'Mmmm. It's been tough on him, this sperm thing. He needs to know it's okay.'

Adam came back from his business conference full of beans. I had really missed him when he was away. I mean, we had been married a long time and it wasn't perfect, but I was used to having him there. A bit like a scrap of rough skin on your hand that sometimes you wished wasn't there but you touched all the time anyway. I got Mother sorted and made a special dinner of steak and kidney pie – homemade, not bought or anything. I think he was pleased to see me.

'What a great conference!' he boomed as soon as he got out of the car. 'Look what I got you!' Adam handed me a bumper sticker. 'I thought we could put it on the fridge.' I looked at the bright red message.

*Smiling wins more friends than frowning!*

'Isn't that true, Eve, isn't that just so true?' He bounced in telling me how much value he had got from learning that *Your attitude determines your altitude* and *Whatever the mind of man can conceive and believe it can achieve.*

He was so busy conceiving, believing and achieving that he never even asked what I'd been up to. Actually we had a lovely evening and there was even some hint that we might head upstairs for an 'early night'. It had been some time since Adam's 'injury' and he hinted he might finally be ready for that 'test run', but then we got into a bit of an argument. The conference had spent some time planning a new ad for the Stalwart Security Home Alarm System and I'm afraid I didn't like it at all. The front cover showed a dark, shadowy figure of a man with the words,

> *This man might be a mugger,*
> *This man might be a burglar,*
> *This man might be a rapist.*

Then you opened it up and there was a picture of a smily face and the reassurance,

> *Or he could be the man from Stalwart Security*
> *with your new home alarm.*
> *Stalwart Security –*
> *Keeping You Safe as Houses*

Adam was thrilled. 'Isn't that great? I really think it says everything about the need for this kind of product.'

'I hate it,' I said quietly.

'Don't be silly, darling, you don't hate it. It's exactly right. We spent two days on that. You should have seen some of the brainstorming sessions. It's perfect. Everyone said so. We're going to do a leaflet drop to every house in Edenford.'

'I don't think that women should be frightened into buying something. You shouldn't keep telling women that they can't go out, that it isn't safe.'

Adam didn't understand and I didn't know how to explain. Things were starting to change. There seemed to be a male thing happening and a female thing happening and somehow I was caught in the middle of it. I was and so was John.

## *Subterfuge*

> And when they rose early in the morning, and the sun shone
> upon the water, the Moabites saw the water opposite them as
> red as blood . . .
>
> (2 KINGS 3.22)

After many sessions, my psychiatrist has finally voiced something close to an opinion. 'I presume the deceased, John . . . Antrobus, opposed your plans for the refugees.'

'Why do you?'

'It was important to you. Did he object? Was he unpleasant?'

'I wish he had been. No, it was John being so damned nice that put a spanner in the whole thing. At least everyone else thought he was being nice. I don't now.'

We had been collecting for about three weeks. Everyone in Edenford had been helping and Adam, even though he's not mad about people from abroad, had promised the full support of the council. Then things started to go a bit wrong.

First, I lost the WI Flower Arranging/Candlestick Competition. No surprise there. Doris won with an extraordinary display of daisies, sprayed green and wrapped around a white candle. She called it Flame of Liberty. There was some talk that she'd cheated and used hairspray to hold the arrangement together. I felt this was rather confirmed when her granddaughter, Tasha, set fire to the wick and the entire creation went up, but everyone decided it was a freak gust from that loose window pane above the piano. Doris got her award and Tasha got rather singed eyebrows. Doris thought I had bad-mouthed her about the whole thing so she was a little tense with me in the shop each day. I think it turned her against me in the end.

Then John turned up one afternoon with a huge bag of second-hand clothes. I think he expected all the old biddies in the shop to swoon and, of course, most of them did. He was very good-looking and he charmed everyone. It wasn't difficult. These were women whose idea of an intimate encounter was a hair wash at Pat's Beauty Spot.

'Just a few bits and pieces,' he chuckled, as we pulled stunning designer shirts out of his bin liners.

'We can really sell these. Oh, John, you are kind,' dribbled Doris.

Everyone was smiling and dribbling when suddenly he reached out to steady himself against the counter.

'Sorry, sorry,' he whispered. 'I think I'm a little faint.'

'Get him a chair! A chair!' barked Mrs Hoddle, who had done years of service with Meals on Wheels and knew infirmity when she saw it. 'Doris, open the door, get air, we need fresh air!' she commanded to the very winds of the town.

Everyone ran in all directions. Tea was made, hankies were pressed with lavender water, Helen Richler tried rescue remedy but John declined.

'No stimulants, thank you.' He smiled weakly. 'Sorry, I'm being pathetic. I always am when I give blood.'

'You gave blood!' Emma Milton squealed. 'That's so wonderful.'

John managed to speak, but quietly so that we all had to gather round.

'It was just an idea I had for all the men. You know we have these little meetings.' The women all nodded. The Centurion Club now boasted nearly every prominent man in town. 'I thought we should all give blood. It's the least we can do what with you ladies doing such wonderful work for the refugees. Everyone must do their bit. After all we have no idea how much will be needed.'

There was much clucking and approving of this idea.

'The man is a saint,' was the general refrain until Helen said, 'Blood? Sorry, why will we need blood?'

John patted her hand. 'Oh, I don't know that we will need it, it's just a precaution.'

'Sorry?' Mrs Hoddle was confused and stopped fanning him with a copy of *The Lady* magazine. 'I don't follow.'

'Well, it's just that these poor, misfit people, who you quite rightly are helping, have been through a lot. They have had very little food, terrible accommodation . . . Who knows what infectious diseases they may have picked up. We need to be ready to help. No one would want Edenford General to be unprepared in the event of some epidemic or other . . .'

'No.'

'Not that it will happen,' he managed weakly. John recovered shortly after that and left. There was a silence in the shop that lasted some time after he had gone.

'I think I'll be off home now,' announced Mrs Hoddle.

'Yes. It is late, isn't it?' said Doris, looking at her wrist even though she didn't wear a watch. It was the beginning of the end.

I'm tired. Tell Shirley that I love her.

Love,

Eve

# Chapter Seventeen

Eve had woken up feeling fat. She seemed to be lying on one side of the bed and her stomach on the other. When she looked in the mirror she saw that she was fat.

The journalist from the *Mail* was trying to get Inge to look at herself. The feature, Why I Never Married, was to be a big spread and the writer was unhappy about doing the interview on the phone. She wanted to meet Inge.

'Body language is so important,' she kept saying, but Inge insisted. The conversation did not go well. No, Inge hadn't had a disastrous affair from which she had never recovered. No, she did not dislike men. The interviewer was relentless in pursuit of Inge's inner life. She belonged to the nation, they owned her, they had a right to know. It was ironic that Inge was made to be so defensive about liking men. She did like them. A lot. In fact, it was because she tried to save Lawrence's boy, Patrick, that she got into such trouble.

After John's appearance a few women had stopped coming to the charity shop. The appeal was still going great guns but there had been talk about disease and the 'risk to the town', and the *Edenford Gazette* had carried an article about TB amongst refugees. Then the Centurion Club passed a motion requesting that Edenford General prioritise blood supplies for residents of no less than five years. They also petitioned for each member's wife to be given first access to any donated blood. The request concluded, 'We will protect our women.' And was then signed by them all.

'What diseases are we worrying about?' Eve asked Adam.

'Tuberculosis,' he said darkly.

'Yes, but you don't need blood for that. You need . . . well, not blood anyway. I don't see what all the blood is for.'

They were both on shaky medical ground so Adam lost his temper.

'Eve, it is my job to protect you and I would appreciate it if you would just let me get on with it.'

'Adam, darling, of course, but we can't possibly need buckets of blood unless the incomers arrive determined to hack us all down with some foreign machete or something.'

Adam looked at his wife and frowned. 'You're right. They could be violent. We don't know why they had to leave their country in the first place.'

'I didn't mean . . .'

Naturally the hospital refused the request, but then the whole thing became another steel leg in Adam's election platform. The *Gazette* was behind him all the way. *Councillor Marshall says – stand up for your town. Don't let others suck your blood.*

Eve was furious. 'I thought you were on my side, Adam.'

'I am. I'm not saying those people can't come here, you know, if that's what you really want, but I do have a civic duty to make sure Edenford is safe first.'

'It is safe. It's so bloody safe that it's boring the arse off me. I can't think of anything I would like better than an intruder in the middle of the night or a quick how's-your-father with some mugger down the bus station. There is no danger here, Adam. There never has been and there never will be. There was no mugging. Nothing happened. No one could be bothered. No one in Edenford needs blood because they are already half dead!'

They were both rather shocked by this. Adam sat down at the kitchen table and Eve made tea as if it had never happened. Then he went to fix a new light sensor on the garage door and Eve went to see if Inge was in.

It was raining when Eve went outside. Horrible grey, English rain. She was soaked in an instant. Wet through to the marrow. Kate answered the door. She looked thin and wore no make-up. Eve's mother would have said she hadn't made the most of herself, but she smiled so warmly that Eve didn't care about that.

'Eve! You're soaked! Come on in. Inge is battling with mirrors.'

In the sitting room, Inge was unscrewing a large mirror from above the fireplace.

'Camie!' she shouted. 'Just in time for a coffee, or shall we have gin?'

Eve stood dripping on the carpet. 'I'm sorry, I must look a fright.'

Kate laughed. 'You'll never know in this house. Inge has taken down every mirror in the place.'

'Why?'

'Because,' said Inge, heaving the mirror off the wall, 'I am sure that part of every day is ruined by people wondering about what they look like. I am sure that a preoccupation about her appearance goes some way towards ruining some part of every woman's day. It's all part of the oppression that is cultivated by the media to make women feel disgusted by their own bodies, and I'm not having it.'

Kate sat down on the sofa and looked up at Inge. 'I don't think there's any oppression in having a straight parting,' she said gently.

Inge shook her head. She was adamant. 'The fact is that every woman is told from the day she is born that no matter what she does with her life, if she is not beautiful then she didn't make it. Life becomes a daily struggle against hair unwanted on major parts of our bodies and remembering what colour the stuff we do want used to be. Camie, give us a hand.'

Eve grabbed one end of the mirror and together they lowered it to the floor.

'There.' Inge dusted her hands and began to put away the ladder. 'Gin and tonic, I think.'

'Just tonic, thanks,' called Kate, as Inge headed for the kitchen. Kate settled back on the sofa. She was thin, very thin and pale. It was sort of frightening and for a minute Eve couldn't think of anything to say. Kate beckoned her to come closer and then whispered, 'She's lying to you.'

'Sorry?'

'Inge . . . about the mirrors. She doesn't give a damn what she looks like. She just doesn't want me to see myself wasting away. Do you want to sit down?'

Eve didn't know if she did or not. She wasn't sure what was happening. She felt uncomfortable and didn't know why. 'I'm very wet,' she managed. Eve looked around for something else to talk about. She had been to Inge's house before, of course, but they had always sat in the kitchen. The sitting room was nice. Sort of terracotta colours with one whole wall covered in photographs of deserts. Acres and acres of sand and dunes and windswept horizons.

'Did Inge take these?' she asked.

'No, I did. It's what I do . . . did. I'm a photographer. Travel pictures mainly.'

Things started to click with Eve. 'With Inge's writing. She writes articles sometimes. I've seen them.'

'Yes.'

How wonderful to travel to the desert together and bring it back for people who couldn't go. 'I'd love to go the desert. I hate the rain. I hate being wet. I'd love to travel.' Eve ran her hand over a photograph of rich, golden sand.

'I once knew a young man who hated the rain. He hated it with such a passion that he began to be afraid of it, afraid of getting wet.' Kate began a story, and like a child Eve found herself sitting down and listening. 'He ran away to the desert and tried to live like a nomad. He wandered the sands and learnt about the birds and the plants. Then one night when he was sleeping, with no warning a flash flood came. It poured through the desert valley in the blink of an eye.'

'He drowned,' Eve gasped.

Kate nodded. 'I know, strange, isn't it?'

'Is that true?'

Kate shrugged and they sat silent, looking at the photographs. A small carriage clock on the mantel ticked quietly. Inge came in with the drinks. She had no tray but carried them any old how under her arm and in her hands.

'Hello, who set the room temperature to gloomy in here?' she enquired.

'You did when you came home,' laughed Kate.

Inge bowed to her friend. 'I am the Queen of the Grump.' She handed Eve her drink.

'I shouldn't really,' Eve said feebly. 'Not at lunchtime.'

Kate looked at Inge and replied, 'You never know how many lunchtimes are left.' Eve didn't know, so she bumbled on asking Inge why she was grumpy.

Inge plumped down next to Kate and smiled at her old friend. 'Oh, it's nothing. Bloody press driving me mad. Keep asking the wrong questions.'

'The wrong questions? What do you mean wrong?'

Kate looked at Inge and nodded for her to go on. Inge smiled and shrugged her shoulders.

'It's nothing. They want to know why I never married and I never know what to say.'

'Tell them the truth,' replied Eve in all innocence.

Inge blushed, but looking straight at her oldest friend said quite clearly, 'I can't, Eve. If I tell them I'm gay they'll take me apart.'

Gay. Eve was sure no one had mentioned the word to them at school. She thought about Susan Belcher and the cobblestones and how innocent it had all been then.

'Right,' she said, and they carried on with their drinks. Perhaps it should have been uncomfortable but it wasn't. Inge wasn't Inge Holbrook to Eve. She was her friend. She was the girl who had carried triumph as captain of the netball team while Eve stood at the side and cut up the oranges for the break. She now knew that Inge, her friend Inge, was a lesbian.

When she left she kept saying it to herself. She didn't think it was a very nice word – lesbian. Eve looked down the street at the other houses on the estate and realised the place could be full of them and she wouldn't know. It had never occurred to her. She had thought you could tell by looking but you couldn't. She had seen them both wearing skirts sometimes. Kate and Inge were a lesbian couple. She wondered how that worked with no man. Who was in charge? Then she wondered if that meant she thought Adam was in charge, which was silly. There was no reason why Kate and Inge couldn't manage perfectly well. You don't need a penis to take out the rubbish. What was it that had made Inge who she was? Had she had some bad experience with a man? That couldn't be enough. If all the women who had bad experiences with men became lesbians, there'd be a lot more of them.

John was just running up to the house when Eve came out. He saw her leaving Inge's and waved as he got to the driveway.

'Eve,' he called. 'Looking lovely.'

She was looking wet.

'Isn't that Inge Holbrook's house?' he asked, looking across the drive. Eve nodded. 'Quite the celebrity. Not your sort I would have thought.'

Eve didn't feel like a chat. 'What are you doing running in this weather?' she asked, looking at his tracksuit soaked in sweat and rain.

'Every day without fail. Good for you, you know. If I have the time I run three or four hours a day.' He patted his flat stomach. 'I'm adding ten years to my life, you know.'

'Maybe, but you are spending them running.'

John frowned at her reply for a brief second and then laughed. 'Very good, yes, very good.' The laughter stopped as if turned off and he was serious again. 'Listen, Eve, I'm so sorry about the whole blood thing. I do think it's got out of hand but I hope you know I was just trying to be helpful. I had no idea people would react the way they have.'

'You could stop your wretched club passing silly motions,' Eve said irritably.

John took her hand and held it as he looked her straight in the eye. 'Oh no, I can't. I may think they're wrong but the men need to make these decisions for themselves. It's because men today feel so powerless that we need groups like the Centurions. It's done William so much good. You wouldn't want me to take that away from him, would you?' Before Eve could answer he added, 'Can I borrow a towel?'

'Sorry?'

'I'm working with Adam, and I thought I'd just freshen up first.'

'Right. In the airing cupboard.'

John went into Eve's house to shower.

Eve decided to walk to the shop to get some exercise. The rain had passed and it was turning into a nice afternoon. The route into town meant she passed the Hoddle house. Horace and Betty had the largest house on the estate. It was built in a hacienda style and was apparently identical to their one in Spain. Perhaps having two houses exactly the same stops you getting confused in the night. Mrs Hoddle was in the front garden cleaning out her bird bath. It was a massive affair. More of a bird health spa really. She was very particular about it.

'Afternoon, Betty,' Eve called cheerfully. It was summer and it was sunny. Apart from being fat, Eve did feel quite cheerful. The town would get over its obsession with blood and they were doing very well with raising the money for the pool. She thought about Inge and Kate.

'Ah, Eve,' Mrs Hoddle muttered, while her rubber-gloved hands scraped away at any suggestion of actual bird occupation in the bath. Soap suds flew from her fingers.

'Bird bath looks good.'

'Yes,' she said, pleased. 'Well, it's the least I can do.' That in fact turned out not to be true. Providing a bath for passing flocks of feathered friends was the most she could do. She stood up and snapped shut the lid on her Jeyes cleaning fluid. 'Eve, I shan't be coming to the shop today.'

'Why? Are you ill?'

'No. Horace and I have had a long talk and I just can't support you on this any more. I love this town and it's too big a risk.'

'Look, the blood thing has got out of hand—'

'The blood is merely a side issue, although why people can't say where their own blood is to go . . . Have you seen this?' She held up a leaflet. The world had gone leaflet mad. Eve thought for one horrible moment it was yet another one of Adam's. 'It was sent to Horace by someone from Dover. They know about refugees. It's where they sneak in, you know,' she said darkly.

The leaflet was entitled Dover the Land of Plenty and subtitled Refugees – 33 reasons why we should send them back and close the door.

Betty stabbed at the brochure. 'Look at Number thirteen and have another think,' she exclaimed.

Reason 13: Pregnant refugee mothers only want brand new equipment for their offspring. Are these infants entitled to hold a British passport to success now that they have been born in our local hospitals?

'Betty, how many babies can there be? Isn't it better that they're born here with a chance than in some country where their parents might get beaten up?'

Betty tapped the leaflet again.

Reason 21: No medical checks on refugees – with the knowledge of their promiscuity and selling sex for money, who is to answer for the epidemic of venereal disease that will undoubtedly become rife.

Betty jerked her head up and down like a bird with a particularly resistant worm. 'Do you want to run the risk of one of those diseases?'

'Well, no,' Eve replied, 'but then I wasn't planning to sleep with any of them.'

Mrs Hoddle looked at Adam's wife. 'These are facts, Eve, and you can't get away from them.'

'I don't know what a fact is any more. My son says there are facts but we forget what they are because all facts are interpreted.'

Betty gave a loud sniff at the very idea and turned on her heel to go back inside. A small bird flew down and landed on the edge of the bath. It stooped for a second and then flew away. Betty had forgotten to refill it.

Pe Pe was coming up the road in her convertible BMW. Her model good looks and radiant smile in the flash car could have been an advert for success. This was a woman who never had a panty-pad that leaked. A woman whose teeth had little cartoon stars on them when she looked in the mirror.

'Eve, hi!' she beamed. 'I was just coming to see you.'

'Pe Pe, how long have I known you?'

'I suppose it must be about four years.'

'Do you ever frown?'

'I can't. Hop in.'

Eve didn't feel like going to the shop any more but she didn't hop in. She wobbled in and they drove off. Eve had a vision of Barbie with her Mrs Potato Head friend.

Mother was calling out when the women got in. 'Who ha! Who ha!' Eve tried to make her comfortable while Pe Pe just stood smiling in the doorway.

'Who ha, who ha!' yelled Mother. Eve knew she wanted the commode but she wasn't really concentrating. As Eve moved to pull her mother up under her shoulders, Claudette the cat launched from nowhere. It was hard to know who was more shocked, Eve or Mother. The old woman weed on Eve's new trainers and blue trousers. It wasn't her fault. She couldn't see a thing. Her glasses had been in her handbag and were covered in horseradish. Eve thought about getting her a plastic handbag to put food in. She thought about putting her in a home, like the woman at the party had said. She thought about a lot of things.

Suddenly Mother stopped her howling and looked straight at Pe Pe. She pointed at her and said quite clearly, 'Baby.' It was the first real word she had produced since the stroke. Neither Pe Pe nor Eve knew what to say.

Afterwards Eve sat in the kitchen just wanting to weep. Pe Pe sat looking at her sister-in-law.

'Come on, Pe Pe, you're the Queen of Self-Help. I have a mother who keeps gravy in her handbag and has managed to pee on my entire wardrobe. I have a kamikaze cat who wants at the very least to maim me and I am living in a town where everyone is either about to be mugged, burgled or infected with VD. What am I supposed to do? You must have the cure.'

Pe Pe just sat, smiling. Then slowly, across her smile, tears began to descend from her eyes. It was bizarre. She looked completely happy, but tears just kept pouring down. Eve didn't know what the hell was going on.

'What is it? What's happened?'

'It's definite. William can't have children. He'll never have children. We had the report. I shouldn't have opened it without him but I couldn't wait, and now I just can't tell him. He won't cope. He just won't cope.'

Pe Pe sobbed, still smiling through her waterworks. It was like a rainbow behind a waterfall. As Eve debated what to do, John appeared in the doorway wearing nothing but a towel around his waist. He was young and had muscles you could bounce pennies off for sport. His hair was newly washed and hung in little damp curls around his head.

'Sorry, thought someone might need help.' He dripped on the lino.

Pe Pe gasped for air and carried on smiling.

'Pe Pe's just . . .' Crying and smiling Eve wanted to say but she couldn't. John reached for a tissue on the kitchen counter and moved towards Eve's unreal sister-in-law. Gently, he began to wipe her tears. Neither one of them said a word and Eve sat there thinking that men and women could probably do without each other if it were not for the annoying business of reproduction. After a moment's mopping, John turned and went back to the rather critical matter, Eve thought, of putting some clothes on. Pe Pe sat sniffing and then finally went home without ever asking Eve how she was.

Adam and John went out to bang on doors when Eve finally went along to the charity shop in the late afternoon. Eve watched Adam set off. Edenford was not that big a town. She was sure he must have visited everyone twice.

Eve arrived at the shop determined to see the Romanian project through but Doris Turton simply wouldn't hear of it.

'I must say that I am surprised at you, Eve,' she began. 'I would think that you of all people would know that Susan Lithgood was a very religious person.'

'Well, yes, but—'

'These people, they're not Christians, are they?'

'Well, I don't know, but—'

'I think they may be Muslims.'

'I don't think so.'

'I don't think they want our help. I've seen them on the television and they do nothing to endear themselves to us.'

'They're not panda bears.'

'They just want our benefits, that's all.'

'I don't think anybody popped over here from Romania on a whim. They need our help. We've got room. What about the old swimming baths? We all agreed they would be perfect.'

'They've been sold,' said Emma the Knit.

'They can't have been. Adam promised—'

'The swimming baths are not the point,' said Doris, sniffing. 'This is a Christian town with a Christian tradition and we are not about to have that disrupted by people who want to come here and sit outside WH Smith with their hands out.'

Eve left and bought a packet of light Silk Cuts, but after she'd smoked two she threw up in the sink. She wiped her face and went to sit with her mother. Mrs Cameron stared out of the window as Eve tried for the kind of conversation they had never managed to have.

'What do you suppose people would fight about if there were no religions? I can't say I've got time for it myself. Too many years freezing to death on a Sunday at school. Imagine not giving to children because their parents are some other religion. The shop committee has decided to write off for affiliation to the Cats Protection League. I told Tom. Did you know that bad Buddhists are either reborn in hell or the wombs of cats?'

# Chapter Eighteen

When Kate went into hospital for more tests, Inge probably knew that they were heading for the final pass. Even taking all the mirrors away wouldn't hide the truth. The cancer of the womb had been there for some time but now it had spread and there was no going back. Inge and Eve sat in the corridor of Nightingale Ward at Edenford General.

'What do you think is next, Camie?' Inge asked Eve, as she sat still waiting for news late into the evening.

'Oh, I expect they'll think of some more tests and then—'

Inge looked at her chum. 'I don't mean that. I mean next for Kate.' She tried to smile. 'They say the Gauls used to lend sums of money to each other that were repayable in the next world. That's how convinced they were that the souls of men are immortal. I don't know. I think you have to live in this life and not the next, but Kate believes. She really does.'

And Eve thought about that and wondered if it mattered for the next life that she hadn't even managed to live in this.

Adam was away and when Eve got home she lay in bed trying to read the book Pe Pe had given her at the tennis party. It was called *Attitudes of Gratitude – How to Give and Receive Joy Every Day of Your Life*. It claimed to be a sourcebook for less stressful, more joyful living. The author was absolutely adamant that it was possible to be grateful even in times of pain and hardship.

Eve kept thinking about Kate and she found the book hard going. *When I first got involved with voluntary simplicity . . .*

What the hell did that mean? Voluntary simplicity – giving up the car? Not having a cleaner? What about restaurants and films? It turned out it was about making deliberate, thoughtful choices, about designing your life to coincide with your ideals. Eve guessed it meant that it was no good waiting around for someone else to make things better. That there was no point in blaming others if you didn't get what you wanted.

Adam was beside himself with excitement when he returned. The *Daily Mail* had picked up on his campaign. Under the headline Adam and Eve of Edenford was an article about putting the family back in the heart of the town, about the men looking after the women and a huge picture of the two of them taken at William's party. Eve was falling towards the camera at the time and Adam was trying to stop her. Eve thought it looked as though he held her strings in his hand. The article was across the page from an in-depth report on a parrot from Berkshire who was said to speak Swahili and two pages away from a large spread on why Inge Holbrook had never married – she had been busy, she had a career, perhaps the footballer Mark Hinks (also oddly not married) had never asked her, etc.

Eve was beside herself with fury. 'Adam and Eve of Edenford! Are you quite mad?'

'I don't write the headlines, Eve. I think it's rather a nice picture.'

'A nice picture! Five seconds after that was taken I had my face in their shag-pile.'

Adam sat drinking his coffee. He didn't understand his wife. Eve tried to be calm. 'Adam, what happened about the swimming pool?'

'I'm sorry, Eve, it was a good offer. The council wanted to accept. I did try.'

'Who bought it?'

'That church over by the river. The Ten Commandments place.'

It was Shirley's church. Shirley's church had taken Eve's dream.

Eve stopped working at the charity shop and Mrs Hoddle stopped speaking to her. In fact, she cut Eve quite dead at the wet fish counter in Sainsbury's. It didn't stop her deciding to get on. When Shirley asked her mother to go to the Church of the Ten Commandments with her, Eve said she would. Shirley thought Eve might find God, and Eve thought she might find out what they planned to do with the pool.

It was a Tuesday morning and from the kitchen Eve could see the wisteria flowering on the garden wall. It was not a great day. Her mother had yet again weed everywhere, supper was going to be late and Adam was busy rehearsing his Shirley Bassey. By then his upcoming performance at the golf club had started to take over their lives.

Adam and Eve had both had a lot of sleepless nights before he finally settled on 'I Am What I Am' as his piece. Eve had thought making his mind up would have a calming effect but the tension seemed to mount daily. Anyone who didn't know about raising money for the golf club would have thought he was preparing for Covent Garden. Eve was trying to be supportive but unfortunately she had been forced to the conclusion that Adam wasn't terribly musical. After some weeks' rehearsal he could now sing his song backwards, and indeed much of the time sounded as if he was, but it wasn't enough.

Eve was peeling the parsnips, soaking Mother's underwear and thinking about homosexuals, when Martha arrived at the back door. Since her return from Bangkok she had never visited Eve's house so it took Eve by surprise. In fact, she hadn't spoken to her sister since Eve had knocked her out during the self-defence class. Eve made her coffee and she sat at the kitchen table while her housewife sister got on.

'Eve, I've been thinking,' began Martha.

'Hmm,' Eve said. She had been thinking too. Since Inge had moved in, Eve had realised she wasn't sure what she thought about homosexuals. She didn't think it had ever come up before. She wasn't sure she'd ever met one and as for the boy ones, well, it was silly, but her main question was why, if you had a penis of your own, would you want another one to play with?

'I need to get something off my chest,' said her younger sister, who had never confided anything to Eve in her life.

'Of course.' Eve plunged the parsnips into the bowl and straight on to Mother's urine-soaked gusset. In just a few minutes of mindless activity she had managed to forget that they were there. Eve looked down at her handiwork and wondered what the impact of wee was on parsnips. She wondered if anyone else would ever know or if she could just serve them up anyway. She wondered—

'Who ha, who ha!'called Mother. Eve knew she wanted a drink but she hadn't the energy. Martha was oblivious. She never visited her. She never sat with what was left of Mother.

Martha began to weep. Eve had never seen her cry. Martha had the gift of parading through life with no regrets and Eve didn't know what to do. She just knew that somehow she would get some of the blame.

'It's about . . . Mother,' Martha sobbed. 'I can't bear it. I should never have been made to live in that house again.' Eve let the remark about the house go, took off her rubber gloves and sat down. Martha carried on weeping. Perhaps she was much more moved by their mother's illness than Eve had realised.

'It's all right, Martha. I think she'll improve. Maybe if you sat with her sometimes . . .'

'I can't,' sobbed Martha. 'I can't.'

Adam poked his head into the kitchen. 'Everything all right?' he asked.

'It's Martha,' Eve said.

'Ah,' he replied, as if that explained everything and went away again. Eve got Martha some loo roll from the downstairs cloakroom and waited for her to settle. The crying slowed and finally she blew her nose very loudly and said, 'It's all my fault. It's all my fault.'

'Don't be silly. Mother had—'

Martha banged her hand down on the table and shouted, 'Will you listen?' She had always had a temper as a child, so Eve thought she probably would. Martha took a deep breath.

'Do you remember when I got into all that trouble at school? In the fourth form?'

Eve did remember because she could have died at the time. Eve was in the fifth form. Inge Holbrook was Head of the Year and Games Captain. Eve was not the brightest, not the best, but doing all right. What she didn't need was a sister causing trouble below her. Martha was fifteen at the time. She had always been promiscuous, but when she was found giving the games class sexual instruction in the sports-equipment room, using herself, a girl from the third year and a hockey stick, things blew up badly. Mr and Mrs Cameron were called to the school immediately and rumours flew across the playgrounds. Everyone was sure that Martha would be expelled, but she wasn't.

She never told Eve what happened. Until then. Her parents went into the head's office, where the headmistress, Mrs Hintle, was beside herself. Martha related the story.

'She was furious. I knew I would be chucked out and I just couldn't be. It would have been too awful. Mrs Hintle sat behind her desk and said to Mum and Dad, "Although Martha is one of our brightest pupils, I have no choice but to expel her from the school. Martha, do you have anything to say?" So I asked to see her on my own. I thought it would be confidential. I thought it would get me out of it. You have to understand how desperate I was. It mattered to me. You weren't academic, it was different for you.'

Eve looked at her sister, her flesh and blood, and realised she knew nothing about her. 'What would get you out of it?'

'I told Mrs Hintle . . . that I needed help. That I was so interested in sex because . . . because—'

'What?'

'Because Dad . . . interfered with me.'

'You didn't!'

'I told her it was confidential. I told her not to tell anyone. I just thought she would be sympathetic. I never thought she would do anything. Just let me stay.'

'But it wasn't true?' Eve demanded. Martha hung her head.

'No. I was just trying to get out of trouble. Everyone wanted an explanation, so I gave them one.'

'What happened?'

'Straight away she called Mum and Dad in and started telling them everything. Dad went pale and had to sit down, and Mum started yelling at him. Mrs Hintle said of course she would get me help and I wasn't to be blamed. Mum wouldn't speak to Dad and it went on for weeks until I couldn't stand it. Finally, I told Mum the truth. That he had never done anything. Never touched me, and he came in while I was telling her. She listened and then she said, "You're my daughter and I believed you. I would do anything for you. You're my daughter." And I felt terrible and they never recovered. That's why Dad hated her. Because she believed me and not him. He stayed for you but he hated her from then on. That's why he left her nothing, that's why she . . .'

Martha began to cry again and Eve sat. Her mother had chosen Martha over her husband. Would she have done the same? Would she choose Shirley over Adam? After a while Martha calmed and wiped her eyes.

'Thanks, Eve. I feel better now. I had to tell someone.' She stood up to leave. Then she told Eve she was going back to Bangkok. That she had thought she could make a go of it back here but she couldn't. She reached out to hug Eve, who just sat there motionless. The sisters touched briefly and then Martha was gone. She left behind the burden of her past, which Eve had known nothing about.

That evening Theresa Baker phoned. She said even though Martha had gone, the women still wanted to hold the study classes and would it still be all right to have them in her mother's house? Eve went to let them all in and Theresa, bless her, was really trying to keep the thing going. It made Eve so mad with Martha. She had started something. She had made the women think, and now they didn't know what to do about it.

'Why don't we watch a video of me giving birth?' Theresa asked as soon as they had sorted the food and drink, to which Eve replied, 'Well, mainly because you're all eating.' They were having an Italian night provided by Fran, and Eve doubted anyone would have kept the lasagna down.

The discussion was low-key. The women had their own group now but they weren't at all sure what to do with it. Without Martha to give them focus they floundered about in the feminist fog. Then someone suggested they needed a project. Something to get them going and it was Theresa who suggested the bypass.

'It's going to go right through the woods,' said ferret woman. 'We should do something.'

There were general murmurings about Mother Nature, the power of trees and what a wonderful discovery aloe vera had been. Eve promised her support but soon left them to it. She could not bear to be in that unhappy house.

# Chapter Nineteen

20 January
Holloway Prison for Women
London

Dear Inge,

## *Bypassing Edenford*

... when you give alms, sound no trumpet before you ...

(MATTHEW 6.2)

I can't tell you how wonderful it is to hear that Shirley has started talking to you. It sounds like you need it too. Adam won't discuss anything when he visits. Not that he was able to before. I remember one Tuesday evening when I'd got back from one of the women's meetings. I was sitting having coffee when Adam sidled into the kitchen. He had the same look that Tom used to have when he'd just eaten something from the coal bucket. Naughty but thrilled.

'Eve, I've been thinking.'

'Mmm,' I replied, thinking that thinking was overrated.

'I've been thinking about Shirley,' Adam confided.

'She's fine. She's having dinner with John.'

'Yes. Not that Shirley. Not daughter Shirley. My Shirley. My song.'

'Shirley Bassey. Right.'

'Eve, you know how much I admire Shirley and I want this to be "fun", like Horace said, but I don't want anyone to think it's not a serious tribute.' I nodded. Well, what was there to say? 'So I think I've decided that I really can't give the full flavour of Shirley unless I actually dress up as her.' I stopped my reverie on root vegetables and looked at my husband. He was quite flushed and as excited as I had ever seen him.

'The thing is, I would need your help. There are things I don't know. I mean, sequins of course, but what sort of dress, and where would we get it? Shoes, I think, might be tricky, but apparently there are shops where . . .'

Once Adam had broached the subject of dressing up he couldn't stop himself. Over lunch we had endless detailed conversation about the denier of stockings and whether Shirley generally favours a pearl nail varnish or plain. We hadn't talked so much in years. Odd that the sort of conversation I thought I might one day have with my daughter, I was having with my husband. Adam was glowing as he polished off the parsnips.

'I haven't told the committee about it. It's going to be a surprise. I wonder if I should write and tell Shirley herself? As a tribute. You know how much I love her. We named our daughter after her.'

We had also named our son after Tom Jones but I didn't see Adam practising his hip swivels and stuffing socks down his crotch. That night he sat on the bed with his hands protecting his lap. The bedroom looked quite different now. Adam had stopped growing his avocado plants on the windowsill. The avocado plant which I had tried to sellotape back to life had died. Adam had been very upset.

'Eve,' he demanded one morning as he stood before his felled vegetation. 'How could this possibly have happened?' It was a tone of voice that 'will be obeyed', so I told him.

'Let's see . . . oh yes, I had just had a rather tense encounter with Simon the postman when a projectile speculum shot out of my vagina and shredded the plant with a single blow from forty feet away. I tell you, if I could serve like that at tennis we'd be champions at the club.'

He gave me one of his looks and never mentioned it again. Without saying a word, he moved all the plants from the bedroom and filled up the little porch off the kitchen with them instead. I think he was too embarrassed to ask what a speculum was. He hates not to know anything, and he didn't know. I left it lying casually on the coffee table on top of his copy of *Security Monthly* for ages and he never so much as commented. Somehow the plant death seemed to make Adam determined to take more charge in the house.

'Eve,' he said, while I was sorting the laundry, 'I have made a decision. I don't think we should have the *Guardian* delivered any more.'

'We could get a different paper,' I said, counting out his socks.

'No, it's not the paper. It's the principle. I don't think it's helpful having all that foreign news flooding into the house. I think it upsets you and I don't want to pay for it any more.'

I stood looking out of the window with his clean underpants in my hand. That was when I realised. I didn't have any money. I'd never had any money. It was not mine. It was Adam's. It was all Adam's. It had always been Adam's. I couldn't do anything unless he said. That night I couldn't sleep. I stood in my kitchen in the dark, looking up to the woods behind the town.

The next day the women's group were up amongst the protesters. They brought food and blankets. They made some very nice signs in support of the woods, clean air and plants in general.

The general consensus at the Centurion Club was that the women's study class had to be stopped. Not just the protest. They had to be stopped from meeting at all.

'It's causing a division in the town between some of the men and their wives,' Adam explained when he asked me to stop letting the women use Mother's house. 'The men feel they are getting blamed for things that are not their fault. The people of Edenford need to work together.'

'And,' I added, 'the men are not getting a hot supper on Tuesdays.'

'That doesn't help,' agreed my husband, surprised by my understanding. 'By the way,' he said, 'I shan't be in tonight. It's my turn for escort duty.'

'What?' I swear we were speaking different languages by then.

'Escort duty! I told you! The Centurions are offering escorts to young women out for the evening. Making sure they get home all right. It was—'

'John's idea,' I sighed.

He was everywhere. John was niggling away at every inch of our lives.

Adam had gone out on escort service when I got word from Tom that the contractors and the police were about to make their move. I called Theresa to gather the women but she wasn't home. None of them was home. I ran to get you, and Patrick was there and we ran, all of us, even Kate, up to the woods. Remember? All you could hear was those huge diggers and tractors moving forward. The headlights swinging into the woods and my Tom standing there in front of his tent, not moving. Nobody came to help and we weren't enough. The earth-movers just ploughed forward. It was as if they didn't see that anything was in their way. They wrecked everything – the bluebells, the trees and then Tom's tent. This two-ton machine just ploughed through the tent and it was so surreal. All Tom's animals flew in the air as the canvas ripped and shredded round the marching machine. Death flew about and we could do nothing. It was Patrick who found the box with the dead ducklings inside. They had been completely crushed. He stood there crying and Tom put his arm round him and he was crying too. And no one came to help and the man in charge said to me, 'It's progress, Mrs Marshall, you can't stand in the way of progress.' And he had legal papers to make it all right. Legal papers from Hogart, Hoddle and Hooper.

Tom came home with me and he was desperate. Sobbing like a little boy, but I couldn't help him. I couldn't make it all right. He went to his old room and wouldn't come out. I wanted to help him but I was scared. My son was broken and I couldn't mend him. I couldn't care for one more person and make their life whole again. I just didn't have it in me. I was so sad for my son and so terrified that I was supposed to look after him. I felt like I was choking. Drowning. Theresa Baker finally called at about ten when she got my message. She had been out to dinner. All the members of the Centurion Club had taken their wives out to dinner. Odd that they had picked that one night. And I was angry and I got angrier. You know. You were there. Kate was there. Tell Shirley. Tell her what happened. Then the phone went again and it was the police. Adam had been arrested.

I don't know if Shirley ever understood about that either. He had been on escort duty, waiting at the pub for any woman to phone for help but no one had. Anyway, come closing time he felt he hadn't really done anything. He's a good chap so he started to walk home but he was looking out for women on their own. Well, you know he's had this trouble with his . . . bits, so he was holding himself as he walked. There was nothing to it but he went up to this woman waiting at the bus stop. Anyway, it was a complete chance thing. She turned out to be a friend of Theresa Baker's. She'd seen all Adam's leaflets and it had made her rather wary. None of this was helped by the fact that Adam did have his hand on his trousers. She was very tense so when he came near she screamed, kicked him in the groin and called to a police car that happened to be passing.

The police cleared it all up, but it caused talk. You know what people are like, saying there's no smoke without fire. When I went to collect him he could hardly look up.

'Oh God, Eve, what will people say? What will they say?'

And I think about that. I think maybe I stopped caring what people would say.

Love,
Eve
PS I found this for you and I really like it.

> Behold, I am toward God as you are:
> I too was formed from a piece of clay.
>
> (JOB 33.6)

Funny that it's giving me some comfort.

*Fact – 220,000 gay people were killed in the German concentration camps of the Second World War. It was the second largest group after the Jews. When the war was over all survivors of the concentration camps were treated generously and given reparations. Everyone except the homosexuals. They were told that they were ineligible for compensation as they were still technically 'criminals' under German law. Fearing further discrimination the survivors found they had to keep their identity secret so none were able to protest publicly.*

I didn't know.

# Chapter Twenty

The morning after the death of Bluebell Wood and Adam's arrest, neither father nor son emerged from their rooms. The *Daily Mail* kept phoning to speak to Adam until Eve had to take the phone off the hook. She found herself alone downstairs with no idea how to heal the hurts in the house. She had nothing to occupy her but chores and more chores. She took the newspapers out to the recycling box in the garage. Adam's election posters and paints were all over the floor. He had spent weeks of his life on this so he could call himself 'councillor' and tell everyone about family life, and now, perhaps, it was ruined.

Eve stood looking at his campaign materials and in that moment she made up her mind. She would never work at Susan Lithgood's again. She didn't like cats. Snooty creatures. Eve spoke out loud to the empty room, 'You can't imagine them starting a shop for us if we were in trouble, can you?'

However much the women of the community were behind the Cats Protection League, Eve knew she wasn't about to sort other people's smelly old clothes to sell for ten pence to buy KiteKat for stray animals who'd savage a bit out of your leg as soon as thank you. Eve opened a great tin of red paint. If Susan Lithgood could start her own charity then so could she. Eve Marshall's Mission to the Children was on its way and it was partly the mission that drove Eve to Shirley's church.

The Church of the Ten Commandments was very modern, very

Scandinavian. It looked like a religious franchise in William's shopping mall. It was very large with banked seating in a three-quarter circle rising high above a central stage of light wood. The place was packed. There must have been several hundred people there when Eve went. She wore her blue dress because it was church and it was Sunday, but she stuck with the trainers. She really liked her trainers and was less and less interested in what anyone else thought. Eve stood outside waiting to go in. A very modern sculpture dominated the front entrance. It was made of white stone and showed Jesus smiling and holding out his arms to a small group of children. It should have been lovely but it had a slightly sinister look to it. In defence against the ever-present pigeon population of Edenford, the church elders had had the sculpture made birdproof. Three-inch spikes of clear plastic stood in relief over the entire edifice. They stuck out from the top of Jesus's head and his hands, from the clothes and shoulders of the children. Suffer the children, thought Eve, especially if they fell on the sculpture.

She was surprised to see Kate and Inge heading towards the church. Kate leant on Inge's arm. She looked pale under her tan and thin, very thin. Eve didn't say anything. She hated the idea that people might think she was friends with Inge because she was famous. Inge had no such inhibitions. Meeting Eve again had been one of the best things that had happened lately.

'Morning!' called Inge. Kate smiled and waved.

'What are you doing here?' grinned Eve.

Kate whispered to her. 'I thought I'd better introduce myself to God before I meet him in person.'

Inge laughed. 'Yeah, yeah. Actually Patrick asked us. His dad's the priest. Not your regular haunt, is it?'

'No, my daughter, Shirley. I think I told you – she's been saved.'

Kate was about to say something when a woman in a dress fresh from a Sunday supplement advert swept over.

'Inge Holbrook! Inge Holbrook! It is, isn't it?' She almost pushed Kate aside in her desire to get to Inge. 'I can't believe you are here. Well, I can. I mean, it doesn't surprise me that you walk with us, but I can't believe we will actually worship together. This is thrilling. Will you stay for coffee?'

'Actually I'm with my friends.'

The woman looked Kate and Eve up and down. 'Yes, well, I suppose they could come too.' The woman took a good look at Eve. 'Mrs Marshall, isn't it? Very funny piece in the *Mail* about your husband.' Before Eve had a chance to reply the woman took Inge by the arm and began to lead her towards the church. 'I wonder if I might take this opportunity to talk to you about an event we're having . . .'

Inge looked back helplessly at Kate and Eve, abandoned on the path. Kate smiled and shook her head. She turned to Eve.

'You will help her, won't you, Eve? She can't manage. Everyone thinks she can run the world but she really can't. She'll need you.'

Eve took Kate's arm and they moved into the church together and sat down. A handsome man with greying hair was walking amongst the congregation, shaking hands and hugging as he went. Inge had been placed in a prominent position right in the middle of the main seating. The man made his way to her and shook her warmly by the hand. By the time Kate and Eve arrived to sit beside her, Inge felt she had met the entire six hundred people in the building.

'You all right?' whispered Kate.

'I told you I didn't want to come,' hissed Inge, still smiling at everyone.

The handsome man stopped at the front row where a woman and Patrick were sitting together. Patrick had cleaned up for the service and looked quite a different boy. He wore a brown suit and tie and looked much more the nearly man that he was. The greying man smiled at the woman and then pulled Patrick into a long embrace. The congregation settled down and the man stepped up on to the stage. In his hand he held a well-worn Bible and a sheaf of notes.

'My name is Lawrence.' His voice boomed from a bank of speakers behind the congregation. It was the very voice of God. 'My name is Lawrence, Lawrence Hansen. I am the pastor of this church and I am so glad you all came. So glad!'

There was a slight whoop from the audience as Lawrence opened his arms to welcome everyone. 'Now, if anyone is new,' he said, 'I would like to introduce you to my family . . . this is my wife, Joan . . .' Joan stood up and waved at everyone. 'And this is my son, Patrick.' Patrick was less keen on the waving but managed a nod from his seat. Lawrence stood looking at the boy for a moment and then looked up at the assembled ranks. 'And I would introduce you to the rest of my family, but there are hundreds of you so I don't think there's time!'

This familial inclusion got a little round of applause, to which Lawrence gently held up his hand both to acknowledge and stop. Patrick turned in his seat and searched the crowd for Kate's face. When he found it, they exchanged a little wave and the boy turned back to his father.

'So I am here with my family,' continued the sermon, 'but why have we come together? It's a lovely summer's day. What are we doing inside?'

'I was beginning to wonder myself,' Inge whispered to Eve. Eve wasn't listening. Her eyes were fixed on Shirley. Her daughter was now a big part of the church. She had joined the choir and sat angelically in white robes near the front to one side. John faced her in his dark blue suit. He was ready to do service. He was near Shirley. Eve hadn't made the robes, she hadn't heard her rehearse, she hadn't helped her join. None of it was anything to do with her. Between mother and daughter a huge divide of people sat listening to the pastor.

'I'll tell you. I am here, we are all here, to share the good news. Good news! Isn't that great? Couldn't you all do with good news?' There was a general murmur in the rather young crowd. Yes, good news would be nice. He held up his small bundle of notes. 'I have here the sermon I planned to preach today. I think it was a good sermon. I shouldn't say that but however hard I try the Lord doesn't seem to have purged me of all my vanity.' Lawrence smiled at the vast congregation and the regulars laughed. He smiled again. 'I think it was a good sermon but I am not going to share it with you.' Lawrence took the papers and slowly shredded them on to the stage. The word of God snowed down on the pine floor. There was some general whispered discussion at this but Lawrence held up his hand.

'I am not going to give you that sermon for I believe I need to speak to you today from the heart.' He looked out at his flock and Inge knew that he really did believe it. In his eyes you could see that he was so sure that what he was about to do was not only right but good. It was mesmerising to watch. Eve saw Inge lean forward in her seat. Perhaps Kate had been called to hear this. Perhaps it would make everything all right. The preacher seemed to look straight at Eve and her companions and only at them.

'I was shaving this morning and I was listening to a programme called *The Moral Maze* on Radio 4 . . . because that's the sort of old fogey I am.' Lawrence smiled and there was a ripple of laughter from the assembly. He was charming. 'A panel of learned people were debating euthanasia for people with terminal illnesses. People who are suffering ought to be able to kill themselves – that was the basic argument. They debate something different every week – abortion, genetics, surrogacy, that kind of thing. And there seems to be a general notion that people should do what's right in their own eyes. You do your thing, I'll do mine. Sounds very tolerant, doesn't it? Almost very Christian. But as I stood there looking in my shaving mirror, I felt confused. I felt confused because I did not know why the debate was taking place at all. Why?'

Lawrence gave a long pause and he held aloft his Bible. 'Because I've read this book and if you read this book then there is no moral maze for you to get lost in. It's all here. From beginning to end, from Genesis to Revelations, the Bible speaks of God's way and man's way. Now, man and woman can choose God's way or not. You have a choice, but the choice is clear. God is the giver of life. We all know that and we also know that it is a sin to commit murder. Thou shalt not kill and that includes yourself. It is not your life to take. It is God's.' Lawrence strode across the wooden floor, his shoes making resounding thwacks of emphasis as he spoke. Suddenly he stood still and put on a high pitched woman's voice. 'But Lord, I have to die, I'm in pain, I'm suffering.'

He grinned and everyone smiled. 'Do you think God doesn't know about suffering? He gave his son to us – can you imagine that? Is there a greater gift? And he gave us this.' Lawrence held his Bible aloft once more. 'We have here a complete manual to tell you the way forward about absolutely anything that could happen in your life. We live in a technological age and yet I can't even find such a book for my computer. What a gift this is!'

There were several muted hallelujahs and some half-hearted hand raising. It was revivalist but still essentially British. Lawrence stood stock still and stared down at all his people for an uncomfortable minute.

'Now, I once had someone in my flock who was confused about their sexuality and they came to me. Did I love them? Of course. Did I love their temptation to sin? No. Why not? Because God tells me so. Look in here . . .' Lawrence flicked open his Bible on the large wooden lectern.

'Leviticus, chapter eighteen, verse twenty-two – You shall not lie with a male as with a woman; it is an abomination. Leviticus chapter twenty, verse thirteen – if a man lies with a male as with a woman, both of them have committed an abomination. This is part of the Holiness code. Leviticus first says it in chapter eighteen and then again just two chapters later. Why does he need to repeat himself? Because it is so important. It is clear – God says it is a sin. There are no grey areas of sexuality. It is just wrong. But some people will say that I am being old-fashioned. That gay people can't help it. They're born that way . . .'

Lawrence wove his way through Sodom and Gomorrah as

Eve sat listening. Although she was sitting next to Kate and Inge, although she had understood that they were a couple, none of what was being said seemed to apply. Kate sat unmoving as Lawrence spoke. Occasionally she glanced at Patrick but mostly her eyes bored into the speaker. He was very compelling.

Eve looked at her daughter and thought what a comfort it must be to feel you are right. To have God on your side. She wasn't sure of anything any more. She felt stupid. It had taken Inge with her life, and Adam with his mugging to make her realise the universal fact that what you read in the papers is not the truth. What was truth anyway? In the news, day after day, were endless accounts of individuals and nations who were convinced that they were right, their actions were just, that it was divine will.

Lawrence kept quoting from the Bible as if it were the truth. A helpful woman next to Eve, ever mindful of lost sheep in the flock, opened her own Bible and passed it to Eve. She pointed to the text Lawrence was using and smiled.

Eve hadn't read the Bible for years and her eyes glanced down at the open book. This was her daughter's guiding light. There was all that stuff about men lying with men that Lawrence was covering but there also seemed to be things that probably didn't happen every day any more. There was a lot about sleeping with beasts, which must have been a positive menace back then, it was absolutely forbidden to 'give any of your children to devote them by fire to Molech' and there were a few rules about sleeping with your uncle's wife that seemed a bit Ricki Lake. Eve decided she was stupid about the whole thing.

'Inge,' she whispered across Kate, who refused to be distracted. 'Who's Molech?'

Inge frowned and whispered, 'What?'

'Molech. Who's Molech?' Eve pointed at the passage in the Bible. 'It says in here you're not to devote your children by fire to Molech. Who is he?'

Inge shrugged and turned back to listen.

Lawrence moved from the past into the present. 'Let me tell you a story. Imagine that you have a son, who you love, and he is thirteen years old. He is just the right age to begin exploring his sexuality. He goes to school and one of the lessons required by the government includes information about Aids. Aids is a terrible plague and the school decides to get some people with this terrible affliction to come and speak to the class.

'Now, two speakers come to the school and both are homosexual. They are young, they are dying and the young class of teenagers feels very sorry for them. The speakers explain about their kind of sex in order for the young people to understand how to avoid getting Aids. Students are instructed in all the details of protection, and they make it sound fun. The speakers talk in slang and seem hip and trendy.

'The next year, your son – who is now fourteen – has more sex education in school. He is told a famous lie – that ten per cent of the kids in the class are homosexual. He is told not to worry about who he 'fancies' because one sexual 'orientation' is as acceptable as another. No one mentions that for thousands of years homosexuality has been considered deviant behaviour. That it has been against the law of man for many years and has always been against the Law of God. No, your son is told that a homosexual is born that way and can never be heterosexual.'

Patrick never moved. He sat completely still in his brown suit, listening to his father. Kate watched him and she never moved either.

'He is given the impression that we in the churches and synagogues, we parents are old-fashioned and don't understand. That many famous people were homosexuals and anyone who does not accept homosexuality as the same as heterosexuality is homophobic.

'Where is your boy in all this? Well, he's fourteen. What's he doing? He hangs around with his friends and, just like me at that age, he is still a bit uncomfortable around girls. Now let's say the school, trying to be helpful, give out a sheet and ask all the students to mark their 'sexual orientation' by putting an X next to homosexual, bisexual or heterosexual. Your son, who is a nice, sensitive boy, has been given too much information and he doesn't know what to answer. So he doesn't check anything. This worries the teacher. Maybe he has a problem so she asks him if he'd like to talk to a counsellor. He doesn't know why but thinks he had better agree.

'He sees this counsellor who suggests that he contact a Gay and Lesbian Youth Hotline. He's on a treadmill now. He rings the hotline and the person who answers the phone invites him to their community centre. They suggest that he doesn't tell his parents where he is going – just to say he's going over to a friend's house.

'After several meetings at the centre, others there begin to talk about "coming out" to their parents. Then some older guys invite him to the movies. Later, his new friends invite him on a camping trip, and one night on that trip an older guy comes into his tent and begins to touch him. It feels good. He believes that homosexuality is okay, and now he's sure that he is a homosexual.

'Back at home, the counsellor helps your son become secure in his homosexuality, and they plan how they will tell you, his unsuspecting parents. At the age of fifteen your son tells you that he is a homosexual. Is this just a story? No, that's how it can happen. Your son wasn't born a homosexual. He was recruited.

'And what does God say about this? Read St Paul – one Corinthians, Chapter six, verses nine to ten. *Do you not know that the unrighteous will not inherit the Kingdom of God? Do not be deceived; neither the immoral, nor idolaters, nor adulterers, nor homosexuals, nor thieves, nor the greedy, nor drunkards, nor revilers, nor robbers will inherit the Kingdom of God.*'

Eve leant across to Inge again.

'I don't understand. I thought God loved everyone.'

The helpful woman beside her gave the only reaction to Eve's comment. She patted Eve on the hand and whispered, 'He does. It's because he loves us that he wants the best for us.'

Eve felt bewildered. This didn't seem like a very nice message. Where was the nice guy with the beard reaching out to her? Was he really willing to let some children grow up believing themselves to be evil? Undeserving of God's love from birth to death? Lawrence was sweating now and pacing furiously towards some kind of climax.

'You can watch the Mardi Gras from Sydney or see people on television talking about "gay pride" but you only have to read the ancient story of Sodom and Gomorrah and you know what being gay actually is – it's a manifestation of a depraved nature. It is a perversion of divine standards, and nothing will change that.' The bringer of the good news stopped and took a sip of water. He never looked at his son or his wife. He was transported to a higher plane.

'Okay, what if you still find it hard? What if you need some rational explanation as well? That's all right. If you want to be scientific about it, let's do that too. Let's think about biology. If a man and a woman come together before God they are able to create something so precious – new life. Can homosexuals do that? No. You know what they say – God made Adam and Eve not Adam and Steve.'

This caused much laughter as Lawrence burst his rather serious bubble with a boyish grin. Eve looked around the room at the gathering of mostly young men and women. So they were all here to make babies. That was why they had come. Adam and Eve of Eden had done that and now it was Adam and Eve of Edenford. But in her heart Eve knew that she and her Adam had thought different things from the beginning. She thought you could have sex with someone if you really loved them and Adam thought you could if they'd let you. Was that what she had been created for? As a bearer of children? What about Tom's all-female fish in the Gulf of Mexico? What about those Amazon mollies? Lawrence steamrollered through her doubts.

'And what do we say to all those people who would change our minds? Are we homophobes? Do we hate our fellow man? No! We surely can love their souls but we must be vigilant against their wicked agenda! The unrighteous will not inherit the Kingdom of God! Let us join together and sing hymn number four hundred and eight.'

Everyone smiled as they stood, they smiled as they sang, they smiled as they hugged at the end and they smiled as they shook hands with Lawrence on the way out. It was the most smiley group of people Eve had ever seen in her life and she envied them. Outside the church a group of teenage church members were accosting passers-by on their way to B&Q or whatever. A middle-aged, middle-fat, middle-class woman like Eve trundled past in her coat of many seasons.

'Excuse me, wouldn't you like to be enlightened?' asked the smiley people. The woman never broke stride.

'That's very kind,' she said, 'but I'm afraid I just don't have the time.'

Lawrence stood outside his church in the bright sun and chatted to his flock. His son approached and Lawrence pulled him close. They stood hugging and Eve, Kate and Inge could see such love. There was no doubt that the father who gave his only begotten son truly believed he was doing the right thing. Shirley and John were caught up in a group of friends, all laughing and smiling. If it was so clear then why couldn't Eve see it?

Inge was surrounded by people getting her to autograph bits of paper, the back of old phone bills and even a couple of Bibles. Lawrence stood in attendance, receiving his own praise from the congregation. He hugged his people and made idle chatter with the TV star who had entered his flock.

'Perhaps we could persuade you to read in the carol service as well?'

Kate stood shaded under a tree. She looked at Patrick who looked away and pretended he didn't know her. Eve wanted to ask Lawrence about the swimming baths. Whether her group could have them. Whether God wouldn't want the charity to have them but she couldn't get to him. John came over.

'Let me take you to your car, Eve,' he said. He took her arm as if she were in imminent danger of falling over.

'I wanted to ask about the baths. The pool the church bought.'

John tutted. 'I know, Eve, I'm so sorry for you, but the church will be needing it. They're going to do baptisms, full immersion, so they just can't have it empty.' They got to the car with its snapped aerial and trailing balloons. 'Thank you for coming. It's meant so much to Shirley.'

When Eve got home her house was silent. Her mother slept in the dining room, her son would not come out of his bedroom and Adam had departed for a security conference in Birmingham. He hadn't wanted to go. He wanted to lock the door on his shame, but Eve had persuaded him. He had done nothing wrong. He had to carry on.

Eve sat in her kitchen as the light faded from the day. It was dark when the doorbell went. Kate stood on the front step. She stood outside the security gate and Eve couldn't open it. Kate was sobbing and clinging on to the bars to hold herself up. No matter how hard Eve tried she couldn't get the gate open to let Kate in and in that moment she hated Adam and his bloody security. Eve tried to hug her friend through the bars but it was hopeless and she was in such a state that Eve was afraid to leave to come out of the back door. Kate could hardly speak. Her whole body was eaten up with crying. That was when Eve found out about Patrick. Lawrence's son had been found dead in the school basement. He had hanged himself.

# Chapter Twenty-one

25 January
Holloway Prison for Women
London

My dear Inge,

## For Better or for Worse

Let Marriage be held in honour among all . . .

(HEBREWS 13.4)

The shrink wants to know what I've been thinking about. Actually he'd like to get right inside my head if he could and have a good rummage.

I tell him, 'Brigitte Bardot.'

And he says, 'Sexually?' which is ridiculous. The man can't get his head out of other people's trousers.

I never know where to begin with any of this. You see, they have the tabloid papers in here. Everyone reads them. That and *Hello!* magazine. I don't know why. It couldn't be further from real life. Anyway, there's been a good deal in the papers about Brigitte Bardot and her particular batty problems. Now I'm not all that interested in the intrigues and wherewithals of the famous but lots of the girls on the wing are. I never tell them that I know you.

'You seen about Brigitte Bardot?' they say to me in the lunch queue, so I have to have a look and I do find I read on. Well, I am curious about how much people can live with on their consciences. I am plagued with my conscience and I am not sure it is always a good thing. I don't think Martha is. In fact, I'm sure she isn't. Not because she has religion, she just isn't and I envy that. Why didn't I get that clear head instead of her?

I used to think I had to let every pushy swine on the road nip in ahead of me or they wouldn't think I was a nice person. Now I realise, of course, they don't give a monkeys about me anyway and if we were in New York I'd have been shot by now for slowing down the car behind. Anyway, for those of us who lack religion, the guidelines for the conscience are a tricky business. There's a woman in here who's had such a difficult life that she says to me, 'Eve, I know it's not right but I can't remember what it is I'm supposed to feel bad about.'

Which brings me to Miss Bardot. She feels bad about animals. So bad that she has given up her career, her money and her jewels to save rabbits from perfume trials, dogs from cigars and ferrets from inflammable kitchen equipment or whatever they use ferrets for. Brigitte (if I can be so familiar) has also given up her home to the critters, but they are letting her live there till she's dead, which I call downright decent. So there we have this caring, sharing woman who has deserted her good looks and glamorous life to mess about with cats and spend a life covered in dog hair. Good for her. Then she falls in love with and marries a National Front politician. Now I know you can't help who you fall in love with. You meet the most unlikely person when you least expect it and bam! – your body is awash with chemical impulses, teeming hormones and sweaty palms. But if you then learn that this person 'adheres to views that you personally find reprehensible', as Martha would put it, would you go on to marry them? Bardot says she hates his politics but she loves him. So how do you separate the man from the message, particularly if he is an up-front, campaigning tub thumper?

Love is a curious business. I would have thought that when people hold very strong political views, that's a big part of who they are as people. You can't just say, 'Oh, it's a phase. He doesn't really mean it,' if he is a full-out campaigner. Yet Adam was and I loved . . . love him.

'Did you love Adam? Were you awash with him?' the psychiatrist persists, and I don't know what to say.

'I'm not sure. I was young. Just eighteen. I do remember thinking that marriage sounded more fun than biology A level.'

How odd to end up pregnant with a mortgage just because you were once bored by the details of the aorta.

I didn't know what to do about Patrick. It was the religion thing that was so difficult. I had never really thought about it. I suppose I'm C. of E., but I'm not sure that counts. Shirley says it's not so much a religion as a commitment to cream teas and fêtes, and I think that's true. Both my mother and my daughter believe, believed, and I didn't get it.

'How did Patrick's death make you feel? What did you do?' My shrink feels he is homing in on something.

'I went to Safeway's. They're open twenty-four hours now. After Kate had gone home to wait for Inge. I offered to go with her but she looked unwell and I think she wanted to be alone. I was so angry by the time I got the gate open that I had to do something.'

'So you went shopping?'

'No. First, I went through all the old newspapers in the recycle pile.'

'And?'

'I cut out all the pictures I could find of the famine in Ethiopia. All the kids with big eyes and bulging bellies, all the close-ups of ribs and pleading faces and I took them with me in the car. To Safeway's.'

'What did you do with them there?'

'I put them all over the counter of the delicatessen and I left.'

'Why?'

'I don't know.'

I had wanted to talk to Adam about it but we seemed to have lost the knack. He phoned from his hotel.

'Hello, darling,' he said. 'I won't chat for long because it's very expensive.' I was glad he'd phoned, but it wasn't a great conversational opening.

'Yes.'

'Quite nice hotel really. Very nice selection of biscuits with the in-room tea-and-coffee-making facilities.'

'That's nice.' We paused for a moment. 'You know Lawrence Hansen?' I asked.

I could hear Adam opening a ginger snap. 'No.'

'He's the priest at Shirley's church.'

'Oh, yes.' He crunched into the biscuit. 'No, I don't.'

'His son died.'

'Oh, I'm sorry.' There was a pause. 'I'm glad Shirley's found an interest,' he said, and then we rather ran out of things to say. I don't think men and women do chat all that well. Not that men and men do any better. Adam and Horace have known each other since they both started first school. They feel they've been intimate with each other if one of them admits his stamina on the squash court isn't quite what it used to be.

'Eve?' said Adam. 'I'm so sorry. I didn't mean—'

'Adam, you didn't do anything wrong. It was a misunderstanding. The whole town had just got too wound up about safety. We are safe. Nothing has changed.'

'I didn't mean any harm. I was trying to help.'

'I know.'

'And now that poor woman . . . well, I mean . . . her husband is on the golf club committee. This might mean the end of the captaincy.'

Tom finally came out of his room and I made him some hot chocolate. We sat with Mother, listening to her wheeze in her sleep.

'Maybe I should take her to Lourdes,' I said. 'Maybe there could be a miracle.'

Tom picked at the skin of his drink and sipped quietly. I looked at my boy. My strange, silent boy, and thought maybe I hadn't let him talk enough.

'What do you think about gay people, Tom?'

'Nothing really,' he said. 'It's just people, Mum.' He looked at me. 'I'm not.'

I think we were both embarrassed so I pretended not to understand.

'You're not what?'

'I'm not gay, if that's what you were thinking.'

'No . . . I—'

'Would it matter?'

'No . . . no.'

'I wouldn't mind. I wouldn't mind feeling all that . . .' Tom put down his drink and moved to go upstairs. 'You should think about the lesser snow goose.'

No one spoke to me in English any more. The lesser snow goose? Was it possible to lose all reason very, very slowly? 'Why?'

'They've done a study in California. The lack of available males in lesser snow goose colonies often results in the homosexual pairing of female birds, laying eggs and successfully raising chicks. It seems that after the males contribute semen, they don't have any role that a female cannot play equally well. In fact, they're not sure what males are good for – in an evolutionary sense, of course. It's interesting. The birds may just like it that way.' Tom stopped in his lecture and looked at me. He looked about seven and my heart nearly broke for him. Tom and Adam, my lost boys. I wanted to help them and I didn't know how. I felt helpless with the people I loved most.

'Mum?'

'Yes?'

'Do you think I'm wasting my time? It does no good, does it?'

'I think you're the best.'

Tom went back to his room and I sat looking at his cup on the table. I had taken the cloth off since Mother had arrived and it was becoming covered in rings from coffee cups and medicine bottles. I ran my hand across the surface.

'Take a miracle to get those off now,' I said to Mother. It was the sort of subject she would have liked, combining as it did housework and the work of the Lord. I sat there thinking. You know how those Jehovah's Witness people always call just when you're going out or in the bath or have just put the Shake 'n' Vac out on the carpet and you just want them to go away? Stupid really because, I mean, just then would have been a really good time. If they had knocked at that moment then I would have probably invited them in.

'Come in, come in. God, I can't believe my luck – we were literally just out of belief when you happened past. Been through all the cupboards, hadn't got a thing in the house.' Helluva product, instant salvation. Maybe Mother and I both needed Lourdes. She had sacrificed her marriage for her daughter. She had believed Martha and it had ruined everything.

For God so loved the world he gave his only begotten son . . .

(JOHN 3.16)

They've put up a lovely stone for Patrick in the churchyard. I looked Molech up in the encyclopedia. It says he was a god 'to whom child sacrifices were offered by the Israelites in the days of the monarchy'. Some people think he was actually Milcom, the national god of the Ammonites. I like the idea of having a god called Milcom. (We've got a milkman called Malcolm, which is nearly the same thing.) Or he might have been Maluk or even Yahweh, the God of the Jewish people. Anyway, it says in the old *Encyc. Brit.* that the Israelites were apparently so appalled by the practice of human sacrifice 'that they tried to blot out their shame by changing the name of the god from Yahweh to Molech, as though human sacrifices had been offered only to a foreign deity'.

So they changed history. Maybe one day, when Shirley looks back on what I did, she can do the same.

Love,

Eve

PS Thanks for the offer but I don't think you should come back for the trial. I just need to get this done.

# Chapter Twenty-two

A few nights after Patrick's death, Kate called and asked if Eve would come for a glass of wine. The circumstances were terrible but the invitation still gave Eve a little flutter. She had dreamt of phone calls like that. Friends just ringing for wine and a chat. Adam had come home from his conference a chastened man.

'I need to do something, Eve. I need to make things better.'

Eve was pleased. Pleased for him, for herself and for the town, but Adam was only thinking about himself, about his reputation. It was what people thought that mattered, what they had said, what they might say.

'I need to show the golf club what I can do. I need to make the revue spectacular.'

Intent on his social rehabilitation from sex fiend to social entertainer, all Adam wanted to talk about was sequin size. Eve had got him some dresses from the Hospice Charity Shop for his big number, and he was very preoccupied with trying them on. Tonight he wanted to do a bit of a fashion parade while Eve mixed them a gin and tonic. Eve knew he wanted her to stay home but she went anyway.

Kate was sitting quietly on the sofa and hardly moved when Eve arrived. Inge let her in and poured the wine. There were snacks but no one ate them. No one really did anything until the doorbell went. Inge answered it and Eve could hear her in the hall.

She did say, 'I don't think it's appropriate,' but weakly. The next thing Eve knew, John Antrobus was standing in the door-way. He smiled at Kate and turned to Inge.

'Oh, Miss Holbrook, you're such a boon to this community. Kate? I'm John Antrobus. I know you've had a horrible time. I've brought someone to see you. Someone who needs to talk to you.'

And then he stepped back and there was Lawrence. Pastor Lawrence, Father Lawrence, standing, looking desperate and pale, but somehow noble.

'I am Lawrence Hansen,' he managed. 'I am the Pastor of the Ten Commandments Church. We met briefly on Sunday. My son . . .'

Kate looked at him and said, 'Come in. Come in. We need to talk. Come in.'

Inge did try again. 'Kate, I really don't think—'

Kate's eyes never left Lawrence. 'No,' she said. 'It's fine.'

John seemed to have taken on the role of host. 'Lawrence, Kate Andrews, Inge's . . . flatmate, and I think you know Eve Marshall, Shirley's mother?'

'Of course.' Lawrence nodded as Inge moved into the room.

'Please sit down,' she said. 'Would you like a glass of wine?'

Kate got two more glasses and red wine was poured and handed out. Everyone sipped for a moment before anyone dared say it.

'I'm so sorry about Patrick,' said Inge. There was general murmuring then. Everyone was so sorry about Patrick. It was so awful. Lawrence nodded and almost fell down into an armchair. John smiled at Eve and perched on the arm of the chair. Then he opened the can of worms.

'Lawrence wants to find out what happened . . . to Patrick. He knows, Kate, may I call you Kate? . . . that you and Miss Holbrook were close to him.'

Kate nodded. 'Yes, yes I was.'

'I need to know who he had been speaking to. Someone is responsible for what happened to my boy. If he hadn't been told he was gay . . .' Lawrence faltered.

'No one told him he was gay.' Inge nearly rose from her chair but a look from Kate checked her. 'He was worried about feelings that he was having. He was confused.'

Lawrence frowned. 'There was nothing to be confused about. I know young people get passions but he knew what was right. I told him, I tried to help him.'

Inge leant forward, 'What did you tell him?'

'I told him he would grow out of it. That it was a phase and that he must not give in to it. That the Lord was watching over him all the time.' Lawrence was getting angry. 'Who did he talk to? Do you know? Look, I'll be frank. People have been talking and we know there was a young man.'

'A young man?' Kate leant forward. 'What young man?'

Lawrence shook his head in despair. 'I don't know. Some young man up in the woods. He was seen with his arms around Patrick. He had very long hair.'

Eve sat up and looked at the priest. 'That was my son Tom.'

Lawrence paled. 'You can just sit there when it was your own son who led my boy to his own destruction?'

For a brief moment Eve thought she would explode. She rose from her chair and it took all of Kate's strength to get her to sit down again. Eve tried to stay calm. 'My son has done nothing. He is not gay.'

'Would it matter if he were?' asked Inge quietly.

'No, of course not. All I meant was—'

Kate came to the rescue. 'Tom was comforting Patrick. That's all.'

'About being gay?' Lawrence persisted.

'No, about the death of some ducks, actually,' replied Kate. 'Look we know how you feel. We loved Patrick too, but I think you have allowed other people to make some presumptions.'

Lawrence looked from one woman to the other. 'Maybe some things have been said that shouldn't, but I need your help. I need to know who talked to Patrick. Was it someone at the school?

That was where he . . .' Lawrence's voice faltered to a halt. Kate spoke gently to him.

'I don't know about school but I know what his friends said. His real friends. He was worried about being gay. He was worried that it wasn't just some phase. That he felt too strongly about it for the feelings to go away. His friends told him what it would be like if he didn't grow out of it. That life would go on. He was told that being straight isn't the very essence or the heart of being a good human being. He was told that it didn't matter.'

'It didn't matter because some bloody poof teacher somewhere just couldn't wait to get his hands on my boy. That's why he killed himself at the school. Some bastard sodomite who just kept drawing Patrick along, telling him that it was okay so that eventually he could seduce my son. I know how it works. I know what happened.' Lawrence was losing control but Kate needed to be clear.

'What would have happened if he had grown up gay, Mr Hansen?' she asked quietly.

'He couldn't have. It's a sin. It's a sin. I'm a minister.' Lawrence bowed his head. You could have reached out and touched his pain. Eve could hardly bear to look at him.

'So he would have lost you and God?'

'My son was not gay. I am telling you that there is some viper in that school who was feeding Patrick ideas that—'

Kate raised her hand to stop him.

'What is it that you want, Mr Hansen?'

Lawrence took a hanky from his pocket and mopped his brow. 'I'm sorry, I'm sorry,' he said. John patted him on the arm.

'It's all right.'

'You were close to my son,' Lawrence pleaded with Kate. 'Please, I want you to tell me the name of the teacher or whatever who did this to him. I want to know the man who could find it in his heart to drive my son to his death. I want to know that nothing . . . happened before he died.'

'Is that what this is about?' Kate's voice trembled as she spoke.

'You want to know if your son was *intact*? Is that what matters? In all this, is that what you think about? Well, Mr Hansen, you can sleep well because there was no man. I talked to your son. I told him those things.'

Lawrence looked at her and then shook his head. 'No, it can't be. Patrick told me it was a gay person he'd spoken to.'

Kate nodded. 'That's right.'

Eve had never heard a deafening silence before. People talk about such a thing but she had always thought it was one of those artistic licence things. It isn't. It was quite something. Lately John had taken to sucking on his teeth the way Adam did and that was the first sound in the room followed by him muttering, 'But you live with Miss Holbrook. She's . . .'

Kate nodded again.

John nodded. 'I had no idea. I'm so sorry.'

It would probably be fair to say that what followed was a socially awkward moment.

No one wanted to hurt Lawrence. He was bereaved and everyone felt his pain, but he had come for some truth, and Kate, dying Kate, had provided it. The shattered man of God slowly rose from his seat. Perhaps he had no other defence left. He held his Bible aloft and began to declaim, 'You harlot. You whore. You will be punished. God says that *the cowardly, the faithless, the polluted, murderers, fornicators, sorcerers, idolaters, and all liars, their lot shall be in the lake that burns with fire and brimstone* . . . Revelations, Chapter twenty-one, verse eight . . . uhm . . .' Lawrence was getting a little lost in his desperation to have the revealed truth on his side. 'Uhm . . . *many live as enemies of the cross of Christ. Their end is destruction, their god is the belly, and they glory in their shame, with minds set on earthly things. But our commonwealth is in heaven, and from it we await a Saviour* . . . Philippians . . .'

'Don't you do that in this house!' boomed Kate rising and going to stand right in front of the pastor of the people. She was tiny and frail but there was no lack of power in her determination.

'Don't you bring your prejudice in here and say that it is God's work.'

Lawrence held the Bible up in front of him and tried to continue, '. . . *our commonwealth is in heaven . . .*' but Kate put her hand out firmly and clutched the holy book between them.

'Philippians, chapter three, verse nineteen, I know. I know because it is wonderful and I will not have you use it to justify your petty prejudices.'

Lawrence faced her on the hearth rug like a gunfight at the OK corral.

'I really had no idea,' John muttered again, looking at Eve but getting no reply.

A battle began to rage. Inge was on her feet trying to get Kate to sit down.

'Kate didn't do anything to your son except try help him.'

'Help him? My son is dead.'

'Maybe he couldn't fight you and your quotes at the same time.'

'I cannot change God's word,' screamed Lawrence. 'It's in here.' He banged the Bible down on the mantelpiece so hard that the little clock bounced backwards. Kate picked up the book.

'Is it? Is it? Where? Let me tell you. There are nine biblical citations which are usually trotted out about homosexuals. Four of them actually just forbid prostitution by both men and women. Two others are part of the Holiness code and I will give you those. Leviticus . . .'

Leviticus. Eve remembered Leviticus. Lawrence had mentioned him at church.

'. . . does explicitly ban homosexual acts but he also prohibits the eating of raw meat, planting two different seeds in the same field, wearing garments with two different kinds of yarn, having tattoos, committing adultery and sexual intercourse during women's periods. Cracking rules, aren't they? Do you keep to all of them?' Kate eyed Lawrence's clothes. He was wearing chinos and a sweater. 'Surely that's not cotton and wool you're wearing at the same time, Pastor Lawrence?'

Lawrence was faltering. 'I will not argue the Bible with you. You only have to look at Sodom and Gomorrah to—'

Kate threw open the Bible. 'Oh yes, Sodom and Gomorrah – that old chestnut. Let's see . . . Genesis . . .' She flicked to the beginning of Lawrence's Bible. 'Two strangers come to Sodom to spend the night and a crowd of men gather outside Lot's house and shout, "Where are the men who came to you tonight? Bring them out to us that we may know them." Know them? What does that mean, Lawrence?' Lawrence started to reply but Kate didn't give him a minute. 'No, let me help you. The Hebrew word "to know" is yàdhá. It can mean to have sex. In fact the word appears in the Bible nine hundred and forty-three times but only ten times does it refer to shagging and always heterosexual shagging, except possibly this time.' She looked straight up at Lawrence with anger burning through her. 'So, let me get this clear. This would be the one time in the whole Bible the word gets used in this way?'

'Why are you doing this?' faltered Lawrence.

'Because he is my God too and I absolutely believe that he would not, will not, turn me away. I will not let you make him something he is not,' replied Kate quietly. There was a slight pause and then Kate cranked up the heat again. 'Look at it, Lawrence, don't you think it's bizarre about Sodom and Gomorrah? The Old Testament has a perfectly good word for homosexual sex – shákhabh – but it isn't used in the story.' Kate turned to the rest of the group as a sort of aside. 'Shákhabh also refers to bestiality, which, of course, we know is so close to the same thing. So we are supposed to believe that this one time the word "to know" means men wanting to have sex with complete strangers, is that right? How about if it just meant "get acquainted with"? You know . . . get to know? Couldn't it? I think it's possible.'

'I don't have to listen to this,' stammered Lawrence.

'Kate, please,' pleaded Inge.

'No. He came in here damning us and I won't have it. Sodom

and Gomorrah – it's a famous story so you would think everyone in the Bible would agree about it. All those bum boys killed by God. It's a great bit of gossip, except Luke says it's about inhospitality, Ezekiel says it's about failure to take care of the poor and St Paul, who hated poofs, never mentions it at all. Let me tell you the real sin of Sodom, Pastor Hansen. For thousands of years in the Christian West homosexuals have been the victims of inhospitable treatment. They have been condemned by the Church, been victims of persecution, torture and even death. Because no one understood the real crime of Sodom and Gomorrah – shunning those who are strange to you – that crime has been repeated every day to gay people across the world. If Sodom and Gomorrah is about gay people, then Jonah and the Whale is a treatise on fishing.'

Lawrence was wide-eyed by now. It was an impressive performance by Kate, and Eve could see that even in his grief Lawrence was having to think.

'I didn't come here to be bullied,' he managed.

'And I don't want to bully you. I just don't have any more time to be patient with this nonsense,' replied Kate, surprisingly gently.

Inge tried to intervene. 'Kate, that's enough.' But Kate turned on her.

'You have no idea what is enough, Inge. I don't want you to live like this when I am gone. I am trying to help you too.'

John murmured, 'Like you helped Patrick?' It was a mistake because Kate started up again.

'Yes, like I tried to help Patrick. John, you're a bit of a God botherer . . .'

John blushed and clearly wished he had never opened his mouth to be drawn in to the fracas. 'Well, I . . .'

Kate held open the Bible. 'What happens to Lot after Sodom is destroyed?'

'Well . . . uhm . . .'

'Lot runs away with his wife and daughters while all that brimstone and fire rains down on Sodom. Then what?'

'His wife looks back and gets turned to a pillar of salt,' Eve said, pleased that she had remembered something.

Kate waved her hand at Eve as if to accept the contribution. 'Then what?' she persisted. 'It's been a bad day for Lot. His city's been destroyed, his wife is a pillar of salt, he's got two daughters, God's in a horrible mood . . . what happens, John?'

'I don't remember,' John replied.

'Lawrence?'

'It isn't the point of the story. I didn't come here to debate—'

Kate was not to be diverted. 'I'll tell you. Lot and his daughters go up in the mountains where he gets drunk and then what does he do? Lawrence?'

'He sleeps with his daughters,' faltered Lawrence.

Sleeps with his daughters! Eve thought. It was all mind-boggling. Like trying to catch up late in the day with a rather racy television soap.

'Lot sleeps with his daughters,' agreed Kate. 'But, and here's the nice part, he's so drunk that it's not his fault. "*The first-born went in, and lay with her father; he did not know when she lay down or when she arose.*" Not his fault but still not very nice, is it? And what does God do? More fire and brimstone? No, there isn't even a rumble of thunder—'

John stood up. 'I don't think we should stay. I think it's enough.'

Kate grabbed him by the arm and held him tight. 'It is not enough. Is that the lesson? Is that what parents do?'

Lawrence shook his head. 'I'm sure your parents—'

'My parents haven't spoken to me for twenty years. I might as well be dead to them, but a young boy, your son, is actually dead, and it didn't have to happen. I will not stand by and let Inge take the blame, or worse, let it happen to someone else because that is supposedly the message from God. How can it be? Inge and I are a couple. We are an offence and what will happen to us? Are we going to be visited by divine wrath because we love each other? Are there going to be earthquakes in Edenford?

Floods, famines, outbreaks of pestilence? Or are we too refined for that? Maybe just a bad case of rose blight. Actually, maybe we'll be all right. The Holiness code only condemns male homosexuals not female. Women are only condemned to death if they have sex with an animal and we haven't done that for ages.'

Lawrence stared at her with desperation in his eyes. 'St Paul said—'

'Oh, St Paul didn't want anyone to have a good time. All those bloody letters he wrote. Did you ever ask yourself why no one ever wrote back?'

'Jesus said that we are commanded—' Lawrence tried again but Kate wouldn't let him.

'Jesus said nothing about it. He never mentioned gays the whole time he was here. We are commanded to love, that's all. It is an absolute divine command to live a life of love.'

Tears began to flow down Lawrence's face. 'I loved my son. I was doing what was right . . .'

Inge reached out and touched Lawrence on the arm. 'I don't doubt it. Maybe Patrick would have grown out of it. It's possible. Maybe he would have just settled his feelings. Maybe if he had thought everyone was positive for him. That's all Kate . . .'

Lawrence wiped his tears. 'She told him to be gay.'

Now Kate had had enough. 'No, I didn't. I just tried to let him talk. To be himself. I loved your son. I gave him some of the last hours of my life as a present. I simply told him to live. Nobody was trying to get him to be a killer or a dope fiend. Nobody was trying to get him to be anything except himself.'

Things seemed to have calmed down when Lawrence suddenly snatched his Bible from Kate. 'I will not be seduced by you. I will not listen to you. I know what you're doing. You're trying to blame me. Well, you can't. I did what was right. I did what I had to do and your . . . lover . . . she killed my boy. I will see this put right. I will see that it never happens again.'

Lawrence was screaming now and Kate was fighting right back in his face.

'What's the worst that might have happened to your boy?' she yelled.

'You would have made him gay.'

'He would have lived. He would have . . .' At the height of the battle, Kate's onslaught was spoiled by the slightest choking sound. A noise caught in her throat and she reached to clutch the mantelpiece but missed and grabbed Lawrence's arm instead. He had no choice but to help her as she slowly sank to the ground.

'Oh God, oh God . . .' Inge leapt across the room to hold Kate's head. 'Kate, Katie, Katie . . .' But there was no reply. Kate lay insensible on the floor. A tiny, pale figure with no fight in her whatsoever. For once John was useful.

'I'll get an ambulance,' he said.

Eve ran and got a cold cloth while they waited. It wasn't long before the siren wailed outside.

Lawrence had sunk down, motionless, into the armchair clutching his Bible. John patted his arm. 'I'll take you home,' he said, and then turned to Eve. 'I'm so sorry, I had no idea.'

John led Lawrence from the room and there was silence. Inge was crying and Kate was just lying there.

Inge was rocking her and repeating over and over again, 'Kate, you shouldn't have, you shouldn't have.'

Inge said she would call Eve and took Kate to the hospital on her own. They departed and left Eve bewildered and slightly breathless. Eve watched the ambulance leave and wondered if there was any mention of lesbians in the Bible. She didn't think so but then there wasn't much about women generally, apart from getting the blame for a few things. She thought about William and Pe Pe and how much humans all revere sperm and maybe that was something to do with it. Lesbians didn't have sperm so they didn't really count. The real miracle was that, despite everything, all the obstacles, Kate and Inge were happy together.

Eve ran, she ran back to her house and up the stairs to Tom's room. She didn't even knock. She burst in and found him sitting on his bed staring out of the window. He was crying and she ran to him and held him in her arms. Tom sobbed and sobbed. He cried for Patrick, he cried for the woods and the baby ducks and he cried because he was in his mother's arms and it was okay. When at last he calmed he stayed where he was, nestled in Eve's embrace. Eve sat in her own thoughts until at last she said, 'Tom, do you know about Sodom and Gomorrah? Do you know what happened afterwards?'

Tom sat up and wiped his nose on his sleeve. A boy never fully grown. 'I don't really care,' he said. 'The real sodomites in our time are those whose greed and quest for power have brought war and poverty to millions of innocent people. They are destroying the planet and there is nothing I can do about it. Mum?'

'Yes?' said Eve, who could not help him.

'Would you wash my hair for me?'

It was a simple task but so lovingly done. She washed and trimmed his hair and then put him to bed. Her boy, her beloved son.

# Chapter Twenty-three

Inge couldn't cope any more. Kate was dying and there was nothing she could do. She sat night and day by her partner's bed until Kate finally thought of some trinket or other she wanted from the house. She sent Inge to get it. She sent Inge to get some air.

A silver Volkswagen Golf was sitting outside the house when Inge got home. A tall, blond woman and a photographer got out. Before Inge was halfway out of her car the photographer was snapping at her. Her instinct was to hide but perhaps for once in her life she had had enough.

'I know you've been sitting here. I know. I've seen you,' she said to the woman who stood notepad at the ready. 'Why don't you get a proper job? Write something useful?'

The woman reporter wasn't listening. She eyed Inge and held up the article about her not being married.

'I just wanted to follow this up. I just wanted to check a few things.'

'Well, don't,' spat Inge. 'I'm gay, okay? I didn't marry because I don't want to. I am a lesbian. Okay? Are you happy now?'

The woman shrugged. 'Sure. That wasn't what we came about.'

'It wasn't?'

'No. Paul Roe's statement.' Inge looked blank. 'The BBC have issued a statement saying they're updating their image and no one who has presented for them in the past will have their contract renewed. We just wanted your comments.'

'So why have you been watching me?'

'We thought Mark Hinks might be here. The footballer. Everyone said you were secretly going out.' The reporter suddenly felt with a rush that Christmas and Easter had arrived on the same day. 'Is he gay too?'

Barry confirmed the news. *Don't Even Go There!*, the new panel game where people taught their pets to perform impersonations, was about to be announced. As part of their *New Talent* search the BBC was releasing a thousand silver balloons from their premises across the country. The first person to catch one and phone in would be taking the chair. Jenny Wilson, Creative Controller of the BBC Talent Team, was waiting for the call. Inge's contract would not be renewed.

It was Eve's second trip to Edenford General in a year. She never went to the hospital. She didn't even go when the babies were born. Both her children had been born at home. Kate was on Rachel Ward but in a private room. Eve brought some flowers. They had been for the church but now there didn't seem any point. The little room was lovely. It had the standard hospital view over a graveyard but otherwise it was very calming. Inge sat in a small winged chair with a plastic covering in case of accidents. She looked dazed and did not speak.

'You flash thing, Kate,' Eve said, as she popped the flowers in an inappropriate vase. 'Going private, eh?'

Perhaps Inge was just exhausted. She had slept at the hospital every night since Kate had been admitted. 'Hardly,' she said.

'It's the rumours,' explained Kate.

'Rumours?'

'Yes, apparently it's sweeping the town . . . Inge, could you provide a drum roll please?' Inge smiled a little and banged on the end of the bed with her hands as Kate announced, 'I have Aids.'

Eve felt panicked for a second but was too polite to leave. 'I thought you had . . . cancer,' she faltered.

'Relax, Eve, I do, but that doesn't stop a good rumour. It's been doing the rounds ever since that article came out with Inge's rather bold statement. I killed Patrick and now God is killing me with Aids.' Kate smiled at her partner who sighed.

'It's God's punishment on gay people. It's what we all get, all gay people, except, irritatingly, lesbians.' Inge poured Kate some juice as she spoke. 'So either God is a lesbian or he just doesn't care.' She gently lifted her lover's head and helped her to drink.

There was that word again. Lesbian. Eve didn't like it but she did like Kate. She didn't know why. She just did. She watched them together. It was kind. It was love, and that was all that mattered.

Kate lay back on her pillow as Inge wiped her mouth. 'I'm glad you came, Eve,' she said. 'I need to ask you something. I need you to be Inge's friend. There won't be anyone else.'

Inge tried to shush her but they both already knew that Kate on a roll was unstoppable.

'I want you to help her organise the funeral.'

'What about your family?' Eve asked.

'They won't come. I want something simple and my mother is very 'High Church' – you know, Catholic without the pope, that kind of thing. She's a warden in her parish and there's a constant whiff of candles and incense about her. She wouldn't approve. Anyway, she doesn't see me. Not since she found out about Inge.'

'That's sad,' Eve said.

Inge laughed. 'Sad but not surprising. This is a woman who refused to visit for two months after Kate decided not to have velveteen curtains in the lounge.'

Kate nodded. 'Despite all the guarantees of them wearing well.'

It was another world to Eve. People abandoning their children like this. 'What did she say to you? About Inge?' she asked.

'She said I must choose between her and "that dyke". You

wonder how a woman from Surbiton knows a word like that.'
Kate looked at Eve. Inge was holding Kate's hand and stroking
her face when the nurse came in. Eve thought something had
happened because in an instant Inge let go and moved away from
the bed to look out of the window.

Eve didn't understand. 'Why did you tell your mother? I mean,
she didn't need to know. I didn't know.'

Kate smiled. 'It mattered to me that my parents knew how
much I love Inge. That they approved, that they understood.'

Inge sat down and shut her eyes. 'There was no excuse for
them taking it so harshly. They didn't even know me,' she murmured.

Kate smiled at Eve. 'I do think perhaps it was a mistake to tell
them on the day of the Royal Wedding.'

'Which one?' Eve asked, as if it mattered. She had watched
them all with her own mother.

'Fergie and what's-his-name. You should have seen the palaver.
Mother had decorated the whole front room with bunting made
of red, white and blue napkins from Tesco's, hung over strings
from the tomato plants in the garden. I hadn't really wanted to go
but Inge was away working and . . . anyway, we were watching
telly – me, Mum and Dad in total silence. Mum's very royal. It
was a great event. The presenter was droning on . . .'

'*And there she is. The golden carriage at last coming into view
of the cathedral, bearing the fairy-tale bride to meet her prince.
She goes in plain Sarah Ferguson and will emerge in the sunlight
a duchess*.'

'Isn't it wonderful?' Mrs Andrews said, brushing crumbs of
sausage roll from her husband's front. 'True love.'

Kate coughed. 'Mum. I wanted to have a word about me and
Inge. You know, Inge, my flatmate. The thing is . . .'

Kate thought at first that her mother hadn't heard. The organ
music swelled so loud as she explained how she felt about Inge,
how happy she was and how wonderful it was, that she felt sure
only the progress of the virgin bride had taken her mother's

attention. Nothing was said until well after the final wave on the balcony. The fairy-tale couple went off to live happily ever after.

Mr Andrews had risen to turn off the television. Kate's mother had slowly put the hand-knitted cozy on the teapot and risen to her feet.

'Come along, Harold,' she had announced, 'Mrs Bentley has invited us for sherry to toast the royal couple. Say goodbye to Kate. She won't be coming again.'

Kate's father had stood still for a moment and then left the room. Kate thought he had stroked her arm as he left but she couldn't be sure.

'Mum, don't do this,' Kate had protested. 'Talk to me.' Her mother put on her cardigan and picked up her bag.

'You may be very clever and book learned but even you cannot expect us to talk to the dead.' And with that Kate's parents walked from her life.

Eve, Inge and Kate sat in silence for a while after Kate finished telling her story. Eve saw that both the women were exhausted and she needed to think. Why had Kate told her that story? Why had she told her mother? Perhaps you never stop thinking you can always turn to your mum. What could her children do that would make her walk away from them? What could she do that would make them walk away from her? At that moment Eve knew that she didn't understand Shirley's life but that that would change. She would try harder.

Eve looked up and saw Pastor Lawrence standing in the door-way with John. John raised his hand and said quickly 'Now, Eve, don't get upset. Both Lawrence and I were distressed about what happened and we're here to put it right.'

Lawrence moved towards the bed and looked down at Kate. 'Hello, Kate.'

'Lawrence. So you finally saw things my way, eh?'

'No, but I was in the area and I wanted to see you were still fighting.'

Kate grinned at him. 'Sure.'

'I understand you asked Reverend Davies to visit you,' he said.

'Yes,' Kate said evenly. 'I believe he was busy.'

'Did you want to see a priest?'

'Yes, yes I did.'

'Will I do?'

Kate looked up at him. 'Why, Lawrence, why?'

'Because he's your God too.'

Eve, John and Inge left Kate and Lawrence together for about half an hour. John and Eve sat silent in the corridor while Inge fell into an instant deep sleep. At last the door opened and Eve could hear quiet conversation.

'Give my love to my son and remember, try not to give St Paul too hard a time. Bless you, Kate.'

'Thank you, Father.'

Lawrence shut the door behind him and stood looking at us. Inge awoke to find him weeping uncontrollably. No one said anything and he left.

'Thank you, John, thanks for that,' Eve said. It had been a good thing. She could see that. Good for both of them.

John shook his head. 'Oh no, that was Lawrence's own idea. I didn't do that but I did phone the Andrews.' Neither Inge nor Eve were quite sure they had heard what he said. 'Kate's parents. You remember when I was there at your house that night,' he nodded at Inge, 'Kate said she hadn't seen her parents in some time? Well, I was sitting in my office yesterday looking out the window towards the pub. There were these two little girls waiting endlessly outside in the street for their mum to come out. They had been there for hours when their mother finally stumbled out, yet they hugged her with abandoned affection and I thought about Kate. I mean she is her parents' child. I thought, you know, whatever the issues were in the past they deserved the chance to say goodbye. I thought her parents should know. I thought they should know before she went. I thought it was best.'

Kate's mother came on her own the next day. Kate had deteriorated rapidly. Eve was changing the water for the flowers when she arrived. She knew it was Mrs Andrews, as she had Kate's Caribbean complexion and she never stopped crossing herself and muttering psalms all the way down the corridor. Inge didn't want to let her in but Kate was really too weak to protest. The cancer had grabbed her and now the tubes and monitors that relayed her life held her in place ready for the end. Inge wanted Kate to find peace so she didn't argue.

'She said I was dead years ago,' said Kate with a sigh, reaching for her lover's hand. 'It can't make any difference. Let her make her peace.'

Inge had left the small, private room and gone out in the corridor to prepare Mrs Andrews for her child's deterioration. It had been years since she had last seen her. Inge had lived with the changes in her lover on a daily basis but the photographs in their house showed a different Kate from the one Mr and Mrs Andrews had turned away. The hospital corridor was dark with just a single slant of light from the small window above the intensive care sign. Kate's mother sat on a plastic chair clutching her handbag.

All Inge managed was 'Mrs Andrews?' and then the onslaught came from nowhere. Mrs Andrews was a tall woman and she rose and launched herself at Inge.

'You, you . . . murderer.' Eve thought for a minute she was going to grab Inge by the throat but the onslaught was verbal and fierce. Venom spat from her lips.

'She never would have got sick . . . down . . . there . . . if it wasn't for you. You are evil. The devil is manifest in you. I hope you get cancer and die. Don't smile at me, you hussy, don't you dare . . .'

Mrs Andrews launched herself at Inge so that Eve had to step between them and push the older woman away. Inge sank down on to the linoleum floor and stared at her lover's mother. Mrs Andrews returned to her seat as if no interruption had occurred. She didn't go into Kate's room but just sat there. Eve took Inge away to calm her down and not once would Mrs Andrews catch anyone's eye. She just sat reading and rereading the wall poster on stress and related heart disease.

Inge was ranting in the cafeteria. Everyone was looking. This was, after all, Inge Holbrook, television personality and newly discovered lesbian. Eve tried to get her to quieten. 'Fucking woman, fucking woman. Maybe I'll go back there and seduce her. Shall I? Isn't that what we do? Aren't we so persuasive that anyone put under the slightest pressure will turn gay? Isn't that right, Eve?'

'I don't know anything about it. It's your choice—'

'My choice? My *choice*?' Inge's voice rose in anger. 'Why the hell would I choose to be something that horrifies my parents, that could ruin my career, that my religion condemns and that could cost me my life if I dared to walk down the street holding hands with my partner? My choice? To live in the closet. To watch everything you say, everything you do, making sure no one guesses the truth till you're exhausted and frightened and think you're going to lose your mind. Why would anyone choose that?'

'I don't know.'

Inge stopped shouting and sat down. She reached for Eve's hand and held it tight. 'Because you don't choose who you fall in love with.' And they sat holding hands.

When they came back from the cafeteria, a young doctor had just appeared carrying Kate's notes. He was new on the ward. Until now the doctors had given Inge all the information they could about Kate's condition. Now she was ignored.

'Mrs Andrews?' the young intern enquired. Mrs Andrews nodded, entirely composed. 'I'm afraid your daughter's condition is deteriorating. Are you the only family?'

'Yes, I am.'

'I wonder, could you sign these forms?'

As they busied themselves about the papers, Inge slipped into Kate's room. She reached for her hand and was there when the heart monitor faded to a single tone. Mrs Andrews appeared in the doorway.

'She's dead, isn't she?'

These were not words either Inge or Eve could form in their minds. A mobile phone rang. Mrs Andrews pulled it from her bag.

'Hello, Harold. Yes, I'll be home soon. I'll tell you when I get home. Goodbye dear.'

# Chapter Twenty-four

2 February
Holloway Prison for Women
London

Dear Inge,

## *Maybe Not Mensa but Tenser*

I have looked out on everything I have made
and behold it is very good.

(GENESIS 1.31)

They let me have all the papers in here and some of the stories are bizarre. I mean, what people get up to. What they spend their time on. A group of Dutch scientists have discovered that people with warm feet fall asleep thirteen minutes quicker on average than people with cold feet. I have cold feet and I don't sleep. I miss sleeping with Adam. Hearing his little noises and knowing he's there if I have to say 'What was that noise?' in the middle of the night.

There are also several fairly thrilling developments in the world of communications – a Professor David Premack of the University of Pennsylvania has developed an experimental language enabling him to teach chimpanzees to 'talk' and communicate with him. We could do with that for some people.

Then a Boston Television station, WBGH, has developed a system for blind people to watch TV. They get a special stereo channel that transmits a description of the action and the sets, narrated during pauses in the dialogue. Why not just listen to the radio? There's so much I don't understand. If dogs are so intelligent, why can't they walk themselves? In Victorian times you used to be able to buy a dog-driven sewing machine. Apparently it was marketed in the 1870s and actually used in some English households. There was this special set of wheels which were moved by a little dog on a leash. The dog trotted round and round a movable disc, pretty much the way asses and horses used to move mill-wheels, and that ran the sewing machine. You see—

'Eve! Eve!' The psychiatrist is losing patience with me. The trial is soon and he still doesn't know what to say. We must concentrate. He has his reputation to think of.

'I'm sorry. I think too much without being very clever. It's a terrible combination.' I put down my sewing and try to concentrate.

'What did you feel when the boy killed himself?'

'I don't know. Angry, confused. I was starting to feel angry about so many things. Not all the time, you understand. I mean, some days I was really good. I did all my duties – looked after Mother, cooked for Tom and Adam, smiled at my neighbours, didn't buy leylandii hedging, and then sometimes I would just be in such a temper. I felt so . . . outraged at . . . everything. And then Kate died and I did know how to help Inge. It was in all the papers. Close-up pictures of her outside the hospital, at home . . . Everyone pretending to be nice but shocked, you know. Shocked about Kate. About the whole gay thing.'

'What did you do?'

'The first thing was that I got on with my mission – raising the money for the refugees to come to Edenford. I thought I didn't have the nerve but the morning after the news about Patrick I was out early, banging on doors and asking for donations for my

Eve Marshall's Mission to the Children. Then I cleared out the garage to store everything and got Mr Ozbal to agree that I could have all his old cardboard boxes the next time he went to the Cash and Carry. I collected quite a lot of things straight away. You see, I think the mistake Susan Lithgood made was waiting in the shop for people to bring things. If you go to people's houses instead you get loads more stuff.'

'And what did Adam think of all this?'

'Not much. He had stopped campaigning for the council. I think he hoped to keep quiet about the security thing and get re-elected on his past record. It mattered terribly. All he did was go to the office in the day and work on his Shirley Bassey routine at night. We hardly spoke except when he tried to stop me going up to watch them building the bypass in Bluebell Wood.'

'You shouldn't go up there,' he said, 'it's not safe.'

'Don't start with that ridiculous "safe" thing again, Adam. I don't want to walk up to the new bypass and keep looking over my shoulder to see if some rapist is behind me.'

'Eve, you are not to go up there. It isn't safe.'

'Don't start, Adam.'

'I am not starting, I am finishing. I know about these things, Eve. I know about security. How do you think I paid for the dinner we just had?'

That was when William and Pe Pe dropped in for coffee. They didn't seem to know it was late and popped round to have an argument of their own. They'd started having counselling at something called Relate. It seemed mainly to involve relating all their problems to me. Pe Pe wanted them to move back to her home in Australia. I tried to make encouraging noises but I didn't think it was going to happen.

William kept pacing up and down. 'I'm sorry, I'm so sorry,' he kept saying, and then, 'Look, we all know it will be fine when Pe Pe gets pregnant.' Pe Pe looked at me and smiled.

Mother woke up and for a moment I thought I heard her call 'William, William!'

'She's calling you,' I said. 'Please go to her.' But he wouldn't so I told him, 'I don't know how much longer I can cope. She doesn't seem to be getting any better. It's not fair, William.'

We have to go home now,' he said. 'Pe Pe!'

'William!' Mother and I called together.

He turned and muttered over his shoulder, 'Now is not a good time.'

## Woman's Work

A good wife . . . is not afraid of snow for her household,
for all her household are clothed in scarlet.

(PROVERBS 31.21)

I tried to talk to Shirley but she had gone sort of gooey and ridiculous. Not like her at all.

'My friend Jane, from school, is getting married,' she said, while I washed and washed Mother's fading clothes in the kitchen sink. 'She's having an all-white wedding with six page boys.'

'That's nice,' I said.

'She's so happy. She just glows. Isn't that nice?' Shirley continued.

'That's nice,' I said.

Shirley had come round to help with Mother but actually she just sat reading *Brides* magazine while I dealt with what needed to be done. Mother had been with us for months. There seemed to be no movement from the social services, William was utterly preoccupied and Martha had already left for Bangkok.

I wanted to travel. I dreamt about it all the time. Maybe, if I ever get out of here, I'll never go back to Edenford. Would you travel with me, Inge?

*Come with me, we shall set off with a light heart, a heavy purse and a merry companion to go amongst the*

*Mohammedans and Barbarians. I shall pack a Gladstone*
*bag for it straps easily to the back of a mule.*

I want to be an unescorted and independent person – a lady
traveller. I want to be like Lady Anne Blunt who rode two thousand miles as a Bedouin from the shores of the Mediterranean to
the Persian Gulf, or Ella Sykes who passed through Persia riding
side-saddle and wearing a golden silk handkerchief that covered
her head and fell about the chest and shoulders to the waist. I
want to try everything. I shall even eat sweetbreads if they are
offered. They say the testes, thymus and pancreas all have the
reputation of sharpening your mind and body. (Testes, apparently, are usually skinned then sliced and sautéed in butter. I've
sent the recipe anonymously to the Centurions.)

I pulled Mother up in her bed and tried to smooth the sheets
while Shirley carried on talking from the kitchen.

'Of course, the whole bridesmaid thing has changed. The
dresses are so much nicer and you can get shoes dyed any colour
to match.' (The wedding magazines were full of ads for hand-
made shoes in any size so I sent off for a catalogue for Adam. He
loved it, but I warned him, 'Don't get too high a heel. You don't
know how long you'll have to stand for.')

Mother's ribs poked into my hand as I tried to lift her. She ate
nothing but soup now. Soup that I hand-fed her. There was nothing of her, but my back hurt from the endless turning and lifting
to make her comfortable. Shirley was jabbering on when out of
nowhere Mother looked at me and said quite clearly, 'I hate
this.'

We looked at each other and I nodded. 'I know. Me too.' It
only lasted a moment and then she was gone again but I knew
something had to be done. Adam was continuously occupied
with his Bassey impersonation. He firmly believed this was going
to be the route back into the hearts of the community, or if not
the community then at least the golf club. I was glad he had an
interest because what with Mother and my mission I was too

busy to keep worrying about him. I needed to be busy. It was when I stopped that I thought too much.

My mission had only been open a few days and already I was being flooded with things. To be honest, I think people give tins of rice pudding and so on not so much to help but because they want you to go away. I'd been sorting boxes for about a week when Adam said he couldn't rehearse in the garage any more. Apparently there wasn't room for his arm movements so he spent all his spare time upstairs in the back bedroom giving his all as the Tigress of Tiger Bay.

He was up there belting out that he was what he was and what he was needed no excuses, when Horace Hoddle came to call. I tried to call Adam but the music was too loud and I didn't want to let Horace upstairs in case he found out about the surprise.

'I'm afraid Adam is a bit busy just now.'

Horace eyed the jumble I was in the middle of sorting. 'I came to see you actually, Eve.'

'Oh.' Horace had never been to see me about anything.

'Would you like some coffee?'

He would, and he sat looking at me while I made it. 'Always had a lovely way about you, Eve. Adam's a lucky fellow.'

I handed him his mug and his hand brushed mine as he took it. He looked so intently at me that I thought for a minute there must be something unpleasant on my nose. 'You're a fine woman, a very fine woman.'

We drank our coffee while we thought about how fine I was. I hadn't been alone with a man like this since Adam and I had been dating. It was very awkward. I tried to break the silence.

'Garibaldi?'

'No, thank you. Eve, if I were a different sort of man then I might be here on a different sort of mission. I have always thought you were very lovely, and my wife . . . but I'm not that sort of man. I am here to help Adam.'

'Sorry?'

'Eve . . . it's about your little . . . idea.'

A dim light began to burn at the end of the corridor of my mind. 'Oh, my mission, you mean.'

'Is that what you're calling it? Yes.' Horace looked for inspiration in his cup of instant. 'It's not a good plan.'

'Well, not yet. You see the pool was sold before I realised but I will think of somewhere else and—' Horace didn't let me finish.

'Eve, you are a good woman. A good member of this community. Adam has had a tough time. It was all most unfortunate because he was doing important things for Edenford. Give him a chance to come back. Don't spoil it.'

Horace stood up and put both his hands on my upper arms. He looked deep into my face and pulled me towards him. I thought he was going to kiss me and I wasn't at all sure what I would do. His moustache looked prickly and rather unpleasant but I was too polite just to say, 'Get off.'

Horace swallowed hard and you could see the effort run down his throat. It was like facing a pelican with a free fish supper.

'I am using all my will power to stand by Adam,' he managed. 'Now you need to do the same. We must restrain ourselves for him.'

Horace gulped another salmon-size lump and left with his words of wisdom hanging in the air.

The women's group were still trying to meet on Tuesdays, although the heart had gone out of it since the débâcle with the bypass. I didn't stay for the chat any more. Just went over and let them into Mother's empty house.

'You're friends with that Inge Holbrook, aren't you?' asked ferret woman in a tone that I just knew meant trouble. Not that I wouldn't defend you, Inge. It's just that I didn't want the need to arise in the first place. Everything was doing my head in. Being in the house I grew up in, Mother's house. Being at a group that Martha had started and not finished. Martha, who fought for women's rights but who had destroyed the life of my father. I couldn't bear it but the minute I turned to go I could hear the women in the room start gossiping.

'Anyway, I hear there's going to be a legal case brought against Inge Holbrook for her partner's assets. Hogart, Hoddle and Hooper are handling it. That nice young man, what's his name?'

'I can't help it. I don't really like lesbians. I don't even like the word. It makes me think of hairy old women with cats.'

Hairy old women with cats. I'm a hairy old woman with a cat, I thought.

When I got home, Claudette was waiting for me. She took one last feline spring at my shoulders and landed in my arms. The cat was dead.

As far as I can find out, there are no references to cats at all in the Bible. No lesbians and no cats. There's plenty about dogs, a lot of sheep and birds and even some dragons, but no cats. They are utterly ignored by God.

## Labours of Love

And as they went along the road they came to some water and the eunuch said, 'See, here is water! What is to prevent my being baptised?'

(ACTS 8.36)

'Do you know about Blaise Pascal?' I ask the psychiatrist. He frowns at me and looks up from his notes.

'He invented the syringe,' he says rather smugly.

'Yes, and the first digital calculator . . . in 1644 . . . and the hydraulic press. I don't know what that is but it was important.'

'Why?'

'I don't know why. I suppose it was needed.'

'What's this got to do with anything?' The closer we get to the trial the more short-tempered my helpmate gets.

'Tom told me about his wager and I like that. It's called the Pascal Wager and it was a sort of bet he had in life. He said that nobody can really prove that God exists, right? I mean, you're clever and you can't. No one knows for absolute certain that

Jesus or anyone was able to make up for our sins by dying or if miracles really do happen. So the trick is, if you're not sure, just get on and believe anyway. Basically it's better to believe than not. I think it makes sense. If you believe and it turns out there is a God and a lovely afterlife and all that, then you're not disappointed when you die. You might even get something for having all that faith. Of course, if you die and there's nothing, just oblivion, then you'll never know you were wrong in the first place.'

I'd like to invent something.

*Fact – in the early 1900s the Los Angeles city fathers were concerned to make accidents in the street less harmful to their victims, so an upholstered couch was fixed to the front of the local trams. The intention was to 'scoop' up hapless pedestrians who got in the way of the public transport. Unfortunately it had the reverse effect and knocked more people to the ground than any tram ever did. I'm not surprised. I mean, you'd stop in the street and stare if you suddenly saw a large piece of stuffed Dralon coming at you. Beware things that are meant to protect you.*

I couldn't seem to talk to anyone any more. Tom looked quite different with his hair washed and cut. He hardly spoke and all the life seemed to have gone out of him. It was a Samson haircut and I regretted it. He sat with me in the kitchen and didn't seem inclined to do anything. Sometimes some of the construction workers would drive past our house towards the woods and tears would come to his eyes. I had managed to persuade him to come down for lunch one day when Shirley came over with John. They were holding hands and beaming the beam of the chosen.

'Mum,' trilled my daughter, 'Lawrence is going to be doing baptisms at the pool next week. He's brought the whole thing forward to help bring the church together.'

John smiled at my beloved child. 'Everyone is so devastated

about Patrick that they could do with some good news, and Shirley is to be among the first!'

'That's nice.' It was all I ever said to my daughter now. 'That's nice.' Everything was nice. My daughter was to be born again. Among the many things I had planned for her over the years, this had not been one of them. I didn't know what I was supposed to do. Was there an appropriate response? Should I suggest a party? Were there Hallmark cards for the event?

'Eve, we'd very much like it if you would be there,' beamed John. He'd *like* me to be there? My daughter was getting born again and she wouldn't need her mother? 'And Tom as well, of course.'

I wanted to be supportive but I was a bit lost. 'I don't really understand,' I said. 'What's it about?'

Tom played with the salad cream while he answered. 'It's a ritual, Mum. They all have the same purpose. They're used to make outsiders of the rest of us and to make the participants feel superior. You should be careful, Shirley. Once you feel superior to others then it's a small step to thinking another human being is worthless and a tiny leap from there to thinking that really they ought to be got rid of.'

This incensed Shirley. 'That is not true, Tom. It's absurd. I love everyone.'

Tom looked up from his examination of the chicken quarter I had planned to eat. 'Then why do you need to do this?'

There was a short pause around the breakfast bar.

'Shirley . . .' prompted John squeezing her hand.

Shirley looked at her brother. 'Because God has called me.'

Tom looked at her. 'How do you know that?' he asked.

'Well . . .' Shirley looked to John who nodded for her to continue. 'I've prayed and I have been shown the way.'

Tom thought about this and then said, 'Okay, so show me.'

John laughed. 'You have to pray, Tom. We'd be happy to pray with you.'

Tom shook his head. 'No, I don't want to be born again. I just want you to show me how God called you. Just prove it to me so I can see.'

Shirley was getting annoyed. 'Tom, don't be ridiculous. Mother, Tom's being ridiculous.'

'We can't show you unless you believe,' explained John.

'Aaah,' said Tom, angry with the world and winding his sister up. 'So, this being born again is unreasonable?'

'It is not unreasonable!' Shirley was piqued now. The beam was faltering. Tom smiled at her.

'Not to you, Shirley,' he said, 'but scientifically. What you believe has happened to you has no reason behind it.'

'Tom!' I warned, knowing we were heading for trouble.

'No, Mother, it's interesting. You see, if you give up reason then you can believe in anything, depending, of course, on your personal taste. Instead of looking for what is true then what one would like to be true will do. And if you feel pushed to justify that belief then that's easy. You just make it a mystery. Shirley is immune from rational attack because we don't understand what has happened to her. Those of us who disagree are, by the very fact that we disagree, proven incapable of making contact with the mysterious source of truth. What Shirley is telling you, Mum, is that she is now better than us and there's nothing we can do about it unless we stop thinking and just believe.'

John's smile wavered but stayed intact. 'We could help you, Tom. Suppose, just suppose, you're wrong. What will you do on Judgement Day when you are called before God?'

Tom stood up and stared at his sister. Then he turned to John. 'I shall look him in the eye and say, "Sir, you gave me insufficient evidence."'

So my daughter was baptised . . . for the second time. The first time had been at the Church of Saint Mary the Virgin of Edenford followed by tea and a selection of fondant fancies. This time it was at the old swimming baths. Adam had to work so he couldn't come but he and Tom sent a card with some flowers on the front. When I got to the baths, John opened the card because

Shirley was busy getting ready. Adam's message read, 'Have fun, love Dad,' while Tom had scribbled, '*Sapiens nihil affirmat quod non probat*,' which John told me meant a wise person says nothing is true that he has not proven. John said he would give her the card later but I doubted it.

It was no wonder the council had closed down the old municipal swimming baths. They were not in a good state. I was told to sit downstairs by the side of the pool in the public seats on the 'away' side for swimming galas. No one on that side had been saved. We were just related. The woman on my right kept crying so I tried to calm her.

'It's all right,' I said. 'I mean, it's not like the Moonies. At least they're not going away to live in some farmhouse on a moor.' But she carried on sobbing.

Across the water, on the 'home' side, were the members of the congregation who had already been done. John sat there chatting and laughing. I thought they all looked rather smug. Lawrence was moving among them in a white robe. I hadn't seen him since the hospital. He looked tired and pale. After a few moments, the two doors to the boys' and girls' changing rooms opened and the 'about to be born again' people appeared in two single files of men and women. Another mother bustled in late and sat on my left.

'Have I missed it? Have I missed it?' she demanded breathlessly. I reassured her.

'No. It's just starting.'

'I was trying to finish the cake,' she whispered. Cake, I thought. Should I have made a cake?

'Oh, don't they look lovely?' she said. The participants were all in white robes. 'I made six of those,' hissed the woman. 'Not easy. All those lead weights.'

I knew I was out of my depth. 'What lead weights?'

'In the hem,' said the woman. 'You know, to stop the gowns floating up during the immersion. I think it's the boys who worry. My son said to me, "Mum, you don't want to get halfway through the thing and suddenly show the gallery who the Lord has been kindest to in the 'private endowment' department.'"

I looked down at the lines of nervous men and women shuffling towards the shallow end. I think some of the mothers had overdone it with the weights because the gowns appeared to be something of a burden. Everyone rather had to drag their feet out of the changing room.

Lawrence climbed down into the water and stood with his arms spread wide. 'Who does the Lord call next?' His voice echoed across the white and aquamarine tiles. There was a short silence as no one, weighed down as they were with modesty lead, seemed to be able to move very fast towards him. I thought the air of reluctance it gave to the proceedings was unfortunate. Lawrence stood unmoved in the shallow end, looking relentlessly holy while the converts pulled and dragged their frocks behind them like hunchbacks of Notre Dame clanking their way to the Lord. It gave the visiting crowd time to pick out our loved ones. Shirley was about halfway down the line of women. Most of the converts had their locker key on a red rubber band around their wrist, which I thought was a nice local touch but it got a bad mention in the paper.

I think the municipal people, who had run the baths for years, had handed the place over on the understanding that all the usual rules should apply. Not that there was any danger of anyone running along the side of the pool in those frocks, but the church had retained old Lionel Stone to stand in as lifeguard. The trouble was that I don't think anyone had really explained to Lionel exactly what the event was. Not that there would have been much point. He was so old and extremely deaf. I think they'd tried to fire him twice but he didn't hear a word they said. Anyway, everyone had clunked forward and got into the shallow end. They stood in a large semi-circle around Lawrence waiting for their moment.

As Lawrence raised his hands again and called for a 'Sign From The Lord', Lionel leant forward and switched on the wave machine. For a brief moment it was rather lovely as the water swirled around all those white dresses, but then the machine rather gathered momentum and things got out of hand. Quite a number of the believers went down in the uneven battle with their fish weights and Lawrence was lost from view entirely until a freak wave suddenly swept him forward and up under the lowest diving board. It took a while to restore order after that and I did feel the ceremony was a bit rushed in the end . . . after the paramedics left.

Shirley looked lovely but I can't say I was really impressed. I mean, she may have gone into the water with the Lord but she came out with a verruca. They don't burn them out any more like Matron used to at school. Verrucas. Apparently they're caused by a virus and they just let them fester.

'You haven't got children, have you?' I say to the barrister. Clearly nothing could be further from her ambitious mind.

'No,' she says firmly.

It's a funny feeling watching your life's work walk into the shallow end away from you. I had had such dreams for Shirley. I'd have dug escape tunnels with my bare hands if it would have got her out of Edenford. Oh, not that it's a bad place, it's just that I wanted her to do all the things I'd never dared. Travel the world and not just a week in Devon on full board with a guaranteed menu. It's my fault really. I kept telling her that we only come this way once and she must look for something special. I wanted her to get swept off her feet but not by a wave machine. I longed for her to fall so desperately in love that she could hardly bear to tell me, her own mother. All those years I sat in peeling corridors listening to the ballet music or the drama lesson muffled behind closed doors and I didn't mind because it was worth it. Because her life was going to mean something. And, of course, it did. I mean, Shirley was very popular at the church. You have to tell her how proud I am of her. It's just that I kept looking at her that day and trying to think 'That's my girl', except it wasn't. It was some young woman with a vacant glare in her eye, weighed down by fish weights and contracting a pedimental infection. I was trying to do something with my life but I had a son who talked to the animals, a daughter living for the afterlife and a husband devoted to the Estée Lauder counter at Boots.

We went for a drink at the Crown and Anchor.

'John and I are moving in together,' announced my wet-haired child. I had another drink.

## Under Suspicion

A friend loves at all times . . .
(PROVERBS 17.17)

There is a new line of enquiry from everyone. It's about my friendship with you, Inge.

'You spent a lot of time with her, didn't you?' enquires Big Nose.

'She was my friend.'

'And you were very fond of her . . .' We leave my fondness hanging in the air. It is what everyone wanted to think. Any woman lacking economic and emotional dependence upon a male must be deviant. It cannot be right. If I am to 'get off' then I must be feminine. I must be rehabilitated to the heart of my family. The female heart of my family. Being a criminal is a boy's thing. Female criminals are either not women or not criminals. I think they are beginning to think I am bad, so now perhaps it would be best if I were not a real woman.

I don't say so but I am beginning to think that psychiatry is nothing but a con trick. You go along to the learned to get help because you feel upset or confused or unhappy, and the Big Nose you've been assigned beavers away until he finds that the cause of the problem is you. Not the world. It's you and that's because it's much easier to try to change you than to change the way things are.

Tom took Claudette from me when she died and took her upstairs. He spent night and day working on her, returning her to the feline poses of her past. I was pleased that it gave him something to do but I didn't go up to his room for ages. I never liked the cat but I couldn't stand to see her splayed open all over a work mat. Tom was fixing her eyes in when I took him coffee one morning.

'Where do you suppose cats go in the afterlife?' I asked him.

'I don't know but they go somewhere,' replied Tom confidently.

'How do you know that?'

'Because a soul is the energy and fire of a creature and you can't destroy energy. That's basic physics. I cut all my animals open and I look and look and the one thing I never find in any of them is their soul, but I know it used to be there. It has to have gone somewhere, doesn't it?'

'It's cold for you in here,' I said, because I was his mother. 'You should shut the window.'

Tom shook his head. 'No. Winter's coming and that's okay. People don't live with the weather any more. They make it hot inside when it's cold out and cold when it's hot. It doesn't make sense.' I put down the coffee and Tom took my hand. He never really touched me so I was rather shocked.

'Mum, you will mind John, John Antrobus, won't you?'

'What do you mean?'

'Just be careful.'

'He's all right. I mean, we don't see eye to eye but he . . .'

Tom let go of Eve's hand and turned back to Claudette's empty eyes. 'Shirley thinks I waste my time,' he said, shoving some Blu-Tack in the eye socket. 'But I don't. I am safe here.'

'Safe from what?'

'The Bala-puthijjana – the masses of foolish people.'

I watched Tom working for a bit. I knew Adam blamed me. Tom wasn't the things he was supposed to be. He wasn't a Centurion – strong, tough, assertive, aggressive, competitive . . .

Was it because I had been soft on him? Or did Adam despair because he showed no inclination to spread his seed? He made stuffed babies not real ones.

Tom was whistling softly while he moulded Claudette back to life. His hands defied their design. They were intended as grasping instruments for man but he made them bring life to the dead. I watched his mouth – teeth, tongue, lips so obviously intended for eating but now whistling one of my favourite songs. A lot of people in town had been busy saying what things were contrary to nature and I understood none of it.

I was drowning, drowning in the desert, but I had things to do. Adam was walking round and round the kitchen in his new high heels. He was getting in a positive lather about his number. Taking it much too seriously. He had reached the stage where he couldn't seem to do anything without doing huge hand movements and looking very wide-eyed.

I went out into the garage to sort my things. Another two bags of stuff had just arrived from Bernice, who was well known in town for her interesting jumble. I needed to get them sorted into my different boxes. I think I could have done a survey on what people have spare in their food cupboards. Nearly everyone seems to have an unopened jar of black olives, one of those flat tins of sardines and an awful lot of rice pudding. Our garage was quite full now and people had even started dropping round, quite out of the blue, with bin liners of old sweaters. The lease on the charity shop had run out and no one really had the energy to find somewhere else, so my garage was one of the few places in Edenford that would take unwashed jumble. I must confess I found the collecting rather thrilling. There was even talk of me being interviewed for the *Edenford Gazette*. I'd only ever been in it once before when the Duchess of Gloucester opened the spectacle factory and I happened to be passing her left shoulder when the picture was taken. Not that I was doing this for myself. The garage was nearly full now with some amazing things.

'All for the refugees?' Adam asked.

'Well, partly to give to them and partly to sell to raise money. Although I did think the two skateboards would probably be best going to the scouts.'

It was amazing what people threw away. What they had spare.

*Fact – the United Sates contains eight per cent of the world's population and yet uses twenty-five per cent of its resources. Prosperity and comfort of the few at the expense of the many.*

Of course, Adam was not happy. He knew Horace had been round to ask me to stop. He said it looked very bad but I didn't care. I was determined. He had his singing with Shirley and I was having my refugees. I was very preoccupied with my work. I had seen on the news that there was a problem with transporting the refugees from Dover and it had kept me awake. I tried various organisations but they all seemed very expensive and then I thought of Stuart Packer, who does small deliveries and cheap home removals. He'd not married and since his mother had died he hadn't got much to do. He got quite excited about getting involved but said his truck had developed an odd clunking noise and he was worried about it breaking down.

Well, it was like a lightbulb went on over my head. My book from the AA and my free socket set. We spent a lovely couple of hours with our heads under the bonnet and fixed the old girl up straight away. We agreed that as soon as I had a place for the families we would be on our way.

'I never thought I'd be doing something important,' grinned Stuart, with bits of grease all over his face. It was lovely. We were both so pleased.

I told Adam and I can't say he took it well. He and I had one of his 'long talks'. He kept saying things like, 'As sure as eggs are eggs this whole thing is a mistake,' and I kept wishing he wouldn't use expressions like that. I mean, what else are eggs going to be? I couldn't concentrate and kept thinking if he so much as mentioned that something was 'cheap at half the price', I was going to hit him.

I think that was how we got on to the money. Adam wanted to know how I was planning to pay for the petrol for Stuart's van. Well, I realised I hadn't even thought about it and Adam must have seen me go all blank because he leant across the table and spoke firmly at me the way he does with new sales staff. 'In all good conscience, I can't let you have a penny for this nonsense.'

I looked at Adam and I wondered what he wanted from me. One minute I was supposed to let him make all the decisions, and the next I was supposed to cope with Tom, Shirley, Mother and the house. A sort of blend between a fragile poodle and a Rottweiler. Adam knew I was unhappy and he was not an unkind man. He reached over and stroked my shoulder.

'I tell you what, you stop this charity thing for me and as soon as I've won the election we'll go on a lovely holiday. Spend some time alone.'

Great idea, I thought. We could go to Romania. There's hardly anybody living there any more.

Adam got up to deal with his avocado plants. I sat looking at the pot plant on the kitchen windowsill. The speculum had reappeared. He'd used it to mend the spout on his indoor watering can. Now he tended his beloved plants with it. I didn't like to tell him where it had been. Soon Adam went off to practise in the spare room. Music soared down the stairs. Weeks and weeks of Shirley Bassey just so the golf club could raise money for some driving-range mats. I was tempted to pay for them myself except, of course, I didn't have any money.

I knew I ought to put Adam first. It was my duty. It was what I did – putting everyone else first. Adam didn't want me to be subservient, that's what he would tell you. He just thought I should do it his way. Women are subservient to men because they made men disobey God. Bloody Eve. Bloody, bloody Eve.

I turned on the television news and there was some war where at 'The Front' soldiers had been raping the wives of their former neighbours and friends. Why would they do that? I suppose it takes a war or a crisis really to know what you think about anything. I sat watching and I couldn't think why. Why did the BBC keep telling me what was going on? What was I supposed to do with all that news? I wrote to the Foreign Office, I wrote to my MP, no one said they would sort it out. What was I meant to do with all that terrible information? I couldn't start *Live Aid*. I didn't know anyone. I'm not anyone. I couldn't just sit and listen any more. I thought if everyone loaded up one van and took some people home then . . . Why did they keep telling me about it if there was no point? What did they want me to do?

Reverend Davies from the Virgin Church came round in the afternoon and stood watching me in the garage. He was very awkward.

'I'm tho thorry, Eve, ith very thad,' he lisped and sprayed over perfectly good food in a box. 'I haf to think of my congregation.'

He had come to punish me. I was off the flower rota. Doris Turton had been to see him. There had been complaints about what I was doing to the town. About my relationship with 'those women'. He left and I sat amongst my things. No one wanted me to do this. They were happy to clear their houses of junk but no one wanted actual foreigners.

I shouldn't say it but I think there's some of that in the Bible. I mean the Jews longed for a messiah but not just any messiah. They were desperate for a Jewish king who would, with the help of God, rid the homeland of foreigners. Once more bring Jewish home rule under divinely inspired law. A place where the old covenant with God could be replaced with a new one and the old Israel removed for the new. Very like the British Labour Party really.

I had tomato salad for lunch but I couldn't eat it. I kept cutting them open and looking for some message inside. I had become my mother.

## Holiday Mood

> Six days you shall do your work, but on the seventh day you
> shall rest; that your ox and your ass may have rest, and the son
> of your bondmaid, and the alien may be refreshed.
>
> (EXODUS 23.12)

I thought about Adam's offer of a holiday. All my married life 'the holiday' had been a rather strange concept for me. I used to find the whole thing made me quite tense as I knew I was supposed to RELAX! and that there was a LIMITED AMOUNT OF TIME to achieve this strange state and I'd better hurry up or I would SPOIL IT FOR EVERYONE and, anyway, it had all been rather EXPENSIVE so what was the point if I didn't RELAX and GET OUR MONEY'S WORTH. Meanwhile, the children were usually playing near the deep end of the pool or the high balcony of the hotel or the balcony over the pool and something unsavoury had taken up residence in the bath. That kind of thing. It was all very draining.

I dream of travelling. The filing cabinets have gone and I am only ever flying my plane. I want to travel on 'a post horse attached to a heavy berlin' even though I don't know what that is. I want to breathe pure, invigorating mountain air. I want to have travel clothes. Clothes just for travelling. Perhaps something old-fashioned. A dress of light woollen material – carmelite or alpaca. A long, voluminous dress with small rings sewn inside the seams and a cord passed through them so that I can draw the whole thing up instantly and stop it knocking stones when I run downhill.

I shall know how to make a bivouac, how to find just the right sheltered nook with a panoramic view where I shall eat alfresco and see 'the distant mountains free from a trace of cloud' or hear the 'roar of the stones which pour from time to time down the cliffs of the Matterhorn'. I shall stroll through deep meadows and uncut flowers, hear waves break on a rocky shore, climb through hills of powdery snow to a view never seen before and come across the egg of a wild ptarmigan. I will hear church bells ring high up in the still air, cross wooden bridges, go to a fiesta by accident with a blue carpet of gentians underfoot. Ahead of me there will be a whole army of distant peaks. I want my mind to be out of breath as I put my face to the heat of a scorching African sun. I shall ride a camel amongst scented yellow mimosa, large fields of sweet lilac vetches and patches of tobacco in full flower. Perhaps I might lodge for a night in an empty tomb. Eat bread and cheese from saddle bags and read the ancient Estrangelo alphabet. I shall stand atop Mount Sion at dawn and see Egypt and Palestine, the Red Sea and the Parthenian Sea, to Alexandria and the vast lands of the Saracens. I shall be an object of curiosity. A white woman who drinks caravan tea flavoured with mint and the faint aroma of ambergris. There will be domes and minarets, the pinnacles of the Holy Sepulchre and the great Mosque . . .

'Think about it,' called Adam from the bedroom window as I headed out. 'We could go abroad . . . Jersey maybe. Ten days.'

The bell is calling me for dinner. I don't cook any more. I do like that. Hugs to you both.

Love,

Eve

PS Now that Shirley is reading my letters, will you show her this? I read it in the paper.

*Fact – to the outside world, Richard Cohen was a very lucky man. He had been Tina Sinatra's first husband and had about £62 million, which was one million for every year he had been alive. I call that lucky. He was lucky enough to live in Beverly Hills and lucky enough to be invited to a very smart dinner party. It seemed that Richard's only real misfortune was that he was allergic to nuts. Still, most people can live with that. He went to the dinner party and didn't have the nuts. He did, however, have steak. Perhaps Richard was lucky enough to sit next to a beautiful woman. Anyway, something may have stopped him paying proper attention to his chewing because he choked on his steak. Luckily enough there was a doctor at the party and, even better, the doctor knew how to do the Heimlich manoeuvre. He put his arms around Richard from behind and jerked hard to dislodge the food. It didn't work the first time so the doctor tried again. Luckily the doctor was strong and this time the manoeuvre worked. Unluckily he was so strong that he broke Richard's rib, which punctured his lung. Fortunately the doctor knew about mouth-to-mouth resuscitation. Unfortunately the doctor had been eating nuts. Richard died and his wife got the money.*

Life's like that, isn't it? I mean, sometimes things happen and there's nothing you can do to stop them.

# Chapter Twenty-five

More and more Eve felt like she was acting in a play. A play where she was never allowed to read the next scene before she had to act it. A play where things happened to her character that were never quite what she expected. Eve needed a miracle. She had spent the afternoon with Inge helping her sort Kate's things. Journalists never left Inge alone for a minute. They phoned with sympathy, they wrote with sympathy, they even yelled sympathy through the letterbox. Everyone wanted an exclusive. One last chance to wring some fame out of Inge Holbrook before she was finally hung out to dry for good. Inge Holbrook was consumed with grief and everyone wanted in on it. They wanted to know the truth about her private life, her festering secret. Eve made tea, sorted things, helped where she could and Inge wept and wept, tears sliding down where there had once been a famous smile. She wept for Kate but she also wept for herself. For all the years of fear and stupidity.

By the time Eve got home, her need for a miracle had become too intense to bear. She needed one for Inge, she needed one for her mother and she needed one for herself. As she turned up the drive, for one brief moment, one happened. Eve could see that the garage door was open but she couldn't see inside. The whole entrance was obscured by a great plume of dust. Inside a single light burned and a man appeared brilliantly lit from behind. He was surrounded by cloud and light. Eve couldn't see who it was but he seemed to hold his hands out to her. Mesmerised, Eve walked towards him. There was snow in the air and behind her the last wisteria faded on the garden wall. She didn't know what she thought but for that moment, at least, Eve believed. Slowly the dust settled and the man walked towards her. He came out of the gloom with a broom. It was Adam. He had been sweeping because that's all there was to do. There was nothing but room to sweep. Behind him the clouds settled and Eve could see that the entire space was empty. The place had been full to overflowing with boxes of clothes, shoes, games, kitchen equipment, food . . . and now it was empty. There was absolutely nothing left.

'Hello, Eve.' He smiled. Everyone smiled. Everyone smiled all the time even when there was nothing to smile about.

'Adam?'

He looked down and found something fascinating to sweep near his wife's feet.

'Yes . . . look, it was for the best. The thing is, it would never have worked and I didn't want you to be disappointed . . .'

'This has nothing to do with me being disappointed,' Eve said.

'I wanted to protect you,' he pleaded. 'No one wanted those damn refugees and it would have caused you such grief.'

Eve looked at her mortified husband. The man who would be king in his community. The saviour of the people. 'Wouldn't have done you much good either, would it?'

'I was trying to protect you. People were beginning to say bad things.'

'Where is it? Where is everything?' Eve managed.

'John got Stuart Packer to take it away . . . to the dump. Anyway, I heard on the news. The government has agreed to the detention centres. There was no one to come anyway.'

Eve sat in the empty garage for ages. It had been pathetic. Thinking she could do something. It was the day of the local election. Adam's day when the people would choose. Finally it would all be over. Adam got dressed in his best suit and sat in the car waiting for his wife but she didn't move. Eve was supposed to be at Adam's side for the 'count'. Tonight was the night the Marshalls once more took on the mantle of Adam's civic responsibility. Eve didn't know what came over her. She never moved. After a while Adam left on his own and Eve stayed in the garage. She never voted. She didn't go and vote for Adam. She meant to but she couldn't seem to get up from the floor. She didn't go anywhere.

Night fell and Eve sat. After several hours Inge came round and she too sat on the garage floor. They didn't speak for a while. Inge's crying had wrung out her body and she had no conversation left. Finally she handed over a letter from the hospital authorities for Eve to read. Inge had been refused permission to know which funeral parlour Kate had been taken to. As she had no legal claim on the body the hospital refused to give out any information other than to immediate family. The authorities referred her to Mrs Andrews' solicitors – Hogart, Hoddle and Hooper. The solicitors had the facts. It was all legal. It was all correct.

'You must have some rights,' said Eve.

Inge shook her head. 'No. None. We weren't married. We couldn't marry. I'm nothing.'

Eve looked at her friend, sitting in shock on the floor of the empty garage. They had known each other for over twenty-five years. They had been young and optimistic together. They had had good hair and no cellulite. They had raced their bicycles over cobblestones never knowing the life they raced towards. Never knowing they would end up imprisoned. Eve knew what some people in Edenford thought. That whatever Lawrence might say in the future, Inge and Kate would always be blamed for Patrick's death. That to some of the town Inge stood as proxy for all that is evil. They hated her and wanted Eve to feel the same. It was a litmus test for being a normal person.

'Who ha! Who ha!' called Eve's mother from the dining room. 'Who ha! Who ha!'

Inge leant against Eve and Eve needed that. She put her arm

around her friend and rocked and rocked her. When Adam came back, the two women were still sitting there. Silent; one smiling, the other holding. Shirley and John were helping him in because he had had a few drinks. Inge looked at Eve and shrugged. Adam saw Inge's smile and he hated her. He saw her hug his wife, his alien wife, and go home.

'A triumph!' he kept shouting. 'A bloody triumph!' The count was not in yet but Adam was clearly in no doubt that he had swept to victory. No one had said anything horrid. It had gone much better than expected. Adam went to get another bottle of something from the fridge when William let himself in with Pe Pe. William was not drunk but seemed even more demented than Adam.

'Evie, Evie, where are you?' he yelled, as he ran from the hall to the kitchen. He stood in the doorway beaming at his family. 'You're all here, how marvellous. Ladies and gentlemen . . . uhhum . . .' William cleared his throat and announced, 'May I present my wife, Philippa Cameron, woman of my dreams and soon to be . . . mother of my child.' William stepped back and put his arm out as Pe Pe stepped into the doorway. She was also smiling. Shirley was smiling, John was smiling, Adam couldn't stop smiling. Everyone was demented with joy except Eve. William and Pe Pe fell over each other trying to give out all the details.

'I think we should have a home birth,' declared Pe Pe. 'Why go to hospital? It's not as though I'm sick. People only ever die in the hospital.'

William shook his head. 'I don't know, darling, I don't think it's safe. It can be very nice in the hospital these days. I think they even do water births.'

'Shirley had one of those,' Eve added, but no one was listening.

John beamed. 'What are you going to call it?'

'Definitely William if it's a boy,' said William.

'I don't know,' whined Pe Pe. 'I really want something unusual.'

Eve didn't like to tell them that with Pe Pe's genes that was almost certainly what they'd get. Eve knew she should be more helpful. It was what was expected. Women were pleased and did pleased things when people said they were having babies. Eve wondered if she would have felt differently if Shirley were having it. The men went off to find champagne in the cellar, Shirley went to try and tell Mother and Eve was left alone with Pe Pe. Alone and confused.

'How, Pe Pe? How are you pregnant? You told me . . .'

Pe Pe blinked at Eve. 'What does it matter? Look how happy he is.'

'I want to know. William doesn't have any sperm. You told me that. What was it – a bloody immaculate conception?'

Pe Pe put her handbag down on the counter and played with the handles. 'Look, it's done,' she said.

'Yes and who done it?'

Pe Pe sighed and looked towards the cellar door where the men had disappeared to find drink. 'Eve, it doesn't matter.'

'Who?' Eve persisted. She had had enough secrets to last a lifetime. Eve thought she knew but she had to hear Pe Pe say it.

'It was John.' Pe Pe lowered her voice and whispered urgently. 'It was his idea and he was so sweet.'

'John? John Antrobus?'

'He just wanted to help.'

Shirley came in to get Mother a glass of water. She hugged Pe Pe and then Eve.

'Mum,' she said, enfolded in her mother's arms, 'I was going to wait but I just can't.' I knew, I knew what was coming. 'John's asked me to marry him and . . . I've said yes!'

Eve nearly choked. 'What about university?'

Shirley stroked her mother's arm. 'It's okay. I'm going to take another year out and then go. Maybe choose somewhere near Edenford.'

'But Durham, Exeter . . .'

Shirley smiled and took Mother her glass of water. Eve could hardly contain herself. She turned on Pe Pe and practically screamed, 'You had an affair with—'

Helpful John, engaged John, appeared carrying a bottle in one hand and Eve's husband in the other.

'Cracked his head, I'm afraid. Bit overexcited,' explained William.

'Who's having an affair?' mumbled Adam, as Shirley came back into the kitchen. Even Pe Pe's fake smile wavered.

'It's nothing,' she managed, looking at John, at William, at Shirley and finally at Eve. 'Eve!' she implored.

And in that moment Eve didn't have it in her to tell the truth. She didn't have it in her to hurt her daughter or her brother.

'No one's having an affair,' she said. 'Now, shall we pour the—' Eve reached for some wine glasses on a shelf but Adam got up and almost stumbled into her.

'It's that woman, isn't it? That bloody dyke next door.' He had had too much to drink. It was all a mistake. 'I saw you . . . the two of you . . . sitting together in the garage . . . leaning on each other.'

Eve didn't know why she felt defensive. She had no reason to but she did. 'Her partner died,' she said.

'Oh, really,' Adam sneered. 'So she's free now. Free to run off with you. Is that the plan? It's not enough for you that people talk about my own son? Now you want to run off with that . . . that freak. Is that it, Eve? What was she giving you that I couldn't? Huh?'

Eve looked at her partner, her husband, her lover. 'You haven't been giving me anything for some time now.' Eve meant support but he took it all wrong.

'I've been injured!' he screamed. 'You know I was injured. How dare you kick a man when he's down? You . . . you slut. You slept with that pervert and now everyone knows. I can't even look at you.'

Eve looked at him and had no idea what she was supposed to do. It was comical really. She couldn't say anything about John because it would break Shirley's heart, she couldn't say anything about Pe Pe because William was so excited and he was her brother and it's what he longed for, she didn't want to say anything bad about Inge, she didn't like the way Adam had jumped to his conclusion . . .

It wasn't the best family get-together they'd ever had.

Eve was outside Hogart, Hoddle and Hooper the next morning before they opened. She stood in the High Street watching everyone go about their business and none of it was anything to do with her. There was a Sold sign up outside the Susan Lithgood shop and a notice in the window welcomed a new establishment providing *Professional Dry-Cleaning*. The notice was so large it gave some suggestion that until now Edenford had had no *professional* dry-cleaning but amateurs in the field had been a perfect pest. The first snow was beginning to fall and Eve was cold. Colder than she had ever been. John was among the first to arrive.

'Eve! What a lovely surprise. I'm afraid I've got rather a hectic morning.'

They stepped into reception where a young typist was busy sharpening her nails for the morning post.

'I need to speak to you now, John,' Eve said very loudly.

'Love to, love to.' He looked around a little agitated. 'But it's not a good time. I've got—'

'Now!' she commanded. 'Or do you want to do it out here? I have one or two matters regarding my sister-in-law that you might—'

'Right, right.' He bundled his future mother-in-law away to his office at the back of the building, moving with the confidence and self-assurance of those who don't stop to think. The place was immaculate. Apart from the bundles of papers tied in pink ribbon on top of a large wooden filing cabinet, it didn't look like anyone worked there at all. There was a silver-framed picture of Shirley on his desk. Eve couldn't look at it.

'Now then, Eve, what's so urgent? Something legal?'

'I know you, John—' she began.

'Of course, you do. Eve, you're upset, I can tell.' He began to oil his way round her. 'The others went off at the deep end last night but I can quite see how this little misunderstanding—'

'No, I mean, really know you. At first I thought it was an accident that you started the rumours around town about blood and Aids and the refugees but it wasn't an accident, was it? You sent Horace Hoddle that leaflet from Dover. You were determined they wouldn't come here. It was you who put all that Adam and Eve family shit in Adam's head, all that Centurion protect-our-women bollocks. And you knew Mrs Andrews would shut Inge out—'

John raised his hands in mock surrender. 'Eve, you're mistaken. I was only trying to be nice.'

'You represent the bloody woman.'

'Well, yes I do now, but everyone is entitled—'

'You thought Lawrence would damn Kate in the hospital, didn't you? That's why you came. To see him give one final judgement.'

John picked up a pencil sharpener and slowly began to work his way through a pile of new pencils. 'Lawrence is a very forgiving man.'

'But you're not, are you?'

John sat back in his chair and for the first time looked Eve straight in the eye. 'Since you ask me – no. Gay people make me sick. All that fucking gay pride, flaunting their fucking perversions in your face. It's a sin and that's all there is to it.'

'So is sleeping with someone else's wife. I know about Pe Pe, John,' Eve said. John stopped his sharpening and looked at her. Then he picked up the framed photo of Shirley and turned it towards Eve.

'Shirley and I are getting married,' he said. 'I intend for her to be a very prominent member of this community. What do you want, Eve?'

'I want to know the name of the funeral parlour where Kate is.'

'I don't think you should get involved.' John attempted one last charge. 'It would be a shame if those ridiculous rumours about you and Inge—'

He never got a chance to finish. Eve banged opened the door to John's office to make sure everyone could hear. 'I don't give a damn what anyone says about me and I am quite happy to tell anyone who cares to listen that you—'

John leapt to his feet and slammed the door shut. 'Look, I can't give you that kind of—'

'Now.'

What Eve learnt from Inge was that her achievement of any kind of self-esteem was an incredible victory against almost insurmountable odds in the society we live in. She was utterly dignified when they went to the funeral parlour. Eve took her in her leaping, objecting car and Inge never said a word.

The whispering funeral parlour attendant was thrilled to meet Inge. He had been a fan, he didn't care what the papers said, she was all right by him and anyway, they wrote a lot of nonsense. He was sure she wasn't 'one of those'. Inge was gracious, Inge smiled.

'I'm Katherine Andrews' cousin,' she told him. 'I'm afraid I need to pay my respects now. I can't make the funeral.'

Of course he understood. She was busy. She couldn't do ordinary things like make time in life for the inconvenient deaths of others.

They had laid Kate out in what appeared to be a British Rail waiting-room. Magnolia partition walls separated her from the rest of the dearly departed and wailing could be heard up and down the corridor. Her face had a strange white sheen to it. Some odd make-up the funeral directors had swiped across a woman who had always liked her face free. She lay in a dress Inge had never seen before. Inge stood and stared at her and Eve realised she was afraid. It was utterly bewildering to be afraid of her beloved Kate and yet she was. She hadn't wanted to come into the room and see her lying there. The more she looked, the less she could see her Kate. The face looked a bit like her but Kate had gone somehow. Eve knew that if Tom cut her open then her soul would no longer be there. Eve knew that Kate, of all people, had had one, she just didn't know where it was now.

'It's a trick,' Inge whispered. 'She looks like some Madame Tussaud's dummy. I don't know that dress. I didn't know she had a dress.'

Eve didn't know what she had thought would happen. That maybe Inge would fling her arms around the body and hug her tight. Now she wasn't even sure if Inge wanted to kiss her. Inge inched her lips slowly down to Kate's forehead. Kate's hair looked stiff and her glasses were missing from the top of her head. A strong chemical smell leapt up from the plain, pine box. As Inge placed her lips on Kate's head her whole body stiffened and Eve knew that even then she still felt fear.

When they left Inge was silent. She was silent all the way home. As she got out she said, 'She wasn't there, was she?' And Eve answered, 'No,' but neither of them knew what had happened to Kate.

Eve had forgotten it was her birthday. Adam was supposed to come home early to take her out for dinner – two meals for the price of one at the Harvester if you ate before seven-thirty. He didn't come but Horace Hoddle sent a note – Adam had lost the election. By one vote. And Eve knew she was guilty as charged.

# Chapter Twenty-six

Dear Inge,

I had the dream again last night. The one with the plane that I have to fly. This time though it wasn't so scary. I still didn't know how the controls worked but I liked looking at them. I ran my hand over them and I wanted to fly, I just didn't know how.

> I tell you that to let no day pass without discussing goodness and examining both myself and others is really the very best thing that a man can do, and that life without this sort of examination is not worth living.
>
> (Socrates, *Apology 382*)

Socrates was put to death for the crime of examining with a truly open mind the most cherished beliefs of the day. I think it could happen to anybody.

We are closing in on the end. The shrink looks at me, the lawyer looks at me.

'Did you? Did you?' they want to know. 'Did you sleep with your neighbour?'

No one actually has the nerve to ask me but it appeals to the gossip in them all. Even the educated think there must be some tabloid explanation. They have not been listening. Not really listening. It is just a soap opera. I think the shrink has replaced his hopes of my case turning into a learned book with the idea that it might become a made-for-TV movie. Tom says the Hindus call this kālī-yuga – it is the age of blackness in which people become increasingly incapable of discerning right from wrong and the beautiful from the grotesque.

Now we can begin to focus on the reasons for my crime. Was I mad or not mad enough? Was I sexually indiscriminate or promiscuous? Had I failed as a wife or mother? How much domestic responsibility did I carry out? Did I mind? Or say that I minded? Do I look like a woman? Talk like a woman? Was there anything about me that suggested I wasn't a 'normal' woman? Could I be treated? Perhaps it would be best to plead guilty. Get it over with. Don't allow the publicity to damage my family and neighbours. They are the 'real' sufferers. They are the ones betrayed by me. They could not be the source of my misery, I am a hapless, guilt-ridden victim of my own uncontrollable impulses.

We have found some excuses: I'm middle-aged, I had my mind on other things, I had no previous convictions, I am needed to run my home . . . I am a wife and mother, therefore I deserve understanding and sympathy and, of course, leniency. I am respectable, middle class, therefore I must be so sensitive that I will be reformed by a minimum of punishment or perhaps no punishment at all. My husband can help, my children will help. I don't need the help of the justice system if I have them at home.

I hate the lawyer most of all. It isn't about justice. It isn't about justice at all.

*Fact – a married person may inherit property without paying inheritance tax. They have automatic rights of survivorship over their partner's estate. They have legal, financial and psychological benefits on the death of their*

*loved one, which are sanctioned and affirmed by the state.
Without the status of legal next-of-kin, a partner may get
shut out of medical decisions or, ultimately, funeral arrange-
ments.*

It wasn't right what happened to you. It wasn't right at all. I'm
so glad that Shirley sees that now. Maybe she will come out the
other end. Maybe she'll be okay. The lawyer wants me to be
quiet in court. To sit quietly and seem as 'normal' as possible.
Don't talk publicly about the case ever. I need to compensate for
my unfeminine criminal behaviour by presenting myself as
domesticated, sexually passive and constitutionally fragile.

What if I am wicked? Maybe I am greedy. Greedy for my
daughter's attention. Maybe I should be punished not treated.
Perhaps I deserve contempt. I must be mentally ill, emotionally
disturbed or in some way abnormal or it never would have happened. I am not to say that I felt there was no choice. That if I
had been a man I would probably have given John a good hiding.
I would have punched him, kicked him, wrestled him to the
ground. If I were a man I would not have killed him.

Tom came to visit me in prison. He sat with me and we talked
about silly things. He'd walked. It's a long way but Tom doesn't
like transport.

*Fact – a young, fast-growing tree can recycle about forty-
eight pounds of carbon dioxide per year. Carbon dioxide is
the principal gas in the 'greenhouse effect'. If you burn one
gallon of petrol that equals twenty miles and twenty
pounds of carbon dioxide. Drive forty miles in a car and
you produce roughly the amount of carbon dioxide a young
tree can recycle in a year.*

I told him I'd been trying to read the Bible to get some help.
To find some wisdom. I told him I had learnt a lot of the passages
by heart but he shook his head.

'That's not wisdom, Mum. Buddha says that a servant of the king may hear the king's words and repeat them to others but simply repeating his words would not make the servant a king. Repeating the words of a wise man doesn't make you wise.'

Tom brought me something. He had been clearing out Mother's house and thought I might like a memento. He put it on the table. It was the Pope John Paul's head that lit up. The Calvinist Prince of Darkness – the corruptible man who could pass off his own thinking as the inspiration of an incorruptible supreme being. What had I learnt? I learnt that no one has any simple solutions to the human condition. That there may not be any solutions at all.

You decided to go to Barbados and I couldn't bear that you were going to leave. I kept thinking about John. '*Fucking gay pride . . .*' Pride . . . what else was a wedding but having some pride? '*Flaunting their fucking perversions in your face.*' I shut my eyes and I could see you drop Kate's hand as the nurse came into the room. I don't write that to make you feel bad. It's just that you had to be free of all that fear, Inge. Kate knew that.

When I went to see you the day you left, you had lost a lot of weight and all your bounce seemed to have bounced away, but you still opened the door as if you were pleased to see me. I don't mean your smile. I mean really pleased.

'Ah, I'm so glad you've come. I'm in the neighbourhood at the moment *promoting* homosexuality. It's a once-in-a-lifetime offer. Come and join us. You know you want to. Be part of a despised minority. Join us and have your parents reject you, your boss fire you, strangers call you names and beat you . . . and if you agree to become a homosexual for a trial period of just ten days then we will give you, absolutely free . . . this carriage clock.' You held up the very beautiful little clock, which had always stood on the mantelpiece in your house. You held it out to me. 'I'm kidding but I do want you to have it. Kate gave it to me and I know it would have made her happy.'

You left and I couldn't bear it.

'Goodbye, Camie, and thanks.'

Goodbye to being Camie. You went away and left me. There was snow on the ground and the tracks from your car tyres stayed for ages. I knew then that Edenford would be sorry you were gone. You had been useful. The whole town had been able to divert themselves from thinking about their own shortcomings by looking at those they thought they saw in you. Everyone needed scandal. I wondered who the town would turn on next. I thought about you and wondered if you would ever go to San Francisco. If you would go and fly under bridges. And I wanted to run after you but I couldn't. I didn't have any money. Then I thought maybe Shirley could get away. I could suggest a short holiday. Give her time to think but I didn't have any money and then the wickedness started and it didn't stop.

I sold Adam's collection of Shirley Bassey records and then, when I realised how much I could get for them, I went home and got all the souvenirs and sold those as well. He spotted the loss pretty quickly. Well, you would do. He had so much of it. We hadn't seen the floor of the spare room in years.

He'd come straight home from work and gone up to change into his full costume for rehearsals, as he'd been doing all week. He still believed that Miss Bassey was to be his social salvation. I'd got rather used to mixing cocktails for my half-hour with Shirley before supper. He stood at the bottom of the stairs in full Bassey regalia – he looked fabulous, diamanté, acrylic wig – and he was screaming at me. His eyes bulging under those extra extension eyelashes I'd got him at Boots.

'What have you done! What have you done?' he kept shouting.

I was just going to explain calmly about needing the money for Shirley to get away when the doorbell rang. In his temper I think Adam had quite forgotten about his outfit because he wrenched the door open to see who it was. It was Horace. Horace Hoddle from . . . the golf club committee. To say Horace looked surprised would somehow fail to capture the moment.

Horace didn't actually speak but in his eyes was everything everyone had been saying – Adam's assault on that woman, Tom's long hair and strange ways, Patrick, you and Kate . . .

I don't know what came over me but as Adam stepped out to explain, I shut the door behind him and locked it. I stood there till long after Horace had left, looking at Adam through the leaded window in the hall. He stood on the front step with the evening sun glinting off his gold lamé.

It was a shame. Backlit by the sun like that with his arms raised and his mouth wide with fury, he was, for a brief moment . . . Dame Shirley. I wouldn't open the door and I think it was a salutary lesson to Adam just how secure he'd made the house. After a while he turned and hobbled down the road to the bus stop to get the 46 to William's house. I watched his retreating evening dress and felt rather sorry for him. He should have listened to me. I warned him that stilettos should never be that tight. It was best for him. Perhaps the trip on the bus would calm him down.

But I needn't have bothered. There was no talking to Shirley. My daughter was slipping and slipping away. She became obsessed with the wedding.

*Fact – the average UK wedding costs £10,500.*

Shirley wanted me to be involved. Of course she did, and I tried. We discussed which shop to place her list at. It was very important. The mere name of the establishment said something about the class of wedding we were having. So, too, did the size of the ring. We discussed invitations, dresses, cutlery . . .

I thought I would go mad. She wouldn't talk about Adam or what had occurred and I realised how much I had ignored of what went on between my mother and father. Big things had happened and I had never said a word. Adam went to stay with William and Pe Pe, while my life turned into a small sub-franchise of *Bride's World*. I didn't understand any of it. The Bible was no help. I had started at the beginning and got as far as the First Book of Samuel. As far as I can understand, it was like this:

David wanted to marry King Saul's daughter, Michal, but David was worried that he was poor and couldn't provide a proper wedding present for a king. So Saul said, 'The king desires no marriage present except a hundred foreskins of the Philistines, that he may be avenged of the king's enemies.' Now Saul was being sneaky because he thought the Philistines would kill David, but off he goes and kills not a hundred but two hundred Philistines and brings back their foreskins, 'which were given in full number to the king, that he might become the king's son-in-law. And Saul gave him his daughter Michal for a wife'. And who do you think dealt with all those unwanted wedding presents when they arrived? Saul's wife, I'll be bound. You can just see her at the wedding breakfast trying to lay out the foreskins on the present table and hoping her second cousin, who married a Philistine, doesn't decide to turn up.

Now that Shirley was taking another year off, she had taken a full-time job at the building society. She worked there amongst the Peps and the Tessas, the endless future plans of Edenford, and on her days off she sat at our breakfast bar making endless lists. A week before the wedding she asked if John could come and stay.

'His lease is up on his flat and it seems silly to keep it on when we're not going to live there,' reasoned my daughter. 'You don't mind, do you, Mum? You've got plenty of space in the spare room, now.'

And I had. Shirley Bassey no longer filled my life. Mother, Tom and I were alone, although everyone said Adam was desperate to come back from William and Pe Pe's.

'I don't think he likes my food,' soothed Pe Pe, as if praise of my skill in the kitchen would make everything better. He didn't miss me, just my flans. I missed him or maybe I missed the idea of him, I didn't know any more. Pe Pe came round with baby catalogues and we were awash with baby bootees and bridesmaids' bonnets. I nearly choked on some of the prices.

'Dad says we mustn't stint on anything, Mum,' moaned my daughter.

'William says I can have anything I want for the new baby and, believe me, I am going to get the best,' announced Pe Pe.

*Dover the Land of Plenty. 33 reasons why we should send them back and close the door. Reason 13: pregnant refugee mothers only want brand new equipment for their offspring. Are these infants entitled to hold a British passport to success now that they have been born in our local hospitals?*

Suddenly I felt sick. I mean, like I was going to throw up. I started to run out of the house. I could hear Shirley calling, 'Mum, Mum! Come back,' but I had to run.

## Lost

I dreamed and behold I saw a Man clothed with rags, standing in a certain place, with his face from his own house, a Book in his hand, and a great burden upon his back. I looked and saw him open the book and read therein; and as he read, he wept and trembled; and not being able longer to contain, he broke out with a lamentable cry, saying, 'What shall I do?'

(*The Pilgrim's Progress* – John Bunyan)

I couldn't breathe. I ran as if I were never coming back. The tears started to come. Those horrible, female tears. Stupid, stupid. I tried to run faster but the water from my stupid eyes blinded me. The women in Sarajevo were not ashamed to show their grief. They wept and clung to the bodies of their loved ones and the cameras filmed and filmed. Women's tears have a mind of their own. They are an uncontrollable part of our bodies but I hated them. My breath came in sharp, jagged pieces. Stupid, tearful, fat, middle-aged woman who couldn't run. A great, use-less blob on the countryside. There was thick snow everywhere. It didn't look like England at all. Everything around me had turned into a foreign country. A great white alien place that I had never been to before. I didn't know where I was going until I fell. In my blindness, I crashed into something which cracked but didn't give and I collapsed beside it.

I lay in the snow, each breath stabbing into my lungs. Could you die in the snow in south-east England or did it have to be some Siberian steppe? Could I just lie there and never get up again? Why not? What possible loss would it be? I could feel the cold seeping through my trousers and it felt good. I remembered lying in a bank of white as a child with my dad. Lying there on our backs, sweeping our arms and legs in great swathes across the ground to make angels in the snow. The tears began to calm and I tried to breathe again. Slowly I stretched out my limbs into the white landscape. I hurt, I hurt everywhere, but I concentrated my mind. I concentrated on making the most perfect angel, and when it was finished I looked up to the sky.

'What do you think of that then?' I yelled to the man upstairs, to my creator, to Buddha, to anyone who was listening. That was when I saw the bird. It was a short distance away from where I lay and in my haze of tears it appeared to be what Tom had wondered about – a crow with white feathers. I sat up to look closer and scared the creature. It flapped its wings and flew away, black as night without the snow for cover. It was then that I saw what had cracked when I fell. I thought it was a cross at first but actually it was one of those wooden markings they put along the side of new roads. I don't know what they're for. Just two old bits of rough wood slapped together in the shape of the cross. I thought it was a sign. At last I had been heard. I, Eve Marshall, was important enough to have been given a revelation. I crawled towards it and knelt before this holy sign. With my eyes clamped shut and my hands praying like a child, I began to beg for help.

'Okay, this is the fabulous bit of the story where I have a message straight from above to do what I did and you can either claim I'm crazy or wonder if I am touched by the Lord.'

The shrink looks at me. 'Is that what you want to tell me?'

'No, I want to stop that's all. I just want to go back to my cell.'

I prayed and I prayed and nothing. The wind blew along the unmade road and I was alone. I prayed to die, I prayed to understand, I prayed for calm. I did what people have done for as long as there have been people. I couldn't face my life, the truth of my life and so I tried to imagine some way or place or time where it wouldn't exist. I was utterly weak and helpless and what I really wanted was some hero who would come and save me. I don't think I would have minded much whether Jesus, the archangel Gabriel or Batman had turned up.

I looked up to the sky and then along the endless track ploughed through the country for the new bypass. Everything seemed vast and I seemed so small and insignificant. I wanted to understand and what I understood was that it was pointless. No one spoke to me. No ethereal being came down to hover on the digger parked beside me. Of course not. I had done nothing to deserve it. I was nothing. I was no genius that the world would be glad had come. What a ridiculous idea that my brain could come to any sort of adequate understanding of the world and my place in it. It was laughable.

So now what? Make the leap to faith? Jump from not believing to believing because it was safer? I thought about John's kind of Christian where the basic alternative to accepting Jesus into my heart was hellfire. We were back in the playground. I had to play by the rules or I was out. Maybe it would be okay. I just had to put off being happy till I was dead. Was this God's divine plan? Did God even have time to make a plan for me? Of course he did. God was an intelligent, benign creator. He had time for everyone. The suffering was for our own good.

I tried to stay with that thought but my brain wouldn't shut up. It was like I had a little devil sitting on my shoulder whispering, 'If God is so all-compassionate and all-powerful then why couldn't our good be secured without suffering? If it's a test then why did he make us so we needed testing? If suffering comes from disobedience to God, why did he, the all-powerful one, not make it so we can only obey? How come so many religions are based on what God said to people and yet no two beliefs ever got the same message? Did someone get a bad connection?'

I kept trying to get back on track.

'I'm not trying to be difficult,' I yelled to the sky, 'I just don't get it!'

'God is benevolent but his benevolence works in mysterious ways,' came the answer.

'I'll say,' I muttered, as my head filled with more heresy. What if God was just incompetent or a bully? What if . . . there were no more what ifs? I was not going to get a revelation. I could either lie down and die or get on with the lot I had been given.

I think I was exhausted because I seemed to see one of my dreams as I knelt there. I was on a raft. A really strong, wooden raft, lashed together with stout rope. I was alone on the raft but it had everything I needed. The water was calm as I drifted down a wide river. Then slowly the water began to surge and things started to slip from my raft. Things I needed. The waves got worse and soon the raft held only me. Then the raft itself began to break up until I was in the water, clinging to what remained and I knew I had to let go.

I stood up, knowing I would have to say goodbye to everything that had got me through before. The old stuff was gone and there was nothing new to replace it. I had no choice but to do it my own way. I looked at the roadside cross and had never felt so alone in my life.

As I turned to leave, I noticed something on the ground where I had been lying. The snow was white, pure white, unblemished except in the middle of my angel. There was a large patch of red. My life was seeping from me.

## Under the Knife

A cheerful heart is a good medicine,
but a downcast spirit dries up the bones.

(PROVERBS 18.22)

The hysterectomy was easy. The doctor had been pushing me to have it done and I swept in on the much-maligned NHS. Everyone was very sympathetic. Women's troubles. Adam even brought me a present. He'd been to Dusseldorf about some infra-red burglar alarms, so I got a solitaire pendant with a $1 \times 0.01$ carat, brilliant in a 14-carat white gold setting – £35.70 without tax, and two free toilet bags from British Midland. He wouldn't hold my hand since he thought I'd slept with Inge but he did come. Anyway, having my reproductive system whipped out was free and not as bad as I had expected.

## Wedding Day

Hear, O daughter, consider, and incline your ear;
forget your people and your father's house . . .

(PSALMS 45.10)

I didn't get foreskins as a wedding present. They turned out to be much too difficult to get hold of. I got a lace tablecloth and some matching napkins. Tom, however, outdid himself. He came downstairs with Claudette on a large oak plinth. I don't know where her soul had gone but she stood crouched down, just like the cat who had plagued me all those years. Even the glint in her eyes was the same.

'It's for Shirl and that . . . man. For the wedding.' Tom handed the moggy over to me. 'I think Shirley was fond of Claudette.'

I took the creature in my arms and nodded. 'Yes.'

Tom stood there in his usual jeans and T-shirt. 'Are you not coming to the wedding?' I asked.

'I don't see the point,' said Tom.

'No.'

I put the cat down in the hall but it was so lifelike that I couldn't drink my coffee. In the end I took the monster out to the car and put it on the back seat to take to the ceremony. John was just returning from the hire shop with his wedding suit. It was pure white and hanging lifeless on a hanger in his hand.

· 'I think there might be more snow,' he said. 'Look lovely in the pictures. White snow, us all in white.'

'Yes.'

John swung his suit over his shoulder and went in whistling. I could see Mother through the dining-room window, sitting in her chair. No one was ever going to help me with her. Martha had gone back to Bangkok and William had also come to a decision.

'Now that I'm going to be a father, I have had to do some thinking,' he said sonorously. 'It's an important step in a man's life and it has made me think about my own father. He didn't want his money going to Mother and I feel that I must honour his wishes.'

'But he's not here and I am. I need some help, William,' I begged, but he wouldn't listen. The father-to-be.

I went in to sit with Mother before getting ready. I think she'd been dead most of the morning. Well, I'd been busy and hadn't looked in on her as much as usual. Now she had gone to the great Last Supper in the top room. I sat and looked at her. She wasn't there any more but maybe she had given me a gift. Maybe she had meant to let me go. I felt calm until I thought about Shirley. It didn't seem like a great omen for your marriage to have your grandmother die on your wedding day, so I called Tom downstairs.

'Darling, I'm afraid Granny's died.' I whispered so John wouldn't hear.

'Really!' His face perked up like a boy with a new bicycle.

'Yes. You can't have her, but I do need your help.' Tom nodded. 'I don't want anyone to know yet. Now John won't come in here but he might see her through the windows, so I want you to sit with her as if everything is perfectly normal. All right? Just sit next to her and when John looks through the window he'll think she's fine and you're having a chat or whatever.'

Tom went in to be with Mother and I went upstairs to get changed. John was in the shower. He had been in the shower that day Pe Pe was here. I heard the water stop and I seemed to be unable to move. His suit was hanging on the door of the spare room. I moved towards it and put my hand out for the hanger. I was standing there with the suit in my hand when John appeared from the bathroom. He had a towel round his neck and was wearing nothing but white Y-fronts. John looked at me and I think he knew I was near the edge.

'Look, Eve, I only want what's best for Shirley.'

'Why can't you wait?' I stammered. 'Till she's been to university?'

John laughed. 'University? She's not going to university. Eve, I thought you understood. Shirley's marrying me. She's going to be my wife.'

I was smiling, so I think he thought it was all fine. He came towards me and I took off. It was so childish. I thought if he didn't have the suit then he couldn't marry my daughter. You see, if I had been a man I would have just punched him but instead I raced down the stairs, grabbed the car keys and ran outside. I think it took John a moment to react because I actually got to the car before he made it outside. I threw the suit on the front seat and slammed on the ignition. The car was parked in the middle of the drive and I needed to turn around to get out. By now John was racing down the snowy path in his underpants. I shoved the automatic gear lever into drive and jerked forward. It was the jerk that did it. Claudette, stuffed though she was, had one last leap left in her. She flew from the back seat, plinth and all, and wedged the gearbox into reverse. I looked up and saw John right behind me in the mirror.

'So it was all an accident? You didn't mean to run him over? Crush him against the wall?'

'No. I could have stopped it. I could have braked there and then but I just let the car ride back. Back and back to crucify him on my wisteria.'

'What happened then?'

'There was a bump, a horrible soft bump, as the bent car aerial pierced his side. John spread his arms out against the wall and the car pinned him against the wisteria. The dead twigs drooped down on his head, which fell to one side and he was dead. I looked up at the house and I could see Tom sitting in the dining-room window. He had no idea what had happened. He just saw me looking at him so he picked up Mother's arm and made her wave.'

There is a long silence. The psychiatrist looks at me and flicks back through his notes.

'And all this happened after you had the hysterectomy?' he asks.

I nod. That will be it. We had come at last to a conclusion. The hysterectomy. I was hysterical. That was it. There was nothing else wrong. How stupid I am.

Love,

Eve